Micah's Child

By

Lang Buchanan

This book is a work of fiction. Places, events, and situations in this story are purely fictional. Any resemblance to actual persons, living or dead, is coincidental.

ISBN: 1-4033-1874-3 (e-book)
ISBN: 1-4033-1875-1 (Paperback)
ISBN: 1-4033-1876-X (Dustjacket)

This book is printed on acid free paper.

1st Books - rev. 08/16/02

Acknowledgements

From our earliest years, our parents instilled confidence and encouraged creativity in us, and we thank them in our hearts each day. Bonnie and David Buchanan, James and Claire Teed will forever be our inspiration. We also thank the rest of our family members and friends, whose love helped make the fabric of *Micah's Child*. To Don, Sarah, and Don Jr., for being a loving husband and children; they gave their wife and mother the strength to travel unmarked roads.

Special thanks to our spiritual editors, Constance Waterbury and Robin Kazmier, who led us through disheartening times with their unyielding belief in our talents. They were the first to give value to our words.

A deep appreciation goes to our cover design artist, Lori Phillips. Also, to Allen Casey, who introduced us to the wonders of diving, and to Dr. John Worth for his expertise in prehistoric Southeastern cultures.

Finally, we acknowledge our editors and thank them for their input and time spent on our behalf: Mike Garrett, Jeff Orenstein, Madeline Dooley, Dana Miklos, Betty Conner, and certainly Glynda Marlowe. And to everyone else that read snippets of chapters, understood our reclusive attitude, cut our grass when it got too long or helped us in any other way, we are forever indebted.

It would be remiss of us not to recognize some of the writers who helped influence the development of Catherine Faith Scott and Micah Marlowe. A special thanks to Robert Penn Warren and his powerful novel *All the King's Men*; Edward Albee and Tennessee Williams for their strong female characters; Harper Lee for her gift of Atticus Finch; F. Scott Fitzgerald for reminding us of Plato's cave; T. S. Eliot, Walt Whitman, and Allan Ginsberg for their poetic consciousness; Lillian Hellman, Albert Camus and Thomas Carlyle for words that reach the soul; William Shakespeare and Nathanial Hawthorne for works that have endured; and finally St. Therese of Lisieux, the Little Flower, for reminding us all of our childhood innocence.

To those we have taught
and to those who have taught us

I see the veins in the leaves and know the branches and the tree from which they grew. And I know I am the leaf, I am the branch and I am the tree.

-Micah and Catherine-

We journeyed through miles of red clay before I awakened to the ground beneath my borrowed boots, and as I did, sandhill cranes, venturing south, traced in the sky a cross that seemed to defy coincidence.

-Catherine-

We cannot help that we are but a streak of light in existence, but the thunder comes from our own hand. A bitter fruit can become the most beatiful tree.

-Micah-

Prologue

June

I didn't want it to end this way. I didn't want to say "I love you" for the first time in a crowded courtroom under the harshness of fluorescent light. I imagined it so much differently. A warm salt breeze lingers over our bodies as we drink cold beer under the night sky. Our hands lightly touch, and a shooting star drops toward the horizon. You take me in your arms and kiss me so deeply I feel your sighed breath inside of me and smell the spicy scent of soap on your unshaven face, and it's then I say for the first time, "I love you."

Maybe that's why you withdrew from me afterwards. "I love you" should be whispered not shouted, spoken intimately to one person, not yelled across a room in front of strangers. I'm sorry it had to be that way. And maybe someday you'll forgive me for putting you in such an awkward position. I do thank you for giving me your wisdom and your wit; if only I could know the other half of your soul the way you showed me nature's other half. Remember how you made me see the cutter ants, hundreds of them lined up the trunk of the young grapefruit tree? Determined and unyielding, they stripped the fertile limbs of rich and succulent greenery. Like so many handmaidens heaving swollen vessels, the ants patiently displaced half a tree in one evening's seemingly unending procession. Never completely stripping the tree of its leaves, but allowing enough life to remain on the limbs for the tree to renew itself, they died leaving paths full of vegetation as their legacy. It was watching the cutter ants that made me want to grow back the fragments of myself that had been carried away by my own blind shredders. I wanted you to know that.

September

Several years ago, I was crawling along the river bottom hunting for fossils and artifacts in the darkest of water. Sensing a presence, I moved my light forward to see a slight red object resembling a waving rag moving with the current. The murkiness made focusing on anything more than five feet away difficult, so I pulled myself closer till I was perhaps two feet from the perplexing item. During our lives, there have been instances in which something suddenly comes into focus and frightens us, but we refuse to or perhaps cannot move forward. That is exactly what happened when I shined my light a couple inches to the left and saw a smooth white conical tooth. I recognized it as belonging to an alligator, and as I slowly moved my light up and around, the entire mouth came into view. Lying within an arm's reach in front of me was an alligator about twelve feet long, his mouth opened as a defensive maneuver, the red waving rag his tongue. Six inches was all that separated me from crushing jaws and an agonizing death in forty feet of lonely blackness. Its elliptical eyes reflected my light, and I sensed its desire for me to move closer. I looked down and beside my hand was a leathery-clawed foot as large as a baseball glove. By simply spreading my fingers, I could have touched it. My heart pounded in my ears and my focus crystallized. While I slowly backed away and hid in the shadowy waters along the river bottom, I envisioned the creature suddenly appearing from within a rush of stirred-up mud. Going immediately to the surface was not my best option; in the event it followed me to the top, the animal would have the advantage. So, after an indeterminate amount of time, I crawled down river and hoped I was not being tracked. Each log I approached pretended to be my nemesis, but before long, I felt confident enough to swim upward to the boat.

I suppose you wonder why I tell you this story, but there is a reason. I deal with situations such as these and never see the connection with my life above the water. Backing away from confrontation is necessary in the face of danger. Sometimes, however, a day comes along in which fear must be confronted and growth attained by doing so. I wrote earlier of being frightened and unable to move. Because I have been by myself for so long, the thought of sharing my world has become as fearsome as facing the alligator. My heart races as I consider this, but now I fear most the inability to move. There exists at this moment someone who will have more impact on us than anyone else alive. If we're lucky, we will meet that person and if wise, we will find that person. I have been lucky already and now I must be wise. I know where my heart is, and it is with you …

Chapter 1

"Ah, Tess, I'm sorry, so sorry," I whispered over and over to my phantom baby.

I crushed the starched sleeve of Marshall's shirt with my hands and laid it back on the bed next to his other dress shirts. My mind a blank of white fire, I sank to the wooden planks and hugged my knees as I curled into a tight ball. Rocking back and forth, I tried to put out the fire now burning inside of me.

"Get up, Cat," Marshall said, entering the room. "That's not going to help. Come on."

I pulled my hand violently from his and held myself tighter inside my circle. He leaned down and caressed my hair. "Do you want me to get you anything? Water?"

"Please don't go. The bad stuff always comes when I'm alone."

He wiped the tears from my eyes with his manicured fingers. "I'm really behind the eight ball. I can't deal with this right now. Besides, you'll feel better when you get out of the house, play some tennis, talk to the girls. Grading papers will keep you busy. I'll be back in no time."

"You're always leaving me. It wasn't so bad when you left me with the kids, but now I have no one."

"You're not being fair. It's a multi-million dollar acquisition, and I'm the only one to close it."

"Can you leave in the morning instead? One day can't make much of a difference."

"I can't. I have to be there tomorrow night before the board meeting. The deadline is this week." Marshall creased the skin on his forehead with his fingers. "Try to get through this, Baby … for me. It's a big one. After the deal, I'll try to plan a few weeks to work at home. I have the Japan meeting, but that's not for at least a month." He turned to his suitcase. "Help me pack. That'll give us a few minutes," he said with a forced laugh.

"I can't help you leave me again," I said as Marshall half-pulled and half-helped me to my feet. I sat unsteadily on the bed and watched him. "I wrinkled your shirt. Want me to fix it?"

"Jesus Chr …" he caught himself. "No, no, it's alright. If I need another, I'll have Helena buy one. She won't complain about shopping in Paris." Marshall carefully placed the folded shirts and pressed pants inside his luggage. With a hurried pace, he reached into the dresser and pulled out his socks and underwear. As he tucked his briefs neatly away, he suddenly turned to me. "Why now? After all these years?" Marshall scrutinized the mascara bleeding around my eyes and down my face.

"I don't know. Ever since the kids left, she keeps coming back to me. No matter how much time passes, I still wear the mark of Cain. If it weren't for me, she'd be alive. Maybe I should've died too." I pushed my face into my hands and choked on my words. "I let my baby die."

Marshall sat next to me and gripped my shoulders. "You didn't kill her. It was an accident. Don't do this. How many years can you go on like this? It was so long ago. I thought you were better."

"Hug me." He held me close, just long enough for me to feel the beating of his heart. Then he let go and continued packing.

"Why don't you wash your face and get ready for your tennis match? You'll feel better." He glanced over at me and saw the dangerous look in my eyes. "If there was any way I could stay, I would. I love you, Catherine. Always will. But you have to be stronger. For the kids … for us."

"If only I could've rocked her one more time."

"You have two other children. Let her go," he said with a hint of impatience.

"But they aren't here anymore."

"You can see them or talk to them whenever you want."

But the child I wanted now was Therese, my little Tessy, the child I turned my back on, the child who died before my eyes. Marshall would never understand because he wasn't there, and she wasn't his.

"Guess it's time to hit the road. Come here," he said as he held me with one arm and pushed the hair out of my face with the other. It felt safe. "I love you," he whispered in my ear.

"Do you really?"

"You know I do, but I have to go before I miss my plane." He wheeled his suitcase across the floor. "Tickets, itinerary, glasses … I'll call you when I get there." After a quick kiss goodbye, he sheepishly asked if I would be all right.

"I don't have much of a choice, huh?"

"You'll be fine. See you in a couple weeks. Wish me luck," he said just before he walked away from the bedroom. I listened for the sound of the ignition, the opening and closing of the garage door, and the slow rise of the engine as the Porsche slid away from the house. Like a player on a vibrating game board, I moved thoughtlessly to the kitchen bar and poured myself a glass of wine. I sat at the counter twisting the crystal back and forth between my fingers.

"Good luck," I toasted to the empty room. Twenty minutes later, dressed for tennis, I grabbed my racquet, stepped over the shattered glass, and climbed into my Lexus. The tennis courts were about ten minutes away, long enough for me to lose my fragile composure. The car parked, I played with the door handle and tried to sort out my emotions. It's been over for twenty-some years, I thought to myself. You're damn lucky he stays married to you.

As I walked toward my teammates, I thought about running back to the car and driving home to my bed. At least there, I could hide in the comfort of my dreams. But lately even the recurrent dreams of simpler times were turning into nightmares. I was smiling when I walked onto the court, but the lights drew attention to my reddened eyes and blotchy face.

"You okay?" my partner Lisa asked. "You look pretty bad. You sure you can play?"

"I don't know. Maybe if I have some water, I'll feel better."

"You look like you've lost your Lord and Taylor card," Debra quipped. "Have a fight with Marshall?"

"No, not really. He had to leave again."

"And you're upset? You've got it all wrong, girl," Lisa said. "It's better when they're gone. You can do what you want then."

I forced a laugh. "I wish I could see it that way."

"You need to start coming to more of our happy hours, not just on Friday."

"Yeah, maybe you're right." I clutched my racquet tightly in my hand. "I hear Willow Spring's tough. Let's hit a few. I'll be fine." I smashed the ball across the court, warming to the steady rhythm of backhand and forehand. By the time the match started, the burning inside me had cooled. And when the match was over, I had depleted my body of so much energy, I could not think. My legs and arms ached as I sat on the bench outside the fence.

"You played like a machine. Great match, Cat," Debra said as she sauntered off. As an afterthought, she yelled across the parking lot, "Coming over for blender hour tomorrow?"

"Sure," I said with a weak smile. "Sounds fun."

That night I fell exhausted into bed and almost forgot Marshall was gone and Therese was dead.

Chapter 2

To me, trees represent sin, penance, forgiveness, and redemption. Each time a leaf drops to the ground, the intruding light reveals more of the tree. Its existence depends upon these sacrifices returning to the forest floor as they nourish the roots in an endless revolution. I see the veins in the leaves, and know the branches and the tree from which they grew. And I know I am the leaf, I am the branch and I am the tree. Just as the equinoxes reflect the symmetry of day and night, the fallen leaves reflect the symmetry of life and death. My body falls and shrivels, but the spirit stands and grows. Each autumn, the tree sheds its leaves and each spring new ones are born. It is as if all our sins are wasted away. We start anew, virginal, fresh, hopeful … full of dreams and infinite love.

Before Micah Marlowe almost drowned me in salt water, my tree, suspended over soundless Caribbean waters, was, as yet, unfound. Living at the top of the economic ladder, I was at the bottom rung of despair. I was a cryptogram, a jumbled bunch of letters that didn't make any sense, even to me, the one who got the letters all mixed up in the first place. My classroom, however, had always been my inoculation for insanity. It had never before overlapped with my personal life until the day a student, accidentally or not, left a note on a desk. The school week had ended and students filed out either to get on the buses or scurry to the parking lot for their quick escape from traffic. I walked to the back of the room to turn out the lights on that half of my portable classroom and saw a twice-folded, handwritten note. Generally, I would have just thrown it away but not this time. The unrecognized scribble said: "It's started again with my Dad. I have hinted about it with my teacher but not really told him. I wish he were my father." I put the note in my pocket and made a mental reminder to check on it Monday morning. Looking back, I realize now I should have followed up on it right away, but I didn't. I used to think I didn't know why, but now I know. By trying to drown out the memories of my violent past, I prolonged the anguish of a young girl's abusive present. I wouldn't look at the letter again until much later, when I was ready to see it. But by then, my world would change, for the better and for the worse. I would come to know my nightlights, a silhouetted tree and the redemption I had longed for. But not without a price.

#

Two summers after the Olympics, Atlanta was still enjoying its status as celebrity host, even though the city leaders fumed over the continual adverse publicity about the questionable safety of Olympic Park. When outsiders commented the cauldron that held the torch looked like an oversized McDonald's french-fry container, most Atlantans defended its new city marker with pride. It was that same pride that kept most Atlantans celebrating the games long after they were gone. My neighborhood was no exception; if anything, we celebrated more and often on the back of someone's two-tiered deck.

My husband Marshall, a corporate lawyer for a major global conglomerate, traveled weekly to Western Europe or to the Far East. The company would not give me permission to use its name, since Marshall represented the corporation in the century's biggest controversy over feminine hygiene products. The company is still very sensitive over the whole litigious stir and doesn't wish to be involved in another lawsuit involving women and politics. Marshall managed to settle the case rather quickly, saving the company millions of dollars, and the Board of Directors promoted him to handle International Affairs, which meant more money and more time away from home. If he didn't run into any plane delays, Marshall generally arrived home Friday evenings around seven. Usually, by the time Marshall walked through the front door, I had downed three or four glasses of white wine; either I was hosting a happy hour myself, or I had returned from one. Sometimes, instead of coming home, I left a message on the answering machine. "Hey Marshall, it's me. We're over at Monica's house tonight. Stop by when you get home. Robb and Chuck are on their way. Love you, bye." If I slurred my words into the machine, Marshall came over right at seven. But if I sounded sober, Marshall, like most of the neighborhood men, would meander over to the happy hour somewhere between eight and nine. When the men arrived, they ordered pizza for the kids and made sure their wives had a safe ride home. Friday night was something of a witching hour for the women. We drank all afternoon and howled all night.

One evening, though, in early October, I surprised Marshall by being stone sober when he came home. I had just finished the first week of teaching Robert Penn Warren's *All the King's Men*, and having carried the main character Jack Burden around in my head all week, I couldn't face the banal banter of buzzed women. By going through Jack's epiphany, I went through a watered-down version of my own.

So, instead of rushing home after school and checking my answering machine to see where the bacchanalian fete would be that afternoon, I stopped by Kroger's and picked up some tuna and flowers. While the lady in the floral department wrapped my stems of gardenias and star irises, I made my way over to the fish counter. A taxidermy tarpon, his mouth forever gaping, hung above the separate cases of frozen and fresh fish. The slow-moving lobsters in the tank next to the fresh fish case looked too old to be worth the 18.99 a pound advertised on the hanging chalkboard above them. I felt like taking out their wooden claw restrainers, giving some dignity to these bottom feeders, but instead stayed loyal to my fish man and his fingers. Two other boards advertised Nova Lox for 4.99 a tray and the daily special, orange roughy, for a dollar more per pound. I strolled over to the fresh fish case and examined the tuna. The steaks had a nice red color to them and were plenty thick enough for the grill. Behind the fish counter, Stephan, late thirties, lean and muscular physique, graying temples bleached by the sun, beamed his cigarette-stained teeth at me. He had the look of a man who spent weeks on a shrimp boat working the nets nonstop for hours at a time. A man's man. A woman's passion.

"Well, hello, Ms. Scott, how are you today?" Stephan always addressed me formally in public. I'd been coming to see my tilapia and tuna man once, twice, maybe three times a week, sometimes for fish. The two times I saw him in his apartment, and any time we spoke on the phone, he was much less formal.

"I'm as happy as a little clam, Stephan. Especially since it's finally the weekend." My bra strap had slipped down on my shoulder, and I discreetly slipped my hand under my emerald silk blouse and pulled it in place.

"I'll be right with you. I just have one more customer to finish up." The customer, a young overweight mom pushing twin toddlers in the cart, gave me the once-over. I smiled sweetly at the harried, unkempt woman.

"I bet they keep you busy," I felt myself obligated to say. The ends of her thick brown hair were dry and split. She needed a trim badly.

"They sure do," she mumbled. "Jonathan! Sit down! Here, eat your animal crackers." His chubby little hands reached in the cookie box and grabbed more crackers than he could hold. Several spilled onto the floor.

"You're making a mess, Jonathan. No, Chelsea, don't take his cookies from him." Stephan handed her two wrapped packages. "Thanks."

When she left, I reached across the fish case and grabbed a sample cracker with imitation crab dip spread on it. I bit into it.

"Mmmm. This stuff is really good, Stephan. Did you make this?"

"Yeah, I made a batch this morning—it's real easy to make."

"I admire a man who cooks," I said in my best Blanche DuBois imitation.

"I bet you say that to all the guys."

"I'm serious, I really do think it's great that you can cook." Another customer approached the fish case. This time a middle-aged woman in a long jean dress scrutinized the shellfish. Her short hair was sharply angled in the back like a Spanish helmet, and her penny loafers were scuffed and worn—must be an elementary teacher. "Go ahead and wait on her ... I'm still thinking about what I want."

Stephan looked at me skeptically. He had been waiting on me for almost a year before he got up enough nerve to flirt with me. At first, it was a brighter smile than usual and a warm "How are you today?" Later, he commented on the color of my hair and told me he thought I looked like a famous young movie star. His generous compliments drew me to the fish counter more often. One day he mentioned the name of a dive he goes to on Wednesday nights. For the hell of it, I talked my friend Lisa into going to the watering hole with me. The place was about thirty minutes north of Alpharetta in Forsyth County, definitely rural Georgia. The parking lot was full of Harley-Davidsons and pick-up trucks with over-sized tires splashed with mud. We could hear the music blaring before we even got out of my Lexus. On the outside of the short brick building the name SPONDIVITS glowered in large neon lights above the parking lot. A small neon sign advertising Budweiser, the "u" and the "i" burned out, shone in the restaurant's only window. Inside, Stephan was sitting at the bar, drinking a Miller and smoking unfiltered Camels. The head of a hammerhead shark smiled at us from behind the bar. Stephan laughed when he saw me.

"I'll be damn, look who's here, my favorite customer." He put his hand around my waist and pulled me closer. I could smell the alcohol on his breath.

"What can I get ya to drink?"

"What are *you* drinking?" I said.

"Miller Lite."

"I'll have one of those."

"What'll your friend have?"

"I'll have the house Chardonnay," Lisa said.

"You have got to be kidding. Where do you think you *are*, the opera house? You have two choices, beer or hard liquor. Pick one."

"How about a margarita?"

"Now, that's better." He turned away to yell our drink order at the waiter washing glasses in the already dirty water.

"We'll buy the next rounds."

Except for his teeth, he was very good looking in a Florida sort of way. I found out that night he actually lived in Key West for a while, but grew up in Milwaukee. He ended up in Atlanta because he was busted here for transporting marijuana back to Wisconsin. He spent a few months in jail, and when he got out he decided to stay, mostly because he had no money to get home. The beer loosening his tongue a bit, he told me I had beautiful eyes and great legs. Later he switched to Jack Daniels, the shots turning him into an expert on religion, politics, sex and "Mary Jane." He philosophized and waxed poetic until Lisa became bored and we had to go home. Before I left, Stephan and I discreetly exchanged phone numbers. After that, we talked on the phone every week, and I even spent a couple of nights on the futon with him in his apartment. Nothing big. We just mainly kissed, and occasionally I let him put his hand up my blouse. It was very exciting and dramatic—country club maven and English teacher tantalizing the fish man at Kroger's—what screenwriter wouldn't want to get hold of that one? But once school started, I became too busy to pursue our little romance.

"Anything else, Ma'am?"

"No, I don't think so." It was almost seven, the time when families ate dinner. No wonder the store was almost empty.

"So, Ms. Scott, what're your plans for the weekend?"

"Not much. Just a quiet evening at home tonight ... Cook some tuna ... Bottle of wine ... Relax ... Barbecue tomorrow at the Johnson's ... Sunday, tennis."

"I'm off Sunday night."

"Oh, really? What're you going to do with a free Sunday night?" I pushed my bangs out of my eyes, and then ran my fingers through the back of my shoulder-length hair.

"I don't know. Have any ideas?" This time when he smiled, I didn't just see his strong blue eyes or muscular shoulders. I saw Jack Burden, cynical, mysterious, trying to make sense out of the universe. Is there a higher spiritual power? Or is life nothing more than a Big Twitch? "The game's on Sunday night. Maybe after tennis, you could come over for a beer." Stephan knew Marshall's schedule by heart. Home Friday at seven, out Sunday by five.

"Let me have a pound and a half of tuna. Wait. Better make it two. I'm really hungry."

"How hungry are you, Ms. Scott?" I could smell the salty sweat on him and see it on his arms and neck. Not like Marshall, antiseptic, corporate player, Marshall. I took a deep breath.

"Wrap it up. You have other customers." Out of the corner of my eye, I could see two people perusing the fish cases. A young guy with a shaved head leaned over the frozen fish case. Probably a bachelor looking for something he could nuke in the microwave. The other customer, a woman with short generic hair, tapped the fish counter impatiently; she could be thirty or fifty, it was hard to tell. As he wrapped the tuna, he mangled Buffet's *Attitudes and Latitudes.*

"Here you go, Ma'am," he said. My fingers brushed his as I took the white package.

"I like a good beer every once in awhile," I said. I touched my bottom lip with my index finger.

"One?"

"It depends on the beer." My eyes wandered up and down his white uniform. Orange stains lined the sides of his white coat where he must have wiped the fish blood from his hands.

"Excuse me. I'm in a hurry," the woman customer said.

"What can I get for you, ma'am?"

"Two pounds, uncooked jumbo shrimp ... today."

Stephan weighed the shrimp and packed it in a plastic bag. He tore a white sheet of butcher paper from its huge roll and expertly wrapped the shrimp. He smiled at me as he handed her the package.

"Do you still like Miller?"

"Yes."

"Good, cause that's all I got. Still got my number?"

"Of course, silly."

"You haven't called me lately so I figured the only reason could be that you lost it."

The young man glanced at us and grabbed a package of frozen fish before leaving.

"I've been busy grading papers. Teaching takes up a lot of my time."

"So, you gonna call me?" He liked what he saw. And why not? A slim skirt, a push-up bra, a tight blouse that showed. Over forty and I still turned men's heads.

I stared at his sun-soaked face and noticed his eyelashes were almost white. The skin under his eyes was permanently crimped, and deep crows feet extended down the sides of his cheeks. His eyes were bloodshot; too many beers and a heavy menu of drugs. I had no idea whether he was intelligent or not—I did know, however, that he liked working with fish. Maybe surfer boy felt an affinity with the tilapia and tuna because they had been displaced from their ocean home as he perhaps thought he was. Or maybe as he sliced into flesh day after day, he narrowed his life to the heaves of blood on the steel cutting tables behind the lighted glass cases.

"Sure, I'll give you a call." I said it. Like I was available. Like I'd done it before.

He smiled at me again with his stained teeth. It bothered me.

Chapter 3

By the time I arrived home, it was quarter past seven; Marshall could walk through the door any minute. I hurriedly cut and arranged the flowers in a crystal Swedish vase and set them on the cook island. The pink-and-white flowers added a warm touch to the stark black granite counter. I glanced around the kitchen, pleased with the selections I had made four years ago. My kitchen was an emotional montage of purple, red and gold swathed fabric, a cadre for stainless steel appliances and fossilized stone tile. The stepped cherry cabinets with glass inserts showed off my collections of European crystal and Lamoge china. The high ceilings and lead glass windows made experimenting with new recipes and cooking the staples of early-married life more like artistic renderings than necessary drudgery. When Marshall was home, he spent as much time in the kitchen as he did in the bedroom. We left Cincinnati so Marshall could pursue his litigious dream job. He appeased my distress of leaving Sammy and Elizabeth, both enrolled in Midwestern universities, Elizabeth, a freshman at Miami of Ohio, Sammy, a junior at Wittenberg, not to mention the rest of my family and lifelong friends, by giving me carte blanche building and decorating a new home in Atlanta.

A canvas for romantic longing and edgy expressionism, my house heralded my collections of antiques and abstract art; Persian rugs and harlequin-patterned window shades; paintings resembling Monet and those resembling Munch. But it was the fish tank that held my soul. A curved aquarium, four feet high, built center wall, separated the foyer from the great room. The acrylic tank held 640 gallons of salt water and an array of exotic marine life: tangs, porcupine puffer, African starfish, blue jaw trigger, Cortez angel, Auriga butterfly, all kept alive by another aquarium system attached to pipes and tubes and filters hidden away in the basement. Maintenance men came bimonthly to check the coal in the filtering system and to add new salt to balance the salinity of the upstairs tank. An occasional smudge of green algae appeared on the inside of the acrylic wall, but a quick swipe of a long brush cleaned the unwanted contaminant away. Only healthy red algae collected on the crushed pink shells lining the bottom of the aquarium. Adjacent to the tank stood an 18th century English Chippendale gaming table with a glass bust of a woman designed by a recent Italian artist. Her painted yellow hair jutted out to one side as if permanently caught in an ice storm. She had faces on all four sides of her head, her eyes turquoise and marmoreal, her lips red and lascivious. Most of the abstract art came from Italy, the antiques from England and France.

Marshall complained just once about my decorating. I commissioned my painter and eventual beer-drinking buddy Will to design large geometric shapes in ochre, Chinese red, plum and sea green, and then had him tape the colored boards on the foyer ceiling. This project was not easy since the foyer ceiling was fourteen feet high. Standing, sometimes lying on scaffolding, my neighborhood Michelangelo arranged and rearranged the shapes until they looked symmetrically perfect from the hallway where I was standing. He was my medium to the Chapel ceiling. After Will took down the boards and then painted the exact shapes on the ceiling, I had the builder design the foyer lights so that the colors could easily be seen from the outside. The first week after the house was finished, Marshall and I took walks at night just to see the painted ceiling through the second floor window above the front door. Marshall grumbled that we would be considered the wackos of the neighborhood; I marveled that something so incredibly beautiful came out of my imagination.

"Cat? You home?" Marshall bellowed. I heard him slam the heavy glass door behind him.

"In here," I yelled from the kitchen.

When I entered the foyer, Marshall, suit coat slung over his arm, was watching the nasso tangs and angelfish glide by in their small ocean. "Hello, little buddies. You doing okay? Has mommy fed you today?" From the Chippendale table, the Mediterranean blue eyes of the lady's head peered vacantly at me. No matter where I was in relationship to the glass head, a pair of eyes followed me.

"I was just about to change into my jeans." I placed my hand on his back. "Did you have a good week in Paris?"

"Work is work. Where was the drunk-fest tonight?"

"I don't know—I haven't checked the answering machine." I stood like a statue waiting for Marshall to at least look at me.

"Do you think the puffer's moving a little slow?"

"I haven't noticed ... I really just got home."

Marshall finally turned and faced me. "How was your week, Cat?" Marshall loosened his tie, his white shirt impeccable even after the long plane ride.

"Fine. I taught my favorite novel *All the King's Men*. The kids couldn't get over Lois, his wife. They thought it was pretty funny that as soon as she started talking he divorced her."

"Hew, I could use a cold one."

"Did you get to do any fun things in Paris this time?"

"Not really. You know how it is—from plane to board room."

"Marshall, aren't you even going to kiss me hello?"

"Oh yeah, sure ..." He quickly brushed his lips across my cheek. I wouldn't really call it a kiss. Marshall turned toward the aquarium and studied the corners of the glass walls.

"Go in and get a beer," I suggested. "I'm going to throw on a pair of jeans."

"We have any of that Corona left?"

"Look in the laundry room fridge," I yelled from the bedroom.

Ten minutes later, in jeans and a silk T-shirt I found in a boutique across town, I charged the kitchen armed with the desire to have a romantic evening. Marshall, however, was sitting at the dinette table, content in reading *The Wall Street Journal*.

"So, how's the stock doing?"

"Could be better." Marshall didn't look up.

"I bought some tuna to grill for dinner."

"Mmmmhmmm. Sounds good."

"Why don't you change and then fire up the grill? I thought we could have some wine first—I brought up your favorite Merlot." I ran my hands suggestively up and down his back. "We can go skinny-dipping in the pool, and, well, you never know after that."

"You know you won't go in the pool, Cat. I don't know why you ever had the damn thing put in." Marshall pushed back the Windsor chair. "I'm going to change."

I uncorked the bottle of Merlot and poured the wine into my favorite crystal wine goblets. The cobalt glasses added to the ambience of the room, making the idea of a cozy twosome cooking together a very palatable idea.

"So what happened at work this week?" I asked when Marshall returned to the kitchen.

"I told you ... same old stuff ... someone's trying to copy our products—there's always some mess to straighten out. What's this?"

"Your favorite Merlot."

"I'm drinking a beer."

"I thought you might like some after your beer."

"Hold the wine. It needs to breathe anyway."

"I thought you liked your job." I spread crushed garlic around the insides of a wooden salad bowl.

"I do ... "

"Then why do complain about it all the time?"

"I just don't like to talk about it when I get home."

"When *do* you like to talk about it?"

Marshall took a long swing of Corona. "Ah, that hits the spot. What'd you ask me?"

"Can I drink your glass of wine?"

"You always do—So what've you been up to all week?"

"I taught all week."

"Sounds interesting." Marshall picked up the paper.

"Do you want me to marinate the tuna?"

"Sure, why not?"

"When do you want to eat?"

"I don't care." Marshall turned on the television. When we built the house, I thought it would be a good idea to have two TVs suspended from the ceiling. Anticipating parties arranged around sports events, I envisioned two games on at once. Now, I wasn't so sure having even one TV in the kitchen was a good idea.

I put the bread cubes in the oven and set the timer for five minutes. Marshall was engrossed in CNN and the *Journal.*

"Hey, can you get me another?" he finally said.

"Sure. You want a lime in it?" When he didn't respond, I reached in the fridge for a Corona and studied the back of his head. Even though he had plenty of curly gray hair in the front, the hair was thinning on the crown. His sunburned scalp was beginning to show beneath the thin wavy strands; even the mole on the back of his head was visible. I used to feel that mole when I ran my fingers through his once-thick hair, but that was a long time ago.

"Here's your beer." I sat the bottle in front of him and then wrapped my arms around his shoulders and kissed him on the back of the neck. For an instant he grabbed my hand; then he let it go. I walked back over to the granite counter and poured another glass of wine. The bottle was just about gone.

I took the croutons out of the oven and threw them in with the Romaine lettuce. I opened a can of anchovies, drained them and carefully placed them among the lettuce leaves.

"Marshall."

"Hold on—I'm listening to this—" Marshall kept his watery gray eyes fixated on the TV set. I studied his profile while tossing the salad. Face tanned from playing thirty-six holes of golf almost every weekend, lean body—Marshall prided himself in not having a beer gut—great smile, large white teeth, Marshall was still a very handsome and sexy man. His powerful position added to his sexuality, at least to some women. Whenever we went to corporate parties, women, especially younger women, monopolized all of his time. The women in the neighborhood liked Marshall, too. They probably were upset that he wasn't at the extended Friday night happy hour that night. He swore he never had an affair, and since I had no evidence to the contrary I believed him. I always wondered why he hadn't. Certainly, he had been tempted with all the women he meets. A martyr complex too deep for either of us to understand.

Sexually driven since my first pubic hairs showed up, I must have inherited my father's genes. According to my mother, he wanted sex all the time. Maybe it had nothing to do with his genes and everything to do with my mother—my father never could resist her. Lately, Marshall didn't have any trouble resisting me. It wasn't always like that.

I often asked for my parents' help, especially regarding Marshall and me, but they never seemed to listen. They died a good five years ago, so I didn't exactly talk to them. It was communication of the mind, half-praying and half-imagining. My parents had one of those rare happy marriages. Heartfelt joy showed on my mother's face when she was with my father. She laughed at his forgetfulness and teased him out of his crabbiness. No one would guess my mother lived with a man suffering from depression. They made love well into their seventies, terminated only by disease and finally death. Long before that, when I lived at home, I knew they "did it" at least three times a week, if not more. I heard them because my bedroom was right next to theirs and the walls were not very soundproof. I remember being nauseated and fascinated all at once. How could two middle-aged people like each other's bodies so much? Breast cancer, esophagus cancer, menopause, old age, my dad's love for my mother never missed a beat.

Since the move, I started begging for their help. Marshall had turned into a stranger and I had turned into an even bigger stranger. The answers never seemed to come. A few years back, Marshall and I tried counseling, but Marshall slathered on the charm and won the therapist over to his side. He didn't know it was at his expense. The therapist made light of my concerns and said I was just experiencing "the usual ups and downs of marriage." I remember thinking if that was true, then, like war, marriage must be another of humanity's barbaric holdovers. The rising divorce rate in the United States could indicate we are moving towards civilization not away from it if you follow that line of thinking.

"Did you want something?" Marshall snapped me out of my reflection.

"I was thinking about the therapist with the banana tits."

"What?"

"Do I need to open another bottle of wine? Or do you want another beer?"

"I'll have some wine. I'll do the fish in a minute." Marshall retreated back to the TV.

"It's tuna ... fish." I emptied the bottle and looked up at the ceiling. Mom, Dad, I prayed. If Marshall and I have a good night tonight, I will not go to Stephan's apartment on Sunday. I really want a good marriage; I just don't know how to get it ... Maybe if we get a hobby together—I will take up golf, and Marshall will read the literature I love, and we'll talk for hours and hours and I will learn what "offsides" means.

"What're you doing, Cat?"

"Thinking."

"Is there something up there I should know about?"

"Nope, it's the same white ceiling."

Marshall shook his head. "While you were communing with the ceiling, I put the tuna on. Ready in ten minutes."

"Great. I'll set the table." I took two candles out of a drawer.

"What are those for?"

"I thought we would have a romantic dinner."

"Oh, Jesus."

"What's wrong with that? Don't most couples have romantic dinners every once in awhile?"

"Did you open that second bottle of wine?"

"I'm doing that now." I filled his glass and mine. "Here you go. Toast? To us?"

"Toast. To us ..." Marshall almost emptied the entire goblet after the first drink. I refilled his glass.

"I'll check the tuna."

"Fine." I lit the candles and finished setting the table.

"Mmmmm, doesn't the tuna look good?" Marshall set the platter on the table. "Where's the lemon?"

"Oh shoot, I knew I forgot something."

"Jesus, Catherine, you buy tuna and forget the lemon? You must be suffering from early onset."

I hated it when Marshall tried to make me out to be an old biddy hen. I was five years younger than he after all.

"That's a crappy thing to say."

"Well, hell ... forgot the lemon?" His voice rose half an octave.

"It's not the end of the world. Why don't you put some tartar sauce on the fish."

"I'm trying to watch my weight."

"Like I'm not?"

"Lemon would've been so nice but not now I guess."

"Well, we don't have any. Here, have some salad." I felt like dumping it on his lap.

"Have you heard from the kids lately?" Marshall said in between gulps of fish. I didn't feel very much like eating.

"No, not lately."

"Why don't you call them?"

"Why don't you swallow before you speak?"

"Now what? I can't eat the way I want to in my own house?"

"I can see the food when you talk. I bet you don't eat like that in Paris."

"Why do you have to act like such a bitch?"

"I only asked you to swallow your food before you talk. How am I acting like a bitch?"

"So much for a romantic evening." Marshall got up from the table and turned on the TV. He poured himself another glass of wine.

"Everything I do is wrong. Is this really only over a lemon?" Marshall retreated into his newspaper.

"Marshall! Put the newspaper down and answer my question!"

"What?"

"Are you having an affair?"

"Not this shit again."

"Well, what am I supposed to think? You never talk, you're always gone."

"It's called work, for God's sake."

"I doubt very much that you are working for God."

"You think you're funny? You know damn well I'm working for you ... so you can have this house, your expensive clothes, cars, country club ... "

"Who said I wanted all those things?"

"Give me a God damn break. You could not ... "

"I want someone who talks to me."

"I *do* talk to you ... it's just that you forgot the lemon."

"What!"

"I'm not home an hour before you start in on something—Is that the phone?"

"Let it ring."

"It might be one of the kids." Marshall got up from the table and walked to the phone.

"Hello? Hey, Neil ... It's still going on? Who's all there? I'll ask. Cat ... We're just finishing up dinner ... Yeah ... tee-off at eight ... No, what? Right out in the open? Damn, I am never around when all the good stuff happens. Shit ... Is Robb there? I don't know if I can take that prick two weekends in row. Hold on a minute. Cat, it's Neil."

"What does he want?"

"Just take the phone."

"Hey, Neil. Party still going on? I think we'll pass tonight. It's been a rough week. We're having a romantic evening ... Mmmmhmm ... We sure will ... I'm not telling ... Hold on a minute. Marshall, Neil said you're a lucky devil ... Okay ... Tomorrow night, I'll be there. I don't know about Marshall. Ha ... Okay, then. See ya tomorrow. Bye."

"I'm going to bed."

"Aren't you going to finish eating?"

"Nah, put it in the fridge. I can eat it tomorrow."

"It's only eight-thirty."

"Long week."

"Do you want me to come with you?"

"I'm going to sleep, Cat."

"But you wanted to go to the party … "

"I have to get up early for golf, remember?"

"Good night, Marshall," I whispered after he had gone. I pushed the empty chair back into its place. What did the builder call this octagonal extension of the kitchen? The morning room, I think he called it. Or was it mourning?

After I loaded the dishwasher, I poured myself another glass of wine, turned off the lights, and slowly walked to the great room. I sunk into the multi-cushioned couch and closed my eyes. My head spun from too much wine, and I had to open my eyes to stop the motion. The lights from the tank cast a prism of jumping shadows on my arms and legs. If I closed one eye, the shadows narrowed; if I kept both eyes open, there were twice as many. Half-closed, my eyes could see flitters of light and color but little definition. Open … Close … Half-close … Open … Close … The blue jaw trigger and Cortez angel gaped at me from the other side of the wall. Yellow, purple, and emerald fish glided slowly past the spiny clusters of painted coral. Like psychedelic sails flapping impassively in a slow wind, the creatures tacked the waters inside the curved wall. Back and forth. All day and all night … until they slowed and hid among the sculpted reef. The tank blurred into moving impressionism. I drank the rest of my wine and set the glass on the white marble coffee table. Something, my movement perhaps, must have disturbed the puffer fish. He frantically swam from one end of the tank to the other. I drunkenly walked over to the tank to see if he had his mouth pulled back exposing his two large teeth, one upper and one lower. Sure enough, his mouth was open. I could hear his teeth clacking together. The only creature in the tank almost absent of color, he was black with white spots. His orange-flecked eye locked on mine. Can he see into my world as I see into his? I gently brushed my hand along the acrylic wall. "Shhh, calm down, you'll be okay … Drink a little wine to go to sleep … "

I struggled into bed and fell into a restless sleep, my dreams jarred by haunting creatures, luminous emerald, blue and purple skin, yellow eyes, imprisoned by a transparent screen. The frantic puffer accused me, so alone in his colorlessness ... I wanted to release him, but to what? His death? His freedom? I dreamed of Stephan peeling the gray slippery skin of dead fish, slicing through muscle and tissue and fat, the dim eyes of discarded heads huddled together in a rubber trash bin, beckoning him. We had something in common, Stephan and I.

Chapter 4

I woke the next morning to an empty bed and checked the alarm clock. Six-thirty. Sometime during the night I had thrown the down comforter off, and the circling fan whisked on full-speed above me. I shivered in my thin nightgown and pulled the covers back over me. I wanted to curl up under the blankets forever, but the smell of coffee disturbed my slumber. Marshall expected me to shuffle apologetically into the kitchen and make everything all right so he could have a good golf game. In the old days we had our best sex on Saturday mornings.

I pulled myself out of bed and went into the bathroom. Surprisingly, my head didn't feel too bad. I swallowed two aspirin anyway, brushed my teeth, straightened out my hair with my fingers, and splashed warm water on my face. Before I slipped into my robe, I flexed my arm muscles. Not too bad—not great though. I made a mental note to add more weights to the machine at the club. The rest of my body was in pretty good shape—my abs could be tighter, but I wasn't willing to give up drinking to have a flat stomach. I tied my robe around me, and then on second thought, untied and let it slip down to the bathroom floor.

Marshall was sitting in the morning room sipping coffee and reading the *Journal*. He was already showered and dressed for golf. "Well, you're up early this morning." I leaned over and kissed him hard on the lips. He returned my kiss and gave my breasts a quick squeeze.

"Neil and I are leaving early to hit a few practice balls ... our games were off last week."

"Sorry to hear that."

"What're you going to do all day?"

"I have a bunch of papers to grade."

"The tuna was pretty good last night." His eyes studied me over the rim of his reading glasses.

"It was okay. Could've used a lemon, huh?"

"Don't start, Catherine."

"Just making a joke." I poured myself a mug of coffee. "Mmmmm, good coffee, Marsh. You have time for breakfast? I could whip up a Spanish omelet."

"I'll just have some cereal." Marshall started to rise.

"Stay there, I'll get it."

As Marshall finished his cereal, I drank a second cup of coffee. The world seemed better in the morning light.

"What's up for tonight?"

"I told you last week ... Neil's house. He's having a bunch of us over for a barbecue. I told Debra I'd bring some wine and cigars."

"Do we have to do something every Saturday night?"

"We could stay home and have another romantic evening." The words came out before I could stop them.

Marshall threw the paper down on the table. "I have to get ready."

"Marsh, I'm sorry. I didn't mean it the way it sounded."

"Go to hell, Catherine." Marshall slammed the garage door as he went out.

Not knowing what to do, I turned to the ceiling. Mom, Dad, why do I have to ruin everything? Why can't I keep my mouth shut? We were having such a good morning ... Is it all me? Is it Marshall? Or does God want me to pay for her the rest of my life?

"Better put your robe on. Neil's here," Marshall yelled from the garage. I ran to the bedroom and slipped back into my robe—my hands were shaking from the coffee, but I did manage to put on some lipstick.

Neil was already in the kitchen when I walked back in.

"Hey, how was the party?"

He placed a hand on his forehead. "It went way too long. My head's killing me."

"You want some aspirin?" I asked.

"I've taken four already." He turned to Marshall. "Ready to rock and roll?"

"I'm ready to get out of here, that's for sure."

"Too much romance last night?" Neil shot an inquisitive glance at me.

"Not enough lemon is all."

Marshall glared at me. "Your lipstick looks like shit. I hate that color. I don't know why you even wear that stuff."

"I wanted to look nice for company."

"Oh, I see, for Neil."

"And for you."

"Will you two cut it out? Man, my eyes are glued shut, any coffee left?"

"Rough night?" Marshall asked.

"Yeah—we got into the vodka when the beer and wine ran out."

"Gee, I hope it won't make you play like shit so I can win a few bills off you."

"I could never drink that much … hell, might make me better." They both laughed.

"You don't take cream, do you?"

"Just black." Neil studied the dark circles under my eyes. "Everyone missed you last night, Cat. The parties aren't the same without you."

"Are they better?" was Marshall's attempt at sarcasm.

"Thanks, Neil." I knew he was trying to make up for my husband's behavior. We would talk about it Sunday morning, when Marshall was away conducting business on the golf course. Saturday was his only real day off. "I'm sure you all managed to have a good time without me." I stretched my arms over my head, feeling the pull of my breasts as I did so.

"I guess it could've been worse."

Despite my ugly lipstick, I smiled at Neil. "It's nice to know I was missed."

"It's almost seven. Let's go." Marshall briefly acknowledged me. "We'll be home late afternoon."

The door to the garage slammed again. Callaways clanked in their bags as they hit the trunk of the Porsche. The engine started and tires screeched against the pavement. And then silence.

I waited awhile before I reached for the phone.

"Hey, did I wake you?"

"What? This better be good! Sheyit … it's only seven-fifteen. Who in the hell is this?"

"Cat."

"Oh, hey, sweetheart. How you doing? Damn, I'm hungry. Just got home an hour ago." His voice brightened but was raspy from alcohol and smoke. "What's going on, you need fish now?"

"Funny, what time's the game on Sunday?"

"Eight. You coming over?"

"Maybe. I have a tennis match; I could come over after if it's okay."

"It's always okay for you, sweetheart."

"Well, I guess I'll see you tomorrow night. And Stephan?"

"Yeah, Baby?"

"I was just wondering ... are the fish ever alive when you get them?"

"Never—they're packed in ice. I unfreeze 'em and make 'em look good in the cases."

"Oh ... I didn't realize that."

"I'm going to have my girlfriend Mary over Sunday, if you know what I mean."

"I'll probably stick to beer ... but you never know."

Stephan laughed. "I bet I can get you to take a few hits."

"Goodbye, Stephan."

"See ya, Babe."

My hands were trembling when I turned off the mobile phone. Still a bit dizzy from getting up too early, I made my way back into the bedroom and fell into the comfort of the warm covers and thick mattress. My mind drifted in and out of tears and sleep. The emptiness hurt more when I was alone. Sometimes I hid under the covers all day—maybe I would get lucky and fall asleep. My sister suggested I go back to church, but I had lost my faith in God and the church years ago. My children and teaching became my religion. Now the children didn't need me as much, and teaching alone wasn't enough to fill the empty place in my heart.

For years, Marshall tried to help me get over my loss. He was the one who pried my fingers loose from the asylum bars and led me out the door. If it were not for Marshall, I would've abandoned life altogether. And there were times when I was sorry I did not. Marshall thought if he loved me enough I would someday be able to put the past behind me and learn to love him. But I had only broken pieces to give him. Marshall felt the loss of the kids—what he couldn't get from me, he received from them. Now that they were gone, he filled his void with work and golf. When he looked at me, he saw guilt; guilt for not loving him, guilt for not loving a man who gave up his life to save a girl whose pain was too deep for tears.

People who knew us did not understand why I accepted his hostility, his coldness. They didn't know that his anger was easier to accept than his love. Nor did they understand why he accepted my flirtatious liaisons, innocent though they were. Marshall and I were slowly destroying our lives—he used work, I used wine ... and sometimes men. But even the comfort of a stranger's arms couldn't keep the past from coming out of its shadows. The voices were louder lately—it was becoming harder to get away from them ... the institution I tried to forget, the painful labor, the incriminating stares ... *Sister Rose, can I have my baby now? My mom said I can keep her ... I don't have to give her away ... my dad said the hell with what the neighbors think.*

Sometime in mid-afternoon I got out of bed and fed the fish. The queen angels and tangs were unusually hungry. They darted to the top of the tank and devoured their food. The puffer carefully eyed his meal before he slowly moved in and nibbled one small piece at a time. Before he finished, he swam around the tank clacking his two teeth together, stirring up the tiny shells on the bottom. What a curious monger you are, I thought.

When Marshall came home a few hours later, I was sipping wine and grading papers. If it bothered him that I was still in my nightgown and robe, he kept it to himself.

Chapter 5

Marshall and I were invited somewhere every Friday and Saturday nights. Usually Friday night was an extension of the neighborhood happy hour, but Saturday we went to a neighbor's house for a cookout if we didn't make it to Buckhead for dinner. The neighborhood cookouts were becoming something of a ritual for me. I would start out in the kitchen with the women, and by the end of the night, I was out on the deck smoking cigars with the men. Not that they were any better than the women; most of them were balding, potbellied, adolescent boors. The ones who weren't grossly obnoxious were insensitive grumps who bitched about how much money their wives spent. You'd think these guys were penniless charity cases the way they carried on. I don't know how many times I had to point out the status watches on their wrists or the Porches and BMW's in their driveways. No, I went out on the deck because I really did enjoy the roll of a good cigar in my mouth. And I liked pimping the men as much as they liked pimping me. The topic of conversation always got around to the same thing: how to make a good martini and which woman in the neighborhood had the best tits. I generally laughed along with the men, my head spinning from the wine and cigar rush. I had no reason to think this night would turn out any differently from the others.

"You think these shorts look wrinkled?" Marshall smoothed out his khaki shorts as if ironing them with his hands.

"They look fine. We're just going to the Johnsons."

"Yeah, but there might be some hot chicks there. I know of one for sure who's coming."

"Who?"

"You, my dear. You look beautiful, Catherine."

"Do I really?"

"I just said so, didn't I? You want to hear me say it over and over."

"Of course I do," I said coyly.

Marshall laughed. He was in an unusually good mood that evening. He had a birdie and an eagle on the last nine, not bad for a weekend golfer. Marshall ran a brush through his lightly moussed hair and adjusted the collar of his golf shirt.

"Ready. Do we need anything besides the wine and cigars?"

"No, I think that's it."

"Do you want a Corona for the road?" Marshall carried a six-pack in each hand.

"No thanks, I've been drinking wine."

We could hear laughter and loud voices as we walked up the Johnson's driveway. Robb Lyman's voice was the loudest, and he also was the most obnoxious drunk. Sometime during the evening, he would again grab one of the guy's butts and wrestle him to the floor. I told Marshall I thought Robb needed to confront a hidden sexual crisis. Marshall did not disagree with me.

"Don't ring the doorbell. Just walk in," Marshall said.

Not wanting to be attacked by the Johnson's potbellied pig, I gingerly pushed open the door and let Marshall go first. Daisy was already in the hallway, grunting and showing her elongated front teeth. I had been bitten once by the pig, and didn't relish spending another four hours in the emergency room of North Fulton Hospital. I steered clear of Daisy as much as possible. Lord only knows why they let that damn pig have the run of the house.

"Hey, Cat, looking great as usual." Neil turned to Marshall. "Great game today, Bud. A birdie and eagle on the last nine. Better than sex. No offense, Cat. You bring the cigars?"

Daisy sniffed the air to see if we had any food. She lifted her thick snout, pink eyes narrow in her large head, gaped mouth squealing for attention. Looking at her straight on, her nose, head and body were a series of concentric circles; her stubby legs seemed too small to carry the weight of her puffed-out body. She scraped her hard feet along the floor as she bucked her bristled hide against me. "Neil, get that pig away from me," I demanded. Daisy had tasted my blood before, and I think she was waiting to get me alone to finish me off. Her squinting eyes gave away her intentions. As if on cue, Debra came running out of the kitchen.

"Hey you guys, where were you last night?" I gave Debra a perfunctory hug, and before Marshall could do the same, she answered her own question. "I guess you two had better things to do." Debra leaned down and hugged Daisy. "C'mon sweetie, let's go in your pen. I've got some yummy carrots to give you." Daisy snorted and snotted in delight as she followed Debra down the hallway. Sweetie, my ass. That's a deranged killer planning ... waiting.

Neil escorted Marshall out to the deck where the men were already drinking martinis. A few were smoking pre-dinner cigars. Through the beveled glass doors I could see Robb grab Rich playfully by the shoulders. Rich pushed him off, almost burning Robb with his cigar. Robb snickered like an adolescent who just got caught looking at dirty magazines. How would you like to live with that? I thought. At least Marshall and I knew the source of our six-headed monster. Not wanting to face the truth, we blindly chopped off one head to see another grow back. It gave purpose to our marriage, much like Sisyphus rolling the rock up the hill only to see it fall again. We had been married long enough to understand what the game was all about. Robb's strange behavior deluded Lisa, however. A sophisticated, worldly man, he had pursued her with roses and candlelight dinners. Because he was an urban planner, he had ties to important politicians and celebrities. She attended a whirlwind of charity balls and fundraisers. But after she married him, even though he puppeteered a Renaissance man for the public world of business and politics, she found herself faced with a husband who cross-dressed and liked to play little boy games. The kind where she's the mother and he's the bad little boy. At least that's what she told us. We held her secret, just like she held all of our secrets, close to our hearts. We were a strange group of women. On one hand, we were cartoon characters sashaying from house to house in our jewels; on the other, we were spiritual indigents huddling behind gated streets in our protective pashminas.

Debra put Daisy's food outside, and I watched the pig struggle to fit through the doggie door leading to the back yard. The coast clear, I followed Debra into the kitchen. The rest of the neighborhood klatch was already there, busily opening and closing cabinet doors, folding napkins, cleaning silverware, preparing the food and condiments. Already trimmed, the chicken glistened on a platter next to the peppered filets. Bonnie Jorgensen, separating leaves of bib lettuce onto individual salad plates, directed the culinary symphony. "Put the napkins and silverware on the buffet. Where does Debra keep her trays? Lisa, see if there's enough ice. One of us might have to get some more. Monica, do you know how to make hollandaise?"

Off to the side, Amy and Rita, engrossed in private conversation, filled the empty saltshakers. The pair was so caught up in their prattle, they didn't realize they spilled salt all over the floor and counter. They all had full wine glasses.

"Hey, Cat!" Debra said in her high-pitched voice. "There's plenty of wine. Pour yourself a glass or two."

"I hear I missed a good party last night. What'd all you Southern belles do? Analyze Shakespeare? Discuss Nasdaq?" I noticed Debra bought new plates. Designer ones from Nieman-Marcus. I'd seen them advertised in the flyer.

"We had *way* too much fun," said Monica. She placed her hands on her stomach. "And I've got the party ball to show for it." She laughed loudly at her own joke. Monica was the only woman there who was truly from the South. She grew up in Charlotte, North Carolina, and met her husband at an advertising agency in Atlanta; he was married at the time, but that soon ended when he met Monica. I often marveled that out of the six couples Marshall and I were the only ones both on our first marriage.

Debra, who had been married once before, was Neil's third wife, and from what I could tell by watching the two of them together, she was soon to be his third ex-wife. Neil married Debra when she was in her late twenties. A few months shy of her thirty-fifth birthday, she knew she was expendable to him. Neil had divorced his other two wives when they turned thirty. Debra lived her life waiting for the day her rich and powerful husband would replace his tarnished trophy. Deb's drinking was a viable scapegoat for Neil; he easily elicited sympathy from all the men. We women understood her drinking up to a point. We all drank too much, and our situations were equally as bad just different. We knew her meanness was the result of a more serious illness. That's why I sympathized with Neil; at least he was aware of his problems. Plus, he was easy to talk to.

"We read the stock exchange in iambic pentameter." Debra's answer caught the group by surprise.

"What in the hell is that?"

"I didn't know Deb was so smart. Aren't you all impressed?" Bonnie said.

"If we could all be so deep."

"Cat, just because we don't teach English, doesn't mean we don't read. I don't go to sleep without my *People*."

"More wine, I hope?" Debra filled all of our empty glasses.

"Voila! The salad's done. How's it look?"

"Too good to eat, Bonnie."

"An epicurean delight."

"Does it look as good as the ones Cat makes?"

"Better—Ha!"

Because Bonnie and I were the cooks of the group, the other women often called us for help when they had emergency guests like their mothers-in-law or husbands' clients. It was with Debra, though, that Bonnie formed her closest bond. Bonnie, a Nordic blonde in her early forties with wide-set blue eyes was genuinely worried and concerned about Debra. A third wife who married a computer mogul fifteen years her senior when she was barely twenty, Bonnie knew what it was like to suddenly feel replaceable. But there was a noticeable difference between the two. Chuck expanded his software business to include computer design, and Bonnie was the artistic brain behind it. Their new business couldn't exist without her expertise and Chuck knew it. As the business grew, so did Chuck's respect for his Bonnie. Their marriage appeared to be one of the more stable partnerships in the group. Unlike Bonnie, Debra didn't provide much in the way of intellectual stimulation. Whether it was because of fate, genes, alcohol or all three, Debra's endeavors consisted of trying to pass the "Are You a Good Lover?" and "How to Tell if Your Husband is Cheating" tests in women's magazines and nervously scurrying around the house battling outbreaks of dirt and disorder. She wore out pairs of rubber gloves scrubbing bathroom grout and heating vents to their original pristine whiteness. Everyday she polished brass doorknobs and switch plates; every evening she meticulously arranged the silverware so it pointed the same way in the tray. Since she did not keep up with world events, she thrived on gossip. No one was immune from her vicious tongue, not even Neil. You never told her anything you did not want repeated. Neil, once enamored of her boyish figure with great looking breast implants, could barely tolerate her ignorance. I could see it in her tired eyes, limp over-processed hair, and marionette-lined mouth. She knew the signs of a man about to leave. After all, she had been there when he left his second wife. She was a desperate woman. I should have felt sorry for her. Debra tried to get what she didn't have—a stable husband who loved her. I never felt like I was breaking up Debra and Neil's marriage. It was already over by the time I entered the picture. I never wanted him anyway. The man I wanted only existed in books ... or so I thought.

The rest of the women had tolerable marriages. Cute little Amy with her tiny body and dark pixie haircut was a second wife, and Tommy was a second husband as well. Their score seemed even, yet on more than one occasion Marshall and I had seen Tommy out with his young secretary. Amy invited Tommy's secretary over for happy hour on Friday nights and she actually accepted once. I wondered if Amy invited her so she could keep an eye on her. We knew Monica put up with a discretion or two from Rich, but she should have expected that going in. She, after all, was one of Rich's indiscretions. Robb tried to lord it over everybody that he and Lisa had the happiest marriage. Lisa had been married briefly in her teens and Robb had never been married before. He didn't know that we all questioned his sexuality, nor did he know that all the women knew about his secret fetishes. Marshall and I wore our dysfunction openly. That's probably why the rest of the group embraced us. It was no secret that he worked all the time and that I was an outrageous flirt. I kept the fish man at Kroger's to myself, however.

"So I hear you had a romantic evening last night," Lisa said.

"I did, yes ... "

She raised an eyebrow. "Well, it's about time. He's never home. Does he still know how to use it?"

"How good is Marshall?"

"Damn good when he wants to be."

"He certainly is," Bonnie said. Everyone laughed and wondered.

"I can't remember the last time Robb got it up. I think he's in the control group for Viagra." Lisa already had too much to drink.

"It's been so long for us, I need the tweezers to find Neil."

"Is it better after your children are gone? We have no privacy with Jennifer and Stacy running all over the house," said Amy.

"Can't you lock the door?"

"They bang on it until we open it."

"I know what I'd do—I'd beat the shit out of their little asses." Debra 's meanness was starting.

"I can't do that."

"Have you tried a time-out?" A new woman, Rita Friske, in her early thirties, had twins, still toddlers. A little young for our group, but her husband Fred was approaching fifty and she had the honor of being his fourth wife. She fit right in. Unfortunately, she was new prey for Debra.

"Time-outs are a fucking joke. A little smack on the ass is worth a hundred time-outs."

"Shouldn't we get the plates on the tables?" Bonnie suggested.

Before Debra could reply, Neil stuck his head in the door. "Time to put the chicken on, girls." Bonnie handed Neil the plate of chicken.

"Tell me when you need to put the steaks on," Debra said.

We all stole glances at Rita to see how she reacted to Debra's attack. She seemed unaffected by the onslaught. She was already gossiping to Monica and Lisa about Debra's methods of discipline.

I joined Amy and Debra, who were setting the tables outside. Bonnie followed me. The men lingered near the grill, caught up in their verbal parlay.

"I knew I didn't like that little bitch," Debra was saying.

"Debra, not so loud. She's just right inside the door."

"She's the woman I told you about—the one who asked Bonnie who the cool people are in the neighborhood."

"If she thinks we're the cool people, she's in for a big surprise."

"Doesn't say much for her taste." We giggled uncontrollably. The wine was really starting to hit us.

"What're you girls cackling about over there?"

"Your big fat ass, Robb," Debra said. "That'll shut the obnoxious asshole up." We laughed even harder.

"The girls think they are *so* funny."

"Hey, Cat didn't hear about Janie last night." Debra and Amy's eyes lit up.

"You should've seen her. She got so drunk she passed out in Monica's bed. Monica and Rich thought she went home, so when they got in bed, there was Janie literally three sheets to the wind. We'll never let her forget it."

I felt sorry for Janie. She wasn't going to make it in this crowd. She was too sweet … too into her marriage and children … the way I used to be.

"Janie was invited but called at the last minute to cancel." Debra rolled her eyes. "She said she had a terrible headache."

"Drink up, Cat. You need to make up for last night," Bonnie said. Tables set, we went back into the kitchen. I poured myself another glass of wine. The buzz made me feel happy.

"Neil said Marshall played great today. It must've been all that sex he had last night," said Debra.

"I doubt that," I said.

"What's all this talk about sex?" Lisa asked from the opposite end of the room.

"Marshall had his putter working yesterday and last night," Debra insinuated.

"How did Neil do?" asked Rita.

"Pretty shitty."

"Well, you now know what you have to do," said Amy. We all laughed.

Our raucous chatter steamed the kitchen like an over-boiling pot. First, sex vaporized over the countertops and sink, then husbands and children misted their way up the cabinets, while neighborhood gossip rose right up to the ceiling. Carole Watts paid way too much for her faux painting ... She could have gotten it for half the cost if she had used Will. The Millers are getting a divorce. The Perlmans don't have any control over their kids. Do you believe Johnathan's language at the pool? Is Francesca still having an affair with her builder? But of course, and her husband doesn't have a clue.

"Hey, ladies, we need those steaks now; the chicken's just about ready. Hey, Deb, hand me the barbecue sauce, will you?" The steam dissipated and then disappeared. The pot turned cold.

We joined the men for dinner on the deck. Marshall was still talking about his great golf game.

"I eagled number ten. Par 5, 550 yards. My tee shot was right down the middle, and then I just missed the trap out front, rolled up to the fringe. I was just trying to get it up close for an easy birdie and damn if it didn't go in. Neil 'bout shit, he was more excited than I was."

Robb patted him on the back. "That's great, man. When are you giving lessons?"

"Yeah, right. It'll never happen again—a birdie and an eagle on that back nine ... fun, though, while it lasted."

"The only thing he needed to make it a perfect day was a hole-in-one." Neil turned to where I was sitting and smiled.

"Of course," I said.

Most of us enjoyed everyone who was not our spouse.

Marshall and I sat with Neil and Debra, Bonnie and Chuck. The other four couples sat at a larger table just behind us.

"Hey, Neil, the steak's great," said Rich.

"Rare enough?"

"Perfect."

"Chicken, too," Chuck said through greasy lips.

"Anyone need more wine?"

"Who else talked to Janie today?"

"Hey, Rich, how was she?"

"I hear she was in bed with you."

"I heard he was in bed with Marilynn."

"If it were Marilynn, there wouldn't be room in the bed for me."

"Have you seen her lately? She looks like a cow." The men roared at Tommy's comment.

My head felt like it was in a vise. I could have thrown a plate at Tommy. "Hey, you guys," I said before I left the table to get more wine. "Keep it down. She just lives right over there."

"Cat, you are so paranoid; there's no way she can hear us."

"I hear that instead of cutting the grass, she just grazes for a while," Robb said.

I wanted to tell Robb I had some leftover panties if he wanted to try them on. Instead, I poured myself a glass of wine and stared at the ceiling. There has to be more to life than this—what do other people do with their lives on Saturday nights? I was beginning to see double, so I closed one eye and walked back on the deck. I sat almost trance-like while the party spun out of my reach. I could see mouths opening and closing ... Waaaa ... Waaaa ... Waaaa ... they seemed to say. Smiles stretched across the faces of men and women whose names I couldn't remember. I could hear flickers of mean jokes about the man up the street who was obsessive about his landscape—the yard man they called him ... then politics ... the immorality of the president ... the public schools with the incompetent teachers ... the kids aren't learning anything ... the teachers have no control in the classroom ... you know what they say, those who can't do ...

"Cat," I heard Marshall say, "I can't believe you are letting these guys get away with this."

I tried to shake my head back to sobriety. "I was having an out of body experience. I was in the Bahamas for a minute there. Get away with what?"

"Slamming teachers."

"Uh-oh, Cat's going to get on her high-horse again."

"No, I'm not. You guys are right. The education system does suck, but not because of the teachers."

"What, then? The taxpayers keep pouring money into the schools and where does it get us? Our kids are lagging behind half the countries in the world."

"How do you explain that the US leads the world when everyone's all grown up? Maybe all of you got wonderful and creative on your own, huh?"

"But what about all the test scores they put in the papers? We're just about last."

"That's not exactly true. Those other countries only use the scores of their top students for comparison." I needed a good fight to sober me up. My neck burned. "Europe and Asia don't even allow most of the population to get a high school education. We educate everybody, not just a select few. The biggest problem I see in the education system is the amount of information thrown at our kids so that they can score well on tests. Hell, if we had time to teach more about life and less about SAT prep, the system wouldn't produce so many fucked-up adults."

"Like who?"

"Gee, I wonder. Do you really think I have all the power to make a child into a well-rounded adult? If you really believed that, you would puke at how much some teachers make and have to survive with a family. Students in my class joke about how much their parents spend drinking and partying. They have no clue what their kids are doing, in or out of school."

"How are their parents any different from you?" Rich asked.

"My kids are away at college; I have the freedom to party, if I want."

"What about the kids you teach?"

"The kids I spend ten hours a day with? The kids I talk to? Listen to? Spend hours at night poring over their papers? Calling them on the phone reminding them to do their homework, because their parents are too busy with their own lives to bother with them?

Where would each of you over-priced salesmen be without the undervalued teachers of your youth?"

"Okay, we give. We were just pimping you. God, you're so easy."

"Her buttons are pretty easy to push. Hey, star teacher, help me make the coffee." I followed Neil into the kitchen while the rest of the women cleared the tables of plates and silverware.

"You feeling okay? You look really pale."

"I need some water. I can't drink wine the way I used to." Neil laughed while he plugged in the coffee pot.

"You want a couple of aspirin?"

"No, I'll be fine."

"Hey, Neil, don't forget the cigars and Grand Marnier," Rich yelled from the deck.

Bonnie brought in a tray of plates and martini and wine glasses.

"Hey, what are you two doing in here? You okay, Cat?"

Every time I argued or became too controversial, Bonnie thought something was wrong with me. Well, maybe something was wrong with me. Maybe I was a malcontent, a social deviant, a disordered personality, a paranoid schizophrenic. I did, after all, spend six months in the loony bin, not that the people in there were much different from the people out here.

"I'm just fine. I have to defend the profession, you know."

"How is school going?"

"School's fine. I'm having fun."

Armed with cigars and a bottle of Grand Marnier, Neil squeezed through the two of us. "You going to teach Edward Albee this year?" he asked as he left the kitchen. He was referring to his favorite play, *Who's Afraid of Virginia Woolf?*

"I couldn't *not* teach that play," I yelled after him.

The rest of the women made their way back to the kitchen.

"Where's the coffee? The room is spinning."

"I need to sober up so I can drive the babysitter home."

"I'm not going anywhere. Pour on the wine," Debra said. Lisa and Amy followed her lead. I wondered how many of them would end up hugging the toilet bowl Sunday morning.

"What do you do with the dumb kids, Cat?"

"I don't have any dumb kids; just some with issues."

"I'm sorry. What do you do with the unmotivated kids?"

"Every kid has something that motivates him. I just have to look harder in some. I suppose I could just sit around and watch them become lazy, fat-ass adults." I hated talking to them about teaching. They really didn't hear me anyway. How can you explain the weight on a teacher's back? One right word or one wrong gesture can change the course of a child's life.

The women started laughing. "I don't have any dumb kids," Debra mocked me. "They just have issues. C'mon Cat, you teach some stupid kids. Admit it."

"What were you, Debra? Stupid or not motivated?" The question felt good to me.

Debra sniggered and spilled wine down her chin. "I was both. It's lucky I didn't get kicked out of school. The teachers all hated me. The frumpy bitches."

"I don't remember a damn thing about high school," said Rita. "It's just a big blur."

"Must be all the pot you smoked," piped up Amy.

"There is nothing better than going to bed with a joint and Walt Whitman," I said.

"Did you date him before you met Marshall?" Rita asked.

"Oh, my God, "said Monica. "Whitman was gay."

"You went to bed with a gay guy?"

Everyone howled with laughter. I couldn't take it anymore—they were all drunk and stupid and I was starting to sober up. I practically threw my coffee cup in the sink and reached for a clean wine glass. I poured chardonnay to the top of the glass, downed half the wine in one gulp and filled my glass again. Fortified, I walked out onto the deck.

"I need a cigar."

"We wondered what was taking you so long to get out here." Rich turned to Tommy. "Throw one of those Cuban babies over here."

Rich cut the end off and lit it for me. After a few puffs, I had to sit down. My stomach felt nauseous and the wine was making me close to blind. Even so, I leaned my head back to search for a corner edge of sky between the trees. A few stars had struggled to come out, or maybe it was only one star. It was hard to tell.

"What do you think, Cat?" Robb said. "Which woman in the neighborhood has the best hooters?"

Not again. Just once, could they talk about something else? Like which woman had the most brains? The biggest vocabulary? The kindest heart? They bored the hell out of me. I looked at Robb and Rich's emerging potbellies and Tommy's narrow-shouldered anorexic body. Neil's jaw sagged more than usual, Chuck's forehead grew higher and Marshall's hair thinner. Under the deck lights, Fred's black dye job shone on his head like shoe polish.

"Actually, boys," I said, "I don't really care who has the biggest tits. I was wondering which one of you has the biggest dick."

I thought Marshall was going to swallow his cigar. "Jesus ..." he started. But the rest of the men guffawed and slapped the railing of the deck. Marshall had no choice but to be one of the boys.

"I tell you what I'll do." I puffed my cigar until my head rushed. "I'll give the winner of the contest the best blow job he's ever had."

"Good God," Marshall blurted as Robb sprayed his beer down the front of Chuck's polo shirt.

"And ... I bet Stephan wins," I predicted.

"Who?" a couple of quickly fading voices said.

"Oh, nothing."

I don't remember anything after that. Marshall told me the next morning I passed out on the deck and had to be carried home. At first, the guys thought I was faking, but when I didn't respond to their provocative remarks, they knew I was no longer in possession of my senses. They tried reviving me with coffee, then Bonnie poured a wine glass of water on my face, and when that didn't wake me, they checked my pulse. Alive but unconscious, I lay sprawled across the newly power-washed deck. Marshall said I looked angelic, like a fallen angel. Neil and Marshall carried me home, Neil grabbing me under the arms, Marshall hooking me under my calves. Apparently, they plunked me in bed, not bothering to undress me or push the hair out of my face. When I woke up, my mouth was dry and my sweaty clothes stuck to my body. I retched a few times over the side of the bed, but nothing came out. I had the mother of all hangovers. Marshall was in bed when I woke up and initially refused to talk to me. My head aching and my eyes burning, I smoothed things over once again. Reluctantly, Marshall told me the whole gruesome story.

"Was everyone laughing when you and Neil had to carry me home?"

"What do *you* think? If you hadn't passed out, I think I would have. Between your behavior and then Robb stepping in pig shit and tracking it all over the kitchen, the party ended rather quickly."

"I'm sorry Marshall. The hooter talk and picking on teachers was really getting to me—if they didn't do it week after week, it wouldn't bother me so much—but I just cracked."

"Jesus, Catherine, none of the other wives say things like that."

"Well, I am a few years older than the rest of them—maybe it's just hormonal … I bet I'm pre-menopausal."

"Go see a doctor then. Sometimes I think the P in PMS is for 'permanent'."

"Okay, I'll go," I sweetly responded. If only a pill could cure what I had.

"Promise?"

"Yes, I promise." Marshall rolled over and kissed me. I reached my hand down under his pajama bottoms.

"Looks like we have a winner."

"Do I get the prize then?"

"Of course."

#

There was a lovely woman who lived in Georgia. In one of Atlanta's finest suburbs. In an expensive gated community with tennis memberships, golf memberships, and social memberships. And families and husbands and wives and children and mothers and fathers and grandmothers and grandfathers and bachelors and bisexuals and transvestites went about their daily lives, doing their daily jobs and lived happily ever after. Except for the lovely woman.

Chapter 6

Neil blasted the horn of his platinum XK8. Despite the coolness of the morning air, he already had the top down. His salt-and-pepper hair wind-tousled just enough to be sexy above his dark glasses and one-quarter Cherokee cheekbones, he lounged behind the wheel as if he expected a young pop star to emerge from the front door instead of a hung over suburbanite on the wrong side of forty. I steadied my hands on the white built-in shelf next to the dining room window, bright sunlight accusing the hints of dust collecting on the artistically placed books, before checking my reflection in the aquarium wall. Bloodshot from the previous night of wine consumption, even my opaque contact lenses didn't provide enough contrast to make the whites of my eyes look less red. My light-green natural shade blended in too much with my almost daily red eyes, so I started wearing the darker lenses. I obviously unwound too much, since my head still hurt, and emptiness and regret overwhelmed me, the nausea shaking my middle body. It was always the same. I withdrew for a few days, busy grading papers, preparing tests, approaching life with a serious high school English teacher air until I was invited again to the Friday, Saturday, Wednesday, or any day of the week for that matter, drunken bash. I continued to numb my despair in the endless nights of getting drunk and acting out.

After applying powdered blush, my skin still appeared sallow, and my hair limply hanging above my sagging shoulders seemed orange instead of strawberry blonde. The night before, under the influence, I thought I was beautiful, witty—brazen enough to joke lewdly about male body parts, smoke cigars, confront the male ego, and challenge the drowning suburban women. But I could not escape the reality of those stark Sunday mornings. None of my degrees, certainly not my charm, wit, social position, or even twenty-five years of marriage and two emotionally healthy children could drive away my guilt over the death of my first child. It didn't matter what I did to my body or my spirit because, in my mind, what happened was unforgivable. Therapy was out of the question. I didn't need anymore "experts" trying to brainwash me. The Catholic Church tried that already, and it didn't work. No, I had to somehow find my own way to ferment forgiveness out of a tiny cold crypt.

As I donned my leather jacket, I regarded the beautiful angels and tangs. So regal ... so peaceful. I couldn't help but smile at them. Wistfully, I walked out to the driveway and got in the car with Neil. Marshall had already left for golf and wouldn't be home until early afternoon to pack for his trip to China. This time he would be gone for two weeks. Robb and Rich were up already, mowing their lawns, carrying around two bloody glasses of the hair-of-the-dog. They grinned broadly as they watched Neil and me fly down the street in his convertible Jag. I hid my pain behind my European sunglasses. "So, are you the winner?" I said as we approached the stoplight leading out of our subdivision.

Neil laughed. "They all said I was."

"I can't believe you guys. You didn't really ... "

"Well, we were hoping ... but after you passed out, we knew it was the wine talking. And then with Marshall."

"Neil, that was a joke even if I hadn't been drinking."

"Actually, the fear of coming in last was greater than the joy of coming in first so we just forgot about it." Neil laughed as we turned onto Georgia 400.

"How long did the party last?"

"Long enough for Debra to call Rita a bitch."

"She seemed fine when I was in the kitchen. She was laughing at least."

"She wasn't laughing when I came home from dumping you in bed. I can't leave Debra for fifteen minutes without her making a scene. I apologized to Rita and Fred and sent everyone home."

"Is she sleeping it off?

"Who knows? I slept in another room."

We sped north toward the foothills of the Appalachians at eighty, ninety miles per hour, the pace set by the competitiveness of Atlanta's fast-tracked drivers. My hair flew uncomfortably in my eyes and the sounds and fumes from too many V-8 engines made the insides of my head feel like burning rubber. I longed for silence and fresh air. Finally, before waves of nausea caused me to puke over the sides of Neil's silvery clean Jag, we veered off the highway and raced up the hilly roads that led to Mt. Yonah. We found an isolated overlook and turned off the road. "This spot's better than the one we found last week," said Neil.

I could barely respond. "Yes."

"This is becoming a Sunday morning ritual, isn't it?"

"Church."

Neil drew me to him and I comfortably settled into his arms. The sheer lithic walls of Mt. Yonah rose above the valley, the lower expanse of green stippled with lemony pale and purple wild flowers. Soft and gentle, like the purring fur of an old tabby, the warm North Georgia breeze brushed our faces. My half-closed eyes fluttered to stay awake beneath my sunglasses.

"Why do you stay married to her?" I asked.

"Money. I can't afford anymore alimony and child support."

My back stiffened under his arms. "How much money do you need? You really mean, you don't want to *pay* anymore alimony or child support." Neil was worth millions. I wasn't going to let him get away with poor-man talk.

"It'd kill me for her to get any of my money."

"She's gonna kill you with stress and get all of it. Besides, if you could have a chance at some kind of life where you didn't have to worry about whether your wife was going to attack someone or not, wouldn't it be worth it? Maybe you could have a real relationship."

"Just because it's Sunday morning, do you have to preach?"

"You married three bodies with great tits. Did you ever think about trying to find someone who could think, and possibly share something, anything? Don't you talk to them before you marry them?"

Neil laughed. "Damn! Talk to them. I forgot that."

"Funny, but I don't get how someone as smart as you could marry such mentally challenged women. Maybe I don't understand how strong the male sex drive really is."

"Maybe I'm not so smart." A migrating cedar waxwing landed on a small oak tree near the railing of the overlook. Two more flew up and perched on neighboring branches. They stood erect, their tiny necks turning sharply from side to side. Their brown laid-back combs and gray feathers blended closely with the gray-brown tree bark and the dull undersides of the leaves. They were an elegant piece to nature's puzzle.

"What about you? Why do you stay?"

I sighed heavily. "I don't really know. Perhaps because Marshall's a good person. Our problems have always been my fault."

"You can't take all the blame. You know the old saying, it takes two."

"In my case it is me, Neil. You don't understand."

"I understand he doesn't make you happy. You need joy, too, Catherine. It's like you're hanging on to punish yourself. You're worth way more than that."

Neil pulled me closer and wrapped both arms tightly around me. I closed my eyes and fell into a half sleep. In my exhausted state, I couldn't fight back the memories that plagued me that day … the memories that wouldn't go away no matter how much I tried to drink and pretend them away …

Red Ferrari … Hart Schaeffer and Marx Blazer … debutante bachelor… Hyde Park Victorian Mansion … hair the color of old gold … disarming smile … heavy mahogany wainscoting … walls oppressed by books … go in and talk to my Dad … I'll be right back …

Come in, Catherine. Try this. You'll like it.

I don't really drink.

Just take a little sip.

Okay.

How do you like it?

It's strong, but it doesn't taste as bad as I thought it would.

Drink up. You're drinking too slowly.

Where did Perry go?

He's running errands for me. He'll be gone for several hours.

I could've gone with him.

Then we couldn't have been alone.

Why are you acting this way?

Just once, he said, I want to see what it is like to be with you.

I don't think we should do this.

No one will know. Let's go in here.

His flesh was loose around his middle, his face lined, broken red capillaries mapped across his cheeks. His breath was labored and he smelled of whiskey. I felt sick to my stomach. He stuck his tongue in places I didn't know very much about. I was only fifteen. He hurt and scared me. I hated him. And I had his baby.

Sometimes that part of my life seems dreamlike … like it never really happened at all. Then I remember the little girl with wisps of red hair surrounding her tiny face, and I force myself to acknowledge that it was real, and Therese did exist. She was a part of my body, and the labor pains cut through me like dull knives, and a tiny five-pound baby did nurse in my arms. But there are some things I do not remember. I don't remember how I got from Maryknoll, a home for unwed mothers, to the hospital. The nuns didn't tell me that my water could break, so when it did, I screamed bloody murder. Sister Rose chastised me for disturbing the other napping expectant mothers. Pregnancy frightened me, but the thought that there could be something wrong with the baby frightened me even more. Once I was in the hospital bed, I do remember my Dad talking to me about different insurance plans. He wanted to calm us both down. Most of the family was there. Scattered outside my door or wandering the hospital. Waiting.

Then my Dad left me all alone. My mother would get upset whenever she was around me; she never came to the hospital. But at least she agreed I could take my baby home. At first, my mother said I had to give the baby up for adoption. Then she thought I should let Perry have the baby, since his family had so much money. I swore to my Dad I would run away with the baby before I would let that happen. Everybody thought the baby was Perry's. Only four people knew the truth – Edward, Perry, me ... and eventually Marshall. In later years, Edward paid me well for keeping him out of jail. I still haven't been able to spend any of his blood money.

The nurse came to check on me. She needed to run a test. She helped me out of bed. She was rude, rough, and not very helpful. When I got back from the test, the nurse helped me climb into the hospital bed. The doctor still had not come, even though the nurse said I was two inches dilated. Sister Rose came to sit with me. She told me it would be a painful birth, because I was so small. I started shaking all over. My family was gone. They were not there to help me when I went into labor. Some physicians did not offer painkillers to unwed mothers back then. We needed to be punished for our sins. There was no soothing spinal or epidural. Instead, my body trembled from the shock of so much pain coming all at once in thundering slashes. It felt as if my insides would rip wide open. I cried out for my sisters and brothers, and then for my Dad. When the doctor finally arrived, he told me to push. The loneliness was far worse than the pain. It seemed strange to have a baby without my family there. I planned on my child keeping me from being alone.

When I woke up after her birth, sterile smells and white-sheeted walls engulfed me. I heard strange voices from the other side of the room, but the closed sheets kept me from seeing the speakers. For a brief moment, it all seemed to be a dream. Then, the nurse handed her to me. She had been cleaned and the umbilical cord cut. I counted her fingers and toes. They told me to try to nurse her. At first, no milk would come. Then, slowly, Therese suckled, but it wasn't enough. Eventually, supplemental bottles of milk were brought for me to give her.

Later I walked up and down the halls. I wanted to wash my hands but couldn't because of the IV. I stood in front of the nursery and looked at her. She was crying. I turned to find a nurse and told her someone needed to check on my baby. She only commented on how good I looked.

My family came to visit me, but not my mother. My sister sat on my bed. She complimented me on how cute Therese was. I gave Cynthia my baby, and the next thing I knew, the whole room was full of relatives. People I never expected to see. A nurse came in and gave me a blanket so that I would not feel self-conscious of my inadequate gown. They started passing my daughter around, and I became jealous and wanted her back in my arms. My Aunt Ruthie gave me a card. It had all of the family's birthdays on it. She had added my baby's birth date to it.

Therese started to cry. Someone passed her to me and she stopped. She had pale skin and dark eyes. They were shaped like mine, not Edward's. No one mentioned Edward. I was glad. He would never touch my child. No one would touch her the way Edward touched me.

But I could not protect her enough. I lied to her, my Tessy …

Your consciousness stirs. You wonder how this could be the same baby who waddled across the touching beach towels, who played patty cake with your friends, who laughed out loud at your monkey faces. They pull her from you and you collapse again. The pain becomes more and more unbearable, and you need the drugs to lull you into semi-consciousness, but the nausea of your empty feelings never goes away. I slowly become a refugee from sanity and leave the world for a small room with a locked window.

Mary Anne told me I wasn't utilizing our time together. She thought I should talk about the baby. She wanted to help me more; she thought I was treating her more like a girlfriend than a counselor. I knew I should talk about the baby but I couldn't. Especially since I hadn't answered all of my own questions. How was I supposed to answer hers? Besides, she was young and had no children of her own. She didn't know what it was like to lose a child. I did not talk to her about the baby; instead, I sat and stared at my memories. "You have to put the past behind you," Mary Anne finally announced. "You can only do that by talking about it. You need to move on with your life. One day it'll be like it didn't even happen." They had a different kind of therapy back then. If you needed too much time to get over your loss, you were considered weak. My mother cried one day after she lost her breast, then she never mentioned it again. But a child is not a breast.

When I opened my eyes, the pure blueness of the sky and the waves of mountaintops seemed like the dream, rather than the reality.

"How long have I been asleep?"

"Oh, about an hour."

"At least my head feels a little better." Neil smoothed the hair out of my eyes and gently kissed me on the cheek.

"Get out of it, Catherine. You're not like the rest of us."

"I don't want to end up like Martha."

"There's no chance of that." Neil laughed. "You have way too much class. If anybody has turned into Martha, it's Debra."

"And are you George?"

"Do you still think George is a latent homosexual?" Neil and I continued our ongoing argument about the characters in Virginia Woolf. We argued about the characters every time we saw each other.

"Without a doubt."

"Then I'm not George. But I still don't buy that he's gay."

Completely awake, I pulled away from Neil and sat straight up. "Why else would George show such hostility towards a sexual woman? I think the reason she goes after other men is because George can't please her sexually. She screams at him so much because no matter how beautiful or sexual she is, she can never attract him. I'm not even sure she suspects the truth about him, which probably makes it worse for her. She thinks there's something wrong with her because he finds her so repulsive. Very unfair, I think."

"I don't think he's gay at all. I think he feels inadequate around Martha because he's such a failure in her eyes. She really is a castrating bitch who goes after younger men because she thinks she's getting old and losing her sex appeal."

"Obviously she hasn't lost her sex appeal and knows it."

Neil put his arm around me. "No, she hasn't lost her sex appeal." He held my hand as we gazed out across the mountains silently, the breeze cooling a bit the heat inside my head. After awhile, Neil put the key in the ignition and drove towards our gated subdivision.

Marshall, home from golf, was mowing the lawn when Neil and I pulled in our driveway. He gave Neil an obligatory wave and avoided eye contact with me altogether. After Neil left, I leaned down and pulled the withered petals from the geraniums on the front porch. I thought about justifying to Marshall my Sunday drives with Neil, but frankly, I was too damn tired to expend the energy. I watched him disappear around the side of the house, the mower softly vibrating across the grass. Marshall found solace carrying out the household's domestic chores. On any given Sunday, you could find Marshall mowing the grass, spreading mulch, folding laundry and washing windows. He started out by holding me up and continued to do so throughout our twenty-five year marriage.

In our initial years together, I felt affectionate towards Marshall and I clung to him out of desperation and even hope. We had fun furnishing our first apartment and inviting other young lawyers and their wives over for fondue and chilled red Gallo. Marshall encouraged me to go to the local university, and somehow I managed to get a teaching degree. Then when I became pregnant with my second child and Marshall's first, the memories came flooding back to me. I cried throughout the entire pregnancy, and though I felt enormous guilt because Marshall was so devoted, I couldn't snap out of my sadness.

Marshall was afraid to leave me alone when he went to work, so he dropped me off at my mother's house every morning. I didn't learn to drive until after I had my third child—and that was only because my father shoved the test booklet in my face and dragged me to the license bureau. I did much better with my third pregnancy because I had my little boy to take care of. I learned how to laugh my tears, and I didn't have a breakdown until I realized that my third child was another little girl. Elizabeth went home from the hospital before me, and when I left the maternity ward, it was not for home, but for another kind of hospital. The kind where the patients either scream their pain or disappear in their pain. I did neither; I had a funeral and buried my pain. I went home because I wanted to love—and I loved Marshall, Sammy and Elizabeth as much as I could. Of course, funerals are never the end, and many days my little ghost would catch me off guard and hints of pain would rise from the dead.

I suppose that's why I clung so tightly to Elizabeth when she was a baby. I held her all day and all night. "Are you ever going to put that baby down?" my dad would say whenever he saw me. I ignored him and rocked Elizabeth until my arms ached. And even after that, I still kept rocking her. Marshall and I kept her bassinette and then crib in our bedroom, because I needed to hold her during the night. It got so bad, that one day Sammy and some of his kindergarten friends came to me fraught with worry. "Mom," Sammy said, "if you don't put Elizabeth down, she's never going to learn to walk." I held Sammy's sweet chubby chin in my hand. His hazel eyes were full of concern, concern that his little sister would be carried around for the rest of her life. He brought his band of brigands to support him. Four little boys, not too long ago toddlers themselves, accused me of keeping Sammy's sister away from the freedom of child's play: climbing trees, running bases, riding bikes, swinging on Tarzan vines. Four little boys, in parachute pants, high tops and whips of licorice in their hands, brought me back to my senses.

"Okay, Sammy," I said. "I'll put her down so she can hold your hands." The boys spent the next thirty minutes encouraging her to stand. Every time they let go, she sat down on her diapers. Elizabeth wouldn't walk for six more months. Sammy walked at nine months. But, once Elizabeth started walking, she became fiercely independent. I guess she'd had enough holding to last her the rest of her life.

My bad days became fewer as Elizabeth started school and as Sammy became involved in sports and music. It was then that my Dad strongly suggested I interview for a teaching job. "You're going to smother those kids, Catherine," he said. "You need to find something of your own so Elizabeth and Sammy can feel comfortable when they have to grow up and leave you."

"I don't know what to do, Dad. Nothing seems to help." He narrowed his deep-socket black eyes at me. "Sometimes death is a reminder of all those who are still alive. No child can ever take her place, Catherine, and I know you had a lifetime of love to give her. But she isn't around for you to hold anymore. You have a choice, Catherine. You can smother Sammy and Elizabeth until they are full of your guilt for Theresa's death, or you can take the compassion you learned from her death and spread some of it around the world.

Teaching will give a part of her back to you." His voice cracked as he talked.

My Dad buried his face in his hands and cried. His words did not make any sense to me at the time, but I couldn't stand to see him cry. "You're right. I need to teach. Will you help me fill out the applications?" Soon after that I started teaching, and my bad days almost completely stopped. Whenever I did have those days I didn't want to get out of bed, Marshall would take charge of the kids and household. If he had to, he worked from the house, juggling soccer practices and spaghetti dinners alongside legal contracts, integrity issues and patent violations.

Whenever we had business dinner parties, Marshall helped me with all the cooking and cleaning. He shopped for all the food and ordered the flowers. He spent his life making me look good to his business associates and family. He didn't have time to have any real friends. I was the one who developed friendships. Over the years I had a few women friends who touched me deeply, but most of my friendships were safely shallow. Not one person besides Marshall and my immediate family knew about the drowning. Not even his own family. Eventually, I learned how to use distractions to numb the pain when it dared to come to the surface. Since the prescription for broken spirits hasn't been discovered yet, I invented my own.

#

It was eight o'clock by the time I finished my tennis match. Lisa and I played unusually well that night. We won most of our games. Even Debra managed to defeat her opponents, despite the four glasses of wine she downed right beforehand. I saved my drinking for after the match. There was no way I could sustain a two-and-a-half hour match even after one glass of wine. Marshall had left already for China and the idea of two weeks by myself bothered me. It always did. Even though Marshall and I barely communicated anymore, I felt more secure with him in the house. The thought of Catherine Faith O'Connell Scott alone in an empty house scared me. Who would distract the voices when they came?

The first night by myself was always the hardest. That was why I looked forward to Stephan's. I thought about rushing home and taking a shower first, but that would take too much time. I didn't sweat that much anyway. So, I threw my tennis racket in the Lexus, redid my ponytail, and drove the twenty minutes to Marietta. Stephan's apartment was about two blocks from The Big Chicken, a thirty-foot tall icon perched right outside the Kentucky Fried Chicken on the corner of Highway 41 and Lower Roswell Road. The hulking wooden bird with rolling eyes the size of radial tires became a directional landmark for most of Cobb County. All roads led to The Big Chicken. Well, most of them.

"Hey, Babe, you look sexy in your cute little tennis skirt," Stephan said when he opened the apartment door. The molding around the door needed painting and a faint trace of an acrid odor escaped as he pushed the screen outward. He didn't look too bad himself, with his blue cotton shirt unbuttoned to expose his tight, muscular chest and a glimpse of tapered waist. As he stepped aside to let me in, my eyes moved up and down his long thighs; I noticed his jeans were unfastened around his waist. His sun-bleached hair wasn't tied back like at work and he was barefoot. He held a Miller Lite in one hand, which left the other free to tuck his fingers inside the waistband of my tennis skirt.

Before I could apologize for not showering after the tennis match, he gave me a long, deep-tongued kiss. Close to him, I could smell and taste his sweat, beer and mouthwash. He ended the kiss by sucking on my bottom lip, then gently brushing his expert lips against mine. A sly grin crossed his face when he pulled away, and I wondered if he realized how I had struggled for a reply to his rough caress. I was so out of practice—Marshall and I seldom passionately kissed anymore. Perhaps he thought it was unsanitary. Face-to-face was such an intimate act, I thought. Therefore, the most intimidating.

"So, d'ya win?"

"Of course," I said confidently. Stephan had my lipstick all over his chin. I wasn't sure how to tell him, but I did have an urge to lean over and lick it off. "Our match went late. I didn't have a chance to shower."

He didn't respond to my comment; his attention was on the television and the game.

"How 'bout a beer? The game's started already. Braves, Mets. Man, do I hate those pricks from New York. Have for a while. I still remember back in the 80's when they were pretty good and rubbed everyone's nose in it. Gary Carter took more bows than Broadway those years." I nodded in agreement but had no idea what he was talking about.

I threw my purse on an old displaced deck chair and followed Stephan into his galley kitchen. Plates were hastily stacked in the sink. Bottles of Jack Daniels and beer cans filled the rubber garbage can next to the refrigerator. The grease-layered stovetop was black with age. Something under my feet created a scratching, squeaking sound that grated on my nerves. Salt, sugar or sand was all over the floor.

"Stephan, where's your broom? I can't stand walking on this stuff—it's getting all inside my shoes."

"What is?"

"Don't you feel all this grit on the floor? It's like a beach in here." He was immune to his unclean surroundings.

"Uh, I don't have a broom."

"Vacuum?"

"For what? It's just me, and I don't care. I'll probably move soon anyway, so why the effort? I think I'm about to be evicted because of my parties. That jerk landlord's just jealous."

I grabbed a loose roll of paper towels and ran water in the sink.

"You *do* have dish soap, don't you?"

"Yeah, under the sink. Hey, what're you doing? Don't tell me you're going to clean."

Heavy black dirt covered the wet paper towels as I wiped the granular debris from the floor. Stephan stopped me when I started to go after the stove.

"This I *cannot* believe. You come over here for sofa time, and I get to watch you clean my floor and stove? Pretty exciting. You know, now that I think about it, my car needs washing, too. Should I get a bucket and rag for later?"

I tried to ignore him but he grabbed me under the arm and lifted me upright. He looked me in the eye. "Don't clean tonight, okay? I'll leave the key and you can come back and make this kitchen-of-the-month, but for now, let's watch the game and have a little fun, alright?"

He led me to the futon, the only place to sit besides the deck chair. Cigarette burns covered the end where Stephan sat. The next inning had started.

"Here, have a beer and relax. Those dipshit Mets need to get their butt kicked. You been to a game this year?"

"Nope, not yet. We usually go a few times. Mostly when clients come into town."

The 60-inch screen TV seemed to contradict its surroundings, but seen with the Bose stereo system, it was easy to evaluate his priorities. These were probably leased or rented from some local store that advertised late at night on public access channels. From the living area, a short hallway led to a bathroom and then into the only bedroom. I hadn't done more than glance in either but the neglected carpeting did not appear as unsavory as one would suppose.

"Why are you sitting over there? C'mere."

I scooted next to Stephan and he put his arm around my shoulders while he took a long drink of beer. The game was between innings, and with no competition, I became the center of attention.

"Man, that's good, good. So how was your weekend? Party last night?"

He moved closer as his hand dropped off my shoulders and slightly down the front of my shirt. I tensed and then relaxed.

"Yeah, a little. Nothing much, really." I wasn't going to get into that mess of an evening again. Yet, the thought of Stephan's reaction to the blow job challenge made me smile. Maybe he would have been the winner.

"Go, go, get outa here ... yes! Home run! Chipper just kills the Mets." He turned to me for a response but I could only grin and grab for my beer.

I had been to enough games to offer, "This looks like an exciting game. The fans are finally cheering about something. Does anyone like New York teams other than New Yorkers?"

"Probably not, but to their credit, they follow their teams even if they do get on their ass when they screw up. People here are too polite to boo much. Somebody could be getting killed on the mound and by the time he gets to the dugout, everyone forgives him and he's off the hook. All the old ladies are saying, 'The poor thing, he tried.' He could be the biggest bum and it's okay."

The beer felt good going down and disappeared quickly. I hadn't eaten for a while and the coolness permeated my insides. Stephan jumped up and got two more Millers from the fridge.

"Here." He thrust the can into my hand giving me no choice but to pull the tab and have another.

Stephan sat with his legs wide apart, his back slouched half way down the futon, his shoulders hunched a bit. His long bangs fell casually over his brows, and he boyishly shook them out of his eyes as he leaned back and took a long swig of his beer. After quickly finishing, he stuck the can on the small glass table in front of us. He indicated for me to do the same. The lights were already down low, not because Stephan planned it that way; the overhead was burned out and replaced with a more accessible lamp clipped to the wooden frame of the futon. Before I had time to readjust myself to the curve of the cushion, Stephan loosened my tennis shirt and ran his hands up and under it. Deftly unfastening my bra clasp, he massaged my breasts while kissing me again. His tongue probed even deeper than before as his mouth covered mine with an almost suffocating effect. The roughness of his strong hands touched my body in ways that made me forget about any dimension except for the present moment. I reacted to his smell, his body and his callousness. For those brief seconds I was lost in his arms.

"I'm about to come ..." He unzipped his jeans and I could see he was telling the truth. One hand on my breast, one hand on himself, he started to groan. I immediately leaned away from him.

"Stephan, I think we better stop."

"You're kidding. You come over here and get me all worked up and then want to stop. Well, you can, but I'm not."

Before I could think of a response, he was finished. A quick retreat to the bathroom and he was back acting as if nothing had happened. The game re-entered his realm.

"Stephan, I think we should talk about this."

"What? This?"

"Well, you know, the sex thing." I really didn't know what to say. I drove over to his apartment, I let him feel my breasts ... what did I expect?

"What's there to talk about? You come over here, we have a few laughs, fool around a bit, but there hasn't been too much of a 'sex thing' as you call it."

"Well, you hardly know anything about me except that I'm married. Doesn't that bother you?"

"Sure as hell doesn't seem to bother you. I could tell the first time I met you, you were looking for a thrill. It's easy to spot. Besides, you got it made ... husband that's gone all the time, shitload of money. You can do whatever you like with whomever you like. The kind of life I would love. Give me a rich wife with a tough bod, and I'll never stop smiling."

"What do you mean, you could tell I needed a thrill?"

"I didn't say *needed; you* did. I said you were looking for a good time. And you found it, so I guess I was right, huh?"

Stephan was beginning to irritate me. Could his other talent in life besides cutting fish be picking up women with this 'look'? The shark always looks for the weaker fish, and I was beginning to feel like a sick mackerel.

"Is this all you ever want to amount to?" I had to fight back and preserve some dignity.

"I'm okay with things. School's boring so I could never go that route, and I have a job that pays alright." His attention was now on the bottom of the ninth with the Braves trailing by one and the bases loaded. I quietly slipped off the futon to get my purse from the back of the deck chair.

"Hey, where you going? The game's not over. Besides, I have a nice stash of Mary Jane we can kick back with. Sound good?" His gaze remained fixed on the game.

"I don't think so. I have papers to grade and it's late."

"Whatever. You comin' by this week for fish?"

"Probably not." I pulled the door behind me and realized Stephan would be out of my life forever. Glancing back, I wondered how I could have ever come here in the first place, and why it took more than one time to figure out what a Neanderthal he was. Either he had been on his best behavior, or I was blinded by my own illusions. Jack Burden he was not; he was more like Lois, the lightweight hoyden Jack divorced when she finally started talking. At least Stephan taught me that Jack Burden is and always will be just a character in a story. At least that's what I thought when I drove home from Stephan's that night.

Chapter 7

In the second grade, Sister Mary Richard, our music teacher, asked me to mouth the words to the *Ave Maria* when our little class had to sing in front of the bishop. Apparently, I did not know how to carry a tune. Up until that point in my limited life, I loved to sing—I actually thought I had a great voice. Sometimes after school, I would stand in front of the apple tree in our backyard and sing so loud and hard, my lungs hurt.

Our next-door neighbor, August Roseman, one of those people remembered as perpetually old, caught me singing one day. He laughed and wheezed me into such embarrassment I never sang in front of the apple tree without first checking to see if old Gus was outside with his cane. But after Sister Mary silenced my voice, Gus never caught me singing to that apple tree again. Instead, I climbed the tree and hid among the thick leaves and rotting Indian summer apples. I stopped singing altogether except in large crowds where my tuneless notes would fall soundless on the resonating air. Yet, I never lost the intense desire to stretch my vocal chords across the world.

And, one day, after I let my baby drown, I was sitting in the loony bin staring out the window, and a girl a few years younger than me and a boy about her same age flashed across my mind like moving pictures. I quietly gazed into the space around me watching them act out their lives. They came to me often back then, a respite from the all-consuming anguish and guilt, and as quickly as they came into my mind, they would disappear. I never knew exactly when they would come back, but they always did. It was easy to get away with staring at nothing in the loony bin because everybody did it. No one really watched much television in there, though some watched when it wasn't on. What was going on in our minds seemed less of an illusion than the waves across the blaring machine. For almost thirty years, the dreams had interrupted my mind, sometimes in an unending sequel, sometimes startling jolts out of sequence. Or maybe they were not dreams at all, but old memories coming back, time intersections when the past crosses with the present. Over time, the stories revealed the little girl's extraordinary voice, and later, her eventual fame as an opera star. Yet she lived out her last years alone, sequestered in self-imprisonment. I wondered if her crime was as bad as mine.

The answer to my question would come not long after I met Micah Marlowe. As fate would have it, Micah Marlowe crossed my path the Monday morning after Marshall left for China, and Stephan went back to being the fish man at Kroger's.

I believe there are no coincidences. That certain people come crashing into our lives because our deceased ancestors can watch us smash our heads into the same wall only so many times. Driving home from Stephan's, I envisioned my dead mother and father peeking through the clouds and saying to each other, "We've got to do something about Catherine Faith O'Connell Scott." I could hear my mother complaining to my father, "Jamie, she is not the inquisitive little girl who sat on the toilet seat and talked to you about the nuns while you soaked in the tub." Jamie, forever pulling on his youthful chin, admitted to Lola that she had a point.

"That girl of ours is playing with fire. If she thinks life burned her before, she is going to be fodder for the incinerator if she doesn't find some way to get back on track."

After much thought, my father smiled. "I know a man who will bring her back. Someone she met a long time ago."

"Oh, Jamie, I don't know if this is going to work," bemoaned my mother. "After all, he is different."

"It didn't seem to matter the last time, Lola."

"Well, he *certainly* is no saint. You might just be adding to her problems."

"Catherine Scott lost her faith in saints years ago. She needs someone she thinks she can analyze."

"Well, she certainly will have no problems there."

"Thank you, dear."

"But Jamie, what about—?"

"My dear, you know God tolerates all his saints and sinners. Catherine finally will learn that forgiveness, not hate, is the other side of love."

I wished for the boy of my past memories, a child who slipped into my consciousness every time my persistent nightmare became unbearable. The thought of meeting the tow-headed boy again eased the ache in my heart. It was as if a soothing hand from heaven reached down and held my pain.

#

She giggled at him behind the falling-down outhouse. His legs were entangled in fishing line, and he cussed up a blue streak as the hook embedded itself in his big toe. "Damn! Jesus Christ! Hey! Somebody help me!" He gingerly tried to pull the curved hook out of his skin, but the barb wouldn't budge without doing damage. So now, not only did he have his legs entangled in the string he used for a makeshift fishing line, but also he had to hop on his right foot in order to move. Every time his left toe touched the ground he would yelp like a puppy. This tow-headed boy was a curious and ridiculous sight to the girl.

She was staying at her Aunt Sally's Kentucky horse farm in the summer because her parents believed she needed a holiday from city life. As a twelve-year-old, she much preferred the exciting sounds and sights of her riverboat city to the stillness and sameness of the farm. The smell of fresh cow's milk made her want to keel over; she'd rather be switched than to drink the warm thick milk. At least the visit gave her a break from the unrelenting singing lessons with Herr Doerleff. She had been blessed with a beautiful voice, and her mother forced her to attend lessons every day after school when she'd rather be jumping rope with her girlfriends. She used to last the longest at double Dutch on the school playground, but lately she lost to even Lily Lowmiller, physically the slowest of all her friends. When she told her mother that she did not want to go to Herr Doerleff's apartment anymore because he smelled of Limburger cheese and screamed at her when she sang a wrong note, her mother accused her of being lazy and slapped her across the face. Later, her mother told her that geniuses often display unusual behaviors and it was to be expected of Herr Doerleff. He was a renowned opera teacher and would make sure his best pupil would be rewarded. She did not know how to tell her mother about his strange behavior, and even if she could, she knew her mother would not listen anyway.

Leaning against the wall of the moss-covered outhouse, he again attempted to pull the curved end of the hook straight through the skin of his toe. Pain elicited another yelp while he lost his balance and tumbled like a rotten pine tree. The brown-eyed little girl could not contain her laughter any longer. Her giggling became louder and louder until she was laughing from the bottom of her belly.

He staggered back to his one foot, reached around the rotting outhouse and yanked hard on her auburn pigtail. She tried to push his hand away, but he held tight and pulled more. Knowing full well that she had the advantage over him, she punched him hard in the stomach as he lost balance again and fell on his face. "Oh, shit! Oh, shit!" he yelled. "My toe! You made me hit my toe!" Tears streamed down the boy's face as the hook pulled even more against his skin. Seeing an opportunity, the little girl reached down and grabbed the curved end of the hook and with a quick motion, pulled the straight end of the hook out of his toe.

"Silly!" she said. "You were pulling the wrong way." She untied the apron from her pinafore and wrapped one end around his toe. "My name is Nellie Krumplebeck. What's yours?"

"Help me get this string offa me," he drawled. "I'm David and I don't care much for girls, especially one with carrot shavings for hair and a name that sounds like sumpen my pa would name his mules – hah, Krumplebeck."

"I guess you don't need my help, then. Goodbye."

"Hey! Come back. I'm sorry, but you did knock me a goodun. You can help if you wanta."

"You talk funny," she said as she pulled the string from his arms and legs. "Doesn't your teacher make you annunciate your syllables?"

"I don't get to do much schoolin'."

"No wonder you can't pronounce your words right."

"Everyone round here 'stands me just fine – I ain't a stupid Yankee like YOU."

"I guess we're so stupid we won the war."

"Yeah, I bet you're so smart you can wipe your own butt, am I right, am I?"

"That's vulgar – you need to have your mouth washed out with soap – David – Dumkoff!"

"David Wesley, you sissy girl." With the pain in his toe completely forgotten, he picked up a handful of stones and started throwing them at her feet, one at a time.

"If you don't stop that, I'm gonna punch you again."

"You have to catch me first, grump ole' Krumpy, my daddy's mule." He laughed gleefully as she chased him into the tobacco fields and behind an old curing barn. She caught him by the arm and swung him around and around.

"Freeze!" she said. He halted on his tiptoes, torso twisted, arms outstretched like the Halleluiah ladies in the choir. "Unfreeze!" she then commanded.

"Now its my turn!" He swung her right arm so hard, her shoulder hurt. "Freeze!" he yelled.

Instead of freezing, she grabbed his hand, pulled him around the corner of the tobacco barn and kissed him on the cheek. "Your face is as red as this barn," Nellie said. Suddenly, she ran away as fast as she could, her copper-colored pigtails flying furiously behind her neck.

His pre-adolescent voice cracked as he called after her. "You best not come back heyuh tomorra!"

#

Monday mornings saved my sanity. In the hollow space before dawn and the buzz of the alarm, I lay awake reviewing the plans for the day. I searched for ways to jar my students out of their complacency. What words would catch their attention and make them stop for a brief moment in lives nailed down by peer and parental pressure? In Advanced Placement English, we had already spent three days last week discussing Robert Penn Warren, and we needed at least three more days to fully discuss style and theme.

I wanted a provocative quote—one that would appeal to the students' emotions as well as their intellect. In the early morning calm, my slumbering mind ran through the pages of *All the King's Men.* Over the years, the novel had become my bible, its words momentarily releasing me from past and present self-judgments. Warren acknowledged man's moral dilemmas and held them as man's superiority over nature's other life forms. No other animal found itself struggling with honesty and dishonesty, faithfulness and betrayal, forced love and forceful love.

Ah, love, the way to an adolescent's heart. My mind stopped dead center on the page dealing with Jack Burden's realization of love's powerful and god-like effect. After kissing Anne Stanton for the first time, Jack contemplates love while sitting on Anne's porch. He says, "So maybe she was up in her room trying to discover what her new self was, for when you get in love you are made all over again. The person who loves you has picked you out of the great mass of uncreated clay which is humanity to make something out of ..." Could I get my students to love themselves the way they wanted to love others? My three classes of Honors Lit would continue group work on individual sections of Walt Whitman's *Song of Myself.* I needed to do something exciting with Whitman. But what? In Adjusted Curriculum the students wanted to read *The Scarlet Letter* like the Honors kids. That was a problem. How would I keep them awake through all of Hawthorne's symbolism and Puritan bashing?

My mind drifted in and out of the day that would be. Two sets of papers graded ... don't forget to hand them back ... talk about dangling participles and misplaced modifiers in Honors and AP ... The *Howl*! My mind buzzed with the alarm. I threw off the sheets and ran into the den to find my college American lit book. I have to run to the copy machine as soon as I get to school, I thought. I would run off the first few pages of Ginsberg's *Howl* and compare him to Whitman—the 1950's beat poet and the 1850's patriotic poet—pessimism and optimism—both ahead of their time—both celebrating the formerly uncelebrated. I'll have my students write their own Songs of Self in their own style about what is meaningful to them ...

By the time I arrived at school, I was frantic with ideas. Since the AC kids had problems with reading modern English, much less the archaic style of Hawthorne, I had decided to teach *The Scarlet Letter* as if it were written in another language. The language of 1850 Eastern United States.

In the first hours of the school day, the office became a hub of frustrated receptionists answering a constant flow of parental phone calls, administrative assistants writing admittance slips and early excuse notices for long lines of beleaguered students, teachers checking mail and bemoaning the constant trail of paperwork that needed to be filled out before noon, and administrators behind closed doors taking silent breaths before the onslaught of student discipline problems, faculty/community liaisons, and endless meetings grappling with educational reform and ever-scrutinized test scores. The office stayed so busy in the mornings, people offered only a "Good morning" as they scurried past each other. The inattentive forehead could easily careen off a heavy door suddenly thrust open.

The most accessible copy machine was located in the main office in front of the teachers' mailboxes. A large oak table stood between the machine and mailbox slots. A sign-in sheet called to each of us and like good little sheep, we answered. What must have been a very valuable pen was chained to the table. Before I signed in and checked my mailbox, I threw open the top of the Xerox machine and placed Ginsberg's words on the freshly-Windexed glass. While the copies stacked neatly on the receiving tray, I searched through my leather book bag for my plan book and student papers. In the rush to make ninety copies before classes started, I found out later, my grade book fell out of my bulging sack onto the mailroom floor. Organized, aligned, and sorted out at home, I was a fumbling, unkempt mess at work. My life as a teacher meant I was in a constant state of change, thereby in a constant state of disarray.

My mornings were unusually rushed because I taught in one of the thirty portables erected around the main building to catch the overflow of students. It took a good five minutes to walk from the main building to the portables. Since the portables had no plumbing, I tried to be sure I used the bathroom before school started. But sometimes the lines to the employee bathrooms were so long that often I either waited until after first period to go, or I used the smoke-filled student restrooms. Over the years, the employees out in the portables either developed strong bladders or bladder infections.

Tecumseh High was so large teachers were lucky to know the twenty or so names of all the people in their individual departments. If we knew anyone from another department it was because we made a conscious choice to know that particular person. So, when Micah Marlowe knocked on my portable door with my grade book in the middle of my first period class, I vaguely recognized his face, but did not know his name or what he taught.

My first period class was my Adjusted Curriculum class. The title meant exactly what it said, a curriculum adjusted to fit the needs of students with learning disabilities, emotional problems, communication difficulties, Attention Deficit Disorders and any of a number of subtle, unidentified dysfunctions that keep students from learning. I often wondered how any person could learn in the so-called mainstream classes. After years of teaching, it occurred to me that everyone has learning disabilities. Isn't it the very nature of our individuality that we learn at different rates and in different ways? The old idea of classroom management, desks all in a row, the only noise in the room the sound of a teacher's lecture, should be tossed out alongside the rest of humanity's worst torture devices. Unmotivated students often mean incompetent teachers shuffling through reams of worksheets and lectern notes. I had thirty-one students in my class, twenty-six of them males. They gave me more frustration and more reward than any other group.

The worst behaved but smartest student in the class was Joey. He was a large sixteen- year- old with bright red hair. Every morning he blustered into class, knocking desks around, grabbing the smaller guys around the shirt collars.

"Hey, Baby Cakes!" he greeted me every morning. "How was your weekend? Man, I'm too hung over to do anything today. How about we all just take a nap?"

We had just finished reading and watching *One Flew Over the Cuckoo's Nest.* During the two weeks or so we worked on the novel, the students and I transformed the classroom into Nurse Ratched's psychiatric ward. It was an easy transformation, and the students very quickly understood the term "microcosm." All the students had character roles, and because he could not speak or read many words of English, Bdaija, a student recently transferred from Nairobi by the First Baptist Southern Church of Alpharetta, played the part of Chief Bromden. He was allowed to push a broom around the classroom anytime he wanted and to chew the ever-forbidden gum in class. Bdaija smiled constantly as he swept under our feet and around our desks. Joey was a natural for Mr. McMurphy and he played it to the hilt. Not only did he have red hair, he was the best reader in the class. As Nurse Ratched I pursed my lips and took Joey on. The students loved it as Joey and I got into power struggles inside and outside of the text. Attendance was the best ever during those *Cuckoo* weeks. I hoped *The Scarlet Letter* would prove half as popular.

After Joey quieted down, and Jose, a fair-skinned kid whose Mexican mother had married a waspish Georgia banker, finished his cavorting with the five females, I assembled the class in the "therapy" circle leftover from last week's role-playing, and told the students that Nurse Ratched had been fired, and that they were all free to leave the "ward." As a symbolic ending to the novel, I told the students to move the desks out of the circle and put them anywhere in the room they wanted.

"Anywhere in the room?" Joey asked. "I want to put mine outside. It still feels like a nut house in here."

"Hey, Joey McMurphy, aren't you sposed to be gettin' a lobotomy or did you already?" Jose asked while the others snickered.

"The desk may go outside, as long as you come back inside," I said.

"At least I got a brain to take a piece from," Joey replied as he took his desk outside the portable. He did not lose too many verbal battles. By the time he came back in, the rest of the class was settled in desks scattered all over the room, and I already had finished our mini-lesson on nouns and verbs.

"Where should I sit? There aren't any more desks."

"I guess you'll have to sit on the floor, unless you bring your desk back in."

"Crap. I'll get it. I can't sleep on this floor. It stinks like Jose's feet."

"Hey, man, when you smell the floor *and* my feet?"

"Shut up, José."

I watched them peripherally. Joey left the room to lug his desk and chair up the portable steps; Jose leaned forward on his elbows, a large grin on his face.

"Miz Scott, is *crap* a noun or a verb?"

"Actually, it could be either a verb or a noun, depending on how you use it."

"But you said nouns are females and verbs are males. How can *crap* be both?"

"It's AC/DC. Ain't that right Ms Scott?"

"What about AC/DC?" Joey asked. He dropped his desk in the middle of the floor and slid in the chair behind it.

"Sorry, Joey," I said. "You missed the lesson."

"You missed it, Joey. Verbs are males because they act up in front of the female nouns."

"What are you talking about?" asked Joey.

"The class has decided that the verbs are males and the nouns are females."

"Yeah," said Shanna, a pretty blonde with a sassy mouth. "We all sit around while you verbs act out and make fools of yourself. Ms. Scott said the verbs get it on with the nouns, but the action verbs know how to do it right."

"You're not allowed to say that in class. What kind of teaching is that? You could get fired," Joey said.

"Well, that's what the class voted on. The majority of students thought it would be easier to figure out the parts of speech, if we had an interesting association. Tomorrow we'll do the same with adjectives and adverbs, so if you want to give your opinion, be in class and not outside. And stop fussing. You talk more trash than anyone in here."

"Whatever, I hate grammar. I'll be sleeping anyway." He folded his arms across his desk and lay his head face down inside of them.

Jose saw an opportunity. "We also voted that you need a reverse lobotomy, to put some back in."

"Be nice, Jose."

"Hey, Ms. Scott, *screw* goes both ways."

"How would you know, Jose?" said Shanna.

Joey lifted his head. "*Drunk* goes both ways," he said. The rest of the class laughed and Joey put his head down again.

"What're we gonna read next?" asked Peter, a timid boy with severe acne.

"Remember last week when you asked what the Honors Juniors were reading? And you said you wanted to read the same novel? That's what we're doing next. *The Scarlet Letter*."

"Hey, I saw the movie. It has a bunch of sex and stuff in it," said Jose.

"The book is very different from the movie."

"Any sex in it?"

"Oh, yeah, it's got a lot of sex in it."

"You English teachers must be sex-starved." Joey lifted his head again. "Every year since junior high, that's all my English teachers have ever talked about. Everywhere they look, they see a phallic symbol."

"A what?"

"What's a frolic symbol?" Allen, a tall, skinny kid squirmed in his seat. He always smiled when he asked questions. I didn't know if he caught his own joke.

I chose to ignore Allen for the time being. The students waited for my reaction. "I don't think it's just English teachers who are sex-starved. It appears that the entire human race is since sex has been the topic in literature, including the Bible, ever since man started creating stories. Even some children's stories. 'Cinderella', 'Sleeping Beauty'—who knows what else—deal with the attraction between men and women."

"'Rapunzel,'" Joey offered through his pillow of arms.

"We read *I Know Why the Caged Bird Sings* last year. That was about rape and stuff."

"Sex leads to bad things like 'rape and stuff,' but it also leads to some good things like love and marriage."

"And babies."

"Family."

"Okay, okay. Get on with it. What's the book about before I fall asleep again."

"We don't have to write about this book, do we?" asked Melanie. This week her hair was lime green.

"What do you think? Gee, this is a Language Arts class. Reading, literature and oh, yeah, writing. This story involves a beautiful young woman who is shunned and punished because she committed adultery, but the man goes free."

"Isn't that the way it always is?" said Shanna. "The men get away with it, while the women pay."

"That's because we are superior," said Jose.

"You men are all dependent clauses. Tell them, Ms. Scott." Monique, one of the school's few black students remembered my "battle of the sexes" grammar lessons from last year.

"A dependent what?" asked Ryan, Jose's sidekick.

"I had Ms. Scott last year, and she pointed out that women are independent clauses, and you men are dependent, just like in everything. Always cleaning up you all's mistakes."

"We need to get started sometime today," I said. "The books are piled up on the table over there. If you want to read the book, go on up and take one."

"You mean we don't have to read it if we don't want?"

"Only if you want credit," I said.

"She thinks she's real funny," said Jose.

"She's a teacher. They always try to be funny," said Joey.

"Hey, Ms. Scott, why 'd you pin that red letter on your dress?"

"Look at the book cover, idiot. She's going to turn into a schizoid again," Joey responded.

"Joey, the names we call people are often reflections of how we secretly view ourselves."

"I thought your degree was in English." Joey smirked at me across the room.

"Anyway, if you look at the book cover, you will see, as Joey pointed out, the woman is wearing a scarlet A."

I explained to the class what the A meant and about the harsh Puritan laws, which included the stocks, whipping post and, of course, the public wearing of letters to signify the person's crime. I talked about Puritan philosophy and how in their communities there was no separation of church and state. "And that is why the entire community was involved in Hester's sin," I said. "Sin was everybody's business because an individual crime could bring the entire community down. That's why the punishment was so harsh and so public. Have any of you been embarrassed because your parents yelled at you when a friend was over?" Most of the class knew what that was like. "Then think of how much worse it would be to stand on a scaffold in the public square and have the eyes of the entire community on you for breaking a law."

"They still do that Ms. Scott. We have *Court TV*."

"What about public executions?"

"We can go to trials and watch."

"What about those live police stories—the camera's always in the criminal's face."

"Anybody watch *Survivor* last night?"

"That's not the same."

"Yes, it is. Isn't it, Ms. Scott?"

"Those are all good points. So, maybe we haven't changed that much since the days of the Puritans, and that is what I want you to pay attention to as we read the story. What does Hawthorne say about human nature? Are there any issues the Puritans faced that we still have today? I'll write those questions on the board, and I want you to copy those down in your notebook so you can refer back to them as you read the novel. A hint—these questions would make for good writing topics, hint, hint."

"This book doesn't make any sense," said Joey. "I can't even get through the first sentence. What's all this bullshit about the Custom House?" He threw the book on the floor. The rest of the class waited for me to react.

"Hey, can Joey wear a scarlet D for doofus?" I repressed a smile amid the eruption from the class.

"As long as Monique wears a scarlet S for *slut*." Joey always had an answer.

"Look, Joey," I said in my firm teacher's voice. "That kind of language is unacceptable. You're smart enough to know that. You will not call anyone in this class a slut, and you will also not use profanity without my permission and expect to stay in my classroom. I know you understand everything I said, so I see no need to discuss it any further. However, I do understand your frustration of reading Hawthorne's introductory 'Custom House.' A lot of people have experienced the same frustration. That's why we're skipping it and starting with chapter one, 'The Prison Door.' By the way class, much of the book could be frustrating to read. His style is very different from the postmodern style of today's books; he did live in the 1850's. So, we are going to approach the book as if it were written in a different language. When you are done copying what is on the board, open your books to chapter one."

As I was speaking, I noticed that all eyes were on the portable door behind me. When I turned to see what the class was reacting to, a tall man in a gray suit entered the room. "Are you Mrs. Scott?" he said in a low-pitched Georgia twang.

"Yes."

"I'm here to get a grade for a student. It's needed right away in the office. His mom is here."

"Sure, hold on." I began to search for my grade book in the usual places.

"Hey, Mr. Marlowe!"

"It's Mr. Marlowe!"

"Hello, ladies and germs."

"Tell Ms. Scott about the eye trick you showed us."

"Hey, Mr. Marlowe, our English teacher has a pornographic memory. The verbs get it on with the nouns in her class."

"Do you have your faggy trick teeth with you?" asked Joey. There was a sudden lightness in Joey's negativity.

"You still have yours I see," Mr. Marlowe responded. Joey only laughed.

My searching turned from a casual fumbling around my desk to a frantic closing and shutting of my desk drawers. Before my anxiety could get too high, Mr. Marlowe held out the dog-eared navy book.

"Looking for this? You left it in the mailroom this morning. They asked me to bring it out. Couldn't resist. Sorry."

I wanted to thank him but felt somewhat annoyed at his behavior. "Thanks, I think."

"Hey, I need help with the math homework you gave us," dark-haired Tiffany said. His attention turned to our common student. "You need to go over those problems with everybody today. You're pushing too hard, Mr. Marlowe. What do you think we are, rocket scientists?" She was the most serious student in the class and seldom responded to any of the classroom chatter. Her casualness and joviality with Mr. Marlowe was surprising, to say the least.

"Well, I guess I'll just have to do that, then. You all seemed to understand it enough yesterday. Talked me into quitting early so you could listen to a river diving story."

Tiffany smiled widely and looked across the room at Jose. "It's Jose's fault. He always wants to hear your diving stories."

"I understand the problems," Jose defended.

"That's not what you told me," said Tiffany.

"We'll talk about it in class. I've interrupted Ms. Scott enough." Micah Marlowe's eyes were clear and blue beneath his gold wire-rimmed glasses. He had a full head of graying hair and high cheekbones. Deep crevices lined the sides of his face. He was quietly handsome.

"It's okay. I run a flexible class here. If you want to help Tiffany with her math, that's fine. She's a good student, she can catch up later."

"It's your lucky day, Tiffany. You get to work with me two times in one day." Tiffany giggled. "We thank you, Ms. Scott." Mr. Marlowe pushed a desk next to Tiffany's, while she shuffled through her backpack for her math book.

"Okay ... Where were we? We just started to discuss the archaic language of Hawthorne. Does anyone know what archaic means?"

"I'll look it up."

"Does it mean big long sentences?"

"In a way."

"I found the word. It means 'old, out of style, not used anymore'."

"You told us not to write gobblegook," said Joey. "Why does he get away with it?"

"Gobbleygook, Joey. That was the style back then—long descriptive sentences."

"Like lawyers use."

"I hate long sentences that don't make any sense."

"Shut up, you fags, I already said that. What do you think gobbledygook is?"

"Joey, you can't use that language in here."

"I didn't use profanity."

I overheard Mr. Marlowe tell Tiffany, "The most elegant proofs are the shortest."

"Alright, everyone, I just heard a quote that's worth writing down."

"Another one?"

"I'm going to put on the board. I want you all to copy what Mr. Marlowe said in your notebooks. Then we can rewrite Mr. Hawthorne's long old-style sentences into our most elegant way."

"Man, who let him in here?"

"You made more work for us. Don't you have a class to go teach?"

"She drives us crazy with this crap."

Bdaija got out of his chair and grabbed the push broom from the corner of the room.

"Hey, we're done with that book. You're not Chief Bromden anymore," said Jose.

"Ms. Scott, is the class room still a loony bin?"

"The whole school's a loony bin, and the teachers are the looniest," said Joey. Mr. Marlowe's chuckle at Joey's comment resonated more like a low hum than a laugh. The rest of the students laughed along with him.

"Okay ... Okay ... Bdaija, put the broom down and copy the phrase on the board. We are *not* in the loony bin anymore. You judge for yourself whether or not the characters in *The Scarlet Letter* are crazy. You are now all Puritans in Boston, Massachusetts in 1642. You are standing ... pretend ... around the prison yard waiting for Hester Prynne ..." I pointed to my chest." ... to walk out of the prison door. She's been locked up for three months because she committed adultery. When she emerges, she is carrying a tiny baby in her arms."

"What's her husband say?"

"He doesn't know about it. He sent her over from Holland while he stayed behind to finish up important business. He was supposed to join her right away, but hasn't been heard from in years. No one knows what has happened to him. So, she ended up pregnant and they knew it couldn't be her husband's."

"Busted."

"She should have gotten an abortion."

"They didn't have abortions back then, you idi—" Joey put his head back down.

"Well, actually, Joey, they did, but they weren't very safe. So, like I said before, the Puritans often had criminals wear letters for symbols of their offense. For example, if you were a horse thief, you might wear the letter T. Hester committed adultery, so of course she wears the letter A. You all are an angry mob waiting for Hester to come out the door. That's why your desks are all out of order."

"Can we stand, then?"

"You can stand later, when you don't need to write."

"When will that be, ever?"

"Are we going to actually read it? All you do is talk."

Joey managed to get another chuckle out of Mr. Marlowe. Jose had made his way over to Tiffany and Mr. Marlowe, so now he was helping two students with their homework. I should have been annoyed at the intrusion, but actually I welcomed having another teacher in the classroom. For a brief instance, I scanned the threesome. This is the way teaching should be, I thought. In tandem, one offering special help, while the other continued with the larger group.

"I want you all to stare at the portable door and imagine you are waiting for Hester to come out."

"What's she look like?"

"Oh, she's beautiful. Long dark hair, black eyes, rosy cheeks."

"Yeah, baby."

"Who'd she do it with?"

"Shut up, and let Ms. Scott read."

"I'll read the first sentence, then you write it in your own words, your most elegant proofs." I cleared my throat, and read in my most sonorous voice. "'A throng of bearded men, in sad colored garments, and gray steeple-colored hats intermixed with women, some wearing hoods, and others bareheaded, was assembled in front of a wooden edifice, the door of which was heavily timbered with oak, and studded with iron spikes.'"

Mr. Marlowe would have left without my noticing him had not several students interrupted my reading.

"See ya, Mr. M. Glad you finally got your telescope back."

"I'd like to beat the face in of the student who stole it," said Jose.

"Ya'll be quiet. Ms. Scott is reading to you." He placed his finger to his lips.

I walked over to the back door of the portable to thank him again for bringing my grade book to me. "Thanks. If I had lost that … "

"My name is Micah," he said. "You have quite a few of my students in here." Micah Marlowe's face remained impassive as he talked, his voice a slow monotonous drawl, yet there was a powerful presence about him hard to miss. "You work well with my … our kids," he said. "Keep pushing them. They need it. They want it." For an instance he smiled, the constriction of his mouth controlled and contained. "Stop by my room sometime after school and we'll talk." His eyes searched instead of lingered, his movements understated as he opened the portable door.

Before I could say anything else, Jose yelled across the room. "Hey, Ms. Scott, we only have about twenty minutes left. Could Mr. Marlowe stay and tell one of his diving stories?"

"Yeah, Mr. Marlowe," said Monique. "Ms. Scott has never heard any of them. Tell the one about getting lost in the woods with your buddies."

"No, man," said Joey. "We've heard that a hundred times. I want to hear the one about the barracuda."

"Mr. Marlowe might want to get something done this period, instead of wasting his precious time on all of you. Plus, you didn't write your elegant proofs yet."

Mr. Marlowe closed the door behind him and walked back into the portable. "If ya'll write your proofs like Ms. Scott asked, I'll tell the barracuda story … if it is alright with Ms.Scott."

"Sure. Okay, let's hear those proofs," I said. I felt a bit caught off guard.

Amid the students' words, I glanced over at Micah Marlowe. His stillness unnerved yet intrigued me. He appeared to be around forty-years-old. He could have been five years younger or older.

"There was a door," Allen volunteered.

"Bare women watched the door. They were in the hood." The class laughed at Jose's response.

"Puritan men and women stood in front of a large door."

"Hey, Ms. Scott, you listening to us?"

"I'm listening. Those are great."

"Even Jose's?"

"I suppose."

"Gee, thanks."

"I got the best one," said Monique. "Old men with beards and big hats waited with the women around a big oak door. Yes!" She circled her fist around while barking.

"Hey, Miz S., we're running out of time. How many ways can we redo one lousy sentence, anyway?"

"Okay, okay. Joey's right, read chapter one tonight. It 's all yours Mr. Marlowe."

Micah Marlowe pulled the high stool I had sitting next to my desk to the center of the classroom. He slowly and deliberately seated himself on top of it, resting his left foot on one of the bottom rungs. He cleared his throat and readjusted his glasses. He took a few moments to apprise the students, as if trying to figure out what their reactions would be before he told his story. His methodical movements made me uncomfortable. When he had absolute silence, he finally began.

"If it were not for my good buddy Joe Doughty, a marine biologist from San Francisco, I would have a big red scar running from the top of my eyebrows to the middle of my head." Marlowe ran an index finger up and over his forehead.

"How wide would it have been?" asked one of the students.

"About as wide as my pinky finger, at least. Anyway ... "

"Can we have a closer look at your head?" asked Peter.

"Well ... no. Now, hush." Micah cleared his throat and started again. "A few years back one summer I took some kids from this school to Eleuthera, a small island in the Bahamas. We adventured like Robinson Crusoe at a house in the middle of nowhere that sat on a little ridge just above the dunes. Neat place. Anyway, we needed a new barracuda skeleton for teaching purposes cause the goofy dog had eaten the last one. We were drift-snorkeling up at the cut between our island and the next, just north, and this barracuda about four feet long had been following us all day. I hung around at the back of the group with my spear gun. Do ya'll know what a Hawaiian sling is?"

"Not really," Joey responded for the group.

"Well, it's a spear gun with no cord attached so you have to be really accurate. I shoot for the gills, but my aim was a bit off and all I did was hit 'em in the stomach. Now he's swimming away with my spear that costs about $35 so I grab at it and one second later, all I see is a big mouth and lots of teeth. He hit me right between the eyes and glanced off my mask and just laid me open. I swam in a bit and staggered to shore. I yelled at Joe, 'Hey, I need some help out here' and when he saw me his tan turned white. He said I looked like the devil himself with my blood-red face. Every time my heart would beat, blood would ooze out of a cut from here to here." He traced his finger from just above his eyebrows to the top of his head as he stepped down from the stool. "We got the bleeding stopped and piled back into the truck and headed for home. It took about an hour-and-a-half to get back. The roads were pretty bad. Well, since we got back too early anyway, the guy who owned the place was gone and the key to the medical stuff with him. The only doctor-type around was the vet and he was out of town, so off we bounced to the local hardware store in the village a couple miles away. On one of the dusty shelves, they had some dental floss and needles used for fixin' sailcloth." The class and myself moaned at the image foreshadowed. Micah paused for effect, then eased himself back onto the stool. Not a single student had his head down, not even Joey. "Now my head was hurting more and more from all the running around we were doing, and the towel was almost completely saturated with blood."

"I'm surprised you didn't pass out," I interposed.

"Quiet, Ms. Scott. Let him finish."

"She always has to get her two cents worth in," said Joey.

"We only have a couple minutes left," added Jose.

Micah laughed at the class. "You're the ones doing all the talking, not Mrs. Scott. Let's see, where was I. Oh yeah ... so now they have me sit down at the kitchen table and pour some whiskey on my cut and in me. One of 'em holds the cut together and the other tries to push that sewing needle into my scalp. It hurt like a sucker but wouldn't go in. So, now what? Well, back they go to the dirty old hardware store and sittin' on the shelf behind the register is an old bottle of Superglue."

"No way. This is made-up."

"Serious, this junk really happened. On my momma's grave. It's time to go so I'll make it quick. So, one of the students held the cut tight together while Joe ran a bead of glue down it and tah-daaaaah, it worked! Now, you can look at my head."

The students rushed forward as the bell sounded. "See, hardly a scar. A medical miracle."

Some of the girls held their heads. Even I was cringing a bit.

"That is so gross, Mr. Marlowe," several students said.

"No way. That's too cool," Joey said as he grabbed his books.

"Can you tell us another story today in class?"

Micah smiled playfully at the class' reaction. "So when do you all suppose we cover the chapters in the math book? Any of ya' all willing to come to school on Saturday and Sunday then?"

"We can do both, Mr. Marlowe."

"Both Saturday and Sunday?"

"No, cover the chapters and listen to your stories."

"I told you, as soon as we finish chapter five, then a story, maybe."

I really liked Micah Marlowe. He struck me as a skeptic with a shy personality, full of unrehearsed and natural charm. Self-assured and calm, the words fell easily from his mouth in a slow, mellifluous stream. His style was so different from mine. I was in constant motion, darting here and there, my mind spinning like the wings of a hummingbird, my voice high, almost shrill at times, exploding with manic energy. Yet despite or because of our extreme styles, we were able to reach students many teachers could not. My heart went out to Micah Marlowe that day, though the reasons were beyond my grasp at that time.

"Can we continue reading tomorrow? We already know a bunch of people are watching the door."

"Are we going to read every paragraph this way?"

"No, just the beginning one to get you started."

"See ya tomorrow."

"Bye, Baby Cakes."

I turned around to say goodbye and thank Mr. Marlowe, but he had already left. I felt disappointed, but prepared my desk for the next class. Yet, Micah Marlowe's visit stayed with me all day long—he haunted me through *All the King's Men* and my three afternoon classes of Walt Whitman. I sensed a familiarity about him that came from a place deep inside, a place deeper than this lifetime, an ancient place collected in the unconscious waves of the brain passed down through centuries of nature's blood struggles. And then I knew I had to evacuate the emotional past, those spiritual struggles evolved from nature's origins. "If you could not accept the past and its burden, there was no future," Jack Burden told Anne Stanton, his lover, his betrayer, his wife. It is one of life's idiosyncrasies that we can spend twenty-five years with a person and not get past the epidermis, yet we can spend ten minutes with a stranger and see clear down to the viscera. I had to find Micah Marlowe again.

Chapter 8

As fate would have it, I didn't see Micah Marlowe again for two weeks. My dentist and good friend Dr. Craig had Lou Gehrig's disease, and it was getting progressively worse. The day Micah Marlowe found my grade book I received a phone call from Craig's wife.

"Craig's dying," she said, her voice broken by tears. "I don't think he's going to make it through the week. You stayed with him after most of his patients left. He really appreciated that. I thought you might want to say good-bye to him. Cat, I need to warn you. He looks pretty bad. He's lost a lot of weight … I haven't seen him smile for weeks … He still hasn't made peace with himself."

Craig and Summer lived two streets down from me, so it was easy to drop by at a moment's notice. I knew the disease was progressing, and Craig had relinquished his practice. Back in May he had called to tell me about his new dental partner and had set up a time for me to interview her over coffee. She had gone to medical school with Craig and proved to be not only a close friend of Craig and Summer's, but also a competent and compassionate dentist with a sense of humor. Little did I know that by October, she would be the only dentist in the office.

It had been almost two years since Craig first told me he had been diagnosed with the disease. Heather, Craig's dental assistant, had just finished polishing my teeth with baking soda compound. I was wiping the abrasive drool from my chin just as Dr. Craig walked in the room.

"Hey, beautiful," Craig said. "I want to floss you all over."

"I'm ready for your strong, capable hands, Doctor."

"Speaking of hands," he said. "Mine are not doing so well. Look."

Craig held his right hand out in front of me. It shook like an old man's.

"That's great … a dentist with shaking hands. It's a good thing I'm not having a root canal."

"Catherine, I don't know how to say this … I guess English will work." He smiled ironically. "I've been diagnosed with Lou Gehrig's disease. I'm the luckiest man on the face of the earth." Craig sat in the swivel chair next to the desk and faced me at eye level.

"Lucky?"

"I was just ... oh, forget it." He looked exhausted. "I've been notifying all my patients. It's not bad enough now for me to discontinue my work. It's in the beginning stages, but it is a degenerative disease. My nerves are dying. You might not want my shaky hands in your mouth."

"You can put anything you want in my mouth for as long as you want."

Dr. Craig laughed. "That is a dangerous thing to say, Cat." His face grew serious again. "I am telling all my patients to look for another dentist."

"I'm not leaving you. We are in this for life."

"Well, that's not much longer."

"Craig, I am so sorry. If there is anything I can do ..." I awkwardly climbed out of the dentist's chair and threw my arms around him. I felt the shudder of fear run through his body. "I love you and Summer. You are two of the best people I know."

"Say something funny. This is getting too morbid for me."

"Did I tell you I always flash my breasts for dying men?"

Dr. Craig laughed. "How many dying men have you known besides your father? "

"Of course I wouldn't be so sacrilegious as to flash my father—especially since my mother lost a breast. The first person I ever flashed was Nick; he was one of the Lower Price Hill Rats who hung around with my girlfriend Judy. He was the James Dean of the Hill ... the Leader of the Pack. He died as a result of a horrible car crash—he was in a coma for weeks—I had just turned seventeen at the time and had this tough-ass philosophy that I would do whatever I wanted whenever—the hell with being the good little girl."

"So what about the flashing?" Dr. Craig brought me back, the disease forgotten for the moment.

"Judy and I sneaked into his hospital room, and we both flashed him, hoping that would bring him out of his coma. It didn't work, but Judy swore she saw some movement under the sheets. Then about ten years later I flashed Artie, my girlfriend Cheryl's husband when he was dying of cancer. I flashed him so he would feel better. It did made make his dying easier. Cheryl begged me to do it."

"And now your dying dentist."

"You don't know that, Craig."

"Don't I?"

I searched Craig's wide blue eyes to see how he was facing the certain nearness of his death. They revealed a resigned anxiety, a tentative hopelessness. The rest of his long face bowed down in cynicism, his thin lips curled in suppressed hysteria. He had a beautiful and supportive wife, a six-year-old little boy and twin girls not yet a year old. The prospect of leaving them was hard for him, I knew. Was it only a few years ago I interviewed this man who would so profoundly affect my life? A man who would cause me to examine my own life and force me to take hold of the grit and girth of the earth. I placed my fingers on his lips to erase some of the bitterness.

"Your life is a good one, Craig. You made a wise choice when you chose Summer."

"And she made a shitty one."

"I think you know Summer would not trade the years she's had with you. Hell, you're not dead yet. Who knows what new cures will be found in the next year. Medical technology can make leaps and bounds overnight. That's the one good thing about the fast pace of high-tech these days. Speaking of which, are you ever going to examine my teeth?"

"I would, if you ever stop talking long enough. Open wide and let me see those sexy molars."

Craig had been my dentist since I moved to Atlanta. I met him at our first country club picnic two summers before the Olympics. As I watched the tremors in his skillful hands, it saddened me to think of the way he was that July afternoon. Tall, great smile (of course), exuberant, muscular. Bonnie Jorgenson introduced him to me. "He's a great dentist," she said. "He's very gentle."

"I have to know someone very well before he sticks his hands in my mouth. I have had really bad experiences with dentists in the past."

"I'm a Stanford graduate. What else do you need to know?"

"How about meeting me for a drink sometime next week, and I'll bring my list."

Dr. Craig laughed. "Are you serious?"

"I always interview my dentists. If a dentist will not take the time to get to know me, then I cross him off my list."

"I heard you were a character."

"Thursday at Spinnakers? What time do you get off work?"

"How's seven?"

"That's fine."

Dr. Craig shook his head and smiled broadly. "Do you want me to bring my diplomas and dental books?"

"Just yourself."

I really didn't expect Dr. Craig to remember to meet me Thursday or even to take me seriously, so I called his office after school the day of the meeting. "You still meeting me at Spinnakers?" I asked.

"Of course, I am. Why, can't you make it?"

Later at Spinnakers, he confessed he would not have shown up had I not called him. "You're really serious about getting to know your dentist."

"I've had too many bad experiences with dentists in the past to go to somebody I don't trust. I've had my tongue cut, a tooth pulled without Novocain, and so many painful fillings that I vowed when I could make my own appointments with the dentist, I would choose only the kind, gentle ones. I got the idea to start interviewing dentists from my dad. When my mom's oncologist suggested she get radiation treatments for breast cancer, my Dad suggested she get a second opinion. So, before I got my teeth checked the next time, I was about ten, I asked my dad if I could get a second opinion. He said, what are you going to do, go around and interview all the dentists in Price Hill? And that's what I did. Well, not all of them, but more than three. And, I found someone who at least listened to me when I told him dentists really scare me."

That afternoon I found out many things about Craig. I found out he grew up in Connecticut, attended public schools, started as quarterback for his high school team, married the girl he took to his senior prom, and graduated from Stanford University. Except for a mother who was a busybody and complained too much, he had an unexceptional childhood and a decent high school experience. He did get caught smoking and drinking at the junior high Christmas dance, much to the chagrin of his parents. His father was not much of a disciplinarian, but would use the belt occasionally if his wife pressured him into it. His father did get out the belt after the junior high Christmas dance fiasco. That didn't deter him from drinking and smoking the rest of his high school years, however. He stopped smoking when he decided to go to dental school, though he still liked to drink. He had been invited to the neighborhood shindigs but from what he had heard, they involved too much drinking for him. He attended the St. Mary's Episcopal Church every Sunday with his wife and children, and read books by Thomas Moore to heighten his spirituality. The highlight of his life was his family.

But Craig was not the least bit self-righteous or dull. He was quite the opposite. Gregarious and witty, most people found his company entertaining. He loved his wife, but enjoyed the company of other women. His wife was secure enough to ignore his flirtations, and she laughed along with him when he joked with other women. With Craig, going to the dentist became more of a spiritual experience than a painful one.

And Craig did take more than a neighborly interest in me. Because of teaching, I had to make my dental appointments at the end of the day. And since I was more often than not one of Craig's last patients, he would suggest getting a beer before we headed home. We had some of our best talks then. Craig suspected that I was troubled, but he was not the kind of man who asked for details. He listened to my childhood stories about the Sisters of Charity and the run-ins they had with my Irish father. Sometimes we would talk about our favorite books, or he would bring a book with a passage marked and ask me what I thought about it. He was a fan of T.S. Eliot, and once when I brought *The Love Song of J. Alfred Prufrock* to the office, he cut my examination short so we could rush to Spinnaker's to discuss the poem.

In the bar, I read to Craig my favorite lines. Leaning my body close to his, I stared hauntingly into his eyes: "'And I have known the eyes already, known them all ...'" I swept my eyes around the bar. "'The eyes that hold you in a formulated phrase ... '" My voice deepened, and I sat back in the booth. "'And when I am pinned and wriggling on the wall, then how shall I begin to spit out all the butt-ends of my days and ways?'"

"You are so sexy when you read Eliot. Let's go back to my car so I can ravish you."

"Shut up, you sex maniac. Here, find your own lines to read."

Craig leafed through the poem until he came to a line he remembered from having read the poem in college. "'I should have been a pair of ragged claws scuttling across the floors of silent seas,'" he quoted. "Coppola used that line in *Apocalypse Now*, remember?"

"Yeah, the journalist. Right before Captain Willard meets Kurtz," I said. "Every time I read this poem, I get shivers down my spine. Do you think Eliot's life was a hell of loneliness?"

" Eliot married, didn't he?"

"People can be lonely in marriage."

"Here's a great line," Craig said. " 'And indeed there will be time to wonder, "Do I dare? And, Do I dare?" Time to turn back and descend the stair, with a bald spot in the middle of my hair.' "

"And do you measure out your life in coffee spoons, Craig?" I teased.

"Sometimes I wonder about my life, Cat. 'Do I dare to eat a peach?' Have I disturbed the universe enough? Have I taken enough risks? My life seems too perfect—beautiful wife, great kids, thriving dental practice."

"I hope you dare to eat a peach. You're a dentist for God's sake. Plus, you risked going out with me. I don't think you know how capable I am of disturbing the universe."

"That's what I like about you, Cat."

For Craig, I was the woman he would have had an affair with if he were the unfaithful type. In a strange way, I took care of any urges he might have had in that area, not literally, of course, but I created enough fantasies to keep him out of trouble in his spare time. At least that's what he implied on more than one occasion.

"Is there any question who has the best tits in the neighborhood?" Craig asked one time after I told him what the men joked about at our neighborhood get-togethers.

"And who would that be?" I returned the question, feigning innocence.

"You know damn well those guys in the neighborhood are dreaming about yours."

"I don't understand why men get so fired up about these things," I said, cupping my hands under my chest. "Must have something to do with the Oedipal complex Freud says you all suffer from."

"How about a quick shot sometime, Cat?"

"You already have a shot," I said, glancing at his vodka martini.

"Not that kind of shot. I mean the kind with your blouse unbuttoned. Just one quick look will keep me occupied for a long time."

Every time he asked for a shot I would laugh and suggest different places and times for Craig to get his peek. It was harmless flirtation more playful than sexual, but it bound us humanly and wantonly together.

And now Craig was dying. Some of us disturb the universe more through death than in life, yet others just disturb—like Micah. When I hung up the phone with Summer that late fall afternoon, my mind was yet searching for reasons why a reserved math teacher could affect me so much. Maybe the quiet Micah Marlowe entered my life at just the right time, a time not so burdened with the excessive demands of emotional survival, a time that had let in enough distance, or possibly his constrained personality reminded me of that sadness that was so constrained inside of me, or maybe I was seeing Jack Burden again and the hope that I could resurrect the withered leaves of a life forgone. I fought against the idea that Micah Marlowe was just another fish man.

With these thoughts in mind, I entered the Coulters' house. Summer had converted the great room into Craig's living and sleeping quarters. Summer immediately hugged me and whispered that she had just finished feeding Craig. "I need to wipe his mouth before you see him. Wait here a second." From the foyer, I saw Summer lean over and tenderly wipe Craig's face. Next to his bed stood a table, filled with brown plastic pill bottles, cotton swabs, half-filled water glass, thermometer, and paper spitting cup. I heard her whisper something to Craig and could see him shaking his head dejectedly. Summer walked slowly to the foyer. "He doesn't want you to see him like this, Cat. I'm sorry."

"Oh for heaven sakes," I said. "This is ridiculous. If he thinks he is going to get rid of me that easily, he has another thing coming." I thought for a minute. "Summer, would you like to take the kids out somewhere for awhile? I really would like to talk to Craig alone. It might be easier that way."

"That might not be a bad idea. We could all use a break. I could take them to McDonalds. They'd like that, but it might be awhile, and I don't want to leave Craig too long."

"I'll stay with him until you get home. And Summer, don't worry about a thing, I'll take real good care of him."

"I know you will. Thanks, Cat, I'll tell him ... "

"No, you just go on ahead; no sense in making him get used to the idea twice."

Summer left and I crept into the sick room. When I saw Craig, I understood why he did not want to me to see him. The shock on my face could not help but show. He had lost at least fifty pounds and his face was gray and emaciated. He looked worse than my seventy-eight-year-old father did on his deathbed. He lay on one side, his thin arms crossed under his chin, his legs and torso curled into a fetal position. When my gaze reached his eyes, he turned his head from me. He waved his waiflike arm for me to go.

"If you think you are going to get rid of me that easily, you have another thing coming, sweetheart. A promise is a promise."

Craig had a hard time turning his head around to face me, but when he did I thought I saw a knowing glimmer in his eyes. "Dr. Craig, I think we have had enough talks about life to know where true beauty lies. Your body doesn't quite look like Arnold's, but that is not what I am seeing right now. When I think about how you lived your life, I see a combination of Richard Gere, Mel Gibson, Robert Redford and Harrison Ford all rolled into one. You could not be more beautiful to me than how you are right now." Craig just stared at me expectantly. I felt like I had to continue. "You know Craig, some people walk around this earth like they are already dead. You were, I mean, you are ... have been really alive, you did dare to eat that peach, Craig ..." I was stopped in mid-sentence by Craig's moaning. I knew I wasn't making much sense and was eating both feet at the same time. He tried to lift his head and I noticed he was limply pointing at me with his finger.

"What is it, sweetie?" I said softly.

"Dying." He strained to get the word out.

"I know you are, sweetheart. And I will really miss you. We all will." He lifted his trembling hand an inch off the mattress and strained to raise his head.

"Breasts," he said. "Dying ... Breasts ... Dare disturb ..." There was nothing wrong with his memory, it seemed.

"Oh, I get it. You want me to ..." I smirked knowingly at him. "You devil, you. Well okay then," I said.

Facing my former dentist now my patient, I moved as close to Craig as I could without blurring his vision. The bodice rippers I had read in high school came to mind as I undid the pearl buttons of my eggplant-colored blouse. In those fantasies of long ago, a tall, dark, handsome man would want me so badly, he would not be able to wait long enough to unfasten the fifty or more tiny cloth- covered buttons of my high collared shirt; instead he would rip open my muslin blouse and ravish me. Reality had always been much more raw if not more dramatic than my fantasies. So, for the third time in my life, I undid my own buttons for a dying man.

Carefully, I laid my silk blouse on the end of Craig's bed, and then unlatched the clasp on the front of my bra. The hook got caught in the red lace, and it took a few moments for me to untangle the clasp. Craig's eyes grew wider as I struggled to make this event go as smoothly and naturally as possible. The clasp finally unleashed, I slid my arms out of the silk straps and let the brassiere fall to the floor. The sun eased its way in through the southern exposed windows of the great room, and I stood tall as my naked chest flashed in the waning afternoon light. Unbound, my breasts felt heavy and ripe against my body, compassion darkening the hushed rose of my fleshy aurioles.

Using all of his strength, Craig raised his head and smiled wide enough for his teeth to show. When he fell back down, I leaned over and hugged his emaciated body. He felt like a frail old woman to me. When I reached my lips up to his, I realized he was trying to speak to me. "Catherine," he said barely above a whisper. "Beautiful ... "

"I'm glad you think so ... "

Craig shook his head. "Everywhere ... beautiful," he struggled to say. I squeezed his hands and said goodbye. I knew I had to leave before he saw me cry.

Dusk had already overshadowed the front of the house, and I stood at the dining room window waiting for Summer and the children to return. Craig had fallen asleep, my visit exhausting his limited energy reserves, his words vitalizing my forgotten stores of hope.

"He's fast asleep," I said to Summer as I was leaving. "He handled my intrusion like the trooper he is."

"You always make Craig smile. You are welcome here anytime you want. Thanks, Cat."

For the next ten days, I devoted myself to Craig and his family. I came directly home from school, dropped my books and papers on the kitchen counter, fed the fish, and went directly over to Craig and Summer's. Sometimes I sat with Craig, who barely opened his eyes or spoke any more, as Summer helped Chad with his letters and fed the babies. Other times, I watched the children while Summer sat with her husband. I did not make it to any of the happy hours those days, and even though I was invited, I declined Monica's invitation to her Saturday night Halloween party. Instead, I pulled out my sewing machine and made a Spider-Man outfit for Chad and angel outfits for the twins. Halloween night, Summer and I pulled Craig's bed into the foyer so that he could see the children's costumes as they came to the door. Most of the children thought he was a ghoul, and in a way I guess he really was. That would be Craig's last Halloween. He died the Friday before Marshall came home from China.

Marshall appeared glad to see me when he arrived home, but I was so distraught and occupied with Craig's death that I barely noticed Marshall. I don't remember much about that weekend, but I do know I didn't grade any of the research papers I promised my Junior Honors students I would get to over the weekend. They let me hear about it in class on Monday. To make up for it, I let them have a reading day in class. I had just introduced *The Great Gatsby*, and they had the first four chapters due by Wednesday. They were overjoyed and I finished grading fifteen papers. My mind stayed busy until seventh period, my planning time. Even though I had prepared myself for Craig's death, I still really missed him. I hurt for Summer and the children but felt powerless knowing there was little I could do to ease their grief. And I also hurt for myself. Not just because I lost a good friend and dentist, but also because I lost a compassionate person who calmed my mind by his mere presence. He may have wished he had taken more chances, but the choices he made were honorable ones. He led a gentle, caring life full of loving family and friends. He found his peace early in life; I had as yet found mine.

It was only fifteen minutes into seventh bell, and I knew I had to get out of my portable, so I grabbed the few papers I had corrected and walked over to Micah Marlowe's classroom. My students explained to me earlier that he had erected a birdhouse outside his portable so I knew it would be easy to find. I also knew he had a trig class seventh because some of my honors students were in his class.

If he were busy then I would leave; if not, I would use the pretense of handing back my students' papers to stay and visit for a while. Maybe we would plan some time together after school to share ideas to use in both math and literature. Or maybe we would just talk.

The furthest portable from the main building, Marlowe's rectangular corrugated box stood aloof in a patch of high grass and gravel. His tract extended into a small yard on the side of the portable adjacent to the student parking lot, facing away from the permanent classrooms. In the center of the yard was a rustic wooden birdhouse atop a four-by-four stuck in the ground. About ten feet to the left a green paint-chipped birdfeeder was placed upon an embedded steel post. Small seedlings were growing from the birdseed that somehow escaped uneaten. Telltale signs of bird droppings graced the roof and periphery of the feeder. As I approached the worn wooden steps leading to the aluminum door above, I could hear a congenial hub of voices mixed with Marlowe's mock exasperation. "How many times have I told you to keep the string taut? No wonder the calculation won't work, you knuckleheads. Some of you have either the victim being nine feet tall or the murderer being a midget, both of which are wrong. Now watch."

Configuring a trig equation on the dry erase board, Micah Marlowe at first did not notice my presence in his classroom. I drifted over to the left-hand corner of the room and sat in a tired straight-back Shaker chair, more reminiscent of the flea market circuit than a high school setting. Student desks hugged the back wall; the students themselves, dressed more for mountain climbing than studying, haphazardly sat or reclined on multi-colored blocks of carpeting glued to the floor. Stretches of butcher-block paper splattered with red distorted circles lay among the scattered groups of adolescents. Scissors, meter sticks, calipers, and unraveled string were on the long sheets, momentarily forgotten as the students listened intently to Marlowe's careful instruction. If any of the students did notice me, they kept it to themselves, either so engrossed in Marlowe's lesson to care about an intruder or too respectful of their teacher to cause an interruption.

My chair was tucked next to a black metal file cabinet covered with a multitude of stickers, most of them from *Star Wars,* one of the eclectic themes running through this anomaly of a classroom. I had a clear view of Marlowe's desk positioned diagonally on the opposite side of the room. Suspended above his desk were *Star Wars* models: X-Wing, Tie-Fighter and the A-wing. Situated on top of his desk was a scale version of the Hubble Space Telescope. The rest of his desk was confusedly stacked with papers, books and what appeared to be minerals and crystals. Next to this, a long picnic table held tanks filled with lizards and fish and one ant farm. An assortment of bones filled the remaining table space.

My inspection of Marlowe's room was cut short by the intuitiveness of recognition. I could not exactly see Marlowe's eyes; the glare of the fluorescent lights caught his glasses, and I could only see the distorted reflection of myself where his eyes should have been. I smiled weakly at him as he continued talking to the class.

"So, you have gotta measure the major and minor axes carefully, then go through the trig steps and I'll help you again after you do that. I'll come around to help, and don't take forever. This crime has to be solved before class is over."

The lesson through for the moment, the students resumed their chatting and measuring.

"Mr. Marlowe, is that your girlfriend?"

"What?" he said. By the way he stiffened, I could tell he knew exactly who they where talking about if not what.

"I'm his sister," I smartly said.

"No, she's not. She's Ms. Scott, our English teacher. Are those graded papers for us?"

I ignored Micah's stare for the moment. "Yes, they are. And when Mr. Marlowe wants to hand them back, he can." I turned to the very still Mr. Marlowe. "Do you mind handing these back before the end of the period?"

"Leave 'em on my desk. They can get them when class is over." Before I could say anything else, he abruptly turned and walked to the other side of the classroom.

"Ms. Scott, do you have my paper graded too? Do you know if I passed? How were my references?"

"Hey, get to work. You can do English stuff later."

I whispered to Patrick. "I have your paper graded. It was magnificent." Patrick breathed a sigh of relief.

"I'm glad I don't have you for a teacher," one of the other students said. "I can only take one hard teacher a year." The pony-tailed student bobbed her head towards Mr. Marlowe.

"Ms. Scott's cool," said one of my own.

"As cool as me?" Marlowe said over my shoulder. He appeared more relaxed when I turned to face him.

"Sorry to barge in on you like this. I just thought if you had a minute, you or I could pass out these papers. I did not quite get them graded over the weekend. A friend of mine ... "

In the middle of my apology, Marlowe veered around to a student who needed his help. "Here, hold the string like this and now measure it." He looked up at me. "Don't worry. As punishment for interrupting, you have to stay or at least come back and tell us about Edgar Allen Poe. What'd you get? Okay, then that should give you the approximate point of origination."

I decided I was in the way and tried to catch his eye before I left. I finally gave up and headed toward the door.

"Hey, where are you going? Don't you even want to know what we're doing, and why Poe?"

"Well, yes, as a matter of fact, I do." Secretly, I was relieved he asked me to stay. The thought of spending the rest of the day alone in my classroom gripped me in its anxious vise. There was some comfort being with this strange but gentle man.

"I'm trying to show the students how trig is used in forensics. A buddy of mine is a medical examiner, and he showed me how he figures the exact point in a room from which the blood emerged." He related to me how the evening before, using watered-down red acrylic paint, he simulated blood spatter on large pieces of packing paper. Actually, he shook the bloodlike substance on the paper with his hand. Micah had come up with the idea to show the connection among forensics, trigonometry, and even literature. He showed me the copies of Poe's "Murder in the Rue Morgue" he had used to enhance the project.

"How did you have the time to incorporate literature into your math class?" I asked.

"You make time. I held back the last five pages of the short story," he said. "We read a little bit every day during the last few minutes of class. We did that for about a week. If they wanted to know the ending they had to pick up the last pages from me and read them at home. Most everybody did. It was a great way to show the class how even Poe recognized the part science and math play in solving crime."

"I don't know too many math teachers who teach Poe in their classes. I wish I knew enough about math to incorporate it into my literature classes." As I smiled up at Micah, his skin took on a glow I had not noticed before.

"Well, Ms. Scott, I would be glad to help you with that dilemma. Math is a part of all of nature, including human nature. You teach Emerson and Thoreau, right?"

"Of course."

"They both write about math in nature. Emerson talks about Man Thinking in "The American Scholar." He says the whole is greater than the sum of the individual parts. That's math, albeit a different kind. There's a mathematical reason the spiral of a seashell elicits wonder and a sense of beauty. Symmetry is the basis for all existence."

"I suppose it makes sense."

"Not sure who, but someone once said, 'God is a mathematician.' It's in everything. Look, I have to get to work here."

"Sure, no problem." He turned back to his students while I looked closer at the curious items spread out on his desk. I held one of the crystals in my hand and could see the math involved. The deer bones would take some explaining, but I was willing to listen to this math teacher unlike the many of my teenage years.

Around his students, Micah was in his element. His voice was fuller, his mouth relaxed, his stance full of self-assurance and fatherly maturity. As he continued to teach, his enthusiasm and earnestness washed the tightly controlled lines of anxiety from his face, the sharpness of his jaw softened by the love he felt for his subject. His depth and impassioned words touched me. I wanted to tell him so. "I would have loved having you for a teacher," I said to myself. Then I impulsively added, "Maybe I still can."

Micah squatted on the balls of his feet, his strong forearms exposed beneath the rolled sleeves of his cotton blue shirt. His meaty fingers smoothed the crinkled edges of a long sheet of paper as his deep voice instructed, scolded and soothed. What is your secret, Micah Marlowe? I thought, as I watched him scrutinize his students' work. How can your face light up one minute and then disappear into itself the next?

I wound a leftover piece of string around my index finger, feeling its rough texture on my skin. It had been a long time since I played with string— cat's in the cradle, walking the dog, tin cans with telephone lines, and paper kites tied to light wooden crosses. Once when I was eight-years-old and it was my turn to bring treats to my Brownie meeting, I dismantled my kite because I needed the string to wrap marshmallows. The night before my troop meeting, having heard my mother and father complain about the financial hardship of sending five children to Catholic schools, I knew I could not ask them to spend money on treats. So, I took down a roll of yellow toilet paper from the bathroom shelf, pulled apart my kite in the utility room and found miniature stale marshmallows in the kitchen cabinet under the sink. I carefully wrapped the marshmallows in folds of yellow tissue and tied them with the broken pieces of string. Before I went to bed, I placed twenty-five tiny packages containing ten marshmallows each in a brown paper bag, and hid them behind the furnace next to the coal bin.

After school the next day, I skipped to my Brownie meeting twirling the brown bag as if it were a baton. The Brownie meetings were always held at Cathy Cavin's house; her mother was the troop leader. After hopping down the basement steps two at a time, I situated myself in a corner, watching Barbie Briarton run around the room, demanding all the girls' attention with her loud voice. Eventually, the leaders quieted us down. We said the Brownie pledge, sang several songs, and divided into groups for the day's project. After about an hour, several of the girls shouted they were hungry and begged for the treat. "Who brought the treat today?" asked Mrs. Cavin, our Brownie leader. Everyone looked around the basement room. I walked over to my brown paper bag and passed out the wrapped marshmallows. Several of the girls started snickering, and Barbie Briarton loudly voiced her disgust.

"Stale marshmallows! I'm not eating these! I'm hungry. When it was my turn, my mother baked cupcakes." Some of the girls felt stale marshmallows were unfair; others said they would never eat anything that was wrapped in toilet paper. The leaders were no better. I could hear them whispering to each other. "What mother would let her daughter wrap marshmallows in toilet paper? What kind of snack is this?"

Mrs. Cavin, brownish-gray hair teased into an overblown bouffant, motioned for me to go upstairs with her. "Cat," she said, shutting the basement door, "do you have anything else at home that you can bring?" I knew we didn't, since my family rarely had treats or sweets of any kind in the house. But I was too embarrassed to tell the truth, so, stalling for time, I let Mrs. Cavin take me in her car and drive me to my house. Watching her tightly pursed lips, I became acutely aware I did not actually live in a house, but a small unit attached to four others. My street was overrun with parked cars; the rundown garages next to our building were full of old sofas, washing machine parts, rusted old cars with bald tires and miscellaneous junk the neighborhood children used for play. Reluctantly, I walked into my whitewashed cement unit. Clothes were piled on the living room couch, and my mother was furiously shaking starch out of an old Pepsi bottle over one of my dad's long-sleeved work shirts. "I thought you had Brownies this afternoon," she said. My mother, red scarf wrapped like a turban around her rolled hair, a few bobby-pinned bangs sticking out the front, barely looked up from her ironing.

"I haven't gone yet. I came home to use the bathroom first."

"The Cavins don't have a bathroom?"

"I like to use ours better." I went into the kitchen and opened the bottom cabinets hoping against hope to find a brand new bag of cookies or candy. The same cans of tired old peas and lima beans stared back at me. I was too short to open the cabinets above the sink, and I spent the day in my room several times already for standing on a kitchen chair to reach them. I was fairly sure we did not have any treats anyway, so the risk was not worth it. "Hey Mom," I shouted. "Do we have any cookies or anything sweet?" I folded my hands and prayed for a miracle, but she answered in the negative. "Okay," I said.

Mrs. Cavin stared at me expectantly as I walked down my porch steps. She saw right away I had nothing in my hands. "My brothers ate them all," I lied. "My mother baked fresh Toll house cookies for our snack today, and added peanuts and raisins and everything, and my brothers just ate all three dozen because they thought I completely forgot about them." Somehow it felt safer to lie to Mrs.

Cavin than to explain to my mother why I needed the treats. Mrs. Cavin must have known I lied to her.

"Well, didn't your mother give you money to buy more cookies at the store?" Defeated, I played with the hem of my Brownie uniform. "Well, I'll buy them, for the love of God," Mrs. Cavin said. "Some people."

We walked into the bakery of the IGA, and I had to keep my head down, because the day before I had tried to buy a dozen donuts with a handful of acorns. After packing up a dozen donuts, the bakery ladies had not appreciated my unusual barter. Mrs. Cavin impatiently purchased three-dozen sugar cookies, and shoved the bags in my hands. "Here," she said. "Tell your mother she owes me three dollars."

When we returned to the meeting, the girls were hollering for their treats, and Barbie Briarton said in her loudest voice, "Did these cookies come out of the toilet like the marshmallows?" All of the girls except my one and only friend Susan McKenna started laughing, while I impassively handed out the cookies. I could hear Mrs. Cavin whispering to Mrs. Elmbrook in the far corner of the room. "Do you believe that? She didn't even give her money to buy more cookies after I took her home." I noticed that Mrs. Cavin's orange lipstick ran into the smoker's lines around her mouth. For the rest of the meeting, I walked around the room retrieving my kite string from the red and yellow linoleum.

I had not thought about Mrs. Cavin and the marshmallow fiasco in years. It was hard to believe that little girl ever existed. Holding Micah's string in my fingers, I had a faint realization of the ingenuity of the child who was I. A slight smile crossed my lips as a buried shame lessened a little.

The end of the day announcements of bus changes and practice cancellations caught me by surprise. The school day over, the students rolled up their projects, put calipers and rulers back in their respective boxes at the front of the room, and curled remnants of string into small balls and placed them in a plastic box resting on a small metal table behind Micah's desk.

Micah voiced last minute instructions before the final bell. "Make sure your name is on your paper before you put it up. Not there, Kelsey, on the desk. And hey, don't forget the dive meeting tomorrow morning. Tell your parents about it. Just a couple spots left." The computerized bell reverberated sharply, and students rushed towards the front and rear portable doors.

"See ya, Mr. M."

"Bye, Mr. Marlowe."

"What time tomorrow morning?"

"Thanks for bringing our papers, Ms. Scott."

"Chow, Mr. Teach … Ms. Teach."

I very easily could have left without causing any awkwardness. Instead, I stayed and waited for Mr. Marlowe to usher his students out the door. Left behind in his classroom for a few minutes gave me time to check out the rest of his classroom unobserved. The trig equations still cluttered the dry erase board, but now I noticed newspaper clippings of important events clipped to the board's sides. A quick glance indicated articles that were mainly related to sports and astronomy—the announcement of the last lunar eclipse and another indicating a meteorite shower. Tacked above the board were posters of dolphins and sea turtles. Literary quotes were strung among the dive posters, most of them recognizable ones from Southern authors. But one by Thomas Carlyle stood out. *If you go as far as you can see, then you can see further.* A curious quote. A deep one. I wondered why he chose it. Still curious, I made my way to the back of Marlowe's room and next to a timeline of historical events from the late 1700s to the present, a round plastic clock advertising Viagra graced the wall.

"I see you found my good-luck clock. I get one free with every case," Marlowe said and smiled.

"You certainly do have an interesting room," I said trying to deflect the statement.

"Did you see my Eleuthera posters? They should remind you of the story I told your class."

"They do. I suppose you have a Civil War map of Roswell because your great great grandfather fought in the Civil War, and, let me guess, the archeology posters and all the artifacts. Are you secretly Indiana Jones hiding out as a math teacher? I promise not to blow your cover."

Micah shook his head. "You're too sharp,Lois. I have been dee-scovered."

"Just call me Cat."

"Is that short for anything? You have nine lives?"

"Cat's short for Catherine and I think I have well exceeded nine lives, Mr. Marlowe ... Micah."

"Well, Cat," Micah pointedly said, "you're partially right about one thing, I had two great-great-grandfathers fight in the war of Northern aggression, one on each side. My mom's family has lived in Georgia for years, and her great-granddaddy fought for the South. My dad's family hailed from Kentucky, near the Ohio border, and his great granddaddy fought for those other guys, but I'm still proud of him. He fought for a belief too."

"From the sound of your accent, I would say you're more Rebel than Yankee."

"You are correct again, Lois. My mom and dad raised me as a true Southern boy. I don't have any great love for Yankees."

"So does that mean you weren't really serious about planning some classes together?"

"I have an incredibly high tolerance level. I can take one or two of you at a time with relative ease now that my therapy about that is complete," he said.

"Oh, thank you so much, Mr. Marlowe, for tolerating a Yankee heathen such as myself," I feigned with mock drama. "Would you like to hear my Blanche DuBois impression?" I said.

"I'd rather not. You Yankees butcher the Southern tongue, when you think you are sounding so Suuuh-then.""

"Well, sir, I always have depended on the kindness of strangers," I said in my interpretation of Blanche's mellow Mississippian voice.

"Well, Blanche, that will get you sent North on the next train. You need to hang out at some local joints and just listen. You can pick it up."

"I didn't think I was that bad."

"Well, actually, you are."

"So what's with all the bones and rocks?" I asked.

"It's a hobby of mine. See this?" Micah walked over to the table with the tanks and Riker mounts. "It's a mastodon tooth. This here is the bone of a sloth, millions of years old."

"Where'd you buy them?"

"I didn't. I found 'em. A buddy of mine and I go diving in rivers for them, usually in South Carolina, though we have found some really good fossils down in the Flint River, south Georgia."

"Did you find these there too?"

"We find these all over. You know what kind of teeth these are, don't ya?"

"Shark teeth?"

"Megalodon."

"Mega ... what?"

"Megalodon. These guys lived millions of years ago. Good thing cause some were big as a bus. They're extinct now."

"How fascinating. Can I hold one?"

"Sure."

I held the five-inch tooth in my hand, the gray tooth and curved black root almost completely covering my hand. "Are these easy to find?"

"Not one that big. It's pretty dark on the bottom of most rivers. If I don't find any teeth with my light down there, I'll have to push-feel through the mud with my hands. I've had more luck that way finding the big ones."

"Sounds pretty creepy to me."

"It can be if you let it."

"I could never do that," I said.

Micah laughed. "It does get scary sometimes, especially when I get my hose caught in an old tree trunk or encounter an alligator."

"Hose? Alligator?"

"Yeah, we don't use tanks. We run a compressor that feeds air down to us through hoses and sometimes we see alligators. They haven't bothered us too much yet."

"I can't believe anybody would dive in rivers for fun." I picked up a Riker mount of arrowheads. "Did you find these in the river as well?"

"Some of them, but most of them I found around here. I found this point walking the shores of Lake Allatoona, and these just 'bout a mile from right here."

"You just find them lying around?"

"You look for a construction site. With all the building going on in Atlanta, there have been plenty of places to look but it has to be elevated and near a creek, someplace where the Indians would have camped, where anyone would want to live, actually."

"I've never gone looking for arrowheads before. That's something I could do."

"Well, maybe I'll call you the next time I go. "

"Make sure you do. But tell me, what does all this have to do with math?"

Micah reached for a fan-like device of various colored and knotted cords attached to a base rope. "Do you know what this is?"

"I have no idea."

"It's a quipu, model of one. The Incas used this device as their bookkeeping system. They used the knots to store information."

"That's cool."

"Yeah, but know what? No one has broken the code of the knots. An entire system of math and logic is hidden in the strands waiting to be discovered."

The opening of the front portable door halted our conversation. A pretty female adolescent with long flaxen hair and short skirt entered the room. "Did you remember that I was coming for algebra help, Mr. M?"

Micah's face softened. "Of course, sweetie. I wouldn't forget. Sit over there. I'll be with you in a minute." Micah turned back to me. "I guess we'll have to catch up later. I can't turn down a student who wants algebra help. She's one of my squirrelly ninth graders."

"No problem. Well, this is all very interesting." I glanced at my watch. "It's a good thing your student showed up. If I didn't leave soon, I'd miss happy hour."

"Well, Ms. Scott, Cat, I wouldn't want to keep you from that."

"When do you want to get together and plan a math and literature lesson?"

"What time do you get here in the mornings?"

"I can get here early if you want. How about 7:30 tomorrow morning?"

"I can't do it tomorrow. I'm having a meeting for the kids who want to go on my yearly diving trip. This year we are going to Honduras. You should come to the meeting."

"No thanks. Diving is the last thing I ever want to do."

"I'm talking about pretty diving, not river diving."

"I hate the water," I said. "What about Wednesday morning, then?"

"Sure. Grab some coffee and meet me here. How could anyone hate the water? It's beautiful."

"That's your opinion. Okay, see you Wednesday then."

I had gone just a few feet outside the portable when I heard Micah call after me.

"Cat!" I stopped and turned back towards his portable. "Do you still want me to call you if I go looking for points?"

"I'll be mad if you don't."

"Don't you mean angry? I thought you taught English."

Chapter 9

For years, physicists and cosmologists have sought one formula that explains the universe for any given situation at any given time. Maybe the study of human behavior would provide the missing link to prove the Unified Field Theory. After all, in any given situation, certain emotional factors present, a human being will behave in a predictable manner. Take a woman who through unexpected circumstances has begun to awaken to the forceful voices of life and death, surround her with slumbering phantoms of fear disguised as friends, and the answer to the equation will always come out the same.

I have to believe that anyone who had just witnessed the painful death of a close friend, and the courage and devotion of his loving wife, and who later found solace from an impassioned math teacher in a badly designed trailer, would have acted as I did that Monday afternoon. I longed to reveal myself to my circle of neighborhood friends. I needed to tell them how I felt about Craig's death, and how he touched a part of me, the holy, uncorrupted part of me I had not acknowledged in a long time. I wanted to tell them about Micah and his classroom and his creativity and the higher purpose teachers are called to. I wanted to tell them how it is possible to dive in rivers and find prehistoric bones and teeth, and how right down the street from us are tools of ancient civilizations. And, I wanted to tell them about Nellie and David, and my dreams, and my shame, and the small glimpses of hope I experienced over the last few days. But they weren't ready to listen, because they couldn't really see me.

And how can I blame them? In the recent past I needed my friends to admire my hair, my clothes, my figure, and aspire to look like me. I pretended to be cool, "with it," so I could be invited to the wildest neighborhood parties, my phone ringing constantly as testimony to my growing popularity. For years I hid behind my own intelligible lies that expensive things made me happy, that I had an uneventful childhood, that I married my college sweetheart and that I was content with the *status quo*. Even that I voted Republican. But a death and a fifty-minute class period changed the degree, altered the angle, however small, of my illusions.

Unfortunately, my circle of friends did not want to know anything more than idle, and sometimes vicious, gossip. Trophy wives soon to be turned into sad cartoons, their futures hung precariously before them. Their cute little whines would become incessant nagging, their nails obnoxiously red and long, hair one shade too orange, cheeks puffed with collagen. Already, many of them had given their essence to wine, tennis and private investigators. I got lucky. My soul was on the edge of being uncovered. They fought as hard as they could to hold me back, but it was too late. I too clearly saw them for what they were, and in them too clearly saw what I had become. And in the end they had to let me go, for misery loves company, not lecturers.

Initially, I needed to walk into Debra's house as if I were the star of the party. If I acted too much out of the ordinary, I knew I would lose my audience. So, after school, I threw my teacher's skirt and blouse on the floor and soaked in a whirlpool full of scented bubbles. After the half-hour soak, I took great pains to look beautiful in my short green worsted jacket, black velvet jeans, several thousand dollars worth of jewelry and shiny fake brown contact lenses. I gelled my highlighted blonde hair until it was just one notch short of big. I was ready to take on the world … at least the world of my gated community.

It was not unusual for me to stir up trouble. Ever since the blowjob challenge, a certain amount of outrageous behavior was expected of me—which was no problem. I could male-bash with ease and share sexual techniques without batting an eye. All my safe friends thought I was hilarious and encouraged me to drink more and more wine. The problem was that the more I drank, the more I had a tendency to drop my façade. Usually, I stopped drinking before all my inhibitions wore down, or else I passed out. This time I did neither.

By the time I arrived at Debra's, four cars already lined the driveway. Wine in hand, Debra answered the front door. I casually peeked around her as I followed her into the kitchen. Last time I had come by for a quick visit, Daisy had sprung a surprise attack on me. That infamous day, while Debra rummaged through the house for our new tennis schedules, I felt something brush against my leg. I looked down and almost jumped out of my shoes when the 'something' turned out to be a snout full of bared teeth attached to a stout stubby body. I tried to sweet-talk that smoking hunk of pork tenderloin, but that riled her up even more, so with a burst of action, I sprinted for the door. Daisy, snorting and clacking on the floor, was right behind. She seemed to enjoy the chase before the kill. I rounded the corner and headed into the hallway. I escaped, but my shoe didn't. Daisy somehow managed to grab the end of my heel in her teeth and rip it from my foot. As I stood and watched, the deranged pig killed my shoe with gnashing teeth and low grunts. My blue pump never had a chance, and it was over in seconds. Her look of satisfaction was almost a smile but actually more a smirk as I think back. I vowed that one day the antelope would attack the cheetah. One day.

"Well, hey there, Miss Catherine. We were wondering what was taking you so long. We've been here since three," Debra now said.

"You guys have a two-hour head start on me. Where's the wine?"

"Hey Cat. I heard about Craig. What is Summer going to do? Marilynn told me his business hasn't been doing too well."

I took a long drink of white wine. Debra's comment made me angry. "Well, I guess not. He's been dying for a year. What did you expect? He all but lost his practice."

"She's worried about Summer. How's she going to keep the house. Did Craig have insurance?" Bonnie defended.

"I don't know. Maybe she'll get lucky and have to move out of this neighborhood," I said.

They were all too drunk to be offended by my words. I could say almost anything and they would just laugh. For a few odd moments, I had the feeling that I was really talking to more wine bottles not people.

"I like your boots, Cat," said Rita. "Did you get those here?"

"Marshall got them for me on one of his trips. Maybe in New York. They are real alligator—dyed of course."

"I hope they died."

"Lucky alligator—immortalized as beautiful boots," said Lisa.

"I wonder what we are going to be immortalized as?" I said. "What could our skin be made into?"

"Cat could be made into prophylactics."

"Gee, thanks."

"No, Cat would be better as a jock strap."

"Only if it were made out of silk."

"We're going to end up as dust, no matter what," said Bonnie.

"Didn't the Nazi's make lampshades out of the Jews' skin?" said Monica.

"How horrible."

"It's true. Can you imagine Shari's skin as a lampshade?" Rita joked.

I poured myself another glass of wine. "That's not even funny. In fact, it's downright scary," I said.

"Come on, Cat. I was just having some fun. I like Shari. I don't care if she's a Jew."

"Fun? Do you realize what you just said?" Were we always like this and I had been too drunk to notice? I would have thrown my glass at Rita, if Janie and Marilynn had not come in the door just then.

"Hey Janie, glad you could make it, girl," Monica practically screamed.

"Marilynn, have you lost weight?" asked Rita.

What a bitch, I thought. Rita knew damn well Marilynn hadn't lost any weight. Both Rita and Debra played the game of putting people immediately on the defensive. They were experts at sweetly attacking an individual's insecurities, especially if that individual were female. I quickly downed my second glass of wine, and immediately poured another. Sipping from my lipstick stained glass, I too loudly pronounced, "I *hate* the suburbs."

"How can you hate the suburbs?" chirped Lisa. "Laurel Hills is the best place Robb and I have ever lived. Where else would we find all this?"

"All what?" I said.

"These happy hours, pool, club, all our friends. The children always have someone to play with, and we have our tennis league. And our husbands get along so well," she added.

"Everything is so casual here. If we feel like cooking out, we just call someone up, and the next thing you know there's a party. We even celebrate each other's birthdays," said Monica.

"Big damn deal," I said. "Jesus, you act like this is all there is to life. All any of you ever think about is tennis, cooking out, birthdays. That was a great birthday party of Robb's, wasn't it? It was really fun getting thrown out of Rio Bravo's because we were all so damn drunk. And Debra, it was so fulfilling watching you and Neil scream at each other in the parking lot. It sure made me feel lucky."

"That was only one night. And what about you? Offering blowjobs to the men. How are you any different from the rest of us?" Debra defended.

"That's the point. I'm not and I want to be."

"What's so wrong with us? Here, have some more wine. This is getting good," said Rita.

"This is what is wrong with us." I held up my glass. "We substitute a wine high for joy, passion, ecstasy. I don't want to spend my life getting drunk every afternoon in someone's kitchen. We drink so that we don't have to see the truth about our shitty lives."

"We don't do that. Sometimes we get drunk around the pool," said Monica. Everyone thought that was funny but me.

"What about thought-provoking nights under the stars? Listening to some good music every once in awhile? Have any of us ever discussed a good book or play?"

"We've done that."

"No we haven't. We run out to the pool, the tennis court, each other's houses. And the only things we talk to each other about are who has the best cleaning lady, where the best place is to get our nails done, who has the best dirt on our so-called friends. I'm sick of stumbling around like a blind idiot."

"Cat is deep."

"Even assholes can be deep, if they wish," I said.

Overdosing on eyebrow pencil, Rita, a St. Mary of the Woods' graduate, proudly exclaimed. "I'm not deep at all, and I never will be. I like being shallow. It saves my skin." The drunken paper dolls exploded in laughter. It was too much.

"Why in the hell did I think any of you would listen to me? At least I realize my life is boring … at least I get out during the day. "

"You're so much better than us, Cat," Debra smirked.

"Why don't we change the conversation," said Barbara. Wide-eyed Janie agreed with her.

"No, I'm not changing the conversation. I can't believe that not one of you in this room is bothered by your life. Didn't any of you ever want to go fishing with Hemingway and chat on the boat? Or to ask Walt Whitman what it was like to be gay in the 1850's, or wonder what it was like making love to Picasso? Don't you want to rebel and yell and laugh at the plastic lives we live? Don't you ever have an inner longing to create something?" Then I said it. The word that finally got a reaction out of them. "Aren't you ever *bored*? Aren't you ever *bored* with your husbands?"

"No, my husband's not boring," said Janie. "I love my husband."

"Well, my husband's boring," I announced with finality.

"You're the one who's boring," said Bonnie. "I can't believe you would say that about Marshall. He's so devoted to you."

I violated a rule as old as Eve herself. I would have been better off describing the color and flow of my menstrual cycle. It seemed to them I had it made. My husband did not fool around, handed me all the money and freedom I wanted, and was reasonably in love with me. As a well-treated wife I should make myself beautiful, offer unlimited sex, and speak of him in public as if were a god. Whoops. I really screwed up. It must have been that third glass of wine. I decided I had better have a fourth.

"Maybe I *am* boring," I finally said. "But I know I am not as boring as all of you."

"Like all your talk about education isn't boring. And your damn lecturing. You have a lot of nerve saying Marshall is a bore. At least he's fun."

"You're right," I said. "He is rather fun, isn't he? Maybe I meant to say that *your* husbands are boring."

"Even Neil?" said Debra. She was so drunk she could hardly stand up. She had propped herself up against the refrigerator.

"Neil is the most boring," I said. "In fact, there are so many boring people around here, I'm leaving. I am sick of spending my time hanging around with slugs. Actually, I could have a better conversation with slugs than any of you."

I could hear them talking about me as I stomped out of the kitchen. "What a bitch. Don't ask her to the happy hours any more."

"She's just drunk. She'll be laughing about it tomorrow."

"Poor Marshall."

"Cat never could handle her wine."

I could hear them still talking about me as I walked toward the front door. Then the scraping of wood and a dark peripheral movement caused me to look to my right. A small twist of black hairy tail and the ham hocks it was attached to protruded from inside the opposite end of the kitchen from where the cackling hens sat.

Daisy's attention was on the group as she watched for a dropped morsel or perhaps another innocent unwary shoe. She did not see or sense me. A magazine from the coffee table was in my hand before I could think and with the grace of my antelope counterpart, I crossed the room in two long strides. A Stephie Graf backhand for a winner set about a series of actions that bring tears to my eyes even today. A squeal like a fire alarm burst forth as hooves ran in place on the slick floor. Gaining her footing, the black barrel shot off across the kitchen towards the now also-screaming drunken women. A flurry of flailing legs, chairs falling and still-squealing pig made me hustle to the door before I could be discovered. The last thing I heard above the chaos was "Oh, my God! It's Daisy, and she's shitting all over the place! It's everywhere! Auuugh!" I closed the door and smiled all the way home. I never mentioned to anyone my role in the disaster and the incident never came up in conversation. But I know they suspected me.

The rest of the night, however, was all a blur. Marshall came home around seven; it was one of the rare weeks he did not have to travel. I had passed out on the couch, and when he woke me, I felt a terrible sense of emptiness and loneliness. An overwhelming pang of guilt gripped me. I had hurt Marshall so much ... so much. He deserved better than me. I had vowed never to act out again, but could not seem to stop. "Marshall," I said. "Will you hold me?" When he did, I told him I was a terrible person, and that if he wanted to leave me, I would not fight him. I would not even take any money from him.

"It's just the wine talking," he said. "You are not a terrible person, and I do not want to leave you. Come on, get up. Go to bed. You'll feel better about things in the morning."

"Marshall, I'll find someone for you. Do you want a blonde or a redhead?"

"Both. Now go to bed."

"But Marshall ... "

"Put your arms around my neck." He lifted me off the couch and carried me into our bedroom. He gently laid me on the bed, and tucked the covers around me.

"Marshall."

"Yes?"

"I wish I could run away."

"Did you go to the doctor yet?"

"For what?"

"For hormones. They'll make you feel better."

"There's chicken salad in the refrigerator if you're hungry."

"I'll find something," he said as he walked out of the bedroom and closed the door.

I think that's what we said to each other.

#

In the hours just before dawn, I awoke with a dry mouth and wine headache. I arose out of bed and clumsily walked to the bathroom to find some aspirin. My eyes felt dry but at least my stomach did not feel nauseous. Good sign. I would only have to contend with a mild hangover in the classroom instead of a raging one. I settled back under the covers and eventually the aspirin eased my head, yet I could not fall back to sleep. Fragmented images of previous times reeled through my mind like fast improvisations: Marshall's strained face ... Sister Rose's accusing eyes ... my mother's curled hair ... Micah's sturdy hands ... then as if out of nowhere, Nellie and David.

David was crying behind the red tobacco barn, his blonde hair covered in sweat, his knickers pulled up awkwardly, shirt half-tucked. She did not know what to do this time. There was no line to untangle, no fishhook to pull out. In between gulps of heavy tears, he hit his right fist against the barn wall, causing his knuckles to bleed.

"You'll have to call the doctor if you keep punching the barn, silly," she said.

"I told ya not to come back! Yankee trash!" His head bent over, he began picking red splinters from the palms of his hands. She noticed the bruised impression in the middle of his forehead.

"Get a whippin?"

"What you care?"

"You had your pants pulled down, didn't ya? Who did it, your daddy?"

He nodded his head up and down.

"What with?"

"What he always uses, stupid. His belt."

"You must have been bad."

"I cain't seem to do nothing right. I don't member most of what he tells me to do. It just won't stay in my head, no matter how much he beats me."

"Are you stupid?"

"I guess so." He wiped the tears from his cheek on the untucked end of his shirt.

"I know a test that will tell whether you are. Want to take it?"

"Why? Just so I'll know for sure that I can't do nothing?"

"Well, if you know for sure, then you can tell your daddy that you can't help it, you've been tested and you are just stupid. Maybe he won't beat you then."

"He's gonna smack me for talking back. You and your damn Yankee test gonna get me in more trouble."

"Name the keys on a piano," she challenged.

"Ain't got no piana, that ain't fair."

"Okay, then sing the notes of a scale."

"Never learnt that neither."

"Gee, well what is nine times seven? You know that?"

"Easy, sixty-three."

"How about eleven times twelve?"

"132."

"Wait a minute ... Yeah, that's right."

"45 times 36?"

He replied 1620 within two seconds.

She found a stick to work out the answer in the dirt. He was right.

"How did you do that so quick? You're cheating."

"Am not, I don't know how, I can just see the answer in my head."

"You know how to multiply by stacking up the numbers?"

"I've seen it but I don't need to do all that. Now who's stupid?"

"You're like the Mozart of math."

"Who? Is that good?"

"He was a child genius who could play the violin when he was three years old. He wrote an opera when he was six."

"Wrote a what?"

"An opera, a story with music. My music teacher Hermann teaches me about them. He's related to the phantom of the opera."

"Who's that?"

"A monster that was burned as a child, and now he hangs around the Paris opera house strangling opera singers who forget the words to his songs. Hermann shakes me when I forget words. He threatens to tell my mother."

"Does your momma beat you too?"

"She takes me in the coat closet so the servants can't hear, and then beats me with a wooden hanger. I still have some scars. Look." She lifted her skirt and pulled down the top of her stockings. Her legs wore the stain of healing blue marks.

"She beat you for not memberin' words?" His gaze revealed an understanding.

"And for the things I told her about Hermann. Try this one. 76 times 134."

He thought for a moment. "Ten thousand, hunnert eighty fo." He was proud of his answer. The dirt revealed his accuracy.

"David, you are not stupid. You are just the opposite. Let's go tell your daddy." She got up to leave.

"No, he won't believe no girl."

"You better start going to school more. You could be smart if you wanted."

"I do want to, but my teachers think I'm dumb. Besides I cain't read much."

"Well, you sure did learn your math. What did they think of how you do your math so fast?"

"They told my daddy I cheated, so he beat me for that. I just miss 'em now so I won't get beat no more."

"If you do all that ciphering in your head, you can learn to read and show them all."

"No one ever taught me much more'n a few words."

"I can teach you, but you have to pay me."

"I ain't got no money or nothing else nobody wants."

"Then you can pay me with a kiss after each lesson. I'll bring my school books and papers tomorrow, okay?"

"Ah have chores to do first, but then, yeah, I'd like to learn to not be stupid."

"You gotta remember your chores. I can teach you how to not forget. Hermann makes me memorize words I don't even know the meaning of. I use mind pictures to help me." She twisted the end of her long braid around her hand.

"Why you got to take them music lessons anyway?"

"Because I have what you call a gift. Hermann says when I sing the angels listen. He is training me to be a famous opera star. I hate him."

"Why don't you go to a different teacher?"

"Momma says he's the best. I don't care if I am a star or not. I like what we sing in school much better than all those arias and operettas he makes me sing. My mother wants me to be a famous star one day so she can bring all her friends to watch, says I will be a great beauty like her mother was."

"You ain't no great beauty yet … more like an upside- down carrot."

"If you knew what Hermann does to me in secret, you wouldn't be so mean."

"Like what?"

"It's too awful to tell."

"Does he whale on ya all the time?"

"He does way worse than that. He locks me in the closet and hangs me by my braids for hours at a time if I forget songs. One time he left me in there all night long."

"Aw, he don't neither. I tried to hang by my feet in the barn and almost broke my neck. Made me all dizzy."

"He does, too. He does."

"That sure makes my beatin' seem like nothing." He laughed, not knowing whether to believe her or not. "I'd rather my pa beat me than do that."

She continued indignantly. "I sure don't know what you were crying about, after what I had done to me." She paused. "Can I take a look and see how red you are?"

"I dunno … with you being a girl and all."

"Showed you mine."

He thought about it. "Well, alright, I guess you can have a quick look." He turned and carefully eased down his pants, grimacing as his cotton knickers brushed his raw flesh.

"Lord, that must have hurt. You have welts raised up high as heaven."

"Okay, enough lookin'." Buttoning his knickers, he proclaimed, "I didn't cry till he was gone."

This time when she leaned over to kiss his cheek, he caught her before she could run away.

"You gonna come poking round here tomorra?" Before she had a chance to answer, he kissed her softly on the lips, the warmth of her breath filling him with unexpected pleasure. Bound by childhood pain, he a bastion of Southern masculinity, she a buttress of Yankee femininity, they stared at each other for what was probably a minute, but felt like hours.

"Something I was wonderin'. Was this phantom always a monster?"

"No, he was once a good person. I guess he still is; he just doesn't know it."

He held her tightly before she broke away and ran far into the tobacco fields.

#

By the time the last bell rang on Tuesday, my head was pounding. I wanted nothing more than to pack up my briefcase and satchel of vocabulary quizzes and essays and rush home to a cozy couch and warm green tea. The day was cloudier and colder than usual for November. Earlier in the day, the wind had cut sharply through my lightweight trench coat as I ran to the main building to grab a salad from the cafeteria. After the noon lunch break, the wind's strength picked up and whipped against the sides of the portable, the aluminum walls noisily clanging like a prisoner's dropped chains. There was no point in leaving immediately after school. I would have had to fight student traffic and bus fumes, making my headache and tired body that much worse. So, I decided instead to jot a few notes about Gatsby, Fitzgerald's shadowy illusion, as the Platonic conception. My cupped hands formed my own cave around my head, blocking out the room's harsh fluorescent lights. I was so intent on sketching out my notes I did not hear the footsteps on the trailer's steps. The rusty door hinges scratched together, escalating the tension inside my head, causing me to look up just as Micah Marlowe entered my room.

"You must have had a hard day," he said. "Are you trying to pull your hair out?"

"I didn't get much sleep last night," I curtly replied.

Micah merely chuckled. "That must have been some happy hour. Did you hang your head out the window on the way to school this morning? Your hair is interesting, to say the least."

I smoothed my hair with my hands. I did not think it looked that bad. Micah's observation about my hair annoyed me. Granted I did not bother to blow my tresses dry that morning, and my coarse hair jutted out into an unwieldy mess of natural curl. But given the rest of me, most men wouldn't have noticed my hair. I guess that's what drew me to Micah in the end. He knew how to see people in three dimensions, myself included.

I didn't have the patience for Micah's observations that day, however. I wanted to get rid of him as soon as possible so I could go home and lick my wounds.

"The wind certainly has not helped my hair any, or my teaching. The kids thought we were going to be swept away, a la Wizard of Oz," I told him.

"At least the rain finally stopped. Some of my students this morning were soaked. I've been trying to get the administration to consider putting up covered walkways from the main building to the portables for years. At least we can stay inside until the rain stops. The students have no choice. They have to get to their classes on time."

"Yeah, well, maybe they need to carry bigger umbrellas." I really did not care about covered or uncovered portables just then. I threw my pen down on my desk, sighed in exasperation, and opened and closed my top desk drawer.

Micah picked up my copy of *The Great Gatsby*. "My students said you were teaching this. They said you mentioned Plato's cave."

"Yes, I did." My voice remained short. I really wished he would leave.

"I do a project in trig dealing with Plato's Cave."

"Micah," I interrupted. "My brain really can't handle any more school crap today. I have a splitting headache."

Micah's jaw tightened, and I knew I hurt his feelings. I really didn't care. I just wanted to go home.

"Maybe we can talk about it tomorrow morning," he said.

"Yeah, maybe."

"But that's not the reason I stopped by. Me and Bobby are going looking for points as soon as the traffic clears. You said you wanted to know the next time we went. I thought you might want to go with us."

"In heels?" My irritability worsened. "If you really wanted me to go, you would've given me at least a day to plan."

"We didn't know we were going until it rained this morning. The best time to go is after a hard rain. I always keep my gear in my truck. I have an extra pair of boots and old clothes if you want to go. You could change here."

"Not this time," I said. "I need to get home. And Micah, I can't make our meeting tomorrow morning. I have too much to do. Maybe another day." Please, Micah, I thought, leave me alone. I just want to go into a shell and hide. Yes, I found you interesting two days ago, but I have too many complex issues to sort out right now to go running around in the mud looking for god knows what. I don't have time for big Boy Scouts.

Micah waited while I packed up my books and papers and turned off the lights. "We'll see, Ms. Scott." I thought I heard a catch in his throat.

We walked out the door together, and after a hasty goodbye, I hurried towards my Lexus. Driving away, I noticed Micah making his way across the parking lot, hands in pockets, looking back over his shoulder. It did not make sense, especially in light of my attitude that afternoon, but I yearned to go after him. I didn't. That was the last and only time I didn't.

Chapter 10

Dew had collected on the windows overnight, and the early morning sun danced pearls and crystals through the leaded glass. The symmetrical patterns waved in horizontal and vertical lines along the walls, a design of nature's making. My head clear, my eyes rested, I lazily watched the play of light around the room before I crawled from beneath the feathery covers. Marshall, already out of the shower, leaned over the dresser searching for his favorite tan socks. It seemed odd having Marshall home on a school morning. I stretched my arms overhead and peeled my nightgown off at the same time. The dancing light made me feel happy, and also, I had to admit, very sexual. Marshall would not take the time to make love, but at least I could get him to think about sex. Naked, I climbed out of bed, and threw my arms around the back of Marshall's waist.

"You want to feel my tits before you go?" I purred.

"Not now."

I slid my hands under him and grabbed his crotch.

"Stop it. What're you doing? You're going to be late ... Ahhh ... don't do that."

"Marshall," I said. "Look at me. Not in the mirror, but here, in the flesh."

Marshall glanced at me and then resumed pulling on his socks.

"Slowly look at me, Marsh." He allowed his eyes to linger over my body. "Come back to bed with me."

"I can't ... Catherine ... you know you have a beautiful body."

"You're breathing hard, Marsh. I need to be touched. Get under the covers with me."

And he did. And we briefly made love, and I smiled when he groaned, and then I breathed in the scent of my own body's arousal, and gently caressed myself until I brought about my own satisfied groans. Marshall had hurried out before I finished. Always the white rabbit, always frantic about being late.

By the time I headed out the door, the sun brightly shone in the foyer, the puffer fish quiet, soothed by the added warmth of the strong rays. It was a glorious November morning, the air crisp, the leaves splendid in their last hurrah of golden color, the purple, yellow, red pansies flourishing in the mild climate of an Atlanta autumn.

Even though I lingered in bed that morning, I arrived at school earlier than usual. For once, I would have a chance to refill my coffee mug for a second cup of caffeine. Micah had beaten me to the large silver coffee maker and came within inches of spilling his Styrofoam cup as he came hurriedly through the doorway of the cafeteria's kitchen and found me coming in.

"How about you wear a bell or something?" he blurted out. "Sorry, just in a hurry. Last year someone knocked my coffee all over me, and I had to look like an idiot all day. Kids thought it was funny and they almost had another reason to chuckle."

"Maybe *you* should be using a bell, especially if you're going to run around the school with hot coffee in your hand." I stood my ground even though I felt guilty about the way I treated him the day before.

He stepped back and with a slight bow replied, "Yes, my master." He so disarmed me with this slip into feigned submissiveness I forgot all about filling my coffee mug.

"You mentioned a lab or something you do with your students about Plato in math class. It sounded really interesting."

The white flag waved, Micah accepted my surrender. "Yes, I do this lab or something about Plato. I started to tell you about it yesterday but someone had an attitude problem. Then Perry Mason turns and says, 'And that someone is *you*.'"

"Funny, very funny, Marlowe. So, how do you do Plato in math? Archimedes maybe, but Plato?"

"Well, last year I was gathering info and applications for Trig class when I came across how trig is used for projection mapping onto curved surfaces. In other words, how can you take a two-dimensional image and place it onto a representation of a 3D object like a doorknob so that the reflections, however deformed, are correct. Have you seen any computer-generated movies or pictures?"

"Yes," I was trying to think of one.

"You know, like *Toy Story*?"

"Okay, got it. And so what's this have to do with a philosopher from centuries ago?" I couldn't yet imagine a connection.

"I remembered from college reading an ancient classic with some story about shadows on the wall created by a fire, something like that. But I did have a pretty good idea of the intent of the tale, which was that the shadows, being two dimensional, represented the real world of 3D. We all see the shadows of others and think we are seeing the real thing. A great topic for many people around here to consider." I could feel a lecture lurking just beneath the surface.

"Am I one of those people?"

Ignoring me, he continued. "Anyway, I knew Charles, our resident Latin teacher and expert on ancient philosophy, would know the story. He told me to find Plato's *Republic*, and sure enough, it was in there. When I read it, I knew there was a great topic for free knowledge day."

"Free knowledge day?"

"Yeah, if I get caught up with what we need to cover, I'll take a day to discuss how the math in the textbook relates to the world around us. The days range from black holes to forensic studies of blood splatter analysis to fractals. A lot of my formers tell me that they remember these days more than anything else ... and they're pretty fun for me. It forces me to learn about things so I can explain them."

"That's wonderful but how do you find the time?" I knew I didn't even have time to grade the paper pile living at my house.

"I don't go to happy hours for one thing. But, I don't consider these assignments extra work. Makes me see the world in a different way and understand it a little better each time. It's also good to let my students see that just about any topic they can think of has a connection to all disciplines."

"Go back to the *Republic*." I should have been heading to my portable, or making a precautionary trip to the bathroom, but the sound of his voice warmed me and I wanted to prolong our conversation as long as possible. The curious snail couldn't help but come out of her shell, much different from yesterday.

"I read from the *Republic* and then have a good chat with the kids about how many of them present only a shadow of themselves to friends and family and how they must seek to see through the shadows of others and get as close to reality as possible. We spend so much time on presenting a good image that we often perceive a person's value based upon outward appearances when their heart is the real person, not the clothes or the car."

"Amen to that," I got in before he continued.

"I ask them if they think truth is even attainable or if what we achieve is merely a pretender of truth. We finish up with wondering if all that we see as reality is perhaps not just a lesser dimension of actuality. It makes for some interesting comments and kids that never speak up much often have something to say. In this suburban atmosphere, I think these topics need to be discussed and it's a subtle way to bring it up. Too many of them don't realize how shallow they can seem because all their friends are also. When in Rome."

"I'd like to hear their response to all that."

The ten-minute bell rang and I still had not gotten any coffee. If I didn't leave soon, I would be late for my first period class. Micah followed me to the coffee dispenser and continued talking.

"I show them how trig is used in plotting coordinates of points that represent images which are two-dimensional, like a picture of a room. When the shiny doorknob is seen up close, it must have the room's likeness on it but in a distorted way. The transition is from a flat surface, the picture, to a curved surface, the doorknob. The math involved in doing this is trig-based and is 2D to 3D. That's the connection. Plato's poor souls are changing 3D into 2D and trying to make sense of it all while mathematicians do the opposite and trick us into seeing what they want us to. It's a fun day that they think is cool. So, at the end, I take everyday items and place them behind a little cardboard screen I devised and onto the overhead. They can't see what they are, only the shadows as projected on the screen. Then they have to guess what the twenty or so things are. Some are easy, but a few are really tough. Makes them think."

Now I knew how Plato and doorknobs came together in Micah Marlowe's classroom. I never would have thought of this but not too many people would have. What else lies hidden in his shadows? That question would wait because the tardy bell indicated that it was time to go.

"Thanks for the lesson, but I really need to go."

We turned away from each other but not before I could catch a twinkle of respect in his eye. He must have appreciated my inquisitiveness about his shadows on the wall. Maybe I reminded him of his own attitude about learning and seeing the world in a different way. At least I hoped so.

That evening Micah called me way too late. I had half-dozed on the couch grading papers, waiting for Marshall to come home from a client dinner, when the phone rang. It was after 11 o'clock; I thought for sure it must be Marshall calling to say the dinner was going longer than expected and he would spend the night in town. Instead, Micah's deep voice was on the other line.

"Hey, you in bed yet?"

"Just about."

"Bobby just called about a great place to go poking around in the mud. It's just behind the new Target on Old Alabama. The rain's supposed to keep up all night and tomorra some. By the time school's out it'll be stopped—perfect for finding stuff. I thought I'd give you a day's notice this time. Why don't you come with us?"

"Well ..." I hesitated. "I might have students staying after school for help."

Micah was not to be put off so easily this time. "That's okay. Just bring old clothes to school and change there. I'll swing by your portable around four. That'll give you plenty of time to help your students. Just listen for my speaker on the truck."

"What about my car?"

"It'll be fine in the parking lot for a couple hours. There's always someone there at least until nine. See ya."

"Wait. What kind of truck do you have?" It was too late; he had hung up without saying goodbye. I tried to call him back, but information said he had an unlisted number.

Marshall came home a half-hour later to piles of clothes strewn all over the bedroom. "How am I supposed to sleep with clothes all over the bed?" he asked.

"I'm trying to find something to wear. Just throw them on the floor; I'll put them away tomorrow."

"She acts like she has nothing to wear," he said to no one. "I've never seen a closet with so many clothes." Marshall stripped down to his underwear and climbed under the covers not bothering to remove the stacks of pants and shirts.

Ignoring him, I continued to root through my closet for something along the lines of Indiana Jones and Diane Fosse. I finally decided on an old pair of khaki green jeans, a red flannel shirt I bought in Jackson Hole, and a fishing vest. At the last minute I threw in a faded green baseball hat with Old Navy printed on the crown.

Marshall was sound asleep by the time I assembled my outfit, so I slipped under the covers like the stealthy Titania next to her Oberon.

I half-prayed to my parents, asking them if Micah truly was of their fateful doing. Micah was a kind and gentle man, but surely he was no saint. Saints do not have early wrinkles and saints do not hold such troubled stares in their eyes. My father would never send me a saint. He knows saints hold my interest about as long as telemarketers, insurance salesmen and gastroenterologists. When I was in elementary school, the only saint that kept my interest was St. Therese. At least she had some spunk. I could see her driving the nuns crazy with all her talk about wanting to choose everything. All the others spent hours on their knees, beseeching crucifixes. It is little wonder that St. Lucy tore her eyeballs out. Sister Mary Timothea said it was because she had such faith in God, she wanted to show Him she trusted He would replace her eyes. I knew otherwise; if I had nothing better to do than stare at crucifixes, I would tear my eyeballs out too, and then for a cover, say it was because I was trying to show my faith in God. St. Lucy, forever immortalized by Francesco del Coss, eyes sprouting from her hands like flowers. I received a prayer card with a picture of St. Lucy on it from one of the nuns at Our Lady of the Assumption (Or, as my Dad liked to call my elementary school, Our Lady of the Consumption). In that picture, St. Lucy held out a golden platter with her oedipal eyeballs on it, gazing up to heaven with her new faith-inspired irises, looking cock-eyed nonetheless. That card gave me nightmares for weeks ; my mother had to finally throw it away.

Unlike St. Lucy, Micah kept his eyeballs in his head. In fact, he seemed to have eyeballs in the back of his head, his vision was so keen. So, my father sent me a man who had one of those second sights, especially where nature was concerned. Micah was a man who could identify all the constellations and planets, see shooting stars quicker than anyone else, and spot tiny land crabs or minuscule fire worms that remained hidden to the rest of us. He knew where to find the best crystals in both Arkansas and Brazil, where to hunt for fossilized nautilus shells and bones of wooly mammoths, where to dig for ginger beer bottles and Civil War buttons, and where to dive for sharks' teeth millions of years old. He could detect a "Jesus lizard" in an avocado tree out of the corner of his eye, or tell you the exact location of a pilliated woodpecker driving down Georgia 400 in his gray pick-up truck at 70 miles per hour. I felt blind as a heathen next to him.

But that knowledge of Micah came later … after Thanksgiving … after Christmas … after winter break … after a long night under the sky on the Tennessee River. Ignorant of what lay ahead of me, I nestled comfortably and safely in the confines of my silk sheets and expensive down-filled blankets.

Chapter 11

In the steely light of the next day, the notion of traipsing around in the mud searching for arrow points and pottery pieces did not seem as appealing. Also, the site Micah wanted to take me to was about a mile from my house, and who knew which of my neighbors would spot me staring at bare ground with two sons of the Confederacy. I had not as yet met Micah's friend Bobby, but Micah told me that morning Bobby was borne and bred in Georgia and had an extensive collection of Civil War guns and swords.

As the school day wore on, I wavered between anticipation and dread. Finally, just before the start of my AP class I decided to cancel. Like the kids, I was really quite skilled at faking illness. In fact that day in class I faked an orgasm. As one of my students read his paper on *The English Patient*, the beauty of his words spellbound the class, as well as me. Initially, I sighed at his interpretation of the author's hand imagery, and because the students chuckled at my reaction, I screamed out in pretend ecstasy when he finished. "Ms. Scott, would you like a cigarette?" one of my students asked.

"Haven't you all ever seen *When Harry Met Sally*?" I questioned. "Meg Ryan does the best interpretation of an orgasm that I've ever seen."

"I don't know Ms. Scott. You did a pretty good job just now."

"I wonder if I could get fired over this?" I asked rhetorically.

The class just laughed. "If you haven't been fired yet," they said, "you never will be." And this class knew me best, since I had them the year before for junior honors, and they had sat through my behavior for two years. Then, I read the "Hollow Men" to them, and by the time I was through reading the poem, I decided to keep my appointment with Micah. Like T.S. Eliot, I wanted to go out with a bang not a whimper. Maybe Micah would show me how to move from the "conception" to the "creation," from the "emotion" to the "response." I had spent too long in my dead cactus land already.

After school, only two of the five students who had asked for extra help showed up. By the time I reworked their thesis sentences for them, the student parking lot had been cleared out and Micah was calling my name over the speaker contraption he had hooked up to his CB radio. "Ms. Scott ... it's time to go," he crooned, the sound of his voice magnified by the PA system.

"What is that?" my students asked.

"I'm not really sure," I said. "But we have to cut this help session short. If you want to come by tomorrow morning ... "

"Ms. Scott ... hellooooo," Micah repeated over the truck speaker.

"We're okay. You helped a lot. See ya tomorrow, Ms. S."

Infuriated, I walked out on the porch of my portable. "You're early!" I yelled. "Give me a few minutes to get dressed."

"Hurry up. It gets dark at six," his loud voice said. I didn't have time to put my outfit together with as much thought as I wanted, but I was too mad to care. I wish he'd shut that damn speaker off, I thought. As I thudded down the portable stairs in my hiking boots, Micah got on the speaker again. "You are too dressed up for walking in the mud, Ms. Scott. All your pretty little clothes are gonna be muddy. I mean *muddy*. We aren't going to some fashion show."

"Will you shut that thing off?" I demanded as I opened the door of his gray Toyota pick-up truck. "The whole school can hear you."

"This thing's great, isn't it?" Micah laughed grinning from ear-to-ear. "You want to say something in it?" He held the microphone close to my face.

"Get that damn thing away from me," I said. "I thought we were going to hunt for artifacts, not play 'Smokey and the Bandit.'"

"You do kinda remind me of Jackie Gleason." Before I could respond, Micah continued. "Don't worry about your clothes. You can wear a pair of my old pants," he said. "Here." He threw a dusty pair of camouflage pants at me. "And leather boots, good lord. You can wear a pair of my rubber fishing boots. I always carry extras." He studied me from head-to-toe. "I hope you know what you're getting yourself into here."

"Don't give me that," I said. "You kept pushing me to go. Now you're stuck with me."

"No kidding, I think this counts as the community service part of my sentence," he said.

As we drove to the recently scraped site, Micah told me a story about Bobby. "You know Bobby is a decorated Viet Nam war veteran, don't you?"

"No, I didn't."

"He's been wounded a couple times, lost his left eye."

"Oh, I am so sorry to hear that," I said. "I didn't know."

"Well, he is rather sensitive about having a glass eye. He feels that people are staring at him all the time because of it. I'm telling you this, so you don't make him feel bad. Whatever you do, don't stare at his eye."

"Of course, I won't stare at him. I'm glad you told me about it."

When we arrived at the site behind all the construction, Bobby was waiting for us dressed in an old army camouflage hat, hunting jacket and military issued black boots. He nodded to us as he took one last drag from his cigarette, then flicked it to the ground and stomped it out. He was shorter than me, and sported a handlebar mustache. "Hey, Coach," Bobby spoke in a deep Southern dialect. "How did Micah ever talk you into this? You 'll sink at least five inches in this mud."

"Oh, Micah used his charm on me," I said, taking small glances at Bobby's eyes. "By the way, I don't coach anything. You must have me mixed up with someone else."

Both Micah and Bobby laughed. "That's just his way," Micah said. "He calls everybody coach."

"Especially when I don't know someone's name. Where's your manners, boy? Aren't you even going to introduce us?" Bobby called Micah "boy" even though he couldn't have been more than five or six years older than Micah.

"This is Catherine Scott," Micah said. "She teaches at the same school as me. She's one of those English teachers."

"Glad to meet ya. Feel free to correct my speech anytime you want. I won't listen to you, but it might make you feel more comfortable out here."

This time I laughed. "When I'm not in the classroom, I don't pay attention to anybody's speech but my own."

"This hill's real slippery, solid mud because of the rain. You can walk way 'round or slide down on your backside. I hope you have old clothes on." The more Bobby tried to hold eye contact with me, the more I kept looking away.

"She has to change first. Go in the truck and put on the pants and boots I gave you. Maybe Bobby has an old army coat for you."

"Yep, you go and get changed and meet us here. I'll get my old coat."

Micah shook his head. "I told her to wear her oldest clothes, and she comes out looking like she's off the cover of *Vogue*."

"I heard that," I yelled. "*L.L. Bean* maybe, but certainly not *Vogue*."

The front seat of Micah's truck was rather tight, even without all the rocks he had piled on the floor. His pants were about four inches too long, but I tucked the ends into Micah's size eleven boots to help stabilize my walking. My hair tied back into a ponytail, I donned my baseball hat, and quickly freshened my lipstick.

"Let's go. We don't have all day," Micah said when I met them back at Bobby's truck. "Put on this coat and follow us down the hill. Here, use this beaver stick for support."

The beaver stick was longer than me and awkward to handle; instead of holding me up, it seemed to propel me forward. After a few attempts to walk down the hill, I decided to leave it behind. I would take a breather and then try to make my way by taking small side steps. Bobby and Micah made it with no trouble whatsoever. They maneuvered their walking sticks to their advantage and glided to the bottom with ease. Not being used to walking down muddy hills, especially ones as slick as this one, much less in a pair of rubber fishing boots that were two-and-a-half sizes too big at least, I took only two steps before my feet slipped out from under me. "Holy shiiit!" I yelled. "I've got mud all over me." Both Micah and Bobby climbed up the hill to help me down. Bobby reached out his hand to help me, while Micah offered me the muddy end of his walking stick.

"Didn't like my walking stick, huh? Whatever," Micah chuckled but hid a bigger laugh. I was too concerned about getting down the hill in one piece to point out to Micah that it was his idea for me to come along on this trip. And that he was very persistent about it. Some people just like to complain, I thought. Waving Micah's muddy stick away, I grabbed Bobby's hand and together we inched our way down the incline. As we did, I couldn't help but get a close look at his left eye. It did not seem any different from his right eye. He had two perfectly healthy eyes. Micah Marlowe had played me for a fool. He must have seen how closely I inspected Bobby's eyes, because when I got to the bottom of the mudslide, Micah was nowhere to be seen.

"I wonder where Micah ran off to?"

"We'll soon find out," said Bobby. He put his thumb and forefinger in his mouth and whistled. After a few minutes, Micah emerged from the trees. I made a point to have excellent eye contact with Bobby, and anytime I found a pottery shard or what looked to be part of an arrowhead, I showed my finds to him rather than to Micah. At one point, Micah came over to us as Bobby was describing how to tell the difference between a plain old rock and a piece of flint that had been worked on, and noted that we were spending more time peering into my hands than into the dirt. "You need to pay attention to what you pick up. You can't be bringing every rock and stone over to Bobby for him to inspect. He'll never have time to find his own stuff."

"Don't pay any attention to him, Ms. Scott. Micah has been living by himself too long to know how to treat a woman. I don't mind helping anybody who takes an interest in archeology. "

"Thanks, by the way," I said loud enough for Micah to hear. "Has anyone ever told you what great-looking eyes you have?" I could hear Micah coughing as he walked to the far end of the scraped site. His coughing continued for some time. "I hope Micah's not getting sick," I innocently said. Bobby, however, had been in on the joke and laughed just as hard as I did at Micah's coughing fit.

I continued to follow Bobby around and after awhile I got used to looking through the red clay myself. Whenever either of us found a piece of flint or quartz that looked as if it had been chipped, we rinsed it off in one of the small pools of water that had collected in the hollowed-out places around the site. After awhile, Bobby said he had to go. "You and Micah still have about an hour of light left. Keep looking. I have a dinner meeting to go to. If I'm late, my sweet thang won't be too happy. Nice meetin' ya, ma'am."

"Call me Cat. Thanks for all the help. Do you have any idea where Micah is?"

"Don't worry, he'll find you. He's a little shy around women. Don't find 'em all, leave some for me."

He damn well better find me, I thought as I watched Bobby disappear up the hill; otherwise, I'm stuck trying to find a ride home in this ridiculous get-up. Covered with mud the way I was, I would most likely be arrested for being some sort of a derelict or lunatic. I rested my eyes on the horizon.

"Stop daydreaming, Ms. Scott, and come on. We don't have all day."

"Where did you come from?" I asked. Micah ignored me and continued walking; so without asking any more questions, I followed him to the turned field on the other side of the creek. After all, this was his territory, not mine. Bobby had taught me how to tell the difference between a stone that had been worn down by years of erosion and a stone that had been chipped and worked by man, but I still felt completely out of my bailiwick. I ventured away from Micah once we arrived at the new field. Since I hadn't had much luck finding artifacts that day, I half-heartedly kicked my feet around in the dirt. I found a comfortable boulder to sit on and watched Micah doggedly tramp through the wet clay. I envisioned Indians sitting on this same boulder, passing time much the same as I. Maybe some Indian child was hammering points out of flint for his warrior father, or an Indian maiden laughed while her baby sister ran around in a field here. My gaze dropped to the ground beside me, and I noticed a smooth curved object that seemed out of place. I yelled across the field to Micah.

"Micah, you need to see this. It looks like something I saw in your classroom the other day." Micah ambled over and examined what I had found.

"Hey," he said, his irritability gone, "you found something cool. That's part of a pipe bowl. See how the inside is darker from ash? Let's see what else is around here. Go slow."

Sure enough, we found more pipe pieces, as well as shards of what were clay cooking pots, stone tools, arrowheads and spear points. "These shards look like they're from the Woodland period somewhere between 1000 and 2000 years old." Micah picked up the pottery fragment. "See this design? It's from a binding rope. The Indians wrapped the wet clay with it, and then fired it. The rope burned off but the impression remained. It's sand tempered, meaning they mixed sand into the clay for stability. See this? It's part of a spear point. You can tell by how it's chipped and beveled on the edges. If you didn't know better, it just looks like another rock."

I held the white projectile in the palm of my hand as I examined the intricate but subtle worked edges. "It's really beautiful. I feel like I'm holding some ancient person's soul. Whoever carved this created a work of art."

"That person was mainly concerned with staying alive, not creating art. But when you think about it, in ancient civilizations their lifestyle was their art. It allowed them to survive. You can tell great care was taken with some spear points and pottery."

"Micah, there's a person behind every one of these points we find. It's overwhelming to think about."

"Not too many people think about that, but I'm sure whoever made this never thought there would be a day two thousand years ahead." Micah's gaze held mine for a minute. "And I'm sure they didn't imagine people descended from another continent digging up their household utensils and calling it art. Even the ordinary people left something of substance behind."

"I guess we don't need to create art anymore to survive. Most of what we make is disposable, even people."

"Maybe art is the only thing that'll help us continue to survive. Hey, here is another piece with a rope design. Let's see if it fits with the one you have."

We put the shards together, and even though it was an imperfect fit, we used our imaginations to fill in the uneven edges. A small find in the scheme of things, but exciting nonetheless.

"Could be this is a bigger site than I thought. I might call my archeologist buddy and see."

"Who's that?"

"John Reed. I met him at Fernbank, the museum. I go with him to work on this other site down near Between."

"Between what?"

"That's the name of the town. Somebody was plowing a deer plot and found this big village. A rare Vinings culture. They have found postholes, pots and even trash pits with stuff they ate. Couple of bodies, too—mostly teeth, though. Red clay eats up bones."

"What kind of food did they find in the trash pit?"

"Anything that gets burned will preserve if covered up. They found berries, squash, little bitty corn, not the engineered kind of today. Deer bones, turkey bones, even rat bones. When you get hungry, food is food. Oh, yeah, and some shells from the river, probably mussels."

"What about the people's teeth?"

"This is kinda cool. Some were found within the outlines of the house. If someone died in the winter time, the only place with ground you could dig in was inside the house. Bet they couldn't wait for spring to get grandpa outside, huh?"

"That's fascinating. When're you going down there again?"

"I don't know for sure. Wanta go?"

"Give me more than an hour's notice. Is this anything?"

Micah turned the glazed white ceramic shard over. "See these hand-painted blue stripes? This is Leedsware, probably early nineteenth century. Cool. Guess there was someone else living here after the Indians. This is a good spot. High enough and with good water. There was probably a house somewhere right in here two hundred years ago."

"And they tied the horses right over there to the barn. Where do you suppose the outhouse was?"

"Downwind, I suspect."

"I wonder what it would have been like back then, milking cows, growing your own food."

"They drank milk right from the cow. How's that sound?"

"Makes me sick. I hate milk. Even when I was little, I couldn't drink it. Mom tried everything— Nestley's, Hershey's syrup, even butterscotch. Nothing helped."

"Yeah, I bet you'll be one big broken bone when you get old. Your momma shoulda popped you with a switch."

"Excuse me?"

"My mom woulda used a switch on me for sure if I didn't drink my milk." Micah laughed.

"My parents never hit me. They would threaten sometimes. I remember one time my mother did put me over her knee. Lark Denzel's mother called her and told her she spanked Lark with a hairbrush because we came home from school an hour late. My mom wouldn't have even noticed if Mrs. Denzel hadn't called. So, for the first time in her life, I think I was ten, she put me over her knee. I was so indignant that I wiggled my way off her lap and yelled at her, 'How dare you try to spank me!' She just let me go and went back to doing laundry. I think she was pretty much tuckered, raising three teenagers and then me."

"Well, that tale explains a lot. That's not how they raise kids in the South. I got switched real good a few times. My grandma even made me go to the woods out back to get my own switch."

"So you could get whipped with? That's awful."

"Ask just about any male raised in the South and he'll tell you the same thing. Dad worked long hours while mom and grandma worked just as hard at making sure the home was taken of. Dad might run the farm but momma ran the house. That why moms are respected so much."

"How'd you know what kind of switch to get?"

"My grandma made me get it from one of the bushes that had long branches. I hated that—fetchin' my own instrument of torture. She kept sending me back. Nope, too short, nope, too thick. I had the biggest red welts on my legs. Man, those would sting. She was tough."

"Some would call that child abuse."

"Yeah, look how undisciplined society is, now that everyone got all sensitive. Shoot, that wasn't nothing compared to if your daddy ever got really mad at you. You might as well just run away from home."

"Oh, my God, that makes me feel so sad. I wish I could take that all away from ..." For a split second I could see a small tow-headed boy with big tears running down his cheeks, his head low in humiliation. I wanted to follow my maternal instinct and cradle the adult Micah in my arms and try to make everything better for him now. In actuality, I did nothing but stare wide-eyed at this revelation.

He half-snickered at my reaction. "It weren't so bad. It kept me in line, I tell ya. I think that's what some of them kids at school need more of. Some of them don't have any idea what self-control means. What're they gonna do when they have a job and a boss? No wonder some get in with the wrong crowd. A good smack when they were younger might have saved them and their parents a lot of trouble."

"Well, I think there are ways of disciplining children that're not physically abusive."

"I don't mean beat the crap out of 'em. Just a reminder that actions have consequences. I'd rather get a switching than lectured to for an hour. I could see you doing that."

"I didn't lecture my kids for hours. They got sent to their room or had a privilege taken away. Then maybe a discussion of right and wrong."

"That means nothing to a two-year old running the streets, but a little hedge limb on the butt will mean something. Besides, sometimes kids that get whippins ain't got anything to take away."

"Well, if the mother watched the child to begin with ... "

"Yeah, right," Micah said, as he walked over to a spot a few yards away, inspecting an interesting stone.

"All I can say is, it's a good thing you don't have kids."

"I just grew up in a different culture from you Yankees." He practically spit out the word *Yankees.* "We believe in keeping our children in line. You break the rules, you know what's coming. Anyway, I have a whole lotta kids each and every day and some of 'em coulda used a good ass-whipping a while back before they got in over their head."

As Micah continued talking, I wondered if Southern graciousness was a gloss to cover up dysfunction. Maybe we up North were too crass to even care about hiding how screwed up we were. It's kind of like the difference in the way families teach their children to regard bodily functions.

"Respect for each other, whether you mean it or not, is highly regarded in the South. Most males born in the South are drilled in gentlemanly behavior early on. Any Southern mother would have been proud to have Rhett Butler as her son, even though she might not want Scarlett as her daughter-in-law," Micah asserted.

"And just what does that mean?" I said.

"Well, two strong-willed women in the same house can lead to another war."

"Can't argue with that. Anyway, why are you so paranoid when I question Southern ways?"

"Cause we are tired of the rest of the nation telling us how to think, act and speak. That's how the Klan got started—all those carpetbaggers comin' down here trying to get our land and 'show us the light.' I don't go for much of what the Klan has done since, but they are not wrong about everything."

"I cannot believe you would agree with anything those racist rednecks have to say!"

"My momma said when she was little, the Klan was about everyone doing right, not just the focus on minorities like those Neanderthals of today. If a white woman came to church with a bruised eye, you can bet her husband would be told about it. If he did it again, well, street justice can be quick and sweet."

"So, is it justice to own slaves and then torture them when the government says they can go free?"

"First of all, my dear, most Southerners never owned a slave, probably less than ten percent of 'em did. Maybe a few plantation owners but, you know," he paused for effect, "if it were not for the factories up No-worth, slavery would never have lasted as long as it did. Who do you think bought all the cotton and wore all the clothes made from it? You're the English teacher. Didn't Thoreau say the North was just as guilty of slavery as the South?"

"Yeah, well, I guess he does talk about that in 'Civil Disobedience.' It seems industry up North made just as much, if not more, than the plantation owners. Indirectly but it still counts."

"No kidding. There's good and bad in every culture; just like there's good and bad in every person. It's just a lot more convenient to blame us I guess."

Before I could ask Micah what the bad part was in him, he threw a small rock into the puddle beside my foot, the muddy water splattering my borrowed pants.

"Hey, you could hurt someone doing that."

"I know where I'm aiming. If I wanted to hit you, I could." With that, he threw another rock into the pocket of mud behind me.

"Stop it, you got mud all over me." This brought a chuckle from Micah.

"How can you tell? Besides, you're the one who wanted to tromp around all day."

I reached down and scooped up several stones and tried to hit him anywhere I could. I missed each time, the next throw worse instead of better. When he started laughing again, I threw all the rocks in my hand at the same time. They scattered all around him. He flicked a stone right on my rear end.

"Okay, that's enough; somebody's going to get hurt." I said this as I threw one last rock at him. It landed several yards behind him in one of the small pools of collected rainwater.

"Not bad," he said, not realizing I was still aiming at him.

"See, better watch it, buddy."

"Try to hit that old tree trunk. Like this. Watch." Micah hurled a piece of gravel at a fallen down oak twenty or so yards away. It thudded into the tree just where the gnarled branches used to spread outward.

I took aim and the rock wobbled far to the right. "You throw like a girl," Micah said, then continued. "Look here. Get a better rock, little bit heavier, and watch. You throw like a catapult. You never did play softball or anything, did ya?"

I ignored the question and threw again, just falling short of the old oak.

"Not bad. Throw a little harder next time." Micah smacked the trunk in the middle.

This time I swung my arm back and forth several times before I finally let go. A slight hollow click ended the flight of the rock.

"I hit it, I hit it! Did you see?"

"What? Oh, no, I wasn't looking … just kidding."

"I'm ready. Let's have a 'hit the tree' contest. Most hits out of fifty?"

"Fifty? I can't even find fifty rocks. How 'bout outa ten?"

I took aim and missed by at least ten feet.

"The object is to hit the tree, right? You still throw like a girl, but I can live with it."

We threw rocks at the old log for what seemed like hours. We lost track of who was winning. Finally I said my arm was hurting and needed to stop.

"Excuses, excuses. Actually, mine is aching. I thought you would never quit." He hesitated and then reached into his coat pocket. "Here, I found you something." When I reached out my hand, Micah placed a black-and-white feather in my palm. The colors had sharp edges, a slender feather almost nine inches long.

"Have you ever seen a pilliated woodpecker?" His hand remained on mine, the feather between our skin.

"I don't really know … maybe … probably not."

His hand closed over mine. "They're endangered. Their feathers are hard to find. It's the largest woodpecker in North America. I haven't found but a few of these; their cousin became extinct this century but maybe these can make it. They are so majestic and beautiful. Seems, though, everything beautiful has a tough time staying out of man's way." He held my hand for several seconds more, then picked up his walking stick. He turned and said, "You know what? I usually keep these for myself." He said the words as much to himself as to me. What a peculiar man he was. One minute he wouldn't even give me his hand to help me down a hill, and the next he grasped my hand as if he had held it one hundred times before. He was mercurial as the day was long—tender and sensitive one minute, gruff and withdrawn the next. I think that was what drew me to him in the first place—his inscrutability. For an analytical person like me, he represented a lifetime's work. I knew I couldn't rest until I got a handle on what made him so invulnerably vulnerable. I had never come face-to-face with a walking oxymoron until now. Nor did I ever encounter anyone, male or female, that could reach down and unearth the trusting child who used to sing to apple trees. I had to grow up way too soon, and until Micah became my friend, I had long ago forgotten what it was like to view the world through virginal eyes. As we walked down the hill to the highway back towards the truck, near the offices and strip malls, I felt as if I had emerged from a land of Indian princesses, Peter Pan and perhaps Huck Finn. Maybe it was *Alice in Wonderland,* but the place I now walked to felt like the dream.

We were over-forty Holden Caulfields; neither of us wanted to return to the world of adult hypocrisy, broken communication and fragmented lives. I tried to forget my bleak and destructive days without Micah, and wanted to revel and bask in the moment like the twelve-year-old of my past life, but I knew that if I were to grow back on life's spiritual tree, I had to discover what was real and good about me. I needed to face the gathering voices inside me and shape them into my life's art. But what you know and what you do are like two islands firmly placed in recognizable proximity, yet kept apart by ever widening waters.

Chapter 12

For the weeks before Thanksgiving, Micah and I went walking together at least a couple days a week. The neighborhood forgotten during the week, the only time I could find for Micah on the weekends was on Saturday mornings and Sunday afternoons. Marshall still liked to go out with our group on Saturday nights, and the time I spent with Micah made the partying and hooter talk almost bearable. Initially I thought the entire group would be disgusted with me and tried to avoid the group as much as possible. Yet they actually sought me out more. I think the neighborhood women saw themselves in me, and I represented what could happen to them if they started to examine their lives too deeply. They weren't ready for that kind of freedom. They admired and pitied me at the same time. I still danced on tables and talked about blowjobs, but I was unmistakably different. I did not need them anymore and they guessed it had something to do with the muddy clothes they saw scattered across my garage floor.

"How'd you get mud all over those your clothes?" Debra asked one Sunday evening when she picked me up for tennis.

"I'm learning about archeology the hard way," I joked. "By walking through the mud. I wash them every third time I wear them. I save on detergent that way."

When I returned home from my days with Micah, my answering machine would be full. The women especially were curious about my new archeology "classes." And Bonnie Jorgenson remarked one Saturday night at Martini's that my skin actually glowed. Even Marshall commented on my behavior. "What do you mean, I'm different?" I asked him one evening.

"I don't know. You seem to laugh more. Did you finally go to the doctor?"

"Yes. But he's a witch doctor, and made me smear red clay all over my body and wear feathers in my hair. Then I drank from ancient waters trapped under the sewers of Atlanta. I know it's kind of strange, but it did seem to help."

Marshall looked at me askance as I sauntered through the house like Nefertiti. For once, I felt like the queen of my own life. Marshall knew that I went out with some math teacher after school for a few hours as well as on the weekends, but to Marshall my absence had to do more with an extension of teaching than the emancipation of my selfhood. He had no idea how much I loved being with Micah. We took many walks along the torn earth behind the highways. Usually we looked for dirt that had been bulldozed on a high area near a creek, a place where Indians would have camped. After parking on the side of the road, we would go tramping up the hill hoping to find sherds of pottery, and quartz or flint arrowheads. Micah often was silent and withdrawn. I did not mind Micah's silence. It gave me a chance to study him more than I could have if we were talking.

Most of our days started out the same, quiet. I paid close attention to him as we donned our boots and trudged up another muddy hill. Then Micah would race ahead, scanning the site for old creek beds, not paying one iota of attention to me. Left to fend for myself, I would waddle through the red clay, stepping in his footprints, trying to keep up with his long-legged stride, a low-country walk. Holding his shoulders rigidly upright, he moved with both his feet slightly tilted outward, while his neck stretched forward, his head cocked to the left as if he were listening for the whispered chant of an old shaman.

But sometimes he would be in the mood to joke. He delighted in making fun of me, especially the way I walked. "You look like you're walking on eggs," he would say. And then he would mimic me, gingerly holding his arms up in the air while shuffling his feet like a geisha. Later, he complained that I never watched where I was going and that I bumped into him all the time. "Go over there and look for your own stuff," he would say. "You don't have to walk where I am looking all the time. If you follow me like a baby duck you won't find anything."

At first I did not think much of his reaction to my bumping into him, but then I started noticing that when I would show him an arrow point or pottery shard I found, he would very carefully take it out of my hand so that his skin would never touch mine. On another occasion, I needed help crossing a log over a narrow river. Instead of giving me his hand, he showed me how to hold on to tree branches to get across. And there was the time with Bobby when he held out his walking stick instead of his hand to help me down the slippery ravine. Yet he had felt comfortable enough to hold my hand the day he placed a feather in it.

Other days we went "rattin' around" along the shores of Lake Allatoona or swamping for frogs up near Cumming. We meandered down roads in his gray Toyota pick-up truck with camper top, the back loaded with rocks he picked up along creek beds, quartz arrow points he rescued from mud floors about to become part of subdivisions, and beaver sticks he found in rivers. He always carried along his hunting caps and several pairs of rubber fishing boots just in case we found a muddy spot or lake or river we wanted to go wading in. I borrowed his boots and his extra hat many a time.

"Why don't cha go to Target and get your own stinking boots," Micah would jokingly complain.

I always answered him the same way. "I prefer walking in yours because I like the way they smell."

And I really did like the way they smelled. They smelled strong like the leathery skin of armadillos, the pungency of long marsh grasses, sage and fennel seed, unpicked purple plums, overripe and long forgotten. Micah himself smelled like all of nature. Whenever we walked through the woods, I stood next to his tall, wiry body, covered from head-to-toe in camouflage gear, green hunting boots, oilskin hat with a feather jauntily placed on the right side of the brim, and I closed my eyes and breathed him into myself.

Even though we barely touched each other, we often communicated through our scents. One day sitting in a field of tall grasses listening to the courting sounds of bobwhites, Micah told me that my smell is heady like wild onions, freshly baked bread, hot butter and the sweaty hair of a child at the end of a summer's day.

Sometimes I called him because I missed his scent, or because I forgot to memorize the exact lines of his cheekbones, or the size of his Adam's apple, or the shape of his mouth under his sandy-colored mustache. "Let's go somewhere in your truck," I would suggest. And when I was finally riding next to him, I wrote his face, his hands, his neck in my mind. And sometimes I caught Micah staring at me, and I worried what he might discover if he examined me too closely. Not just the crows feet around my eyes or the softening under my chin, but I worried that he would come face-to-face with that little girl who fell down the steps and drowned so many years ago. Because Micah was staring at me, I got my original eyes back.

"Your eyes are so dark, I can't see what you're thinking," he said one day while we were driving through the back roads of Cumming, Georgia. "I can't even see your pupils when we're in the shade. You look like the night of the living dead."

I was offended because I thought my bought brown eyes looked attractive; I thought they accentuated the roundness of my eyes. I started wearing the dark brown, almost black, contact lenses because they made the whites of my eyes look less red after my weekend drinking binges. My natural color was so light green that one could almost see through them to the other side. "You certainly know what to say to charm a woman," I said.

"Why is it in the sunlight I can see some green in your eyes? Are you wearing those colored contacts?"

"Yes, I thought brown would go better with my reddish hair."

"Your hair looks more blonde than red to me. I think the brown is too dark. Take them out and let's have a look."

"I can't see without them and I don't have my glasses with me."

"There's an eye place right up the street. Let's getcha some new contact lenses. You can charge them."

"Micah ... "

Before I knew it, we were at Lenscrafters, and I was bending over the counter taking out my lenses. Micah was puzzled, as I knew he would be, when he saw my eyes. "Why would you want to cover up your natural color?"

"I don't know, I just didn't want people staring at me," I lied. "How would you like to go around with eyes the color of limes?"

"Better than night of the living dead."

I was the opposite of St. Lucy. Instead of getting new eyes, I got my original ones back, while my substitute irises crawled like two brown beetles down the drain.

Since it was almost dark by the time I was fitted with my new contacts, we decided to skip the walking and go to our favorite Chinese restaurant. We strolled in dressed like hunters, which we were, and found a booth. While waiting for our chicken with plum sauce, Micah looked into my eyes for several seconds. He then chuckled and spoke.

"Your eyes are the color of salamanders I remember from a while back. The sun would hit 'em just right and you could see a rainbow."

She scooped up the creek water into the jar and giggled with delight as she peered through the glass at her new friend.

"Polliwogs," I said.

"What?"

"I used to catch polliwogs, not salamanders."

"What the hell is a polliwog?" Micah asked while he wrinkled his forehead.

"You know, a frog before it's a frog."

"A tad-pole, maybe?"

"Yeah, whatever. We lived by some woods and Dad would take me walking down by the creek. I guess I was about eight or so. He showed me all about catching polliwogs, as he called them, thank you. Later on, I took my friends there and we would catch jarfuls and wait for them to turn into frogs. They always died."

"Shoulda changed the water. But at least you tried."

"You caught salamanders? Where?"

"Up at my cousin's in Canton. We would stay in that creek for hours, it seemed. He was twenty years older than me but we caught frogs, crawfish and the neatest salamanders." Micah stared over my shoulder at a memory. "We always let them go."

"Twenty years older?"

"Yeah, there were eight children in my mama's family. She's the youngest."

"Didn't your cousin have any kids for you to play with?"

"Nah, he never married. Lived with his mama till he got sick … and died. He left me all his Civil War relics. I used to tell him he was my favorite relic. He was a neat fellow."

"Well."

"Well, what?"

"Seems the men in your family don't marry much, huh?"

"There's only the two of us. Besides, I almost let some woman get me."

"What happened?"

"The hook came out and I swam to safety."

"No, really."

"Maybe one day." And I could tell the subject was dropped. "Your eyes keep changing color."

"I should have kept my others."

"No way. Too fakey."

Micah was smiling at me when the waitress brought dinner.

"I'll have another glass of wine," I told her.

"Please—my ears cannot take it."

"You do your fair share of talking," I said watching Micah dump two bags of sugar into his hot tea.

"You know, you eat like a bird," Micah commented.

"Oh, really."

"Yeah, a buzzard." His laughter brought looks from other customers. I had to laugh, too; it was funny. Actually, Micah was the one always ravenous. Not only did he ravish all of his share but half of mine. It was a wonder he stayed so thin and wiry. I watched everything I ate and still struggled to keep my weight under 130 pounds. Sometimes life isn't fair.

Micah stretched his back and yawned. "Man, I told my kids a story today that is so cool. True too."

"Alright, go ahead. I'll pretend I'm interested."

Micah and his stories. Whenever I was with him he always told some tale. I thought it remarkable that he never told the same one twice. He was a natural-born storyteller. Fact or fiction, he could spin some good yarns.

"This one's true ... honest." Here we go. "One time we ... "

"We, who?"

"Me, mom and dad. We went to a basketball game over in Tuscaloosa. This has been probably twenty years ago, but we stayed at the Scottish Inn. It was downtown."

"How old were you?"

"I dunno, twenty. Hush up for a minute."

"Who was playing?"

"Alabama and Kentucky. We're big UK fans. Can I finish?"

"Go ahead, I won't say anything else."

"Impossible. Anyway," he stretched his neck from side to side like an evangelist preparing for the sermon. "We had a room at the Scottish Inn and it was probably midnight when we got back from the game."

"Who won?"

"See, I knew you couldn't do it. I forget. So about two in the morning, Mom starts shaking the bed, telling us 'Get up, we gotta go, I can't stay here another minute.' Me and Dad are like, 'Go to bed', but she won't shut up. She's walking around wringing her hands, all frantic and everything, saying 'We gotta go, we gotta go.' So we realize we can't sleep anyway with all this commotion going on and give in. We put all our crap in the station wagon and drive toward home at three-stinking-o'clock. Well, after a couple hours Mom's all calmed down and we get a place to stay. The next morning, we come dragging out of bed and turn on the *Today Show*. It's 'bout 8:30 or so and the guy says, 'And now with a report, Kinley Jones.' Well, get this, the picture changes to this guy standing in front of a pile of rubble. He says, 'I am standing in front of the Scottish Inn here in Tuscaloosa. A tornado came through here last night, taking the top floor away and killing two people. Many were injured ...' and other stuff. You could see behind him and the room we had been staying in was just gone. Our mouths just fell open. Needless to say, we listen when Mom has a 'feeling' now. Isn't that beyond weird?"

"That's not true. No way."

"Wanta bet? Ask Mom next time you see her."

"I will."

"Sometimes, I think I have inherited her intuitive senses."

"Like when?"

"Like now. I will be in a bathroom within a minute." He got up and disappeared down the hall.

Catching my eye, the waitress politely came over to our table. "You like anything else?"

"Just our check."

I tried to resume the conversation when Micah returned.

"What other weird stuff happens to you and your mom?"

"Not much, other than the ghosts."

"Ghosts, too?"

"You sure can pester folks. More stories later."

Our check and fortune cookies showed up.

"You don't have to be so rude. I was just asking."

"We'll talk about it when I'm not so tired. Let's go." He rose from his seat.

"Will you sit down?" I said. "We have to read our fortunes first."

Micah plopped back down and started fidgeting with the cellophane wrapper.

"What's yours say?" he asked.

I scanned the thin strip of paper. *Follow the advice of your heart.*

After I read it to Micah, he said, "What if you have heartburn?" He smiled and then followed, "Actually those are good words."

"Just words?"

"Words are only words. You analyze 'em for yourself. You like all that analyzing stuff."

"Me?"

"Yes, you. You want to hear mine?"

"Please, sir."

Micah held his fortune in front of him and smiled. "We dropped your fork in the toilet this morning."

"Yeah, whatever," I said, rolling my eyes, trying not to laugh at his silliness. "Okay, wise guy, read it and no monkeyin' around."

He looked at me over the top of his glasses. "The world awaits those who seek it." His gaze held mine for more than a long pause. Then he shifted position and impatiently wadded up his fortune and put it in his pocket. "It's taking forever for the waitress to bring our change. Stay here while I get the truck." Before I could protest, Micah slid out of the booth and was out the door but not before grabbing a handful of mints from the little bowl beside the register. I remained in the booth until the waitress returned. Marshall and I always left the restaurant together. But then, I reminded myself, I am not in a relationship with Micah. We are friends, and even though my other male friends treat me with much more consideration, Micah does, for the most part, belong to that rare sector of men who have avoided the complicated nuances of male/female interaction, and has remained, despite the thirty-year onslaught of the women's revolution, the quintessential self-contained male.

Outside, a few stars interrupted the dark sky. "What a beautiful, clear night," I said to no one in particular.

Micah stuck his head out of the driver's window. "Let's go. Quit pokin' along and get in the truck."

"I think you've been living alone too long," I said as I slammed the door of his gray Toyota.

"Not long enough," he replied.

We rode over the winding country roads in silence. When we finally reached the school parking lot, Micah needed to go into his room, but I really didn't feel like following. I felt like a pouting child instead of a middle-aged adult, but I couldn't help myself.

"I need to go do some schoolwork, I better go," I told him.

"Alright, I gotta mess around in here for a bit. Feed fish and such. Call me tomorrow."

Before I could reply, he was in the door. I thought he was acting odd but it was hard to tell with him. There was no way to know what he was thinking.

When I arrived home, there was a message from Marshall on the phone. His voice sounded strained and worried as it usually did those days. "Hi, you must be out hunting artifacts with Micah. Hope you found something good. I'll be home Friday around nine." There was a brief pause. "I love you, Catherine." The sound of his voice made my chest hurt, and I poured another glass of wine to drown out the gnawing guilt. Even though my time spent with Micah was innocent enough, I felt like I had betrayed something sacred in our marriage. Maybe it was because I always smiled around Micah, and seldom smiled around Marshall anymore. But most likely it was because I took Micah, not Marshall, to that self-conscious place inside of me.

But Micah Marlowe was not without his demons, and it was his struggle with those very demons that kept him far removed from the mainstream of society. When I first met him, I did not know the source of his demons but sensed he had a secret burden. I knew from the tenseness of his jaw, the lines on his face, and the lowering of his eyelids that he was suffering and did not know how to unlock his pain. He was overzealous about both his work and his hobbies; his creativity and adolescent humor made him a favorite high school teacher; his preoccupation with unearthing fossils and artifacts made him seem strange and isolated. He avoided touch, and the few times I impulsively gave him a hug, he grew rigid and frozen.

As his trust for me grew, he released bits of himself, but the more time I spent with him, the more I wanted to know. We stumbled onto each other by fate, but once our lives intersected, we could not seem to pull ourselves apart no matter how hard we tried. And we did try. At times I thought he was the most wonderful man in the universe, so in touch with the soul of the world, a savant, who because of his intellectual sensitivity resisted the lure of material pleasures and ego-satisfying fame. And in my darker moments, I knew he represented the worst in men hiding with intelligible lies the unintelligible truth. But in the end, he turned out to be another human being struggling with his personal demons or impersonal genes, depending on what branch of science you ascribe to. Ironically, it was his eventual confrontation with violence and death that gave me the strength to take the hidden piece of my heart out of its coffin.

My first glimpse into Micah Marlowe's crawl space came the Saturday before Thanksgiving break. He invited me to an Alabama flea market just over the western Georgia border, and Tecumseh High would have been miles out of the way. Micah suggested I drive to his house instead of meeting him in the school parking lot. "It'll take us about three hours to get there, so why don't you just meet here," he said over the phone. "That way we'll save some time."

When I pulled in his driveway at six in the morning, not only was it dark, but also it was pouring down rain. The newscasters announced over the radio that it was going to storm all day. My lights shone on a 70's white Firebird parked next to the familiar gray truck beneath a carport. Since it was raining, I ran under the carport to the side door, rather than walking across the outside of the house to the front door. Micah opened the door before I could knock.

"Welcome to my abode," he said. "I just made a fresh pot of coffee, want a cup?"

The side door led directly to a modest-sized kitchen with dark green walls. My eyes quickly scanned the room, taking notice of several packages of bread and a bag of russet potatoes piled neatly on top of the stove, dark wooden cabinets above and beneath khaki-colored Formica countertops, a small antique table with two mismatched chairs, and clean plates and glasses stacked on a dish rack. On one side of the table two rubber pails filled with rocks and crystals were placed next to a large Freeware pot filled with brackish water.

"I'd love some. I have a hard time functioning without at least two cups of coffee," I said. "You wanted to leave so early; I didn't have time to make any." I slid into one of the kitchen chairs. "This looks like an authentic Windsor."

"Could be. It's old alright. Mom gave it to me. She found it in an old abandoned house years ago. Used to be when I was a little boy, you'd find abandoned houses all over the South. Some even leftover from the Civil War. My mama and I'd drive all over looking for empty houses. Not many of them around today."

"Where'd you get the other one?" I said, indicating the other chair.

"That? I found it at some flea market. It's older than the other one; I got it for a steal."

"This coffee is really good. I think I'll take a cup for the road."

"I don't think we'll be going anywhere just yet. If this storm continues there won't be much to see at the flea market. Let's wait an hour or two and see what happens with the weather."

"Damn, I got up at five for nothing. I could've slept in for two more hours," I said.

"You can go upstairs and sleep in one of the beds if you're still tired."

"No, no, I'm wide awake now. I guess you'll just have to fix me breakfast and entertain me."

"I've had my pop tart already, but you're welcome to one. Strawberry or blueberry?"

"Do you have any eggs? I make really good omelets."

"There's the fridge ... I might have a few eggs in there." Typical bachelor's refrigerator, the shelves were crammed with half-filled bottles of salad dressings, Tupperware containers of all shapes and sizes, probably inherited from a kind-hearted neighbor, aunt, or a would-be girlfriend, cardboard boxes of leftover Chinese carryout, a full container of milk and a few Coronas. Packets of batteries crowded the fruit and vegetable drawer, while what looked like animal bones in plastic bags filled the meat compartment.

"You have bones in your refrigerator," I said. "Anybody I know?"

"Those are deer bones. I found them in the river. I keep them refrigerated until I can take the time to preserve them."

"Am I going to find anything in here that I should worry about?" I said as I rooted around the lower shelves. "Finally," I said. "I found the eggs." Pushed to the back of one of the lower shelves was an unopened carton of eggs.

"How long have you had these eggs?" I asked.

"Not too long. They can't be any older than a year."

"I'm gonna see if they're any good. Do you have a frying pan and some olive oil?" I asked as I continued to ransack the fridge. "Cheddar cheese and salsa. This could work."

"I don't keep olive oil. I have some butter or a little bacon grease."

"Butter will be fine."

He handed me a pan.

In about ten minutes I had a six egg omelet setting nicely in front of me. I added a bit of cheese, flipped one side of the omelet over the other, spooned on a small amount of salsa, and breakfast was ready.

"Bon appetite," I said, handing Micah a plate with his half of the omelet.

"It feels great to have someone wait on me for a change. Living alone, I'm used to doing everything myself."

"The eggs taste alright?" I asked.

"Just right," Micah said in between bites.

We cleared the plates and loaded the few dishes in the dishwasher. It was raining hard. From the kitchen window the sky appeared dark and foreboding. "You want to go to the mall or something?" Micah said. "We're not going anywhere today. The flea market will be cancelled for sure. It's too far to take a chance. We can turn on the weather channel, but it doesn't look too promising."

"Mind if I see the rest of your house while I'm here?"

"Might as well. Do you want a tour guide?"

"That would be nice."

"I just have to keep an eye on the basement every once in awhile. If it starts leaking, I have to catch it right away. This house is prone to flooding. So, my dear, the official tour begins in the kitchen. To your right is the oven, and to your left is the sink. I keep pots and pans in the cupboards under the sink, and dishes and glasses in the ones above the sink."

"And how much cooking do you do in your kitchen, Mr. Marlowe?"

"I do a lot of cooking, even though it's just a couple things. I make great pizza and spaghetti, and mashed potatoes ... whole pot at a time. One of these days I'll make them for you, with plenty of butter and mayonnaise."

"You put mayonnaise in your mashed potatoes? With the butter? That sounds awful."

"You've never had mashed potatoes with mayonnaise? You don't know what you're missing. Right through here is where I do all my formal entertaining, like when I have someone over for pizza or Chinese carry outs."

"From what I saw in your refrigerator you must do quite a bit of 'formal' entertaining."

"Har-de-har."

The dining room was right off the kitchen and furnished with antiques. A Victorian china closet with intricately carved designs was the focal piece of the room. The table was made from the same dark walnut, as were the chairs, and while massive in size not as ornately carved as the china chest. The walls were painted dark red, with clear acrylic stripes painted on top for a softening effect. Framed photos of ocean scenes graced either side of the chest. They were breathtaking. "These are great pictures. Where were these taken?"

"I took this one in Eleuthera and this one in Honduras, by my favorite tree. If you look closely, you can see the roots of the mangrove tree coming up out of the water, or into, I guess."

"I like how you caught the sunset in the middle of the branches."

"Thank you, my dear. And this is my fish room," Micah said leading me to his living room.

In sharp contrast to the other two rooms, the living room walls and carpet were a stark white. Flanked on both sides by chairs covered in varied shades of sand, the camel-back sofa matched the colors of the walls and carpet, the brocade fabric softening the white-on-white apperanace. Glass and green copper end tables matched the coffee table, and a lighted étagère on the opposite wall was entirely of glass. Two batiks of tropical fish hung over the white couch, a light behind illuminating the brilliant sea colors. Glass dolphins by Frebel sat on the glass coffee table next to enameled and ceramic pastel-colored angel and parrotfish.

"Did you see these?" Micah directed me over to the étagère. "More megalodon teeth like you saw in my classroom, only these are in perfect shape. Look how big these are. Found these diving in Florida rivers."

Next to the teeth were nautilus shells and a large basket sponge. The other shelves harbored more shells, most notably a king and queen helmet, a starfish, and a carved parrot from Costa Rica.

"I got this knife in Honduras. It's carved out of jade. I can't even guess how old it is. One of the old natives I met sold it to me. When I bought it, I thought he must have carved it, but when I got home and looked at it carefully, I could see that it is real old. Could date back to the Mayans."

"It's beautiful," I said. "This whole room is beautiful ... The soft colors of the shells seem to shine against the white walls and glass. I feel like I'm in a prism."

"That's a good way to describe this room. I tried to give it the feel of being under the ocean. It reminds me of a prism under the Caribbean. You really should go diving with us over winter break. You can still go, one of the kids cancelled and I need to fill his space."

"I could never dive. I have too many water phobias to even consider it."

"Once you get under there, it's so beautiful that you forget about your fears."

"Maybe for most people, but not for me. What's downstairs?"

"The library and den. We should go down there anyway to check for leaks."

I followed Micah down a short stairway. Heavy dark curtains covered the entry way to the room, and Micah carefully held them to one side as he waved me into his den. Shelves overflowing with artifacts lined one long wall, while the opposite wall held built-in cabinets filled with books. A large stone fireplace graced the center of the room facing the curtained stairs, an oil painting of the Tennessee River hanging above it. The painting was a scene of the river as it flowed through Chattanooga. Micah told me he had been diving in that exact spot many times. Next to the fireplace stood an iron sculpture of an Indian maiden, and a blue leather couch and cluttered coffee table sat in front of the room's only window. From a distance the coffee table looked as if it were made entirely of wood, but it had a glass top with drawers underneath. The glass enclosed Micah's most precious artifacts: Dutch trade beads, Spanish coins and belt buckles, Civil War buttons, flint arrowheads in perfect condition, and women's jeweled hair combs from the De Soto period.

"It looks like a goddamned museum in here," I said.

Micah laughed. "I found everything in this case and on the shelves, most of it legally, too. There are spots in Alabama and Georgia where you can keep what you find in the river. I just take my chances in Tennessee."

"I would think you might respect the rights of the Indians and not disturb their culture."

"I'm keeping their culture alive. Who is going to see the beauty of their artwork if it is buried in mud under the rivers? Look at this pot

I found. It's in perfect shape—it has to be thousands of years old. I bring it to school every once in awhile to show the kids. I found it sticking out of the riverbank. It would've been a waste for it to go undiscovered. Damn. It's raining hard. You stay here and mosey around, I have to check for leaks."

Micah gone, I felt like a kid in a candy store. There was so much to see I did not know where to begin. Like a magnet, the first place I was drawn to was his books. He had an interesting and eclectic mix of history, science and romance. The titles included *The Prehistoric Indians of the Southwest, The Ascent of Man, Dr. Zhivago,* and *The Life and Times of Einstein.* The complete works of Charles Dickens, all published in 1890, yellowed and brittle with age, appeared as if they would fall apart if you touched them. Leaning against volumes of *Little Dorrit* and *Hard Times,* another old publication caught my eyes. It was thin with a red leather cover. From the large print on curled pages and a few scattered pictures of Indians, I could tell it was a children's book. The name on the cover was *Singing Guns,* the author Max Brand.

"Look at the inscription inside the front cover." Micah was standing so close to me I could feel his breath on my hair. I turned to the inside cover, and written in ink was the name William Faulkner.

"This book was owned by Faulkner when he was busy writing in Mississippi."

"Oh, how wonderful! Where did you get this?" When I turned to face Micah, he was so close that my body touched his. We were in a hug without the arms. He stared at me for so long I thought he was going to kiss me. Instead, he moved away and told me that a friend who was a distant cousin of Faulkner gave his mother the book. She in turn gave the book to Micah, since Faulkner was his favorite author.

"This is an interesting sketch," I said. I was referring to a pen-and-ink of an old man standing in what appeared to be a dust storm. His face was lined, his hand resting on his cheek. "Who did this?"

"I did," Micah said. "It's my grandfather, or what I remember of him. He died before I really got to know him. He was a Georgia peanut farmer, but not rich like the Carters. He had a hard time making ends meet, according to my Mama. There were eight kids in her family for him to feed."

"I can't believe you paint, too. What else do you do that I don't know about? Man, this is really good. Your grandfather's face looks hardened, but his eyes look compassionate."

"I painted these Indians also," he said, leading me to a portrait just to the left of the steps. "The headdress was the hardest part."

"What about these roses? They're beautiful but obviously not your work." I was almost certain he did not do this painting. Brushed in soft shades of pink watercolors, the roses were delicate and very feminine. The petals had the fragile translucency of fine china.

"I just did those last week," he replied.

"No kidding. They seem so ... emotional. You must be in love," I teased.

"I have a lot of love to give, but no one to give it to. So I paint instead. I have a bunch more upstairs. I'll show you sometime."

"Have you tried to sell any of it?"

"No, I just paint for myself. I give pictures away to special people in my life. Mom's got a few."

Micah's momentary sweetness touched me. I wanted to embrace him, but was not sure how he would react if I did. Instead, I changed the subject to more comfortable ground.

"Did you find any water creeping in?" I asked.

"No, not yet. I better call Mom to let her know we're not going. She worries about the weather more than anyone I know."

"It's no wonder after her experience with tornados."

Left alone in the room again, I was free to browse through Micah's collections. Tucked amidst all the books were ginger beer bottles, old inkwells, iron cowboy boots, an African mask, painted feathers, not to mention hundreds of cased arrow points and ancient Indian tools and cookware. He also had an old Civil War knapsack sitting beside his collection of cannon balls and swords from the same era. Curious to see inside the knapsack, I undid the buckle and opened up the top. The only thing inside was a folded piece of notepaper from modern times. I could hear Micah still talking to his mother, so I went ahead and unfolded the note. It was a letter written to Micah dated 1979.

Dear Mr. Marlowe,

Thank you so much for attending William's funeral. You were by far his favorite teacher. He talked about you every day and loved you not only as a teacher, but also as a friend and a coach. He did not think he had much to hope for in life until he was in your class and on your team. One of the only trips he took was the fossil-digging trip to Columbus, Georgia. He talked about that trip for two months. He also talked about your classroom jokes and all the extra things you showed the kids in class. He never looked at a star in the sky until he met you.

I noticed how you had your head in your hands at the funeral. It was not your fault what happened. I don't know why he left without you. If he had stayed, he would still be alive. I have tried my best to do right by him, but as a single mother, I could not afford to live in a very good neighborhood. I tried to protect William from the bad ones here, but I could only do so much. I just wanted to let you know how much you meant to my son.

Forever grateful,
Hattie Jones.

I was holding the letter in my hands when Micah came down the short flight of stars.

"What happened to William?" I asked.

"William who? What are you reading?" Micah grabbed the letter from my hand. When he saw what it was, his face and neck turned red. "Where'd you get this? I had this put away. It's very private."

"It was in your Civil War knapsack."

"I can't leave you alone for a minute without you poking your nose where it doesn't belong. Do you always go looking inside people's things?"

"I just wanted to see what was inside the knapsack," I said. "I wasn't trying to stick my nose in your private affairs."

"I had forgotten all about this letter. Even where I put it. I guess I better find a safer place for it." Micah had calmed down and the redness left his neck. I felt a bit indignant at his reaction, however.

"Micah, I really wasn't trying to snoop around. I can't believe you think so little of me."

"I don't. It's just that I seldom let anybody into my world ... "

"Why me?"

"You seemed like you'd understand."

"Understand what?"

"Me, I guess."

"Well, if that's how you feel, then tell me about the letter."

"No, not now." He turned to the bookcase. "You still haven't seen all my souvenirs from the Olympics and the mastodon bones my buddy Beau and I found last year."

For the rest of the morning, Micah taught me about his collected world that ranged from agatized coral spearpoints to back molars of wooly mammoths. Then when the rain finally stopped, around noon, he asked if I wanted to see the baby bats in his attic.

"Bats? I don't think so. They give me the creeps. I'm afraid they'll fly in my hair."

"Bats are harmless—they help keep the pesky insects away. They're also important pollinators. You must have had some old aunt tell you an old wife's tale about bats getting into your hair. They don't bother with us humans much. And besides, they are *major* cool."

"Don't they carry rabies?"

"Hardly ever. You'd sooner die from a dog bite or bee sting than from a rabid bat bite."

Not knowing what to expect, I followed Micah upstairs and watched as he pulled the attic ladder down. Once we creaked our way up, the ceiling was so low, we had to walk with our heads down through the insulation and slats of wood to the far end by the windows. Hanging upside down by their hind feet were about fifteen baby bats inside the two attic windows. They made tiny squeaks as we came near them. "They're actually kind of cute," I began to say.

"Shhhh ... Don't make any noise. You'll scare them," Micah whispered. We squatted down in silence and watched the babies. We were close enough to see their silky gray fur and short pig-like faces. Their tiny ears turned slightly in our direction, letting us know they were aware of our presence. After awhile, my legs grew tired and I almost lost my balance. Micah indicated for me to lean against him, and when I did, he put his arm around me. We held each other for a long time in what seemed like suspended motion. Micah helped me see the beauty in creatures I once thought were ugly. I felt warm and whole in his arms, and could have stayed there forever. I turned to face him and slowly let my lips touch his. It was barely a whisper of a kiss. He slid his hands over my hair and tugged on the ends. "We better get going," he said. "The rain has finally stopped. We might be able to make it to the flea market and back before you need to go to your party."

"Micah?"

"Yes, Catherine."

"Thanks for showing me the bats. And thanks for showing me everything."

In the truck, we were again just friends hanging out for the day, buddies from work who liked to do things together. We safely pretended there was nothing more. The truth is we were in love, but too frightened to become lovers.

Chapter 13

Monday morning, Micah stopped by my classroom and invited me to ride to North Carolina with him and his parents for the Saturday after Thanksgiving. At first I thought it was an odd request since he knew I was married and had college-age children. But then I really did not act like a married woman around Micah. I rarely talked about my children and never talked about Marshall. Marshall was seldom home and when he was, he never answered the phone. Micah said once he would like to see where I lived, but I had not yet invited him over. With Micah I was in a world apart from my troubled past. I did not want any sadness intruding on the time I spent with him, so I kept my private life under wraps. I honestly could see how Micah would think that I was only pretending to be married.

"We're going to Franklin for the day. Might stop at my cousins'. We'll go down to the mine to look for rubies. Want to go? You could find something good."

"Are they married?"

"Who?"

"Your cousins. And don't say 'to each other.'"

"They were for awhile. Both wives died, so they moved in together. They live way out in the woods and carve some of the most beautiful bowls and furniture in the Southeast. I thought you might want to see some of it."

"Sounds like fun. I hate to miss out, but … "

"We go panning for rubies when we go up there. Earl knows just the right spots to find them. Last year I found a really nice sized one for Mom. Sometimes you find a few good sapphires up there, too."

"You find both rubies and sapphires?"

"They are actually the same rock. Rubies are red sapphires, you know. We're going to leave before sunup Saturday morning, if you want to go."

"I can't go. We made plans in August to go to Kiawah Island with the Johnsons. We already paid our deposit on the condo and the kids are flying down to be with us. I don't think they would understand if I changed my plans and drove up to Tennessee with you. But Micah … thanks for inviting me."

I wanted to say so much more, but I felt awkward and embarrassed. I think he felt awkward as well. We were like two adolescents unsure of how to share our emotions. Plus, how much emotion can a single man show a married woman and still stay within the realm of gentlemanly behavior? And how much can a married woman express her feelings to a single man when she has no intention of leaving her husband? So things stayed the way they were and Micah said goodbye and walked back to his portable.

The days before Thanksgiving were busy, but we did manage to hunt for artifacts once. Micah heard of a new spot near Kennesaw from Bobby and was eager to try it out. So the Tuesday before break, Micah and I teamed up again in his gray truck. He took me to a low-lying area close to the highway. This site had not been scraped like most of the others; instead the earth was tilled, a farm field. Fallen logs lay across the red clay and the stubbles of grass. As my eyes searched through the dirt, I found mostly rocks, even though there were a few signs of quartz or flint chips, possible artifacts. If there were pottery sherds to be found, neither Micah nor I were finding them. It appeared as if the long drive out to Kennesaw was for naught. When dusk crept over the horizon, Micah suggested we start back to the truck. "Bobby must have found everything. Look at these piles of rocks over here. Bobby's mark. He always puts his chips and pieces into neat little stacks—he even left us a cigarette butt. It's a Virginia Slim. Must be him."

"You hear that noise? It keeps getting louder. "

"That's just tree frogs. They get louder as the sun goes down. C'mere, I'll catch one. Be quiet, and stay right behind me."

We walked down a gentle slope and into a bog surrounded by trees. Shrill voices vibrated into a fast series of repetitious notes. The sounds became so piercing and loud I covered my ears. "Don't do that," Micah said. "Let yourself get used to the sounds. It's rare to hear so many at once. You are experiencing a miracle."

I followed Micah alongside a fallen tree just past the edge of the swampy pond. Crispy brown cattails were ready to burst into an explosion of seeds, the slightest wind ready to send hundreds spiraling away in invisible eddies. As Micah inched forward with the stealth of a cottonmouth, I stood still and listened to the overpowering cries of nature's constant tambourine. Micah, now straddling the log, scooted and pulled himself further out. He stopped and examined the underside of each overhanging tree limb or water frond. Lost in the sounds of the tree frogs, I was caught-off guard when Micah held out his hand to me.

"Here."

"I don't see anything."

"In my palm. Look."

In the dimming light I had not noticed the creature in Micah's hand. When I looked again, I saw a tiny frog with an equally tiny pulsating throat.

"You're telling me something *that* little makes all that noise?"

"He's one of hundreds. Hold him." I took the amphibian into my hand and felt his rough, wet skin. "You are such a cute little fellow." The words barely left my lips and the small frog jumped out of my hand.

"He had enough of you right quick. Let's sit and listen." So Micah and I sat on a thick old log in the middle of a swamp listening to the sounds. As dusk darkened into night, their voices became a high-pitched chorus, like the strings of the moon-shaped mandolin and Beijing fiddle in a Chinese opera.

"If you pay attention, nature gives the best performances, free of charge," Micah commented. The sounds grew louder with each moment we were quiet. A few lonely stars graced the autumn sky, and the soft night breeze wavered on the pale of coolness.

My hands were cold and I pushed them in the pockets of my well-worn navy blazer. Buried underneath the torn lining was a heavy square of folded paper that I curiously pulled out. Notebook paper, probably an old grocery list, or forgotten quiz, I thought as I unfolded it. And then in a flash, it came back to me. The note I had found on the desk early in the school year. I had hurriedly tucked it into this same old blazer I carried with me everywhere. I had meant to follow up on its message, but forgot. The words stung as I read them a second time ... her father ... her teacher ... The handwriting seemed familiar ... but then again not. By now, I could easily discern my students' handwriting, but this one was strange, not one of mine. Maybe she ... couldn't be a he ... passed it on to one of my students, and it dropped on a desk in my portable. A quirk of fate. Am I to search for this person? Help her? I quickly put it away, because to find her and ferret out her pain would be to bring up my own all over again.

"What ya reading?" Micah asked.

"Nothing. An old grocery list. It's funny to read the items I needed a year ago. You can learn a lot about people from grocery lists. Like whether they are young or old, overweight or anorexic. Psychologists should study grocery lists."

"You sure are talking a lot about grocery lists. Let me see that."

"Nope. It's disappeared already. Mmmmm. I love this ... the listening ... makes you feel like there is nothing else."

"So, like what you hear?" Micah whispered.

"Yes, I do. It's so great." I could feel his smile in the dark. "Micah."

"I'm right here."

"I wish I could stay here forever. Maybe I'll come back as a tree frog in my next life."

"You'd like that, wouldn't you? Sitting in your favorite tree singing all night."

"Why'd you say that?"

"Which part?"

"Singing. You've never heard me sing. I can't carry a tune, you know."

"It just fit with you somehow."

"Micah, do you ever feel like you may have known me before?"

"Before what?"

"I don't know, maybe in a previous life. Maybe we were related—brother and sister, or mother and son or good friends. Something seems familiar about you."

Micah placed his hand gently under my chin and quietly laughed. "Cat, I feel like I've known you all my life or lives." With that, Micah abruptly stood up on the log. "It's getting late. We've got papers to grade."

"Micah, I need help getting up. Could you give me a hand?"

"If I help you, we might both go in. Hold on to the tree limb."

Disgruntled, I grabbed the tree limb and clumsily pulled myself up. I knew he was right of course; we could have fallen in. But on the other hand, we both could have ended up in each other's arms. The moment had passed, however, so we quietly rode back to Alpharetta in the truck and gave each other a polite hug before we went home.

"Have a good Thanksgiving," I yelled just before I shut my car door. He either did not hear me, or did not feel the need to respond. At any rate, I did not see him again until after Thanksgiving, a Thanksgiving that would ultimately lead me into deep waters.

#

That night I stared at the puffer for a long, long time. He was so still, I was worried he was dead. "Wake up, time to wake up, puffer fish," I whispered, tapping on the glass. Startled, the puffer swam furiously around the tank until he finally settled on the bottom. He clacked his teeth to protest the disturbance of his slumber.

#

"You have one string left on your finger … what did you forget to do?"

"Ah didn't forget nothing. That's for reminding me to meet you."

"Are you remembering to make your lists everyday … and making pictures in your mind so you don't forget what your daddy tells you to do?"

"You sound just like my mama." He beamed at the red-headed girl. "My daddy hasn't had to whip me ever since you taught me them memory tricks. He even said maybe ah'm getting some sense after all."

"Well, let's see if you remember how to read. I sneaked this book out of my Auntie's house, so be careful when you turn the pages. She's only switched me once, and that was one more than I want."

She placed The Complete Works of William Shakespeare in David's lap.

"The … Com … plete. Complete works of … Will … William Shake …"

"Sound the last syllable out." She covered up "Shake" and pointed to "speare."

"Sp … ear … spear … Shakespeare! The Complete Works of William Shakespeare! Our teacher told us about him. He writes plays, don't he?"

"He wrote plays. He's been dead for over two hundred years."

"What'd he write about?"

"Mostly people's tragic flaws. If you think too much, or love too much, or want too much, you will die a horrible death."

"Then yer going to die one horrible death. You think way more'n you need to."

"You only think too much if thinking keeps you from doing anything. Shakespeare wrote about people who went to extremes. They didn't do anything else but think. It's like if I sat on the sofa all day and didn't eat, play, talk, read – just sat and thought all day long."

"Ah'd want to kill you, if you did that."

"You are going to read about a man who wanted too much. He lived in Scotland about a million years ago, and he wanted to be the king of Scotland, so he killed his cousin."

"That ain't right to kill kin. Who'd want to read that?"

"Lots of folks. And he had a really evil wife. She said she would smash her baby's brains out to become queen."

"Well, those folks are crazy. Her husband should have taken her out."

"But her husband was afraid of her."

"Just like my Uncle Burl is afraid of my Aunt Lounette."

"Their names are Macbeth and Lady Macbeth."

"Mac … beth." He rolled the name around on his tongue.

"We're going to act it out. I'll assign the parts as we go along. Since there's only two of us, we have to play a lot of parts, but I'll be Lady MacBeth and you can be MacBeth. Hermann said there's an opera about MacBeth, so maybe we can sing some of the parts."

"Ohhhhhhhh, MaaaaacBeeeeeth, kiiiiiillll yooooooor kiiiiin sooooo youuuuuu can beeeeee kiiiing!" David sang his exaggerated version of an operatic voice.

The twelve-year-old girl fell on the ground laughing. She joined in the silliness. "Ohhhhhhh Maaaaacbeeeeeeth, I willlll beeeeeee soooooo haaaaaaappeee if ahhhhhhhhhh weeeeerrrr queeeeen!" she trilled in a falsetto voice. They sang their made-up version of Macbeth, dancing far into the tobacco fields, the book forgotten.

The sound of thunder brought them back to the old barn. "If that book gets wet, Aunt Sally will kill me!" Nellie said. She grabbed the book, and they both ran into the barn before the rains came. They climbed the steps to the comfort of the high loft and sat facing each other with their knees touching. The good smell of hay mixed with the dusty odor of chickens. Knives of light came through the loft door and through the cracks and knotholes of the barn siding.

"I copied something from the printed news that my daddy sometimes brings home. Do you want me to read it to you?"

"Okay."

He pulled a scrap of folded paper out of his back pocket. The words scrawled across the page in blue ink, smeared blots making the print almost illegible. "If you go as far as you can see, then you can see further," David read. "Written by a Mister Thomas Carlyle."

"What's the farthest you can see?"

"I can see way 'cross the tobacca fields to the edge of the land. But no matter how far I go I can never get to it. 'Sort of like chasin' a rainbow – you just can't seem to find the end or the beginning."

"Mama says that if I work hard enough on my music, I will know more than Hermann. I cried when she told me I have to stay permanently at his school next year; I can only come home holidays. Someday I will sing so well that I can travel all over the world and won't have to ever see Hermann again."

"How come you have to stay at that school, if it's so close to your house?"

"Hermann told Mama that he can't teach me all he knows unless I stay all the time. He has students from all over. Mama says I need to be with all the other students so I can be better than them. She says I have the talent to sing opera even in New York and Paris someday."

"You sure can brag on yourself enough. I told you once 'fore you was so smart you could ... "

"Don't say it! I'm not bragging. I don't mind if I end up as an opera star when I'm thirty; I just wish I didn't have to start trying to be great right now."

"Does Hermann still hang you in the closet if you can't 'member words?"

Nellie put the end of her auburn pigtail in her mouth. "Hermann does bad things." She abruptly stood up and threw hay in David's face.

"What are you doing?" David grabbed Nellie and held her down on the floor of the loft. He took a handful of hay from the bale behind him and stuffed it down the back of her dress. She squealed with laughter as she wriggled from beneath him and scrambled for more hay to throw. They wrestled until they were worn out from the game.

As she lay breathlessly in the hay, she noticed the unfolded paper David had read from earlier. "These words," she said. "I think it has something to do with the future. I can see what I'm going to do with my future. What can you see?"

"I thought I was going to see readin' in my future," he said.

"'Screw your courage to the sticking place,'" she quoted. "Here, you can be the first witch, and I'll be the second and the third."

"'When shall we three meet again.
In thunder, lightning or in rain?' "

They both laughed gleefully as clouds on the horizon coincidentally flashed and rumbled.

"'When the hurley burley's done.

"When the battle's lost and won.'"

"'That will be ere the set of sun,'" Nellie cackled and screeched her lines.

"' Where the place,'" continued the first witch.

"'Upon the heath,'" said the second.

"'There to meet with MacBeth,'" added the third.

"'Fair is foul and foul is fair: Hover through the filthy air,'" the witches chanted together.

David and Nellie read and sang the first seven scenes of Macbeth for the rest of the rainy afternoon. Shadows had moved undetected across the floor of the barn as dusk approached. David jumped up and pulled Nellie to the long ladder. "I told Pa I'd bring in the cows before dark. I don't want him to be thinking I done lost my good sense already." He leaped down the ladder, leaving Nellie at the top to find her own way down with her large volume of Shakespeare.

"You were supposed to give me a kiss for teaching you, remember?" Her words were left on the barn walls, as David was already in the cow fields. Sadly, she climbed down the ladder, and started to walk across the tobacco fields that led to Aunt Sally's gray clapboard house. The horizon yawned pink and gold across the stretch of Kentucky farmland. Nellie felt the slip of paper in her pocket. She leaned her head back to see as much of the sky as she could. "Please God, make Hermann stop," she prayed to the Composer of Horizons. The scrawled words fell out of her pocket as she ran as fast as she could to her inescapable future.

Chapter 14

The car packed with a twenty-pound turkey, cranberries, yams and enough wine and hard liquor to service an entire platoon of soldiers, we started the six-hour trek to Kiawah Island. Not far behind us were the Johnson's in their navy blue limited edition Navigator, carrying their only child in the back seat. Ashley, a quiet, rather brooding adolescent, looked more like a twenty-year-old college student than a freshman in high school. She was Debra's daughter, Neil's boarder. When they were first married Neil wanted little to do with Debra's gawky ten year-old daughter. Interestingly enough, now that Ashley appeared to be turning into the possibility of a sensual woman, Neil started taking frequent glances at the child and more often than before would go out of his way to do small favors for her. He recently began taking her out for driving lessons, especially when Debra was off playing tennis in one of her several leagues. Yet there was something captivating about Neil, and I liked him more than any of the other men in the neighborhood. He maintained that if he had married me his first time around, he and I would still be married. I told Neil one Sunday morning, flying up the highway in his silver Jag, he would never have chosen me in the first place. Granted, I had my issues, but unlike his array of women, I appreciated life outside the walls. Death and bedlam make hard teachers, but they are good ones. Even though I hid behind money, I was not impressed by it. The few times he caught me trying to find God in a far-off star, he couldn't quite figure out how the woman I was then could be the same woman who went alone with him to Beaver Creek.

The year before, all four of us planned a trip to Beaver Creek for spring break. Neil owned a condo overlooking the mountains and knew Marshall and I loved to ski, so it was only natural that he invited us. A few days before the trip, Marshall had to fly to Hong Kong to put out some corporate fire, and Debra's mother suddenly became ill. I already had my ticket and new ski boots, so I went anyway. If Marshall had asked I would have told him Debra did not go with us on the trip, but he was so worn out after his trip to China, he didn't even bring it up. I don't know what Neil told Debra.

The first night together in Beaver Creek, Neil thought it was funny when I suggested fixing a meal in the condo rather than dining out. "You got to be kidding. With all the great restaurants around here? You're on vacation. We're going to take a sleigh ride to the top of the mountain tonight and have dinner in the stars." Neil could not understand why I wanted to cook. I guess that comes from marrying trophy wives who love to sit on shelves all day. I guess that is why I could never (ahem) "do" him. So why did I go to Colorado with a married man who was attracted to young women with skinny bodies and big tits? I guess because he was honest about how screwed-up his life was, and he was intellectual enough to support and understand why I had a hard time living with my lies. Ironically, he helped me out of my despairing desert even though Neil himself was trapped in an arid wasteland of dry intellectualism. And, later, after I started going rattin' around with Micah, and my liquid spirit started to emerge, I knew I had to leave the infertile valley of scarecrows and hollow men. I wanted to be with Micah, not Neil, and immerse myself in breathing waters and sensuous soil in order to stay moist and alive.

The first morning in the mountains, Neil and I were on the slopes by eight. We skied until one, had lunch, and then skied together until the late afternoon. As we were coming off the slopes for the final time, two perfectly coiffed women in designer ski outfits were waiting for us (really Neil) at the bar outside the Hyatt. They appeared as if they spent all day primping. I really wished Neil had warned me they were coming. I at least would have put a comb and lipstick in my pockets. So, exhausted, carrying boots, skis, poles and goggles, I had to face collagen-puffed lips dripping with red gloss. And not only that, I had helmet hair. I thought for a minute about putting my hat on again and pulling it down over my entire face. Instead, I ordered a resort drink called apple pie a-la-mode. It was strong enough to make me forget I even had hair, much less helmet hair.

We sipped our drinks around the crowded stone fire pit. I lost myself in the liquid apple pie, full of rum and whipped cream, while the rest of the group tossed down martinis. One of the breast-enhanced women, I think her name was Ginger, suggested we go back to Neil's place and drink champagne in the hot tub. By the time we got back to the villa, I had had enough apple pie to make subtle jokes about Neil's prime cuts. Before I submerged myself in the hot tub, I enlarged my lips with artistically applied red lipstick, and once in the water, I could not help but notice the buoyancy of the two women. They could not keep their breasts under the water. My own breasts, no small change, hovered just beneath the surface. Directing my scientific finding to Neil, I told him I thought it was interesting saline sacs do not sink. I then started an analytical discussion about the differences between the old silicone sacs and the new saline ones, and whether one felt better than the other. I supposed I would like the feel of salt water ones over gooey silicone breasts. The girls indicated that theirs, at least, would never sag, and I took offense, since mine were no banana pancakes. "If you see any sags in these, you two are hallucinating. Neil, tell me the truth, can men actually get a boner feeling a bag of saltwater?" Neil kissed me to shut me up, and then we all started laughing because Neil's mouth was all red from my overindulgence with lipstick. Not too long after that the girls went home, and I all but passed out in my bed.

I had a hard time getting up the next day for ten more hours of skiing. I begged Neil not to invite those aberrations of womanhood over again. Neil said he would not dream of inviting them over ever again when I was around. My creativity was an embarrassment to him. I told him I was just trying to disturb the universe.

It was hard to believe another year had passed as we rambled down the road towards the South Carolina coast. After five hours of driving, we finally arrived at Cove's Point, the furthest point of West Isle Dunes. The real estate agent I used swore the condo was the best one on Cove's Point, and she was right if she were talking about the view. We had a sweeping panorama of ocean and sky with a glimpse of Vandervorst Island off in the distance. As beautiful as the setting was, the décor in the two-story condo paired East Coast flamingo with used and tattered Mediterranean. And the condo was not in the best shape. The wallpaper was unraveling in the kitchen, the dishwasher did not work, and the inside of the oven appeared as if it had not been cleaned in years. Neil suggested we could estimate the age of the oven by counting the grease rings. Debra ignored the oven and chose to complain about the large hole in the wall next to the chipped marble fireplace. Marshall and I suggested Debra and Neil take the master bedroom and bath, since we sensed they were disappointed in the ambience of the place. Coming out of the master bath, Debra pitched a fit about the missing tiles in the shower stall and the peeling linoleum on the floor. I was extremely apologetic. In hindsight, I should have told her to find a room at the Ritz and stare at the white sheets of a massage table if that is the type of Thanksgiving she craved. Marshall, Elizabeth and I unpacked in the two bedrooms upstairs; we gave Elizabeth the room with the view, plus it was bigger, and Sammy and his girlfriend, flying in on Thanksgiving Day, would be more comfortable in the room next to hers.

By the time we made our way downstairs, we noticed Debra already had emptied a bottle of wine. At least it was not a jug, I thought.

"Didn't you say this was the deluxe condo? I wonder what the other places look like."

Grabbing a glass of wine for survival, I suggested we take a walk along the beach and carry the crabbing net and bucket with us to catch part of our dinner in the grasses under the pier. Debra and Ashley by our sides, Elizabeth and I headed out, leaving Marshall and Neil to catch the end of the first of the many football games that Thanksgiving weekend. We could see Vanderhorst Island across the bay, and I reflected how I wished I could be over there with the descendents of the Gullah people. Debra, at the beginning of her routine evening buzz, talked nostalgically about how she and Neil came down the year before to shop for a beach house on West Isle, and decided to buy a villa with a boat dock so that when they purchase their yacht, they could sail to Bimini or Jamaica. I listened half-heartedly knowing her marriage to Neil was anything but secure. I thought about Robb Lyman's fortieth birthday party and how Debra got so drunk, she crawled under the table at Rio Bravo's and mouthed Robb's penis over his khakis. Neil was so mad he smashed his martini glass on the table and left. Debra screamed that he was an asshole, and the maitre'd kicked our entire table of twelve adults out of the restaurant. I later tried to talk to Debra about the incident, but she refused to acknowledge that it was even a concern for her. She had to. She had no means of support. Besides, Neil provided her with a life she never dreamed she could have—an expensive home in the suburbs, skiing in Beaver Creek, fancy golf and tennis clubs, and the sadistic pleasure of looking down her nose at people. Debra, with her perfect bought breasts, long legs, tanned face, and blonde hair often embarrassed me when dealing with the various workmen she employed to take care of her house. She was rude, cold, and mocking whenever the gardener or painter or pool cleaner asked to use her phone or requested a glass of water. She even refused the laborers the use of her bathrooms.

She also knew she was a bought woman. Neil must have felt cheated when he realized her underlying personality was dark and sarcastic due in part to her chronic problem with alcohol. She really was a miserable drunk. I cannot think of one man who met Neil and Debra who envied Neil because of her. If anything, most men pitied Neil and took bets on when he would finally leave her. For a while, I tried desperately to help Debra. I suggested she read more and keep up with the news. "Your marriage to Marshall is different. He married you because he loved you; he did not try to buy you," she would say. She was right, Marshall did marry me because he loved me, before I graduated from college, before he was making any real money, but the circumstances were different from what most people knew. It took me years before I told anyone the real story of Marshall and me.

We only caught one small crab that Ashley decided to let go, but we had bought plenty of crab earlier from one of the old fish markets just down the road a couple of miles. Debra seemed upbeat and friendly when we arrived back at the villa and seemed excited to make our first night's dinner of gazpacho and crab cakes. Neil fixed his special Bloody Marys made with horseradish while Debra and I picked apart fresh crab legs and chopped vegetables. Debra downed almost an entire bottle of merlot at dinner, but the conversation was amicable, light and even funny. Debra could be gregarious and an excellent storyteller before she consumed that one glass of wine that sent her over the edge into abusive humor and dark sarcasm. We made the mistake of playing euchre after Debra had that one glass too many. Elizabeth was my partner, while Ashley was Debra's. Debra continually criticized Ashley's every move throughout the game and accused Elizabeth of cheating. With angry tears, Elizabeth left the table, the game over. Ashley, humiliated by her mother's behavior, ran out the backdoor. I followed Elizabeth to her room with the hope to offer consolation and salvage the rest of the evening. Eventually, Elizabeth came downstairs and we watched an unassuming movie about a St. Bernard. No one spoke in more than monosyllabic words. Debra smirked while twirling her wine glass in her hand. I thought I heard her whisper to Neil about a whiney little brat. Not soon enough, the movie was over, and I kissed Elizabeth good night, and after noticing Ashley's lost stare, I reached over Elisabeth and kissed Ashley goodnight as well. I knew immediately that I had made a mistake. Drunken beyond control, Debra screamed that I was never to kiss her daughter, that she was raising Ashley to be tough, not weak and overly sensitive like Elizabeth. Neil came immediately to the rescue, dragging the now-crazed Debra to bed. He shrugged at the rest of us as he did so. It was only Wednesday. I told Marshall and Elizabeth that things were bound to get better. I should have taken charge immediately and sent the three of them packing that first night. But it was the time of Thanksgiving, a time for soft hearts and ample forgiveness. I had faith I could ease the tension and juggle everyone's behavior so we could enjoy the rest of the holidays.

The next morning, Neil and Debra, trim and fit in tight athletic pants and matching Lycra tops, laced up their roller blades and cheerfully wished us a happy Thanksgiving. Neil did a good job of keeping up with his thirty-five-year old wife. They skated for over an hour and returned flushed and laughing. I did notice Debra was slightly out of breath and wondered if Neil noticed the dark circles under her eyes. You might want to watch the drinking, Debra, I thought. Neil goes shopping for new merchandise when his wives start to look their age. I was a little on edge when they returned to the villa, not wanting to relive the previous evening's debacle. Yet no one mentioned a word about it, and even though I thought it extremely odd that they acted as if nothing out of the ordinary had happened, I also was relieved. We had a fairly uneventful rest of the morning, Elizabeth, Marshall, and I taking long walks on the beach, Ashley reading on the screened-in porch, Debra fooling around with her pies and stuffing. Mid-afternoon, Neil and Marshall planted themselves on the couches trading football statistics, Debra and I prepared the turkey, and the girls lingered somewhere on the beach. After stuffing the turkey, Debra uncorked the day's first bottle of wine. Elizabeth walked in the door as Debra poured the wine into her glass.

"Can't you wait until at least five o'clock to start drinking? You know how you get." Debra took the dirty dishrag from the sink and threw it as hard as she could in Elizabeth's face.

"Just because your mother lets you talk back to her doesn't mean I have to take your bullshit." Elizabeth ran out of the condo, slamming the door behind her. I ran after her.

"Mom, why don't you say something to her! She is such a bitch."

"If I say anything to her, I will just give her more ammunition to start a fight. I just want us to get through Thanksgiving dinner without a big scene."

"There have already been scenes—last night, today. Why did you invite them to go with us? I hate her!"

"I didn't realize how bad she was. I'm sorry. But Sammy and Jenny are coming in this afternoon and maybe that will take some of the attention away from her. There will be so many people, you won't even have to talk to her, if you don't want to."

"Well, I don't," Elizabeth said emphatically.

Sammy and Jenny arrived an hour later and things seemed to be much better. Debra did make fun of Sammy's dobb kit because he had toothpaste smudges on the outside of it, but he did not seem offended or even to notice her remark for that matter. Right before dinner we all played tennis, a round-robin, until Debra said to Ashley and Elizabeth, "Why don't you girls go back and let the people who really know how to play tennis have the courts."

Ashley's feelings were hurt and I could see the tears welling in her eyes. Elizabeth quickly suggested they go looking for shells and crabs. I left also, leaving Sammy and Debra as partners against Neil and Marshall. Jenny, due to be Neil's partner at the end of the set, abruptly left after ten minutes because she couldn't stand to see the way Debra was flirting with Sammy. She ran to catch up with us.

When the rest of the group showed up at the condo, we opened a bottle of champagne, donned our pilgrim hats and proceeded to enjoy the turkey, dressing, lumpy mashed potatoes, cranberry-walnut salad and an assortment of autumn vegetables. Red and white wines flowed, and we all consumed more wine than we usually would. The cornstalk candles on the table had a short wick and burned out before we finished the meal. We consumed Debra's apple and pumpkin pies with only the reflection of the moon illuminating the table. Debra corkscrewed more bottles while Neil and Marshall poured themselves glasses of brandy. "Do you know how much I paid for these fucking candles?" Debra suddenly flared up against the few minutes of calm. "I paid almost ten dollars a piece for these and they did not even make it through Thanksgiving dinner."

"You didn't even make it through Thanksgiving dinner," I said, the wine loosening my tongue. Before Debra had a chance to respond, Neil abruptly stood up at the table and belched, a signal that the dinner was now over. In the kitchen, Debra donned a pair of black rubber gloves, the synthetic ends ruffled in a red-and-green Christmas plaid.

"Ashley gave me these as a birthday present. Aren't they cute?" Elizabeth and I were thinking the same thing as we watched Mommie Dearest immerse her black rubbery hands in the soapy water. Intently, Debra scrubbed and cleaned the plates before laying them carefully on the drying rack. When Ashley attempted to help dry a dish or put the silverware away, Debra scoffed at her incompetence, and grabbed the dish and cutlery from Ashley's hand, and dried them more vigorously before she carefully put them away. I wondered if she would complain at the way I scoured and rinsed the turkey platter sans gloves. The four of us worked side-by-side in a tense silence. Ashley, Elizabeth and I were miserable. Debra seemed to be enjoying herself. I dismissed the girls when it came time to clean the pots and pans. Debra, loudly slurring her speech, yelled at the girls. "It is only because of Mrs. Scott that you're allowed out of the kitchen. I wouldn't let you off that easy." With that, Debra picked up a handful of leftover dressing and threw it at Elizabeth, most of it missing her.

"You old witch!" Elizabeth yelled, taking a wet dishrag and pushing it in Debra's face. Before Debra could catch her breath, Elizabeth grabbed Ashley and they raced out the door as if they expected Debra to chase them. Recovering herself, Debra poured herself another large glass of wine and proceeded to scour the pans as if nothing happened. She seemed to have no recollection of the previous minutes.

Watching her dry yellow hair and her pursed lips, I thought that indeed she did look like a witch. The thought caused me to start laughing and I could not stop. Tears streamed down my eyes as I assessed the situation. I felt like Mersault after he shot the Arab because the sun was too hot. This Thanksgiving was purposeless, destructive and absurd. The truth is that Debra was a mean drunk and walking on eggs around her was not going to change her behavior. My laughter gave Debra an excuse to break out the hard liquor, and after pouring a large glass of vodka, she obnoxiously declared that we were all going to play euchre. I acquiesced, for what did it matter? A drunk playing euchre is no different from a drunk washing the dishes, or watching a movie, or playing tennis. As in tennis, we switched partners after every game. When the kids came back, they were delegated to the table on the screened-in porch. Initially, Debra and I played Marshall and Neil under the kitchen's florescent glare, while the four kids shuffled and dealt by moonlight. Then somehow Debra and Elizabeth managed to partner against Sammy and Marshall. Debra again was in her mean stage of drunkenness, which also meant that she wanted to win at any cost. My husband and son had also been drinking and neither one of them had any respect left for her. The ensuing scene was inevitable. Every time the opposing team took a trick, Debra eloquently yelled, "Fuck you!" Ashley, on the porch with Jenny, Neil and me, cringed as if hit with a brick at every "Fuck you" from Debra's mouth. Neil became sullen and left the table before we even finished the game. Leaving Jenny and Ashley on the porch, I followed Neil out to the edge of the beach.

"Why don't you do something about her?" I said. "If not for you, then for Ashley."

"Whenever I try to stop her or Ashley, she starts screaming more. It's not worth it; you know what she's like. Remember Robb's birthday party?"

"Then why don't you leave her?"

"She's my third wife. I'm running out of money."

The sound of Debra's laughter echoed along the beach. "Set you, give us two points."

"Excuse me," we heard Sammy say. "That last trick is ours. That's a bower I just laid down. Four points for Dad and me. Ha."

"Fuck you! Fuck you, cheater."

"Fuck you?" Sammy said. "Who would want to fuck you? Not me! Probably no one."

"You're just jealous because your girlfriend has a bigger ass than me!" Debra screamed.

"I can't stand that bitch!" Sammy said as he slammed the door behind him.

Ashley started crying and screamed for us and most of the neighbors to hear, "My mother is always like this! She's always drunk!"

At that point Debra, in her best raging alcoholic form, pushed open the door and slapped Ashley across the face as hard as she could. "You fucking bitch! I am sick and tired of you talking bad about me. You are a spoiled brat! I'll teach you to respect your mother!" She slapped Ashley two more times before Sammy grabbed her arm and pushed her against the porch screen.

"If you touch that little girl one more time, I'll beat the shit out of you." Ashley ran out the door to the beach, Sammy running after her.

"I hate her! I hate her! I'm going to move in with my dad!"

Debra stood blinking uncomprehendingly while I ran after the kids.

"Your mother is the only one who can get through to my mom," Ashley was telling Elizabeth. "Please tell her to talk to her." I grabbed all three children and hugged them until they stopped shaking. I knew I could never talk to Debra again—not while she continued to be such a monster.

We slowly made our way back to the villa, hoping against hope Neil had put Debra to bed. Instead, I found a dazed Debra. "Neil is packing all our stuff. He says we have to leave." In the bedroom, Neil quietly removed all their clothes from the bureau and closet, haphazardly throwing them in suitcases.

I placed my hand on his shoulder. "Neil, we'll bring back whatever you left. Don't worry about packing everything right now."

Neil shook his head. "I'm sorry. I'm so sorry." He made a feeble attempt to smooth things over by offering Sammy his state-of-the-art CD speakers.

"I don't want your speakers, man, but I do think you need to get rid of her. She's a bitch—even before she ripped on my girlfriend." Sammy turned from Neil, tears in his eyes because of the shock of the emotional events.

Five minutes before midnight on Thanksgiving, Neil, Debra, and Ashley drove the five hours home to Atlanta.

"Don't yell at me in the car, Mommy," fourteen-year-old Ashley had repeated over and over. Ashley, who would remain with her mother since her father was far worse; Ashley, who appeared to have every advantage a teenager could have—the best clothes, a beautiful house, tennis lessons, gymnastic lessons, plenty of spending money; Ashley, who would become a varsity cheerleader, a vindictive gossip, a teenage alcoholic, pot addict, and school slut, lived in a secret hell that only my family knew about, and there was nothing (or at least we thought at the time) we could do about it. Two years later Neil finally did leave Debra. He moved permanently to Beaver Creek, and Debra sold the big house in Atlanta. For awhile, I kept in touch with Neil, maybe out of sorrow, maybe out of loyalty, but most likely out of a morbid sense of curiosity. When I heard he married a nineteen-year-old and was paying her way through college, I stopped answering his phone calls and e-mails.

A few weeks after that disastrous Thanksgiving, I did call the child welfare services, but they said the situation was not bad enough for them to interfere. Ashley attended Tecumseh High School, so I asked one of the school counselors to talk to her without revealing specific events, but Ashley indicated that her home life was fine and she had no problems she wished to talk about. She did adamantly state that she did not want to be in my class under any circumstance. When the counselor asked why, Ashley said that I did not like her and would give her bad grades. I tried to talk to Ashley the few times I met her in the school halls, but she always turned around and walked the other way whenever she noticed me.

We were all shaken by the events of the evening. Later on, I found out that my husband laughed when Sammy said that no one would ever want to "fuck" Debra, and even though Debra's behavior was inexcusable, Marshall and Sammy did their part to contribute to the evening's fiasco. For once, I was not part of the scene, and I started to understand how my husband must have felt at the endless dramas I played out at the weekly neighborhood parties.

#

Panting, he lifted her middy blouse over her innocent smooth face and red lustrous hair. Her large expansive brown eyes watched as he undid the laces of her corset and gingerly touched her white upturned breasts beneath her cotton undershirt. As if caressing the Virgin Mary herself, he sacredly slid his hands down to the curve of her waist, and pulled the ribboned tops of her pantaloons down to her ankles and then around and off of her feet. He had waited two years for the young smell and taste of her – two years of watching her in his classroom, listening to the sounds of her pure, sweet voice, hoping to accidentally brush against her young white arms while putting his hands on her waist to teach her how to project her voice. Two years of singing recitatives and arias beside her, breathing in the scent of her breath that passed through her chest and tongue and lips. Then after the previous rehearsal, bolder moves, patting her thigh, smoothing the silken material clinging to her hips, caressing her hand. Afterwards, he started noticing the adoring gazes she gave him, her teacher, the father she never had, her first encounter of a man's attention. Unable to resist temptation any longer, he finally whispered to her after a compelling oratorio. "Come to my room after Elsa's asleep. She will just think you went for one of your nightly strolls along the water's edge if she wakes." He mesmerized her with his soft voice and words. He was after all the older man, her maestro, and she must obey. Smiling as he heard the catch in her throat, he burrowed his face in the softness of her small womb. Aroused by her deep-honeyed aroma, he lifted his eyes towards hers and began to tremble as his body rose above hers. He sang in a half-scream as he penetrated her, not noticing her small startled cries of pain, not remembering he whispered, "Mama, Mama" over and over again as his rhythmical motions started to subside.

#

The next day I woke up early. The trauma of the night before took its toll on Marshall, and he still slept soundly as I quietly slipped out of my pajamas and into some comfortable sweats. The doors to the kids' bedrooms were closed and the only sound was the gentle susurrations of the waves outside. It was barely seven and there was not one other person on the beach. The brisk salty air wakened my senses to the surrounding beauty of sea and sky. The sun was just above the horizon and rivulets of honeyed light poured across the gray-blue watercolor morning. Following the undulating pattern of the waves, tiny peeps scurried backward and forward down the beach. Plovers kept their distance just beyond the ribbon of tidal debris while black-capped sandwich terns hovered over the water like helicopters. Seeing the silver flash of small fish, they folded their wings and dropped headfirst into the sea to snare a morning meal. As I strolled toward them, a group of laughing gulls and royal terns seemed perturbed that they had to move aside for me. Not even having combed their hair yet, they certainly did not adhere to the "early bird" philosophy.

My feet bare, sweat pants rolled up above my knees, I gingerly stepped onto the smooth wet sand and waited for the chilly water to cover my ankles. As the next crest tipped over, I winced and gasped because I'm never prepared for how cold the water initially feels. As the waves subsided, they took with them enough sand to form a trough around my feet a couple inches deep. The retreating water left clusters of empty shells and pieces of former homes rolling down the incline of sand. I had a brief glimpse of a spiral lettered-olive before it tumbled away.

Colonies of tiny clam-like coquinas, their variety of Easter-egg colors dulled by the soft shadows, struggled against the current as they pulled themselves back beneath the sand. They wriggled under my feet as I stood watching the world they knew. Water in, feed quickly, water out, do not get washed out to sea, escape to repeat the cycle. With my back to the ocean, I leaned over to see better in the early light. The next rush of water slid a jet-black shark tooth politely in front of me. Before the favor was taken back, I quickly picked it up. A perfect specimen about two inches long. I felt the urge to turn to Micah and show him that I had found something on my own. Of course, he wasn't there and the gulls and terns didn't seem to care. So I put the tooth in my pocket and continued to walk along the expanse of beach, water, and infinite sky.

My thoughts drifted in and out of last night's debacle, the neighborhood, school, and finally back to Micah. What was he doing at this very minute? Did he find a blood-red ruby? Was he up like me, just walking, thinking? Of me? Does he want me in his life? Mother ... Dad ... help me. Send me a sign. Show me something so glorious that it takes my breath away. I gazed at the sea, and it simply stared back.

I turned away and stepped into the dry powdery sand to trudge back to the villa. Leaning against the gray railing of the walkway, I tried to knock as much sand as possible off my legs. Brushing at my calf, I heard the slightest of clicks and looked down to see that my fossilized shark tooth had fallen from my pocket. As it lay in my palm, I realized how fortunate I was to have been standing there when it came ashore. Hidden for millions of years, only at that precise moment was it revealed, and I could have missed it. But I didn't. Thank you, Daddy.

I wish I could say I chose to change my life immediately, detached myself from the destructiveness around me, sought a new path, and found the depth and spirituality I was missing. Some of those changes did happen, but not because I took charge of my life. I found a new existence because I was forced to find one. By that time, Debra and Neil, the neighborhood parties, Tecumseh High School, and my life in Atlanta were like a pair of old platform shoes, outdated and never worn anymore but too symbolic a time marker to be discarded.

Chapter 15

For the rest of Thanksgiving weekend I went through the motions of enjoying the amenities of Kiawah Island. In actuality, all I could think about was how Debra was going to get home first and therefore have the opportunity to tell the story the way she wanted reality to be. I thought about calling Bonnie, at least, and gently explaining what happened, more to protect my family than any concern with neighborhood gossip, but decided against it. I bided my time until we arrived home.

Almost as soon as we pulled the car into the garage, the phone rang. It was Debra. She said in her sweetest voice, "Do you have the rest of the dishes and wine Neil and I left in the condo? I thought I could come over and pick them up. We have some things to talk about, anyway."

Something in me became very hard, and I knew I did not want her in my life anymore—at least the way she was at that time.

"I'll leave your things on the deck and you can pick them up whenever. Debra, I just cannot talk to you about anything right now. If you get into therapy, maybe join AA and it seems to help, then I'll talk to you again. But not now."

"Well, when we see each other, can we at least have polite conversation?"

"I think I can do that," I said.

The first time I saw Debra after our phone conversation was a week later at a neighborhood Christmas party. When Debra walked into Monica's house, I felt nervous and expected her to be cold towards me. Instead, Debra was ingratiating and kind, and conservatively sipped on one glass of wine all evening. Even though she kept mainly to herself, she did at one point go out of her way to talk to me, and even went so far as to gossip about one of the neighbors and her builder.

"Now Laura's inviting him over to have dinner with her kids. She's flaunting him right in front of her husband." Hoping I would get the hint and play her game of denial, she invited Marshall and me to her New Year's Eve party.

"Why don't you and Marshall come over next weekend and help Neil and I plan for our New Year's Eve party?" I knew she thought enough time had passed for me to get over my outrage at Thanksgiving. She also was shrewd enough to know that if I wanted to be invited to social functions among our mutual friends, I had to operate according to her rules. Debra was without a doubt the most powerful woman in our group. I could not understand her dominance and control, and the only conclusion I could draw was that people were afraid of the havoc she could cause their families, especially their children. What Debra did not count on was that I did not care if I ever was invited to another neighborhood function.

"Debra, what I said over the phone still stands. I cannot be your friend anymore, and it would be hypocritical for Marshall and me to attend your New Year's Eve party, much less help you and Neil prepare for it." Debra acted hurt and offended and moved on to someone else. I fully expected to be the immediate object of her venom. But I underestimated her intelligence. She played it cool and did not release her rage until she found where it would hurt the most. Even Neil tried to mend things between us.

"She's not so bad, Cat. She's just a mean drunk. Why don't you and I go out for a drink, and we'll talk things over."

"There is nothing to talk over. Your wife said some very hurtful things to my family, especially the kids, and I can't set myself up for that again."

"Since when are you so unforgiving?"

"She's hurting her daughter, and she needs to get help before she hurts her even more. Can't you do something for Ashley?"

"I've tried, Cat. Debra's never going to change."

"That's not good enough."

"So our Sunday drives are over?"

"Goodbye, Neil."

It was easy to avoid neighborhood socials and therefore more confrontations with Debra during the three weeks before Christmas. The happy hours and Saturday night get-togethers dwindled during the season, because we were all so busy with shopping, baking Christmas cookies, and decorating our houses. Our weekends were filled with business and customer Christmas parties, school pageants and special church events. My children were home from college for the holidays and provided a reason for me to nest and cuddle at home. Marshall's work slowed down during the month of December, and especially in light of the Thanksgiving disaster, we held each other close as a family.

Even Micah was busy and took a break from his archeological hunts. The first day back to school after Thanksgiving, I ran into Micah walking down the hall with his familiar cup of coffee. The buses were just arriving, so we did not have too much time to talk.

"How was Kiawah?"

"Much different from what I expected, to say the least. How was North Carolina?"

"We had to cut it short. One of my cousins died, so I spent Thanksgiving at a funeral."

"Oh, I'm so sorry. Are you okay?"

"I'm alright. He's been sick for a long time. We saw it coming. I guess we won't be walking much in the woods these next two weeks, what with the weather and getting ready for break. I'm determined to get all my tests graded so I can relax and go somewhere over those two weeks."

"Tell me about it. I have barely started my Christmas shopping. Well, here come the kids, better grab a cup of coffee while I can. See ya."

"Take it easy." We should have walked away from each other but hesitated instead. We were both waiting for the other to say something. I was the first to break the awkwardness between us.

"Do you have time to do something this week?" I asked. "Maybe get a beer or something after school, so we can catch up."

"You ever been to the Varsity?"

"I've driven past it, but no, I haven't."

"Let's go there right after school, and get a PC and peach pie."

"Well, as long as that's all we do, why not?" We were both smiling as we walked away.

"Meet at my trailer?" I yelled to Micah.

He waved his hand in the air to let me know he heard me. He did not turn around; maybe he thought I would change my mind if he did.

#

Built in the forties, the Varsity's red-and-black exterior angled above Interstate 75. The world's largest drive-in restaurant sported a green canopy with carhops, though most modern day visitors preferred to eat inside. It was an Atlanta landmark, serving established clientele as well as out-of-towners. The Varsity claimed Nipsy Russell as one of its first car hops, and Elvis, Jerry Lee Lewis and Jimmy Carter as a few of its visitors. Started by a Georgia Tech dropout who was told he wouldn't amount to much, it sat adjacent to the campus. The hamburger and hot dog joint initially catered to college students, but as the days of car hops and drive-throughs waned, the Varsity grew in fame and importance. During the '96 Olympics, hosts of celebrities dined at the Varsity. Katie Couric even hosted the *Today Show* from one of the many forties-style metal tables.

Sixty years later the Varsity retained its original charm. Not much had changed or been replaced. Only fresh paint had been added to the black-and-red façade, and carhops would meet you as soon as you turned in. Inside, rows of painted metal tables and chairs lined canary-green concrete walls under stark artificial light. A long Formica counter with stainless steel edges dominated the raised black-and-white tile floor in the center of the restaurant. White letters spelled out the menu and prices on black backboard. The price of foot-long hot dogs, chili, hamburgers, fries, and onion rings had risen steadily since the Varsity's inception, yet it remained one of the best bargains in Atlanta, and the lines in front of the counter always were long and crowded. Short-order cooks wearing white aprons and pointed paper hats took orders from a menu that had remained the same for years. Besides the more universal fast food fare, you could order an FO or frosted orange, PC or chocolate milk along with an assortment of individually wrapped pies.

At the counter, not bothering to ask me what I wanted, Micah ordered for both of us.

"We'll have two PC's and two peach pies."

The man turned to workers behind him, "Two peach pies!" In less than a minute the ample milk-cheeked man behind the counter slung two cartons of chocolate milk accompanied by two paper cups filled with ice, and two wax papered envelopes thick with pies across the glass counter top.

"Three dollars," he said.

Micah and I took our PC's and pie to a back table facing a wall with signed photos of local politicians. Micah caught my hand as I started to take the peach pie out of its wrapper.

"It's too hot to eat it like that. Why do you think it's served in a wrapper? You push the pie up a little at a time and eat it like this." Micah held the wrapped pie in his hand as he took a generous bite of the folded hot dough. "That's good. I used to come here as a little boy. Pour your chocolate milk over the ice. Nothing better."

"Sure beats a cold glass of chardonnay," I joked.

"At least this might keep your mouth from running."

"Did you come here often as a kid?" I asked. I was not about to get into a discussion of how much wine Micah thought I drank.

"About once a week Ninelle and I would take a bus and meet my Mama here for lunch. Mom worked at Woolworth's when I was small."

"Whose Ninelle?"

"My black Nanny. Sometimes she'd watch me, and when my cousin lost his job, he watched me for awhile."

"One of your really older cousins?"

"Actually the one who just died."

"How old was he?"

"What is this? One hundred questions? I told you he was almost twenty years older than me. He was sixty-something when he died. He stopped watching me just before my eleventh birthday. It was lonely around the house without anybody, but you know." He changed the subject to talk about different times in his childhood. How he grew up in the country. His dog. His pony Goldie.

"I had to give Goldie up when I got too big for her, so we gave her to a farm down in Newnan. I went back to visit her when I was fifteen. Mom and Dad were with me and when I whistled for her, she came running just like always. She still remembered. That's one of the best memories of my childhood." His eyes glistened slightly.

"You were so spoiled. I always wanted a pony when I was a kid. The only pet I had was a rabbit, and I inherited him from one of my sister's boyfriends."

"It didn't feel like I was spoiled much. My parents got me a pony because I had no one else around. She was just like a big dog. I could sleep in the hay right beside her."

"Were you very lonely?" I looked into his eyes.

"Ah, not really. When you grow up as an only child in a neighborhood with not many kids, you don't really know any better."

"You did have some friends, didn't you?"

"Yeah, at school or on the baseball field. But I kinda got used to being alone. Made it so I feel like I don't really need anyone to get what I need."

"How do you know what you need if you don't know it's there?"

"Yeah, I could see that being a problem," he answered logically. "So, how do you like the PC?" That was all Micah asked.

"It's good. What does it stand for again?"

"Preferred Chocolate... like FO ... frosted orange. You need to get one of those next time. Did you know Nipsy Russell car hopped here?"

"No. I'm not from around here. Did you remember him?"

"How could I remember someone who wasn't even famous yet?" he said. "He was just another face in the crowd."

"I hate to think of you as a lonely little boy. Wish I could have been there with you."

"It really wasn't so bad ..." I could hear the hurt rattling around in him like Old Marley's chains.

"It's okay if it was that bad."

Micah stared at me like he had so many times before, as if he were willing me to read his thoughts. His silence unnerved me. I guess I could have pushed him to tell me more, to reveal those things he and I both knew I saw, but then again, some stories are better left untold.

"Do you know I went through a period where I couldn't walk down steps," I said. "Even the thought of stairs paralyzed me."

"Why?" Micah asked absent-mindedly.

"Because someone I loved fell down. Every time I started to walk down a step or an escalator or stairs, I thought of her and froze."

"Who was she?"

"My little girl. The first little girl." And then the tears came, and I felt ashamed I brought her up in front of Micah. He merely placed his hand on my cheek and stopped the tears with his fingers.

"I think we should go, Cat," he finally said. "Come on." He lifted me up by my elbow and gently pushed me towards the back exit doors. Before he opened the door to the truck, he held me in his arms, his hands searching my back and my waist. He leaned his face down to meet mine and stopped just short of kissing me. I reached my hand to his face and pushed back the skin as if to smooth out his lines. I felt his unwavering eyes scrutinize mine, and for a few quiet moments I harbored the peaceful glow of understanding.

We were quiet riding home in the truck. We had crossed a line of love spoken not with words but with the soundlessness of lips almost touched. By the time we arrived back at the school parking lot, it was dark and the wind was cold.

"Will I see you over Christmas break?" Micah asked as he walked me to my car.

"I don't see how. The kids are home and we're going to be in Cincinnati for most of it." I had failed to tell Micah about the Thanksgiving disaster and how desperate I was to spend the holidays outside the gates of our neighborhood.

Micah's face fell and he put his hands in his pockets.

"Micah, you're a good friend. I think you're one of the best persons I have ever known, and I'm glad you are in my life."

"I think the same of you. Guess I'll see you next year, huh?" Micah turned to leave.

"Not yet." I circled my arms around Micah's neck and kissed his eyes, his nose, his cheeks, and his ears until he laughed.

"You're going to wear us both out."

"If only we could," I slyly remarked.

"We had our chance in my attic," he said.

"Micah, I didn't know you were thinking about anything like that then."

"Weren't you?"

"Maybe a little," I said coyly. "Well, now I can say it. See you next year, Micah. Who knows what the New Year will bring, huh?"

I left Micah feeling warm and happy inside. I vowed to keep those feelings inside of me through the long and frantic days ahead.

#

He stood in front of the gray clapboard house and called her name.

"Hey Nellie! Nellie! Oh Nellie! Is Nellie there?"

A white-haired stick of a woman appeared on the whitewashed porch.

"Well, if it isn't the little Wesley boy, only not so little. Yer jist 'bout grown, lad."

"Hey, Miz Sally. I heard Nellie got off the train two days ago. She too good for a tobacco farmer?"

Miss Sally put her hands on her hip and scowled. "A tobacco farmer? You? It's yer daddy who runs that farm. Yer not that growed to call yerself a farmer yet. Hired hep is mo' like it."

"Mah Daddy's give me almost the whole farm to run single-handed. His rheumatism is slowing him down these days. I'm almost sixteen, anyways." Sally shook her head and chuckled.

"Well, I'll be. You're practically as old as Methuselah, you are. Young David running old Amos Wesley's farm. Lord, give me half his mercy." She crossed her arms and glanced toward the house. "Nellie's grown up too it seems. She's gotten awful quiet and likes to spend her time alone. I don't know if she'll want to run 'round the fields wi'choo no more. She's taking her singing mighty serious nowadays. But I'll tell her you came by."

"Tell her I just want to see her for a minute," David said.

"She heard ya yelling. She said to tell you she warn't coming out today."

David walked up the porch steps and stood next to Miss Sally.

"Can I go in and ask her myself?"

"She didn't seem to want to see you anymore."

Before Miss Sally could stop him, David was in the vestibule of the old house, the screen door slamming behind him. Nellie was sitting behind the piano, lightly fingering the keys. The notes played a melody far away and unfamiliar to him. A ray of sun formed a dusty halo above Nellie's red hair and her maturing beauty startled him.

"Nellie," he said softly. "I heard you came down on the train." When she looked up from her music, her eyes were sadly vacant. Her face was thinner, longer; her skin a luminous white, her flawlessness marred only by dark circles lingering under her eyes. She turned back to her music and flipped absently through the pages. When she finished one book, she took out another and turned page after page in unceasing motion. She seemed not to remember David's presence.

"Nellie, what's happened? Is something wrong? It's me, David."

Her small mouth gave a hint of a smile, and she touched the upswept curls atop her head.

"David," she said barely above a whisper. "It's David."

"How's your music … Hermann?"

Nellie pushed back the piano bench and walked over to the window. She stared outside without speaking.

"Is Hermann still hanging you by your hair in the closet?" he teased.

Nellie put her hands over her face and sobbed. Sally entered the room and glared accusedly at David.

"I told you not to go in. What did you say to her, boy, to make her cry? Is he the one who's made you so sad, Nell? I'll call his father and he'll take care of him good."

Nellie pushed past her aunt and pulled David by the hand.

"We're going out into the fields, Aunt Sally. David didn't make me sad. My mother did. Your fat sister who hoards chocolates and makes her daughter take music lessons from a filthy old goat."

The door slammed behind them as David and Nellie ran out into the fields. Nellie's piled hair loosened and fell wildly down her back as she ran faster and faster through rows of tobacco plants.

"Nellie, stop! Wait for me! Nellie!" David yelled.

After running down endless rows, Nellie finally fell down on the ground, exhausted.

"What's going on with you? You're acting crazy."

Nellie lay on her back and laughed.

"I am crazy, David. I'm completely off my rocker." She became serious a moment later. "This is the last summer I'm coming here. My mother thinks I'm too old to visit Aunt Sally. From now on I have to spend my summers in Europe. Hermann told her he could get me an apprenticeship under some of the best divas in Berlin and Vienna."

"You must have some say-so in this," David leaned towards her concerned, gently picking bits of tobacco leaves out of her tumbled hair.

"My voice is my curse," Nellie said. "If I didn't sing well, Hermann wouldn't do the things he does to me." Nellie violently snapped a tobacco leaf free from the stalk.

"What things?"

"He hurts me all the time … hurts me so much." Tears streamed down her face and she hid her face in her arms.

David pulled her to him.

"You're as limp as an old rag doll. What's he done to you?"

"He makes me sing all the time … He makes me … sing."

"Can't you ask him to stop?"

She smiled at the brown-haired boy. "Oh, you're so innocent, so sweet. I could never make you understand. Is your old barn still there? The one you got whipped behind?"

David's face reddened, "Yeah, it's still there. C'mom, let's climb up into the loft and smoke some leaves."

"You smoke?"

"Of course, don't you?"

"I've never tried it. What's it like?"

"I'll show you."

While their feet dangled over the edge of the hayloft, David rolled several leaves together and struck a match on his shoe. He carefully lit the drying but still pliable tobacco and puffed vigorously on the rolled end until he filled his lungs with the sweetened smoke.

"Here, now you."

Nellie held the homemade cigar and placed the tip between her lips. She slowly inhaled the spicy sweet tobacco smoke, her eyes watering, a muffled cough catching her off-guard. The second time she drew in, she felt a dizzying rush.

Temporarily released from her oppressive thoughts of Hermann and her music, she lay back in the damp hay and took David's hand into hers.

"What are you thinking about, Nell?"

"I was thinking that I want to be friends with you always." He gently took the rolled leaves from her hand and gave her a tender kiss. He pulled his face away from hers and softly twisted her fallen red tresses in his meaty fingers.

"How will I find you if you don't come back here anymore?"

"I'll write you, and when I am done with my apprenticeship I'll come back here ... forever."

"I thought you were going to become a famous opera star."

"Hermann wants me to and so does my mother."

"What about you?"

"I don't know, if it takes me away from Hermann then yes, I'll go to Europe."

"Nellie, sometimes my Pa goes to Cincinnati on farming business. Maybe I can come with him and see you."

"Ask Aunt Sally for my mama's address. She'll tell you how to find my school. It's in an area called Over-the-Rhine."

"I'll find you, Nell. I'll always find you. Time won't matter."

Gray-blue smoke swirled and mixed with dust as streaks of sun sneaked through gaps in the loft. They lay side-by-side until the sky turned dark, and they glimpsed the stars through the rotted knotholes of the roof.

Chapter 16

Christmas came none too soon that year, and the extreme pace of the season kept Thanksgiving a distant dream rather than a reality. As we had done since we moved to Atlanta, the four of us drove to Cincinnati for Christmas. We spent most of the two weeks with Marshall's family in the roomy Victorian home of his youth. But Christmas Eve was always spent with my family, the O'Connell clan, hosted by one of my two sisters in their very modern two-story colonials.

Christmas always reminded me of her. Her drowning, safely buried in the debris of the old neighborhood, remained faintly conscious in the collective of my family. My younger sister Meg, after a few beers, always squeezed my hand too hard and told me she was sorry. My other sister Cynthia made sure to replenish my wine glass whenever it was empty, and my two brothers treated me as if I were twelve-years-old, a safe age, an age that still trusts and hopes. When my parents were alive, my mother held her memory in the sadness of her eyes, but my father told the story of her short life on foggy Christmas Eves. He started telling her story years after her death, when he sensed I was strong enough to listen and needed to listen. After Christmas Eve dinner, he would pat my arm to remind me of our yearly ritual. "Don't forget about our walk," he would whisper as he winked. After the family opened presents, my father and I would walk along the cracked sidewalks into town. We passed homes of friends, the neighborhood grocery store, and the local bar raucous with laughter until we came to the church. We stood silent in front of the Nativity scene and focused on another child for a moment. My father would place his hand on my shoulder and softly ask if I wanted to talk about her. I would silently nod, but actually he was the only one who spoke of her.

She lived long enough to celebrate two Christmases, the most memorable when she was fourteen months old. Her presence created joy in all of us—my parents, my brothers and sisters, me—and she became for us the heart of the season, a child born out of wedlock and pain into familial acceptance and love. The turmoil of her first days turned into peaceful ones, and we could not imagine life without our little baby.

At fourteen months, it was a Christmas of firsts for Therese. Her first visit to Santa, her first awareness of snow falling, her first vision of lighted evergreens. On Christmas Eve morning, my Dad and my brothers traveled almost thirty miles to Oxford, Indiana, to cut down the roundest fir they could find. At home, my mother, Cynthia, little Meg and I unwrapped yellowed paper toweling from around glass ornaments. Therese excitedly screeched and reached out to touch the colored bulbs and glass teapots and stars. We let her open boxes of garland and red shimmering wreaths. The tinsel we left on the shelf that year; Therese had a tendency to put string and yarn in her mouth, and we knew the tinsel would be a shinier form of yarn for her and much more enticing. Meg, who had just turned four, reacted more like a sister to Tessy than an Aunt. And like a sister, she pushed Tessy out of the way more than once as we gathered the Christmas decorations. Very gently, Cynthia and I soothed Tessy's hurt feelings of being pushed out of the way and Meg's growing resentment of Tessy's place as the youngest in the family. We appeased them both with freshly baked star cookies and coconut Christmas cakes. As often as I could, I gave Meg special attention and gifts of my time. It was I, after all, who caused her position in the family to be usurped. Meg, the little crown jewel of the family, now had to share the limelight with a baby born years too soon.

The littlest members of our family appeased, we prepared the house for a tree that would be way too big for our unit's small rooms. Every year, my brothers and Dad would get carried away and lug home a tree that would never fit through the front door. After much sawing and trimming of branches, they squeezed the oversized fir into our undersized living room. In the house they had to cut more branches from the tops and sides, and still the tree took up a quarter of the room. The television had to be brought out into the stairway hall, and we either sat on the floor or pulled out chairs from the kitchen if we wanted front row seats. It was either that or no tree.

Since my family always celebrated Christmas on Christmas Eve, we rushed to get the tree decorated before we had our Yuletide dinner. Unlike Marshall I did not grow up in a large Victorian home lavishly decorated at Christmas with an imposing fourteen-foot tree trimmed with fresh flowers and antique German ornaments. My family, consisting of my parents, two sisters, two brothers, me, and for a while Therese, lived in a tiny attached unit, commissioned by FDR in the late thirties as affordable government housing. Today they are referred to as historical sites, even though that does not make the units any more than what they were. Military in appearance, they were stripped of any decorative ornamentation. Each unit, usually attached to four or five more, had three small functional bedrooms, one bathroom with a tub and a toilet (a shower was a luxury in such utilitarian quarters), rectangular living room, a small kitchen, and since ours was an end unit, we did not have a back door in the kitchen like the middle units until my brother Eugene put one in after most of us left home, and finally a utility room which housed the coal bin, coal furnace, and my mother's washer and eventual dryer. The utility room had lines strung across the top quarter of it originally so my mother had somewhere to hang her wash in the winter, and later they were left up there as a testimony to the wonder of her electric clothes dryer. There were two utility tubs next to the washer and dryer, one of the tubs with a washboard molded into its front.

As a little girl, I remember my mother warming the wooden clothespins in the oven, so her fingers would not freeze as she pushed the wooden pins on clothes hung out to dry in thirty-degree weather. She hated to hang clothes inside, even during the winter. The clothes often mildewed and the wrinkles became too stiff to iron out. Luckily, we never had to explain to the Fire Department how burning clothespins changed the neighborhood.

For Christmas Eve dinner, my Dad stopped at the delicatessen and bought Ray's homemade German potato salad, roast beef, homemade gravy, large dill pickles, and limburger cheese. Some years he bought special pumpernickel rye and goetta to have as well. To me, any food my mother did not make was a treat, not because she necessarily was a bad cook, but because going out to dinner was unheard of in our house, and homemade deli food was the closest thing to going out that I knew. Every year, my mother brought out a special crocheted tablecloth her Aunt Fanny had made and placed it on our metal kitchen table. Next she carefully unwrapped her set of crystal sherry glasses and poured a small amount of red wine in each goblet. We all had some, no matter what our age. We drank to the birth of Christ and to our family and to the Christmas season. Then haphazardly my mother placed the food on the table and in twenty minutes it was gone. Scurrying around after my father and her five children and grandchild, barely taking time to eat, my mother didn't have much flesh to hug.

But that Christmas Eve, the Christmas Eve before her death, we opened presents, as we usually did, after all the dinner dishes were washed and put away and allowed Therese and Meg to stay up past their bedtimes. Because it was Therese's first real Christmas and she had an inkling who Santa Claus was, Cynthia took her upstairs and gave her a bath, Meg following behind, while my brother Eugene donned my Dad's old Santa costume (my dad had gained too much weight over the years to fit into it), and we brought out the presents we had hidden from each other over the last few months. The only presents we did not wrap were Meg's mini-bake oven and Therese's shiny red wagon.

We lived for Meg and Therese's reactions to the presents under the decorated and lighted tree. My oldest sister carried her down, all clean and bundled in a red pajama suit, while Eugene, dressed as Santa, brought in one last present—a brilliant blue tricycle half-wrapped so Therese could see it was for her. At first, Therese shied away from "Santa," and Eugene had to pull down his beard so she could see it was a Santa she knew. But the tricycle was too hard for her to resist, and she ran over and touched the bike while Santa pulled off the rest of the wrapping paper and lifted her onto the seat. He pushed her around our little living room, until Therese started to climb off. Meg, surrounded by tiny dishes, new dolls and a mini-refrigerator and sink to go with her mini-bake oven, quietly went about the business of playing and arranging her new toys. To our disappointment, Therese ignored most of her presents and played hide and seek with the empty garland and ornament boxes we had set beside the tree. But when we turned off all the lights and my dad connected the extension cords and lit the Christmas tree, Therese pointed at the tree and exclaimed, "Look! Look, Mommy. Yights!" All our faces were aglow with the radiance of a fir tree and the love of a family in a little girl's eyes. I remember my sister remarking that the small angel ornament on the top of the tree had a distinct resemblance to Therese. Each Christmas thereafter, that single decoration of satin and glass would bring tears of longing for days past.

Rather than the muted, slow motion grayness of past years, the memory of her flamed with flesh and blood that first Christmas after I met Micah. So the morning of Christmas Eve, I drove west to Lower Price Hill, to the old public pool, to the oblong concrete coffin that held the memory of her hydrous death. The old neighborhood was run down, and I had heard our unit was now a crack house. The pool and surrounding bathhouses, once well maintained with yearly coats of white paint, were a mess of fractured and powdery gray cement. The pool had been closed for at least ten years, and like so many other city recreational areas, there was neither money nor desire to refurbish the facility. Weeds sprouted up in the crevices of the empty adult pool, the shallow end filled with an assortment of soft drink cans and broken beer and wine bottles. The stench of fresh urine pervaded the dank, cold air.

I hadn't been to the site of her death in over twenty years, but that Christmas Eve morning I felt compelled to return. I did not tell anyone where I was going. Marshall and I had just finished our second cup of coffee in the cozy sitting room, snow lightly tapping the outside of the leaded Victorian windows. Marshall solemnly read the morning paper while Sammy and Elizabeth rearranged the many packages under the tall tree in the living room. The rest of the relatives clamored around the kitchen preparing small breakfasts of cereals and dry wheat toast. Without a word to anyone, I set down my coffee cup, wrapped my fur coat around my pajamas and walked out the front door to our car. No one asked me where I was going. I wasn't sure anyone heard me leave.

I drove the forty minutes to the old neighborhood, a conglomeration of government architecture dragged across the furthermost western hills of the city. Intermingled among the worn brick structures was the scene of her holocaust. My ungloved hands gripped the high steel fence that enclosed the old swim club, and my body trembled in the cold as I faced her death once again.

"We need to sit in the grassy area, so Therese won't get hurt," I said.

"That's so far from the pool. Don't worry, Cat, we'll watch her. There are seven of us, eight if Angie shows up. Her parents are acting queer again. They cross-examine her every time she wants to do anything," said Joan. She flipped her long dark hair over her shoulder.

"Five more if the Coryville rats show up. They said last night they were coming," Judy added. She was the wildest of the group, therefore, the one who initiated all the action with the guys.

"Doesn't Kenny have to work on Saturdays?" I asked shyly.

"He and Joe were going to try to get off at noon. They didn't think they could do much more construction work until the plumber came, anyway. Something like that. Kenny and Joe said the old lady who's building the house keeps hitting on them—a regular Mrs. Robinson." Judy laughed at the thought of her boyfriend being eyed by a forty-year-old woman.

"Joe said her body's not too bad for an old broad. Just the thought of him putting his hands on her saggy ass makes me puke." We all laughed at Judy's bold words.

"Therese, come here," Caroline cooed. "You are so cute." Short little Caroline swept Therese in her arms, and the baby held on tightly to Caroline's shaggy blonde curls. "Ouch, Tessy, you're pulling too hard. Just pat lightly, like this. There you go. Hey, do you want to go swinging?"

"'winging. Go 'winging," Therese said in her high baby voice. Caroline held Therese under the armpits and swung Therese round and round, high into the air. Our baby gasped at first, then laughed loudly in delight. Therese had a hard time finding her balance when Caroline put her down. We all laughed at how funny Tessy looked, and she pretended to fall down to gain even more attention.

"Tessy, fall down," she said.

"You're a regular ham."

"Hey, baby," I said. "Show Judy and Caroline how you can do patty-cake." Therese deliberately clapped her two chubby hands.

"There she goes. Yeah, Therese, she can do patty-cake. What a big girl you are. Let's put it in the oven for baby and me."

The teenage girls' giggled as little Therese, my darling of almost two tickled her own tummy and sang in her sweet baby voice. "Pat it and tick it in the w'oven for baby and meeee..."

She was a smart baby and had a large speaking vocabulary for a toddler still in diapers. She could understand most of what was said to her and had no fear of strangers. She loved to practice her words. Her most favorite were "me," "mine," and "no." I was trying to teach her to share her toys with some of the other toddlers who lived in the neighborhood, and while she would let a little friend hold one of her toys initially, after a few minutes, tears would well in her eyes, and she would grab the toy away and say, "Mine." The first time this happened, I tried to make her give the toy back, but Therese screamed and held her breath.

"She doesn't have an understanding of sharing yet," my dad intervened. "Her toys right now are an extension of herself. It will be another year before she understands. She'll learn when the time is right ... just like you did."

But, to me, Therese seemed so much smarter than other toddlers her age, and I spent hours teaching her new words and sentences that she readily absorbed. She learned to walk at nine months of age, and already could manipulate crayons and feed herself. Yet, she was an energetic handful. She delighted in running away from the many adults in her life, and refused to come back when called. My mother, who took care of Therese full-time so I could complete my last year of high school on time, was glad when summer finally came. Therese wore my mother out the last months of my senior year. That summer, I was solely responsible for my daughter. College was looming in my future, so my mother took a three-month hiatus before Therese would become her responsibility once again.

"Cat, wanna meet my friend Amy?" Little Meg stood beside me with another little girl, both in yellow swimsuits with polka dots.

"When did you walk up, Meg?" I said. "I thought you and Amy were going to Coney Island."

"We couldn't go, so her mommy took us swimming."

"Hello, Amy," I said. "Are you four years old too?"

"I can swim by myself," she said.

"Good for you. Do you and Meg take swimming lessons together?"

"We have the same teacher. My mommy said we can have ice cream cones. Come on, Meg."

The two little girls waddled down the cement arm in arm. It wouldn't be long before Therese would be taking swimming lessons and eating ice cream cones with her little girlfriend, I thought.

"Hey, look. There they are! They came. Oh my God! Joe looks so tough. Cat, how's my hair? Does the zit show on my chin? Should I cover it up more?"

"I can't see anything. Your hair looks perfect."

"Can I borrow your lip gloss? Thanks." Judy opened her square makeup box and lay in a prone position before the mirrored lid. She expertly applied the strawberry-flavored gloss to her full adolescent mouth.

"Did you see Kenny with him?" I asked.

"I don't see him. Watson's here though. He's here with some slut. She has on so much make up and hair spray, she's gonna pollute the pool."

"Where's Therese?" For a brief second I panicked.

"Don't get so uptight. Caroline took her over to show the guys."

And there she was on the other side of the pool, her baby-fine red curls shimmering in the sun as she playfully performed for the Coryville boys, Caroline Murphy and Mary Jo Ingram egging her on. The Rats were paying more attention to Therese than to Mary Jo's 38 Ds. I yelled across the pool at the seven of them before I dove into the water and swam to the other side. I placed my hands on the inside ledge of the pool and pushed myself out of the water. I noticed all the Rats staring at me as I climbed onto the slippery cement. I shook the water out of my long hair and pushed it out of my eyes.

"Hey, Cat, how's it going?" Joe said. "Your kid's really cool."

"Mommy. Mommy," Therese said running towards me. I scooped her up in my arms and kissed her fat little face.

"I missed you," I said. "You better stay with Mommy, okay?"

"No!" she said. Everyone laughed, so she kept saying "No" over and over again.

"So, is Kenny coming over today? I heard he had to work."

"He only has to work half a day. If he knows you're here, Cat, he'll be here for sure." The rest of the Rats laughed, and I felt a tinge of embarrassment. I wondered if the Rats knew we talked on the phone every night, and that we made out at the drive-in the week before. Not many guys wanted to date me anymore, and no one knew exactly what happened to me, but Kenny Jergens did not care about my past. He was the leader of the Rats and the Captain of St. Pius' football team to boot, so he could date anybody he wanted, even me, and not lose face. Plus, he was one of the only Protestants at St. Pius so he knew what it felt like to be set apart.

Most of my girlfriends stood by me throughout the whole ordeal of her birth. Like me, they were Catholic girls from low income families, and the fact that one of the rich boys from Hyde Park got me pregnant and wouldn't marry me appealed to their sense of injustice, not to mention their love of unrequited dramas. And that was my first image—a poor Catholic girl whose beauty attracted a rich Episcopalian tennis player. He poured her drinks and took advantage of her, then tossed her aside when she became pregnant. It was close enough to the truth for me to keep my story straight, especially around my dad. He had an uncanny way of seeing right through me. Since the made-up story was almost as bad as the real one, I guessed the pain stopped my dad from looking further. Only Edward knew the truth. And I pretended the truth was a lie, and my lies became my truth. Initially, they became my Gibraltar and over time ... my Golgotha.

"Me go in water now. Ball, all gone." Therese pulled me towards the water.

"It's not gone," I said. "It's here. Come on, Mommy will take you in the water. Later guys."

"Take care of that little girl, Cat. We'll let ya know when Jergens gets here," Jerry Amato said. He smiled as I lifted Therese towards the pool. I had the feeling that if Kenny weren't interested in me, he might have moved in. But who knew, at seventeen I was too marked a woman for most high school boys to date. And, until Kenny came along, I was not very interested in dating anyway.

"We go swim?" Therese almost sang the question.

"Yes. Mommy take you swimming." Therese giggled as I sat her on the edge of the pool. My hand never letting her go, I shimmied my body into the water.

"Ohhhhh. It's so cold," I said.

"Ohhhh. So cold," Therese mimicked.

A few months shy of two, my daughter was fearless in the water. She jumped eagerly into my outstretched hands and threw her head back in childish delight as I swirled her around the water. When she accidentally got water in her eyes and nose, she scrunched up her face and stuck her tongue down toward her chin.

"Yucky," she pronounced. Then her grimace unexpectedly turned into a gleeful grin. "More, Mommy. 'wim me more," she said. The sun was high in the clear summer sky and I could see its reflected sparks in Therese's eyes. I swished her around the water one last time and plopped her down on the pool's edge.

"Cat," I heard Judy call from the side of the pool. "Kenny just walked in."

"Kenny's here? Where?" I yelled back. For an instance my eyes turned from Therese, and I squinted in the sun until I finally saw Kenny. He had a powerful build and a handsome face with high cheekbones and square jaw. His blonde hair fell lazily over his eyes. He had refused to follow the school rule and get his hair cut above his ears. He spent his late afternoons in jug until the football coach bailed him out. He was too good a player to be kicked off the team because of long hair. Eventually, the priests left him alone. They claimed they gave up on him because he was Protestant. My heart raced with the knowledge that he showed up at the pool because of me. He had called me the previous night to ask if my girlfriends and I were going to be at the Price Hill Public.

"I might have to work all day tomorrow," he had said. "But if I don't, I'll see ya there."

I adjusted the straps of my bikini top and then reached for Therese. Only Therese wasn't there. I scanned the deck of the pool and did not see a trace of her. I figured one of my girlfriends had grabbed her and then took her back to the towels or over to the refreshment stand to buy her a treat. At first I was mad they took Therese away again without telling me, but then I reasoned they decided to take her so Kenny and I could have some time together. Whatever the reason, I was the one responsible for her, and I had to find her before I could comfortably talk to Kenny.

Some of the Rats were standing by our towels flirting with Judy and Caroline when I got there.

"Hey, Cat," Jerry said. "Did you see Jergens over there? He's looking for you."

"Cool. I'll find him as soon as I get Therese. Did you see who has her?" I asked Judy.

Before Judy could answer, the lifeguard blew his whistle repeatedly to clear the pool. Still blowing his whistle, he dove into the water and grabbed a small body from the bottom of the pool. Her wet hair clung to her head like red seaweed, and the noisy sunbathers quieted as he gently cradled her to the ground.

"That's my baby!" I cried. "Therese! Give her to me! Give me my baby! My baby!" The crowd shoved me away when I tried to get near her, and I beat my hands against the massive wall that kept me from my baby. As the lifeguard rolled her onto her back, my child stared into my soul with unseeing eyes. He pushed on her little stomach and chest, trying to press out the water. He breathed into her mouth and checked her vital signs.

"Get an ambulance!" he called out.

"Give her to me!" I continued shouting.

"Stay away," the young guard ordered. "She needs air." In tears, he blew again into her tiny mouth, more frantic this time. She lay still, her lifeless body pale and delicate under her matted hair. Her slight arms casually rested on the pavement, the pink straps of her tiny bikini twisted around them.

"Let me try," I heard myself say. I softly held her head in my hands and placed my lips on hers. Breathe, Therese, breathe, I prayed as I tried to pour my life into her. Her lips were cold and wet, and no matter how hard I tried, I could not bring life to Tessy for a second time. Her stillness engulfed me like waves of fire, and I felt the horrible pain of heat choking my throat and blinding my eyes. Then came the horrible screams, like the screams of animals butchered alive, and the screams rang in my ears until the world turned into a wall of infinite whiteness.

The ambulance brought the hope of life with it, and color gradually returned to my eyes. Doctors and nurses came running ... not a lifeguard and an unwed mother this time, not a couple of useless teenagers, but experts, professionals ... gods, oh please let them be gods. They could bring her back. They knew what to do. They held all the secrets of life and death in their hands. And when they lifted her small arm to check her pulse I could see death in their eyes. And I knew then I had killed her. I let her die.

Then I heard the screams again, and I faintly recognized my voice in them.

"Bring her back, bring her back," they echoed in the dark hollow passageways of my brain. "Bring my baby back to life!" My girlfriends were holding on to me, and I saw the shocked expression on Kenny Jergens' face, and then my mother came, and the bags under her eyes were heavy, and I wanted my Dad, and then the fire came and I disappeared into my blank white world.

#

It was early afternoon by the time I arrived back at my in-laws' house. The smell of turkey and cinnamon and ginger filled the house and the darkness of the morning began to lift.

"Hey Mom, where'd ya go?" asked Sammy.

"I had a few last minute presents to get," I lied.

"In your pajamas?" Marshall asked sarcastically. He was an expert at drawing unwanted attention my way.

"Well, I have my coat on. Who cares?" I answered flippantly. By that time the entire household of relatives were collected around me. Their skeptic stares made me want to scream, and I was more than annoyed with Marshall.

"The saleslady in fine china complimented me on my attractive shoes, by the way." Only Elizabeth laughed as I held up my pull-on moccasin bed slippers.

"Cat's always been one of those Catholic liberals," my mother-in-law mumbled. "Your father voted for Kennedy didn't he?"

"Damn right he did," I defended.

"Well, at least your dad wasn't a drunk like some of those Irish. He could tell a good story, though. I liked your dad, despite his liberal views. Now, come help me in the kitchen, honey." Dottie whispered to me as we walked to the kitchen, "I go shopping in my pajamas all the time. Harry has no idea, but of course I wear my regular flats."

Ever since the kids were little we followed the same Christmas tradition—Christmas Eve with the O'Connell's, and Christmas Day with the Scott's. For the four years we drove up from Atlanta, we stayed at Marshall's parents' house, either in one of the rooms in the mansion, or in the small cottage behind the tennis courts. But Christmas Eve night was sacred to the O'Connell clan, and I would have died rather than to have missed one of them. Since my parents' death, my sister Meg took on the onus of hosting the Night Before. By taking over my mother's role as Christmas Eve hostess, my sister in essence became my mother. Her behavior made sense, because not only did she look the most like my mother, she was also the closest to my mother. She could read my mother's moods and knew exactly what to do to elicit her love. Anytime I tried to please my mother, I always ended up making her more closed and withdrawn.

My clearest memory of my mother unveils a hurried woman, her head crowned in pink curlers, washing windows. In my thoughts, I stand inarticulate before her, wishing she would put down her vinegar bottle and cleaning rags to smile at me. I never spent any time alone with my mother, and never remember her telling me she loved me until she was well over seventy. I am not sure why we never bonded as mother and daughter. The only times I felt somewhat close to her was when I was a teenager and we screamed at each other about my friends. Of course she disliked every friend I had and thought Marshall was an impossible jerk. We were very different people. She was athletic, I was dramatic. She read only the newspaper; I read every book I could find. She grew up spoiled by her brothers and father. She was Lolly, the family favorite. She was not prepared to handle the problems that her fourth child would bring.

As a child I often fantasized about the mother I would like to have. She would bake me cookies, kiss me when she tucked me in at night, and occasionally have a birthday party for me.

Looking at old photos, my little self is delicate, quite shy with curly reddish-blonde hair and dominating green eyes. Once when I was seven, my mother caught me looking at myself in the mirror.

"The worst kind of person you can be is a vain person," she said. "Are you vain?" I remember at the time not knowing what the word meant, but because of the way she was frowning at me, I knew I must be whatever she said I was.

"Yes, I am." She turned away from me that day for the rest of her middle-aged life. The irony is I have struggled with my looks all my life. Men, good friends, my sisters and even children have become so frustrated with me because, no matter how beautiful they tell me I am, I never really believe them. I agree with Lillian Hellmann that as we grow older we become more transparent and can see what was once there for us. We begin to feel the ridges of our original lines. I have always had one of those faces that changes with the color of the sky and the reflection of the sun and moon. As a child when people whispered about my beauty, I thought it was because of how I was able to blend myself so well among the wild-flowers or because the sun blocked my ugliness. Deep down inside I knew I was homely, and that has helped keep me grounded and humble when I needed to be. Or perhaps that accounts for all the emotional beatings I quietly accepted until nothing was left of me except the smallest pieces. All my life I have yearned for my mother to ask me what my inner lines are so that she could smooth them out for me.

The happiest time I had as a child was before I realized that my family was poor. My tiny home did not seem inadequate as I danced, made up stories, enacted plays, sang and daydreamed the same as children who lived in mansions and palaces. My parents essentially had three families: Cynthia, Eugene, and Paul when they were in their mid and late twenties; Catherine Faith, me, when they were almost in the middle of thirty; and then thirteen years later they had an unexpected surprise, Meg. Stuck in the middle, I grew up as if I were an only child, minus the attention. My mother had little time for me; my older brothers and sister consumed most of her time, packing their lunches, attending my brothers' football games, and getting Cynthia, my conventionally beautiful sister with blue eyes and blonde hair, my mother's clone, ready for her endless junior miss pageants. Then when Meg came along, she had even less time. Ultimately, I did not feel entitled to my mother's attention or love. I took a very undemanding and passive stance as a child; I never thought of asking for anything. A week after Meg was born, I started my period, and my mother handed me some of Cynthia's old bras and a box of Kotex. My uniform for school was always pressed, and soup appeared on the table every day when I came home from elementary school for lunch. Yet I always ate alone while my mother poured vinegar into hot water and washed the windows.

Like my mother, I loved Meg best of all. I never felt jealous of the way my mother doted over Meg; I understood why she found this baby, child, adolescent and adult so lovable. Meg laughed, smiled, talked, and flirted at the appropriate times. Out of the five of us, Meg was the only one who could get my mother to put down her cleaning rags.

I vicariously felt my mother's love through Meg's eyes. She could entertain my mother for hours with her nonstop stories about her girlfriends, her athletic ability as a soccer star, and antics as head cheerleader for St. Pius' football team. My mother never missed one of my sister's games, soccer or cheerleading; my mother never understood why she heard from Cookie London's mother that I auditioned for a part in Camelot, St. Pius' spring play, and won the role of Guinevere. Because no one in my family had much time for me, I developed my own dream world of Shirley Temple curls and black patent-leather shoes. I had few friends in elementary school and daydreamed through history, geography, and religion. Over time, I developed my own definition of God, and infuriated the nuns when I questioned the sanctity of their Catechism. Early on they marked me as a rebel, and because I feared the marks of their anger, school, for me, became a prison of passivity and boredom.

At least I was given occasional attention from my father on those wonderfully rare evenings when he would soak in the bathtub before dinner. We only had one bathroom, not unusual for the fifties, and he would cover himself with a washcloth and leave the door ajar for those emergencies of nature. I often peeked inside the door and asked if I could come in, and before long the bathroom became a private library for deep talks. Lathering his hairy chest and arms with ivory suds, he told me stories about the Wee Wee Woman, asked me to repeat sequences of numbers both backwards and forwards, narrated the plots of his favorite movies, and asked how the nuns were treating me. Innocently, I would tell him what mean things the nuns, especially Sister Timothea, said to me. The meaner I made the nuns seem, the more attention I received from him. I quickly learned how to exaggerate and dramatize stories to grab a much-needed audience, a skill that has stayed with me all my life.

My eyes opened wider than usual as I enacted the terrible crimes Sister Timothea had committed that day.

"Sister Timothea asked me if I ever carried a cross. I told her no, I hadn't because I'm only seven. Then she made me stand in front of the class so everyone could get a good look at me. 'Seven years old and never had a cross to bear. Class,' she said. 'Catherine O'Connell is a very unlucky little girl. We must hope that she'll be given a cross to bear.'

"I held out my arms and asked her if my cross would be as big as the one Jesus carried. 'Jesus carried the biggest cross of all,' she said. 'But if you're blessed, you'll be given one almost as big. Most of us are given many small crosses everyday to bear. But people who don't have crosses end up with the devil and feel the fire scorch their flesh for all eternity.'"

"Those damn nuns are full of bullcrap," my dad said. "What Goddamn cross does Sister Timothea have to bear? The Pope gives her a roof over her head and all the food in the world. We don't have a fine piano like the nuns have over there in their convent. The nuns are supposed to be taking the vow of poverty. They eat higher on the hog than any of us. She's a wide-ass hypocrite and coward to pick on a little girl. If the nuns talk about anything other than math and grammar, close your ears."

Another time I told him how the nuns said my brothers would go to hell for playing baseball on Good Friday. My father practically stood right up in the bathtub and then quickly caught himself. He coached my brothers' baseball teams, and his father, my grandfather, played on the original Red Stockings team.

"Those damn nuns don't know what the hell they're talking about. They don't have families to raise; they don't have bills to pay. All they have to do is worry about who plays baseball on Good Friday. Those lard-butts are full of crap. They'll give you a good academic education, but they won't teach you a thing about life. Whatever they tell you about heaven and hell is all bullcrap." In class, as Sister Timothea or Sister Richard sermonized about what sinners we were and how God was going to punish us, I whispered under my breath, "It's all bullcrap." And when they asked us to give up our milk money for the poor children who lived in Africa, I stuck my fingers in my ears.

#

My sisters and two brothers raised their families within a ten-mile radius of one another. I was the wanderer in the family who moved hundreds of miles from the vicinity of my birth, my city, and my state. And even though my brothers and sisters welcomed my yearly homecomings, a knot of unspoken tension separated me from them. It had more to do with the emotional gulf between us than the physical miles. For no matter how much I laughed or how successful my life seemed, the stigma of my past burrowed deeply in all five of us. Ever present, their helplessness, pity, and even guilt kept me outside the circle of family gossip, familiar jokes, and good-natured bickering.

Meg tried to recapture the Christmases of past years, but instead of Ray's roast beef and potato salad, Meg baked a ham and made her mother-in-law's recipe for German potato salad. The rest of the females brought casserole dishes of yams, green beans, corn pudding, and homemade apple, rhubarb and pumpkin pies. I brought an assortment of red and white wines, while my brothers provided the beer and the booze. Adults, young adults, teenagers, children, and grandchildren—the family had grown to over forty people—opened presents immediately after dinner. Once the nieces and nephews married and had children of their own, we started exchanging names. Still, the presents under the tree covered the entire floor in Meg's living room. The dishes waited until after the presents were opened and coffee and dessert were served. Then the men vacated the house to the frigid backyard with their brandy, cigarettes, and cigars, while the sisters and sisters-in–law scurried to wash and dry the preponderance of Meg's dishes.

Dishes finally finished, the clan sat and stood around the dining room table retelling old stories, rehashing the glory years of favorite sports stars, and discussing people whose names I did not recognize. Their laughter and shared conversation brought back memories of my childhood home— the comfort of being part of a big family, the loneliness of never quite fitting in.

Christmas dinner at Marshall's family home was a formal affair; the women wore long dresses, the men donned tuxedos. There was only a spattering of blood relatives there, the rest were friends of the family or old business associates. Dinner was served in the palatial dining room on a huge antique table adorned with large gilded candlesticks resembling floral vines frozen in golden motion. We all waited for Harry, Marshall's father, to say his long yet philosophical and loving grace.

"Lord we thank thee for bringing our family together for the holidays. May we always be filled with peace and love for each other and let us remember the others who could not be with us this Christmas season." Afterwards, Addie, the black cook who had been in Marshall's family since he was "knee high to a grasshopper" as his mother Dottie would say, filled our crystal wine glasses, one for white, the other for red, and Harry lifted his goblet of red wine and toasted to family and good friends, and we all followed suit, the ringing of fine crystal initiating our holiday meal. Then Addie, one at a time, brought lascivious platters of food for Harry to serve and pass. Yet even this upper class family, imbued with civility and conservative good manners, was not without its denial and secrets. Marshall's brother Tony, the oldest and favorite son, had not spoken to Dottie in seven years. He claimed that she interfered in his life too much. Dottie blamed Tony's wife Charlene for the loss of her son, but in reality it was Tony who carried the onerous anger towards his mother. When he was a few years out of college, Tony had made some bad investments and borrowed thousands of dollars from his mother to quiet his creditors. Then he started his own insurance business and when that failed, Dottie bailed him out once again. The third time he faced bankruptcy, his mother refused to give him any more money. His family lost their high-ticket home, and he had to withdraw his children from their expensive private schools. Tony's resentment towards his mother worsened over time, and then seven years ago, when Dottie criticized the way he and Charlene were raising their kids, Tony severed his relationship with his mother and the rest of his family.

And even though she thought I came from the wrong side of the tracks and her son was too good for me, she did not detest me the way she detested Charlene. I can't say that I blame Dottie. Charlene was a self-righteous and slavering do-gooder. She was one of those "foot washing Baptists" Miss Maudie described in Harper Lee's novel. She never allowed her children to have candy or soda, kept their rooms immaculate, and never let them play in the mud. She also never touched liquor or cursed and once she had children changed from a tolerably cute woman into an amorphous woman with a closet of jean jumpers. She once called me a progressive mom, and even though I took it as a compliment, I don't think she meant it as one. She knew I allowed my children to have all the candy they wanted, washed clothes as little as possible, and when I did, took them out of the dryer and threw the clothes on the kids' beds. Elizabeth's mantra growing up was, "Mom, why don't we get our clothes out of our bureaus like other kids?" I also encouraged my kids to use the word "fuck" under duress. When my children, who walked the mile home from school even in the rain, came home crying because the McKensie boys were picking on them, I told them exactly how to handle the situation."Now Sammy and Elizabeth," I professorially lectured, "the next time those shit-filled panty waists come near you, scream at the top of your lungs, 'Fuck you!' and they will run home to their mothers. Just promise me you will never use that word unless you really have to. Okay?" The next day I received a phone call from Mrs. McKenzie complaining that my children were using bad words. "Good," I said. "And they will continue to use those words until your snotty overweight boys stop harassing them."

Charlene disguised herself in the sweater-and-turtleneck of good mothering. But her children had too many cavities to count, while my children had none. Charlene's kids grew up fearful and overly apologetic; my kids have more balls than most politicians. One summer at the Cape on a family vacation, Charlene's little daughter Emily confided to me, "My mommy watches everything I do."

"She won't worry so much when she grows up," I assured the little girl. Then we winked at each other and laughed.

Addie nudged my shoulder and asked if I wanted more wine.

"You look like you're in your own little world," she said. "You want a refill?"

"Fill it to the brim, this time, will you Addie?" I jokingly admonished. So, we all passed the vegetables, made more toasts, praised the tenderloin, and pushed endive around gold-rimmed salad plates amidst our soulful attempts to lighten our hearts and conversation for one brief holiday.

Chapter 17

New Year's Day can be nice in northern Georgia, but when we reached Dalton, I-75 was icy and treacherous. It took us almost three hours to reach Alpharetta via the interstates; normally it only took an hour-and-a-half. Marshall and I had decided to return on New Year's Day so it would not be so obvious we turned down Debra and Neil's New Year's Eve invitation. So, facing a gray afternoon sky, Marshall, Elizabeth, Sammy, and I drove into our slick driveway. I groaned when I noticed cars piled in front of Monica's house.

"How are we going to get out of that one?" I wryly asked Marshall.

"Just say we're tired. We rode hours in the car and we're tired. Plus, the kids want to spend time with us before they return to school."

Fully expecting the answering machine to be swamped with calls about Monica's party, I was surprised to find not one single call. I was not surprised Debra and Neil did not call, but I fully expected to hear from the rest of our group. I tried to rationalize the lack of calls by telling myself no one knew precisely when we would be home, but I had an uneasy feeling in my stomach nevertheless. Even Marshall raised his eyebrows, but he was relieved to watch the bowl games in the sanctity of his own home. I spent the evening talking to the kids and cleaning the red algae off the sides of the fish tank. The puffer fish hung glumly around the bottom of the tank, and I wondered if it were sick. We hired one of the neighborhood kids to feed the fish, and there was a good possibility that the fish were over-fed. The rest of the aquarium life looked healthy, though. Maybe he missed our presence.

The week after New Year's the kids returned to university life, Marshall flew to Thailand, and I resumed the winter quarter classes. Micah came by my classroom almost every morning and afternoon. He relentlessly tried to entice me to help chaperone his February diving trip.

"I need a woman to go with me," he said repeatedly. "One of the girls inevitably has female problems, and in the past I've had to scurry around trying to find some female adult to help. It would be so nice not to have to worry about that this year."

"Micah, I don't dive."

"You can get certified down there with the kids."

"I really don't like water ... please don't push this."

"You liked going to Lake Allatoona just fine. "

"Hunting for arrowheads along the shoreline I can do. Plunging my body into the open sea I cannot even fathom, pardon my pun. Only desperation would get me to do something as insane as that," I joked.

And by the end of January, I was that desperate. With the exception of family and school-related phone calls and, of course, Micah, my phone was strangely quiet those winter weeks after New Year's. I attempted to call Monica and Bonnie and the rest of the neighborhood group, but they did not return my phone calls. Rita Friske, the newcomer to the group, finally broke the ice.

She phoned me one evening and apologized for not calling me back right away. Her three-year-old twins contracted chicken pox right after Christmas, and she was up to her eyeballs catching up with housework and errands, not to mention chasing two energetic, though sick, kids around the house all day.

"I'm ready to get out of the house. Why don't I get a babysitter and meet you at Chicago's tomorrow night? Meet me in the back of the bar so we can have some privacy."

I thought it strange she did not invite me over to her house, but I did remember those days when Sammy and Elizabeth were small and how nice it was to get away for an evening. I decided not to push the issue, especially since I was grateful someone in our group would talk to me, and even more importantly I needed to appease my curiosity about why the rest of the group so pointedly shunned Marshall and me.

The bar was dark and located on the far right-hand side of the restaurant. One could easily walk into Chicago's and not even notice its small pub. At first I thought I arrived before Rita and silently slid into one of the high-backed booths. After a few minutes a waitress came over to ask for my drink order.

"I'll wait," I said. "I'm expecting another person."

"Does she by any chance have short blonde hair?" the young waitress asked.

"Yes, she does."

"There's a lady in the back who's also waiting for a friend. You may have missed her when you came in."

And sure enough, when I walked to the back of the bar, there was Rita in the corner of the last booth.

"Rita, I missed you back here. Didn't you see me come in?"

"I must've been on the phone when you got here. Good to see you, Cat. How've you been?"

"A bit confused lately. No one's been taking my calls."

"Yeah, I heard," she said.

I threw my purse into the seat across from her and sat down.

"What's going on? I haven't heard from anybody since we got back from Cincinnati."

"I would think you'd have some idea, Cat."

"Actually, I really don't ... "

"Debra?"

"What about Debra?"

"Did anything happen on Thanksgiving vacation?"

"Well, sure, but what does that have to do with me? It's Debra who ... "

"Debra told everyone about your son and what he did to her."

"My son? To her?"

"Debra didn't blame you at first, but now she's really hurt that you didn't do anything to defend her against your son. The rest of the group thinks you've been pretty mean to Debra. She was crying about it New Year's Eve. She said she wasn't going to talk about it, but couldn't help it."

"What did she say about my son?" I said defensively.

"That he got really drunk and came on to her, and when she wouldn't go along with it, he pushed her against a wall and threatened to hit her. That's when Neil intervened and made everyone leave."

It was worse than I thought. My stomach hurt so bad I could barely get the words out. "That lying bitch. What did Neil say when she said all this?"

"He wasn't there. We didn't tell any of the guys what happened. We don't want them coming after Marshall or your son. Debra asked us to do that for your sake."

"I just bet she did. She's sicker than I thought! How can she lie like that?" I started shaking all over. I grabbed Rita's arms and when she tried to pull away, I held on to her even tighter.

"She's the one who's out of line. She lied to all of you. My son held her against the wall to keep her from hitting Ashley. She was the one who came on to my son. You know how mean and manipulative she is. Why would you believe her? Did any of you think to ask Marshall and me what happened?"

"When you didn't come to the New Year's Eve party ..."

I rolled my eyes at Rita's stupidity. "Why would I? After what she did to me and my family." Before the sentence was out of my mouth, Rita hurriedly slid out of the booth and crouched down behind the bar. I thought someone was about to open fire on us, and I started to hide behind the bar with her. But just before I dropped behind the bar, I turned and scanned the front of the pub. And like Lot's wife I changed to stone. Neil and Debra left as soon as they saw me.

"You can come out now Rita," I finally said. "The coast is clear. Neil and Debra are gone."

"I thought if they saw me talking to you, they'd want to know what we were talking about, and I didn't want to have to explain anything."

"Don't worry about it." I picked up my glass of wine and threw the light gold liquid in her face.

Angry tears streamed down my face on the short drive home. Wonderfully sweet Sammy. How could Debra say those things about him? Yet I knew Sammy would be all right. He lived far away and would remain forever removed from the mean-hearted gossip of the neighborhood. If only I could escape not only the neighborhood, but also my entire life.

When I was in the sixth grade, Sister Mary Gabrielle told us if we place two caterpillars on the rim of a cup, they would follow each other around and around until someone pulls them off. She said each one thinks the other one knows where he is going. Without realizing it, Rita showed me that I was a circling caterpillar.

After my entire neighborhood group turned their backs on me, my life seemed like a robotic nightmare. Even at school I did little but go through the motions. It wasn't that I missed the weekday happy hours or the Saturday night bacchanalian dramas; it was that I could not let go of the lies circulating the neighborhood and the community about my son. I dropped out of the winter tennis league on Sunday nights after the first match because of the incriminating stares from the gossipmongers. Lisa, my league partner, barely spoke to me throughout the entire match and had to force out the words "good game" after we won our first and only set.

The neighborhood debacle should have brought Marshall and me closer together; instead it tore us further apart. Unlike the women, the men in our subdivision continued to call Marshall to play golf and poker. Marshall declined the invitations, yet afterwards blamed me for our problems in Laurel Hills, not outwardly, but through his subtle comments and lack of response.

On one occasion, he didn't bother to hide his resentment. Just home from Hong Kong, Marshall had settled into his Friday night rendezvous with the *Wall Street Journal*.

Chicken waited on the grill while Marshall and I downed pre-dinner martinis.

"Robb called again about getting up a golf game, Saturday," Marshall said between sips of his martini. "And, of course, I turned him down again."

"I don't know how you could even want to play golf with them after all we've been through with this neighborhood."

"You mean after all you've been through. You never know when to keep your mouth shut. If you'd have just left Debra alone and went about your business, things in the neighborhood wouldn't have gotten so bad."

"Marshall ... how could I ... you ... act like nothing happened?"

"You didn't have to bring the whole neighborhood into your act."

"Act? She hurt our children ... and us."

"She wouldn't have spread the gossip if you hadn't made a big issue about it afterwards. You don't know when to quit, Cat. You never have."

"What's that supposed to mean?"

Marshall put the paper down and finally faced me.

"People feel uncomfortable around you. You bring up things that should be left alone. How do you think I feel when you joke with the guys about blow jobs, or go on drives with Neil and now Micah."

"How do you think I feel when you talk about other women's breasts with those assholes?"

"At least I don't talk about it in front of your friends."

"If you mean Lisa and the rest of them, you can say whatever you want. They aren't my friends anymore."

"That's what I mean. You badger people to the point where they can't stand to be around you. You think you can say whatever you want to people because of what happened to you." Marshall got out of his seat, practically knocking over the dinette chair. He tore through the kitchen cabinets searching for a wine glass. I pulled one out of the dishwater and handed it to him.

"What does that have to do with anything?" I poured both of us a large glass of wine.

"You think you are better than everyone else because poor little Cat has suffered so much. You act like no one else in the world has been hurt like you. Well, you know what? I have been hurt. Over and over. By you! All these years I have put up with your shit. I don't care about your little flirtations. It's the way you look at me ... how you just go through the motions ... like how you make love to me."

"Marshall, we could try again to make things better. We could go on a trip together ... so you could get away from work and we could talk ... real talk."

"It's too late for that. I have to pack. I'm leaving for Vietnam in the morning."

"Just retreat into your shell, Marshall!" I yelled. "Don't' talk about anything ... isn't that the WASP way? Pretend you don't see the whole room of white elephants sitting in front of us!"

"Like you want to talk about it? You've brought it up once in twenty-five years—when I was about to walk out the door. How much talking did you really think we'd do then?"

"Well what do you want me to say? That I'm a murderer? A baby killer? A goddamn irresponsible teenager who just wanted to have a life like all her friends?"

"Just because you ruined your life doesn't mean you have to ruin everyone else's."

"You mean your golf game. That's what life is to you. Well, play if you need it so much!"

"I liked hanging around them. And now you took that away." Marshall turned and paced away in long strides.

"You could hang around with me," I whispered. Marshall was too far away to hear me, but the clacker fish floated to the front of the aquarium wall in a rare moment of acquiescence to the tassos and tangs, and from the Chippendale table, turquoise eyes flickered with light under frozen yellow hair.

#

"Oh, sink upon us, Night of Love," throbbed the voices of Tristam and Isolde, the music seething with passion as the lovers ecstatically embraced each other. Her young breasts heaved beneath her high-collared Gibson-girl blouse as she sang the caressing, pulsating soprano. "Night will shield us for aye!" Isolde climactically declared against the coming of death and dawn, her voice ringing boldly with seductiveness and defiance. His trembling voice soaring higher above the rapturous music, Tristam grabbed her around the waist and suddenly pulled her to him, his desperate love for her resounding in the tenor's voice. "Oh, sweet Isolde," he whispered in German. "I cannot even get through one duet with you." She was used to his caresses by now and even though they scared her and she derived no pleasure from them, he was still her master, and she did not know how to deny him what he wanted. She lay on the sofa impassively while he once again lifted her skirts and buried his head beneath her lap. Sometimes it would take hours for his taste to be satiated; other times, he would be satisfied quickly as he hoisted his body above hers to pierce her over and over again in his orgasmic madness. Her legs spread apart, she hoped the percussion would be over soon this time. To ease her pained confusion, she listened to the streetcars and milk trucks clamoring and clanking their way along the streets of Cincinnati's Rhineland. The familiar sounds of bells and conductor's shouts kept her from hearing the timid knock or the creaking of the room's heavy wooden door.

He ran out of the door almost as soon as he had entered. But it was too late. She had heard the cry caught halfway in his throat.

"David!" She pushed Hermann away from her as she ran to the window.

"David, please," she yelled from the opening. "Come back, please!" He stopped halfway across the street and turned towards her voice. Gazing upwards, he cried, "Oh, Nell, why? Why?"

The sound of a screeching milk truck and the high whinnies from its horses told her that David was never coming back. Alarm bells rang as the ambulance came minutes later. The streets of the Over-the-Rhine filled with screaming pedestrians as Nellie stood frozen at the apartment window. She was shocked back into reality as Hermann came towards her, his shirt hanging over his bare legs. "Aren't we going to finish our duet?" he commanded.

"I need to get a prop first," she woodenly answered.

Facing him, she backed into the small kitchen and, when she saw that he suspected nothing, turned and found the knife used for slicing briskets and hams. Slowly, she moved towards him brandishing the knife in front of her.

"What do you think you're doing?"

"I want to sing the death song."

"Melot wounds Tristan, not Isolde."

"She beholds her dead lover one last time, and then falls upon his corpse and dies." Her eyes never turning from his, she turned the point of the instrument towards her throat.

Chapter 18

I had lost my original lines; I was not merely a blurred image of my former self, but a giclee, a print covered with layers of paint to create a facsimile of the original. I was twice removed from myself and didn't know how to find my way back. Marshall's words had hurt, in part because they were true, and in part because I didn't know what to do about them. My tough exterior was crumbling and I did not realize how frayed the threads were that held me together.

Marshall refused to talk about the neighborhood again, and, as planned, left for Vietnam for two weeks. The first Monday after he had gone, I arrived at school early to pick up copies of *Their Eyes Were Watching God* by Hurston. The English book room was empty except for Linda Nevis, my department head, who had arrived early to number a new shipment of textbooks. I had worked for Linda for four years; the first three years not only did I barely speak to her, I really didn't care to speak to her. She was a small wiry woman with perpetually pursed lips who busied herself with endless trails of paperwork. Until recently, she seemed almost invisible to me. But she had divorced Jerry, her husband of twenty years, over the summer, and the English Department was all a buzz with the change that had come over her. This passive little lady had grown somehow large over the summer; she reveled in her freedom and laughed and cried more openly.

At our first department meeting in the fall, she apologized for not really being a part of the group. She revealed to us that she had had ongoing marital problems, mingled in with some physical abuse, and that her self-worth was in the toilet. In part it was because she never had any friends because of Jerry. Whenever they went out with another couple, Jerry would say cruel and hurtful things to her, and the other couple felt so uncomfortable they never wanted to do anything with Linda and Jerry again. If Linda tried to pursue individual friendships, Jerry would make such a scene afterwards it wasn't worth it to her. She finally took a stand, she said, and now she craved all the friendships and fun that had been missing from her life. Little Linda, barely 100 pounds, five-foot tall, surprised not only

Jerry with her courage and determination, but also the entire faculty at Tecumseh High School.

I glanced over at Linda, absorbed in her counting, and wondered why I had not pursued a friendship with her this year. I knew the answer. In part, it was because of being consumed with the death of Dr. Craig and my friendship with Micah, but mainly it was because I allowed my time to be consumed with the neighborhood hype and happy hours. The thought made me sad, and the last four years stabbed at me like old Rome's assassins. Alcohol, pot, cocaine, endless parties, tennis soirees, nail appointments, excessive spending, and infidelity stripped its victims of character, integrity, and hope. We fooled ourselves with our well-scrubbed children, pretty bejeweled women, and GQ-looking husbands. Most of us attended church every Sunday, convincing the world of our happiness, while secretly nursing hangovers, hating our spouses, and wondering what to do with the kids during Sunday night's tennis bash. The women clung to each other like the wailing souls Virgil encountered in Hell, not a day going by without Debra, Monica, Lisa, Bonnie, and I hated to admit it, me, talking to each other on the phone three, four, five times a day. Most of our husbands were either out of town during the week, or came home too late for a real family dinner. The few times one of them did arrive home early, we probably weren't home anyway. We were either at Monica's drinking wine, or at Debra's mixing margaritas in the blender, or at Lisa's slurping down jello shooters. I circled the neighborhood, making my way to the three houses, chasing the demonic hybrid who scratched, skinned and bit our spirits. I suddenly saw with clarity the reason for our camaraderie. We represented the lowest common denominator—drunks, cheaters, liars, gossips, child-beaters. I felt sorry for it all, buried my head in *Their Eyes Were Watching God*, and sobbed hard enough to make my nose run.

I felt a hand on my arm and looked over to see Linda standing next to me. "I hate my life" was the only explanation I could offer.

"Something's been wrong for a long time. You're a wonderful teacher, but I've noticed you're preoccupied lately. Do you want to talk about it?"

"It's a long story … maybe after school one day."

"Does it have something to do with Mr. Marlowe?"

"No, why? How do you know about … "

"It's nothing. Some of the teachers saw you leave school with him a few times. You know how people talk."

"It's not Micah, at all. It's my neighborhood. They all treat me like I have leprosy."

"Do they know about Micah?"

"No, it's not that. It's me, all me."

"That doesn't make any sense. I've always admired you. They must be a bunch of losers." I smiled at that.

"Or maybe I'm the loser."

"You're not a loser. Far from it. Maybe you'd be interested in joining a group I started. It's not a big deal, but since my divorce, I felt I needed a support group, so I asked a few women to get together. We're having our second meeting Friday."

"But what do you talk about?"

"Anything you want—like how crazy your neighbors are, or about your leprosy."

"Yeah, no kidding. Sounds good ... what time Friday?"

"As soon as you can get there after school; I thought we'd need at least two hours. Most of the women can adjust their schedules easier on Friday afternoons than evenings."

"Well, I'll try to be there. And thanks, Linda." I reached down and hugged this strong woman. The world is full of wonderful people, I thought. We just have to open our eyes and look beyond our self-imposed limits.

But by Friday afternoon, I seriously thought about bailing out of the meeting. Even though it was the end of January, it was one of those balmy days that Atlanta experiences in the middle of winter. The sun was out and it must have been around fifty degrees. Micah had asked me to go walking earlier, and had raised an eyebrow when I told him I had joined a woman's group.

"Is this another drinking group in disguise?" he had said.

"No, this is the non-drinking kind," I replied. "We're supposed to vent about our problems and get help from one another."

"Well, see if you can get them to psycho-babble you into the diving trip. It'd do you some good. At least the trip will get you out of Alpharetta for a while, and you never know what you might learn."

"Talk about psycho-babble, Dr. Marlowe. Okay, I'll ask the ladies about the trip. I don't think it takes a rocket scientist to figure out what the answers will be. Should I go on a diving trip when the thought of getting into the water makes my stomach turn? I don't think so."

"Whatever you say, Ms. Scott."

As I cleared my desk, turned out the lights, and locked my portable door, I turned over excuses in my mind for not going to the meeting. *Elizabeth came home unexpectedly from college ... a filling came out of my tooth ... I was just diagnosed with breast cancer ... no one must know my secret shame.* Nevertheless, I put the keys in the ignition and drove to Linda's new house in Duluth. Jerry kept the high ceiling, six thousand square foot house with a circular drive in upscale Sandy Springs. Linda was more than glad to move out of the mausoleum. As I approached the front porch of her modest house, Linda flew out of the door and hugged me.

"I was afraid you wouldn't come," she said in her new voice. The cobwebbed veil began to lift inside my brain, and I glimpsed a slight movement inside myself I had just lately started to acknowledge, a high pitched humming—beautiful sounds, strange words musically swaying beyond my comprehension, cold hands and a longing for someone to warm them. *Che gelida manina, se la lasci riscaldar. How cold your little hand is! He sang to her across the long lighted stage. Let me warm it for you. She finished her aria and turned abruptly from him, her heart closed to all but her singing.*

The rest of the group was seated, the chairs arranged in a halfhearted attempt at a circle. Hmmm, I thought, the old Linda, the married Linda would have arranged the chairs perfectly, even going so far as to marking the circumference with little tabs of tape, designating the exact placement of each leg. I awkwardly took the sixth and last seat and wondered what in the hell everybody was going to talk about. Eileen, psychiatrist and Jungian dream analyzer, appeared the most animated with her big blue eyes, short hair the color of cooked squash and very Atlanta red silk-wrapped nails. Seated to her right, Marie projected the most negativity, arms crossed, head down, crossed leg swinging a mile a minute, showering the room with the kind of impatience smokers have when they have been on a smoke-free plane for too long. The rest of the group simply occupied themselves organizing their day planners, picking their fingernails, and adjusting their bodies to fit the seats. Other than Linda, I didn't know the rest of them very well. I knew that everyone but Marie was involved in education in some way or other, and I only knew of Marie because Linda had talked about her occasionally. She had been married for thirty years before her husband left her for a young thing in her twenties. The once stay-at-home wife and mother, surrounded by her gardening and stock clubs, now had her nose to the grindstone as an executive assistant for UPS. Ester, another English teacher in a different county, used to work with Linda twenty years ago, and Shelly taught college English in our district, but she was fairly invisible because she commuted among three high schools and only spent two hours at each one.

The first thirty minutes we sat around and chatted about our days and devoured a bowl of chocolate and peanut M and M's. Then Linda crossed and uncrossed her legs and finally began the discussion. "I just want y'all to know that Eileen is here as an equal. She is not getting paid to analyze anyone here; she needs this group just as much as the rest of us."

"I'll help any of you work through things if you want, but I hope y'all help me, too," Eileen began. "I don't know if you know this or not, but I am an alcoholic." I could feel the communal surprise from the rest of the group. I knew Eileen as a psychiatrist who worked with some of my students, but I knew very little about her personal life. "Before Buddy died—twelve years ago."

"Who's Buddy?" Marie mumbled, not looking up.

"Buddy was my first husband. He's the father of my two boys."

"How did he die?" I could not help myself.

"He drank too much and drove into a tree. He had it all planned out. He left a note behind before he went out that night." Eileen sounded as if she had said those words many times, but it didn't make the shock any less for the rest of us. Since I asked the question, I felt the need to respond.

"Oh, I am so sorry ... I didn't know. I wouldn't have asked." I stumbled over myself as I tried to show that I was a compassionate and caring person.

"Not many people know." Eileen paused for a minute to maintain her composure.

"It was horrible. Not only because I had two young teenagers, but because I didn't see it coming." Eileen half-laughed. "Talking about denial. My husband, who was one of the best trial attorneys in Atlanta drives into a tree because he lost everything. The son-of-a bitch brought home over a million dollars a year." Eileen shook her head. "Two weeks after his funeral the bank foreclosed on our Andrews Avenue home."

"Andrews Avenue! My God, those are mansions," Marie finally looked up.

This time Linda interrupted, "How did he lose all of his money and you not know about it?"

"You all have to realize I wasn't the same person I am now." Eileen always appeared radiant, well-dressed, happy and much younger than her forty-seven years. She was one of those pretty women that other women envy. She was intimidating to most of us in the room; that is what made her story so intriguing. "I didn't work, didn't have a college degree, nor did I want one. I married Buddy when I was a sophomore in college, and he had just passed the bar exam. The only thing I wanted out of life was to be taken care of."

"So, you spent all his money?"

"No, he lost it gambling."

"He lost millions? On what?" Shelly this time.

"Everything he could get his hands on—dogs, horses, poker. I don't even know what all. One night Buddy said he was going out, and by the time I found the note, it was too late. When I saw the police car in the driveway, I knew."

"Good lord."

"Shit."

"Your poor kids."

"Were they home when the police came?"

"The kids were at Buddy's mother's, spending the night. Buddy made the arrangements for the kids to stay with his mother, so I'd be alone when I found the suicide note. I had been drinking so much by then I guess I was oblivious to the signs. I believe now that nothing just happens. There are hints all over the place. All I could think about were my boys, twelve and fifteen. How was I going to tell them? And then came the financial problems."

"Men are such shits," Marie volunteered. Then she proceeded to tell us the details of her bitter and painful divorce. "Men should be shot once they reach puberty."

"Then they wouldn't be men."

"My point, exactly."

"Richard makes up for all of them," Eileen said about her second husband.

"How did you get from there to here?" I asked.

"I did what I had to do. The bank took possession of my house, and I had to declare bankruptcy because Buddy had run up over twenty credit cards to their max, and there was no way I could pay them off. The boys and I moved in with my folks, and then I really started drinking heavily. I had absolutely nothing, zippo. One of my best friends from Agnes Scott saved me. She's also an alcoholic and took me to my first AA meeting. Between the meetings and wanting to move out of my parents' house, it gave me the incentive to go back to school and get a job. After I got a job as a school counselor, I moved out of my parents' house. Greatest day of my life. Since my oldest was in college by then and I had another to put through, I decided I needed more money, so I went back and got my PhD. I met Richard and here I am."

"And just what do you need help with?" asked Linda smiling.

"I need friends to help me get through the dark days. I don't think anyone ever gets over finding out her husband committed suicide. I worry about the boys and the effects Buddy's death still has on them. If I hadn't spent so much time clubbing and drinking, maybe things would've turned out differently."

With tears in our eyes, we all reached out to Eileen as women are so apt to do. We hugged her and promised to support her in whatever way we could.

"Even if you'd been home baking cookies everyday, Buddy would've done the same thing. You didn't make him the way he was," Ester said.

"Well, at least you found Richard," Marie said in her low, 'I hate the world' voice. "I hope he doesn't turn out like the rest of them. I thought Larry was a great husband too. He was great with the kids, a good provider. We had lots of friends ... and then I find out he's sleeping with his secretary." What else is new? I thought. Fifty year old man can't get turned on by his aging wife and humps his young secretary. Wife finds out, husband is willing to stay, but not willing to give up the extra-marital sex, so the wife kicks him out. The kids hate their dad, dad whines that his ex-wife is alienating the kids from him, leaves town, and now finds a young checkout clerk at Target to bang. Someone needs to write a new script for male menopause.

"You married women better keep your eyes open. Better check their coat pockets, dresser drawers, wallet, suit bags, everything. Men can smile to your face and stab you in the back at the same time." What did Shakespeare say? *That one may smile, and smile, and be a villain.*

"Did you and your husband still have sex when he was doing his secretary?" asked Ester.

"As much as we usually did, which wasn't much. I thought we were doing okay, though."

"I know my husband loves me," drawled Ester in her Louisiana accent. "But he just doesn't seem interested in having sex at all anymore. I'm only thirty-seven, and I need sex." All of us laughed, but, I thought, with some reservations. Ester's husband was well-known in Cobb County. Peter was the minister at a large Baptist church, a graduate of Emory University, a native son, literally a golden-haired boy. I'd seen him in the grocery store with Ester and noticed how thoughtful and kind he was to her. Marshall and I stopped going to the grocery store together years ago; Marshall didn't have enough patience to make it down all the aisles. 'Till groceries do us part' was not in our job description for marriage.

"Maybe he's stressed. He's got a hard job," Linda offered.

"I bet it's that woman in the choir," Marie added.

"I asked him about her, and I really don't think she's his type. Anyway, when would he ever be alone with her? I'm always there."

"Maybe that's the problem," Eileen suggested. "You're always there. That would drive anybody nuts. I'm kidding, but maybe he feels resentful that you're so involved in his job."

"I know, I know, but I'm his wife. I want a leadership role in our church."

"It is his church," Marie reminded Ester.

"It's *our* church. I helped him start it. And now I think he's trying to push me out." Ester talked about her early days with Peter—how they met in college and dreamed of building a church together someday. She also revealed how bothered she was by his dominant mother and withdrawn father. "I'm afraid Peter is closing me out. Like his father closed him out. It's not fair. This is my dream as much as his."

"Maybe if you stay at home where you belong, then the sex will get better." I decided to play the devil's advocate.

"Better yet, show up at the church door in nothing but cellophane," Shelly added.

"Thanks a lot, you guys," Ester chuckled.

"Try talking about blow jobs," I pontificated. "That always does it for us."

"How long have you been married, Cat?"

"A long time ... almost twenty-five years."

"How on earth did you manage to keep a marriage together for so long?"

"You're one of the only ones—"

"Just wait," Marie said. "I was married for thirty years before mine left. Never say never. How do you know he hasn't been having an affair for years?

"I really didn't come here to talk about my marriage."

"So what, then?" asked Eileen.

"Water."

"Water? You having trouble peeing?" They all howled.

"I'm thinking about going on a trip that involves water."

"So, what's the problem?" asked Linda.

"I really don't like vacations that involve water."

"So don't go into the water," Marie and Ester said almost simultaneously.

"But the trip is strictly diving. Other than that, there won't be much to do."

"So, why would you even consider this trip if you hate water? I don't understand," said Eileen.

"I have this feeling I should go. I need something challenging to get myself out of the rut I've been in, and I have a hunch this could be good for me."

"Then go, and if you feel like diving, dive. If not, hang out on the boat," Shelly said.

"Or, go to Arizona and do some golfing and hiking. You don't have to do anything you don't want to do."

"I really like the person who asked me to go. He's a math teacher at our school and needs a female chaperone to help with the girls. It could be fun, plus ... "

"Plus, what?" Eileen probed.

"Plus, the world seems like a better place when I'm with him."

"She's had a few neighborhood problems and needs to get away," explained Linda.

"And maybe it's too soon to say this, but my marriage isn't all that great."

"This could make matters worse," said Marie.

"Or you could make them better," said Linda. "Sounds like you want us to give you permission to go."

"Into the frying pan," said Marie, typical as ever.

"Take it from someone who knows, you need to run your own life. You weren't here last time, but the rest of them heard how for years I let other people dictate my life. Do what feels right to you," said Shelly. "There is no other way to live."

"You never know, you could end up loving the water," predicted Ester. "By the way, what happened in the neighborhood that made this trip so important?"

"The timer just went off," the ever-organized Linda warned. "That ends our session. Remember what we said—no more than two hours, no matter what. Cat will have plenty to tell us next Friday. Right, Cat?"

"Sure. Maybe I'll even make up my mind about this trip."

"And Ester will try her new sex tricks."

"Oh, remind me to tell you something interesting I learned in one of Sidney Sheldon's novels. It works really well," I said.

"Thanks for coming. Everyone's on for next week, right?"

"Sure."

"I'll be there."

"Wouldn't miss it."

#

Friday night I was completely alone. Marshall was still away on business, and even Micah wasn't home. He left right after school on Friday for a weekend dive trip to the Cooper River via his parents' house in Peachtree City. And while cars lined the streets in front of Debra's house, I knew I wouldn't be welcome at the party, nor did I really want to go. I tried calling the kids a few times, but not surprising for a Friday night, they were out with their buddies and, knowing them, would not be home until the early morning hours. So, I made myself some hot tea, put in my favorite CDs and curled up on the couch in front of the aquarium wall and a stack of ungraded papers. Joe Cocker blasted out "You Are So Beautiful," and I circled split-infinitives with a red pen.

And I thought about Micah. We were becoming closer every week, yet what did I actually know about him? I knew he was a good teacher and was really close to his adventure club at school and once a month took the kids exploring for fossils or digging for crystals. He referred to his mother often, but seldom mentioned his father. I knew he grew up south of Atlanta and that his childhood had many solitary days. He barely dated in high school or college, even though he did go out with a few teachers every once in awhile, but none of the dates turned into anything serious. As far as I knew, he wasn't dating anyone at the moment. Yet he wasn't a lonely man; he was a walled man. And I wondered what it would take to get behind those walls, and I wondered what it would take for him to get behind mine.

My mind wandered to the dive trip, and it seemed to me under the silent gaze of the angels and tassos, the trip would be a way to escape my present burdens. The thought of sitting anywhere, even on the bow of a boat, was better than hiding away in the confines of my house and community. The Friday group was a good sounding board, and other than Marie, most thought the trip was a good idea. And being near Micah brought back soothing memories of childhood innocence and play. I thought it was because we did not have the cumbersome past to weigh us down. I didn't suspect how heavily the magnitude of our combined pasts would lean on our self-imposed bars — enough to make them break.

The sudden movement of the puffer fish drew me towards the tank. He hovered near the front glass and stared, perhaps at me but probably at his own reflection. The underwater permanence of his life inside the wall gave me the resolve I needed. You can't escape into the vast wide oceans, clacking puffer, but I can and I will. The machinery from down below bellowed and whistled in my thoughts. I didn't want to be at the mercy of a single switch that could alter and even end my life. Somehow I must find a way to control my own switches, therefore, control my own life outside the tank.

#

Paris was a city of extremes. Beggars, bums, homeless and crippled children hobbled alongside heavily gowned and jeweled women escorted by well-fed men in sweeping black and red capes. A boy, no more than ten-years-old, rested against a wall in the city's famous theatre district. Pedestrians hurriedly passed by him, ignoring the few coins he rattled in his tin cup. As she reached down to add a few francs to his meager bounty, Nellie noticed he had stumps instead of feet and the other side of his skull was missing, leaving a hideous indentation in his head.

Who would allow such a child to sit in the streets and freeze? she thought. Does France not have shelters for such children? "Where is your mother, little boy?" Nellie asked him. Instead of answering he banged his head incessantly against the brick wall until a gendarme came by and pushed him away with his stick. "Allez-y! Allez-y!" he yelled. "Desolee, Mademoiselle," he apologized to Nellie as he placed an index finger against his cap.

"Please, sir, don't hurt him. He was not bothering me," she said in her best French. But when she turned to comfort the young boy, he had disappeared into the crowd.

Nellie walked to find a more uplifting place at the Montmartre in front of the Sacre-Coeur, Church of the Sacred Heart. A chilling yet gentle breeze accompanied a slight drizzle as a musician played strands of Mozart on his cello. Nellie could see the lights of the city from the steps of the church, and above her the leaves of autumn swayed colorfully on the trees. The scenes were symbolic of her life, melancholy enchantment.

The evening before, she sang for the first time on the hallowed stage of The Palais Garnier. The opening rehearsal was flawless. Even the canvas backdrops, which flew up and down the stage on battens, allowing the scenery for various productions to be stored simultaneously, did not distract the performers from the libretto. She had auditioned weeks ago and was selected as part of the women's chorus in Georges Bizet's Lĕs Pecheurs de Perles. *Yet, in her heart, she sang the leading role of Leila as if it were her own.*

Ainsi qui toi me souvien!
Au sein de la nuit parfumée,
Mon ame alors libre, et charmée,
A l'amour n'état pas fermée!
Ainsi que toi je me souvien!

Just like you, I remember.
In the bosom of the perfumed night,
My soul was free, I was charmed,

And was not closed to love,
Just like you, I remember.

One day, Hermann had said, you will receive the leading roles. But oh, how much better she could sing them now, at twenty-three, with the memory of David still held so clearly in her heart and mind. Hermann had moved on to others after she had threatened to kill herself with the butcher knife; she was too old for him now anyway. His preferences were for the very young, male or female. It did not matter.

The excitement of her eventual opening night at the Palais thwarted for the moment the rising venom towards her mother, Hermann, and even the world. Nellie had closed herself off from the other singers, and despite her beauty and talent, had no suitors. If she had, she would have dissuaded any interest they might have had in her. She made up her mind that off-stage she would always be alone. Her bitter resolve gave her extra time to practice and learn the many languages of the most famous operas. Unlike the other young singers, she was not tempted to stay out late and drink the wine and coffee at the cafés and brasseries. She lived with only one purpose in mind – to become the leading diva of Europe and North America. In her young mind, she could see no other reason to live or to hope.

As she descended the steps of the Sacre-Coeur, she wrapped her fur-lined cloak tightly around her to ward off the cold night air. She walked along the streets of the Champs-Elysées and hailed a carriage to take her to her room across from the Palais Garnier. Before she climbed the steps to the small hotel that housed the unimportant singers, she turned to gaze at the magnificent structure across from her. The Palais Garnier was a magical place, and Nellie was not indifferent to its charms.

Crowned with statues that stood in the shadows of the green copper cupola, the theatre proudly towered over the city. Warriors on winged horses waited for a signal from Apollo, god of music, who stood at the highest point of the monument, raising his lyre above his head. Wide rails surrounded the roofs, zinc staircases cascading from them. The ceiling of the entrance foyer dazzled the imagination with its vibrantly colored mosaics, while the Grand Foyer, even higher, awed the most cynical of visitors. Cellars hovered beneath the building, twisting and turning along dark, mysterious paths to the central cellar. If Nellie had followed these paths, she would have seen that there were no ghosts, no phantoms, no lakes but only men with torches in hand guarding a simple water reservoir.

When Nellie finally reached her room, she noticed a letter from her mother resting on her nightstand. Emotionless she shredded the letters into pieces and watched them float out of her tiny window. It was not yet nine when Nellie readied herself for bed and gazed at the cold streets below. Alone in her room she could sing the heartfelt words of Leila, not to Nadir, but to a young tobacco farmer who carried her heart.

In the cloudless sky
Sown with the stars
In the heart of the azure
Transparent and pure
Like in a dream
Bending over the shale
My looks follow you
Throughout the night

#

The following Friday, I practically flew out of my classroom to Linda's house. I wanted to tell the group about my decision to go on the dive trip, and to thank them for their input, even Marie's, for she provided insight into the opposite side, a perfect devil's advocate. I had surprised Micah Sunday afternoon on the way to Lake Allatoona and told him I would help him chaperone his dive trip to Central America. To my disappointment, he showed little emotion when I told him, but later that day he found an almost perfect flint arrowhead and commented that it was his lucky day. "Found a beautiful point and woman to go diving with all in one day" is the way he put it. For the rest of the afternoon, he sparkled with enthusiasm and humor. The sky was one of the most beautiful he'd ever seen, and the trees beyond the lake cast their dark branches in perfect geometric form. When I momentarily lost my green rubber boot in a clump of heavy mud and then put my sock in the mud as well, he laughed hard enough to bring tears to his eyes, and then teased me about it all the way home. Micah Marlowe had turned from an inquisitive eagle scout into a high-spirited schoolboy.

"We all want to hear what happened in Laurel Hills," Linda said after we were all situated in our circle.

"First, I want to tell you all that I have decided to go on the dive trip ... even if I don't go in the water, it'll be nice to get away for awhile."

"Good for you," Eileen said. "I think you made a good decision."

"Way to go, Cat," Linda applauded.

"Are you ever going to tell us what happened with your neighbors?" Eileen asked.

"Nothing all that much. I just told them they were shallow and needed to read more. And I told one of them she belongs in AA and to quit hitting her kid. Then one of them made up a bunch of lies about my family, and now no one wants anything to do with me."

"What kind of people are we talking about here?" said Shelly.

"I guess people like anybody else; they just got stuck somehow. I didn't feel good about myself around them, mainly because of what I had become." I didn't have the energy to recap the Thanksgiving fiasco, so I left it at that.

"Are these the kinds of friends you really want to have?" Eileen pressed.

"No, I guess not. I really was trying to help them. I don't know what's wrong with a little honesty now and then."

"Yes, you do." Eileen pushed even more. "You challenged their behavior. You tried to make them look at themselves honestly, and speaking from experience, when you are caught up in any kind of sick behavior, the last thing you want to hear is how bad it is. You tried to change the game."

"I got disgusted with all the drinking and partying and abuse and I told some people off, and now my former *friends* act like I need the help."

"You do need help!" Eileen said.

"No kidding. I feel so alienated now. I mean, I drive home to what is supposed to be a home, my safe haven, and I feel like I want to cry. And the one woman from the neighborhood who I do go out with hides from me behind the bar. Is it just my neighborhood that acts like this? Is it Atlanta? The world? I can't stand living here anymore. I think my neighborhood's driving me crazy. I keep hearing music in my mind, opera music, I think, in other languages. Then last night I had a dream I was raped by this guy in a Viking hat."

"It was thundering last night," Shelly noted. "Thor's the god of thunder. Viking hat, get it?"

"Were you Thor this morning?" Ester joked.

"Tell us more about the music you hear," Eileen said.

"This isn't a Goddamn therapy session," Marie added.

"I just hear a few notes every once in awhile, sometimes in English and I think Italian or French, maybe German."

"Did your family listen to opera very often?" asked Ester.

"Not at all. Well, maybe in a few Nelson Eddie and Jeanette McDonald's movies or maybe Mighty Mouse cartoons, but that's about the extent of it."

"You *really* need to get out of that neighborhood," said Eileen. And then we all cracked up.

"I'm more freaked out about being raped by Thor than the music."

"Anytime you dream about a god it is part of yourself emerging. Your masculine side is now more powerful than your feminine side," Eileen analyzed.

Linda twisted her watch around her wrist several times. "Right. So what happened at the bar, Cat?"

"Okay, I'll try to make it fast. I feel like I've monopolized the whole meeting." I told them how Rita called me to see how I was doing, now that my former friends were snubbing me. She invited me to have a drink with her at Chicago's, the neighborhood watering hole, and we met around dinnertime. Then I related how Rita hid behind the bar when one of the neighborhood couples walked in; I did not tell them the significance of this particular neighborhood couple.

"That is so high school," said Shelly.

"I hope you punched her," Marie said.

"No, I just threw wine in her face and left."

"I want to meet this chick," said Ester.

"No you wouldn't," I said. "She has those thick eyebrows that are crayoned on."

"Now who's shallow … "

"Sometimes it feels so good … let's move on to someone else for awhile," I said.

"Okay, we can do that. So, Marie, have you met any men lately?" Linda asked.

"Are there any dickless men?"

"New subject. Ester, we haven't talked about your problem."

"Nothing has changed much … I haven't tried talking trash yet."

"What's holding you back?" Eileen asked.

"I don't know. It doesn't feel right. I just can't give myself permission to use that language like you can, Cat."

"Just take that first step, Ester. After that, it's easy."

"I know how she feels. I didn't have the nerve to use that kind of language when I was married to Jerry. I felt like I didn't have a voice. I would want to give my opinion or swear, but I didn't think it would mean anything. I've always admired your nerve."

"Well, thank you very fucking much, Linda," I joked.

"You're fucking welcome," she answered back.

"Well, fuck you all," laughed Marie.

"I love that word," said Ester.

"What word?" said Eileen.

"You know, that word."

"Goddamn it, say the word!" said Marie.

"Why don't we all say it together," Shelly suggested.

"Let's all stand and hold hands and yell the word 'Fuck.'" So, the whole group, all of us in our forties, some closer to fifty than others, stood up, held hands and yelled "Fuck" over and over again. I know I yelled the word close to eleven times; there is something about that word, once you say it, it's hard to stop.

After we stopped laughing and settled down in our seats, Shelly spoke in a voice barely audible. "I sometimes look in the mirror and don't see myself," she said.

"Maybe if you'd eat more, you would show up."

"Marie!" We all apologized for Marie, even though she said what we were all thinking.

"You do look like you've lost a lot of weight," interjected Eileen. "*Have* you been eating lately?"

"I can't eat or sleep. Things are not going well with Aaron and me."

"What's going on?" Eileen asked.

"He tries to control everything. He always has. He won't tell me how much money we have, won't let me help make any of our decisions, even something as small as a vacation. When the kids need help with an idea for a project, his is always better than mine. When we go out and he's around, he won't let me finish a sentence. I'm an educated woman, and he makes me feel like a child."

"Why'd you marry the son-of-a bitch?" Marie again.

"You don't understand. I was an only child of older parents, and my mother was sick from the time I was six years old. I had to be very good around the house for fear of making mother sicker or even die. She lived in bed until she died when I was forty-five years old. Mother manipulated me all her life. She thought I was born to serve her. She never acknowledged me for me, and my father shut himself away in his study and read whenever he was home." Shelly turned to Ester. "I can identify with Peter. His parents sound just like mine. I bet he married you because you're sweet and open. I married Aaron to get away from them but found out later he was my mother all over again. I went from one controlling, manipulative freak to another. Last weekend I just got in the car and drove all the way to Chattanooga. I stopped at a gas station to use the bathroom and took a picture of my face in the mirror to prove to myself I exist." Shelly fell silent while Linda rubbed her back. For once no one had anything to say, not even Marie.

Finally Eileen spoke up. "You do exist Shelly, to us, to your students. We value you."

"You're beautiful."

"He's afraid because he knows you're smarter than he is."

"Do you want us to beat him up for you?"

"Have you thought about counseling?"

"Anytime you need to feel you exist, call me. I'll be your mirror."

"Thanks, you guys."

"Wouldn't it be funny, if the next time you were at a party and he interrupts you, you yell 'Shut up!' as loud as you can? I did that once. Let me repeat, once."

"Yes, but Cat, you can get away with that. The rest of us can't."

"Why the hell not? No one's going to take you out back and shoot you if you stand up for yourself," I said. "Of course, they might nail you to the cross…"

We met the next two Fridays and vowed to continue our meetings after winter break. Linda had thrown us together, and we all came for different reasons with differing personalities, but after a few meetings we felt respect and love for the courage each individual shared, the courage to break through years of illusions and comfortable barriers to get at the truth. For me, the truths we shared those few weeks were more intoxicating than the best chardonnay or merlot. Our dreams, complexities, fears, and triumphs brought us closer each meeting. Suddenly, we were not strangers, but women who shared the desire to plunge deeply into the meaning of our lives. We were middle-age women who wanted a different metaphor; instead of bobbing up and down in the middle of the ocean hanging on for dear life to a rope tossed overboard, we were women who wanted back on the boat, even if it meant swallowing gulps of saltwater, the waves slamming our bodies into the boat's starboard side, creating cuts and scratches on our thighs. We were ready to climb the stern's ladder, shins caught in the rungs, masks on top of wet plastered hair, huffing and puffing, until we stood naturally freckled, a red ring forming around our faces from a too tight mask, flat on the deck, flesh moving freely, unbound, touched by the wind and the sun. And once on the boat, instead of feeling battered and bruised, we would feel real, connected, and grounded on the balls of our blistered feet.

Chapter 19

My newly found world consisted of archeological digs in the rain, barbecue plates and peanut butter pie, Alabama trade days, and a friendship with a man who shared three quarters of his soul with me. The remaining part of him spiraled deeply and secretly out of my reach, and I spent hours trying to twist and tug free what he had buried in his crawl space. One day I peered beyond his bones and skin and knew I had to pull the past from his chipped heart. So, I brushed off my manicured fingers and accepted my fate. We journeyed through miles of red clay before I awakened to the ground beneath my borrowed boots, and as I did, sandhill cranes, venturing south, traced in the sky a cross that seemed to defy coincidence. And like the cranes, Micah and I, along with four fledging adolescents, flew south across the sky in anticipation of the fate that would cross our paths.

Marshall didn't want me to go on the trip, and, so out of character for him, fought against it. But once I had made up my mind to go, nothing could prevent me from renting dive gear, packing my suitcases and getting on the plane. The trip became something of a symbolic first step, a first step towards the truth, towards a higher purpose, towards understanding and forgiveness, and a first step away from the illusions and the lies, away from self-doubt and self destruction, and, finally, the first step away from Marshall, and that is why he drove me to the airport in silence as the sun came up, its red rays appearing as dusty pointillism through the city smog.

When we arrived at the airport Marshall wanted to walk me to the gate, but I wouldn't let him; I wanted the trip to start as soon as possible and with Marshall along the trip could not begin. "Let's say goodbye here. The traffic is going to get worse the longer you stay." I gave him a perfunctory hug and a peck on the cheek; he always looked so sad when he wanted his own way. "Are you going to be okay for the week, Marshall?" I asked.

"I always have work to do."

"I mean ... by yourself, you know."

"You do plan on coming back, don't you?"

"What do you think I'm going to do?" I asked uneasily. "Run off in the Mayan ruins forever? "

"You've been different lately. I'm afraid I'm losing you."

"Don't be afraid of losing me, Marshall," I said. "Be afraid of losing yourself."

"Whatever. Do you really think you're going in the water?"

"I don't know ... and frankly, Marshall, it doesn't really matter right now. Hope things go well at work this week. Now where are you going to be?"

"I told you I cleared this week so I could work in Atlanta. I knew this was your winter break."

"I thought you only cleared your weeks for Thanksgiving and Christmas. When did you start changing your schedule for winter break? Right after I planned this trip?"

"Have a good trip ... and don't drown anybody," he said as he walked away from the gate.

Marshall's statement was cruel, but to his credit, he only threw her drowning in my face one other time, when my Dad took me to get my driver's license. His words hurt me then as they did now, and while his words almost prevented me from passing the driving test, and for many years behind the wheel of the car I fought the fear his words engendered, a fear only few people could understand, I hid my anxiety behind my mercurial driving habits of either extreme over-cautiousness or high-speed recklessness. Watching Marshall leave the airport, his shoulders sagging, his head down, I felt sad and wished the years had treated us better.

In this subdued state, I approached the Delta gate and spotted Micah Marlowe surrounded by four ebullient teenagers, a female duo, one a short husky blonde, the other a tall boyish brunette, both carrying black dive bags on their backs, and two well-scrubbed males, one of slight build with short black hair, the other the same height as the first, but with a muscular build and a jauntily handsome face. Micah smiled broadly, accentuating the lines on his tanned face. He rubbed one hand along the left side of his jaw as if to tone down the hilarity of his expression.

"That was so lame, Marlowe."

Micah rubbed the other side of his jaw. "Right, hysterically funny, you mean. Ya'll jumped back like you saw a Haitian rat."

"Hey," I said. "Sounds like I missed all the excitement."

Micah's expression changed slightly when he heard my voice. "Hey, look who's finally here. Glad you could join us, Ms. Scott. You know any of these here?"

"Only Rachel. I had her last year in Juniors Honors, one of my best students." I turned to Rachel, "I didn't know you were on the trip."

"Yeah, I always go. I was surprised when Marlowe told me you were coming. You never mentioned you could dive."

"That remains to be seen. I don't know if I'll end up getting certified down there or not."

"Joe's planning on it ... but if you're too chicken to try ... Besides, going on a diving trip and not diving is like getting a pair of prescription glasses and never wearing them. Hey, Ms. Scott, this is Stephanie, she's in my Algebra I class, and Jared and Adam are in my trig class."

"We were in his Algebra II class last year and thought we knew all his jokes," Jared said.

Micah started laughing again, and I decided to change the subject to something more neutral.

"Do any of you know what the time difference is between here and Honduras?" I asked.

"Mr. M, are you going to show Ms. Scott your—"

"Hush up, Jared. Maybe later. Let's talk about the time difference. Well, since we'll cross several latitude lines and we're almost to the equator, it should be about four hours."

"Oh, really?" Micah's mouth turned slightly upward, and I thought about what he had said. "Very funny, smart ass. Going south doesn't change times, so how much difference?"

"Two hours. I don't know what kind of chaperone you're going to make, Ms. Scott, talkin' trash in front of the children."

"Just give me a straight answer and I'll be no problem."

Micah acted much differently in the airport than he did when he was in his portable or when we were traveling around together, just the two of us. He seemed to be showing off in front of the kids, acting much like a kid himself. I didn't know what to make of his behavior, but I do know it annoyed me a great deal, especially since the kids, hiding their laughter behind each other's dive bags, played right into his hands.

"I'm going to check to see if the plane is here," Micah said. He abruptly removed himself from the stationary chair and walked over to the gate agent. "Ma'am," he said, "I just want to make sure our flight is on time." The gate agent stared at Micah for a few minutes before she answered, and when she did, she could barely get the words out. The students gasped for breath, tears running down Rachel's cheeks, air spitting out of Stephanie's mouth, Jared and David doubled over in hilarious pain. I could not figure out what the joke was until Micah casually walked over to me and told me that the plane was on time. Then he smiled broadly and displayed a set of teeth that protruded far enough out to change the shape of his jaw line; instantly the teeth changed him from a serene and handsome man to a bumbling and homely hick.

"Good God, what are those?" I asked.

"These are my teeth from the trick store; my old ones were much better. They came with some green colored ones, but I left them in the truck and the sun melted them."

"These are bad enough. I swear, you act like an eleven-year-old sometimes."

"I always wear them on these trips; the kids love them."

"Well, I don't. Will you please take those out before anyone else sees," I said to Micah. "Those are horrible; you don't seem like the same person with those in."

"Either take me like I am or leave me. I think I'll wear these until we get to Roatan. The flight attendants will think they're real. I made sure our seats were together on both planes, Ms. Scott. We can have some fun with these. Come here babe, and gimme a little kiss." Micah moved his toothy face close to mine, but I moved as far away from him as possible.

"Get away from me, you loser," I laughed. "There's no way you're getting anything from me."

Micah wore his buckteeth on the flight from Atlanta to Miami and didn't take them off until we were settled on the Taca flight to Honduras. The teeth had a strange effect on Micah; it was as if they had given birth to a new person, the love child shared by Gomer Pyle and Minnie Pearl. He flirted and parlayed with the flight attendants as they lavished him with attention and smiles; the students couldn't get enough of his goofy grin and down-home jokes and laughed at almost everything he said or did as I winced behind my flight magazine at his adolescent redneck humor.

Overcrowded and over-sold, Taca airlines seated the passengers on a "first-one-there" basis, and after sending the students immediately to the back of the plane to scout seats, we took the only two seats together at the front of the plane. Micah assembled all but his camera gear under the seat, while I squeezed my backpack and dive bag into the overhead bins.

"Do you mind if I take the window seat?" Micah said. "I want to get a good video of the island before we land."

"No problem," I said as I adjusted my seat belt and gathered my reading material around me. "All I plan to do is relax and read a little on the flight." I noticed that Micah was playing with his video gear; he peered through the lens of his camera and focused it out the window and then directed the video camera right towards me.

"So, Ms. Scott, what made you decide to take a trip to Honduras with a math teacher and four of his students?"

"Well, Mr. Marlowe, for one thing, Miss Rachel's also one of *my* students. And the reason I decided to go on this trip? It is because the math teacher you just mentioned pestered me so much about the trip that I said yes to shut him up."

"Har-de-har, okay, enough practice, now I've got it on." Micah cleared his throat. "February 3rd, 1997, first day of our diving trip to Roatan, Honduras. This here is Ms. Scott, marginal English teacher, Tecumseh High School. She's about to get certified and go diving for the first time in her life. Why did it take you so long to get interested in diving, Ms. Scott?"

"Well, Mr. Marlowe, my life with the circus wasn't working out as well as I thought it should be, so I decided to try something different for a change. So I said yes to this trip and I feel pretty good about it. Maybe I'll start saying yes to everything from now on."

"Really?"

I looked Micah straight in the eye and said the most honest thing I had said in a long time. "Yes. I want to say yes to every good thing life has to offer from now on."

As the plane took off from the runway, Micah shifted the camera from me to the window. "And now we are leaving the Miami airport..." I watched him out of the corner of my eye, scanning the sharpness of his jaw and chin and the straightness of his nose. In repose, his handsomeness and singularity was hard to miss; it was curious to me why he would ever wear false teeth customized to obscure his good looks. As he put his camera away, he caught my stare. "Now what?" he said.

"You know me; I'm still trying to figure you out. We've spent hours together and have had some deep moments, but a stranger seeing us together today would never guess it."

"We can't be deep all the time." As he continued to reassemble himself in his seat, I reached for his hand.

"Micah, when people are close, they give some indication of it all the time. But you ... somehow, when you are around students, have to hide it ... "

"Maybe we're not as close as you think."

"We listened to tree frogs together ... and I told you some things ... Micah, I wouldn't have come on this trip if I didn't feel close to you. You're the only person in the world who could have convinced me to go away like this." I would have told him more, that I loved him, that he was my best friend, that I felt peaceful around him, but I wasn't sure the emotion went both ways.

"I like having you here. It may not seem like it, but I notice when you're around, and I listen to the things you say." His lips barely moved as he spoke and his jaw tightened; he lightly stroked the top of my hand with his index finger, his face turned towards mine. My eyes met his steady gaze and I thought I saw emotion as deep as mine, if not deeper, and I had a faint recollection of how paralyzing such feelings could be.

I grabbed his hand and held it tightly. "I understand," I whispered. "Finally, I think I understand."

#

Video in hand, Micah scurried off the plane before the rest of us. He immortalized us on a VHS tape as we climbed down the steps of an orange-and-white 727, our hair blowing in the humid tropical breeze. Of the five of us, I am the first one down the steps, walking tentatively as I lug my yellow dive bag and purple backpack over my shoulders, the wind pushing all my hair to one side, like a bird missing a wing. Because the camera is on, I wave, but my wave is impatient, as if to wave it away. Next off the plane are Stephanie and

Rachel, laughing and flirting with the camera, posing, making faces, having fun, teasing David and Jared who are right behind them. Wearing fishing hats pulled down over their eyebrows, the two boys almost fall down the steps trying to push their dive bags into the two girls. They scream, "Mr. Marlowe, man, we're finally here! Yeah!" Then the tape is a jumble of plane, sky and pavement, a lopsided frame of the two girls, and then the picture straightens out to show Micah with his hands on his hips smiling self-consciously, and then I drop my bags and jump on his back, throwing my legs around his waist, and he acts like he has a ton of bricks on his back, and the girls are laughing while strangers grin widely.

"You weigh a ton, Catherine. I told you not to eat two dinners on the plane. C'mon, ya'll, we have to go through customs." Customs consisted of several small linoleum-covered platforms and a manually operated turnstile that separated us from the single conveyor belt used for collecting luggage. With a cursory glance from the agents, we went through customs fairly quickly. Only one bag was lost, Stephanie's, but the gate agent assured her the bag would be delivered the next day. We excitedly piled into a small ancient bus with rusted doors and blue chipped paint, the open windows offering the only relief from the heat. Our luggage went on ahead of us, bulging out the top of a small flat-bed truck with wooden slat sides, more suited for hauling mangoes than duffle bags. We were ready to take bets on whose luggage would get bounced into a ravine, lost forever. The rickety bus sputtered out of the parking lot and we were on our way to San Pedro's Cay. From the airport, we turned onto the island's main road. On a map, it snaked its way from the northern to the southern end through grassed volcanic slopes and along village-lined shores.

My first encounter with true poverty came as we crested a small hill, and the roadside trees gave way to a clustering of humanity and their weathered shacks clinging to stability. Many on stilts to escape the ravages of hurricanes, unpainted and with tin roofs, they spread out before us by the hundreds. As the bus sped along, the images were quick and disjointed but the emotion was constant and crushing. Even when I closed my eyes, the pain of hunger, lives unnoticed and the image of a hand reaching out seeped through. This initial glimpse of the island came in jolts, the ride was so bumpy, but even so, the windows became our eyes to a world apart.

In silence we contemplated the scenes along the sides of the narrow road: short scrubby trees, occasional vistas of the ocean, multi-colored shanties with clotheslines strung from trees, haciendas tucked away in the privacy of the hills, small farms with roosters and goats, half-starved dogs hanging around the edges of the road and ragged children smiling at the passersby. Sometimes they only stared. There was no denying we were in a third world country. Geographically, we were only a thousand miles away; economically, we were billions of dollars away.

I wasn't sure what to expect from San Pedro's Cay. Since Micah was in charge of the trip I knew it would not be one of those all-inclusive resorts that separated us completely from the people and the surrounding villages. Marshall and I had stayed in resorts that were so enormous, they were countries unto themselves. We could have been anywhere in any warm country in the world. Fancy refuges have a way of making the realities of the host country invisible. They cater to guests who prefer to believe the illusion of Mexico, Puerto Rico or Haiti rather than the truth.

The bus turned down a narrow dirt road strewn sparsely with gravel. On either side of the road were small wooden shacks, sleepy dogs guarding clay pots and an occasional roaming rooster with his harem of scraggly hens. A shallow stream ran alongside the road. Barelegged women were standing in the water up to their knees, wringing out wet clothes, their small children splashing each other or sitting on the bank. On the other side of the stream were broken slabs of red cement, a recreational facility with two iron basketball goals, and a section marked off with faded tennis lines but no nets. A group of local boys were playing basketball while a few small girls watched, suppressing giggles behind their hands. Our world, the world of the bus people, did not exist for them. They went about their daily lives as if we were invisible.

We made a few more turns down the dusty road, until we saw a hand painted sign—San Pedro's Cay. We had arrived. At first it was hard to make out what the resort was like; the rain forest hid the scattered cabanas and wooden dive buildings. But when the bus dropped us off at the edge of a beautiful inlet, I caught a full view of small wooden cabins elevated above the water on stilts, the hills of the rain forest climbing just behind them. More cabins appeared near the top of the hills, and I could see a winding wooden walkway jutting upwards through the trees. Along the inlet's left side, dive buildings, including shops for rental equipment, photography and tank storage, lined the wooden docks opposite the dive boats, some just arriving back from the reefs, some just going out. The pier was full of divers hustling in and out of their equipment, rinsing their gear, hauling dive tanks on and off the boats. For me, a strange and intimidating sight. Before I had time to contemplate the scene further, Micah motioned us toward steep weathered stairs that led to the top of the small mountain we were beneath.

"Have you seen our bags anywhere?" I asked Micah.

"They deliver 'em directly to our rooms. The bags left before we did. I bet they're already there. C'mon, we'll go check."

Approaching the stairs, I noticed two covered docks under which two small fishing boats rocked in tune with the gentle current. Beyond were larger boats, uncovered, tied to the continuing pier beyond the dive boats and just before the bungalows on the water.

"At least our butts are going to get a good workout," I remarked to Rachel.

"This place isn't what I expected," Stephanie said. "Isn't there any place to get a pina colada?"

"You're not old enough to drink," said Micah.

"There's no drinking age in Honduras, Mr. Marlowe. My mom said I could drink if I want."

"She didn't tell me that. Should I call her up?"

"I don't think they have phones around here," said Rachel.

"Ya'll don't want to drink too much," Micah said looking at me. "Can't dive with a hangover."

"This place is so cool," said Rachel. "It's different from any place I ever stayed. When do we get to see our rooms?"

When we reached the first landing, a black man speaking well-articulated English greeted us. "Up this way, please." We all looked up at the wooden steps built into the side of the steep cliff; there must have been about two hundred of them. After a few minutes of climbing, the black Carib spoke again. "Only a few hundred more. Great work-out." He laughed as he easily climbed up the mountainous stairs. Once we reached the top, our guide led us to a large meeting room with open walls and mahogany floors and circulating ceiling fans. Even though it was almost five o'clock, Honduran time, it was hot and steamy and the breeze from the fans was a welcome relief. Below the meeting room were three spacious dining areas, graduated along the sides of the forested cliff, also with open walls and ceiling fans, and next to the dining areas was an open-air bar overhanging the Cay. The entire resort was open to the sea; we could feel the wind and witness the sea from any of the sprawling rooms.

We were given planter's punch with the option of having the punch alcohol-free, but all of us, including Micah, readily accepted the lightly spiked drinks. We were all excited and exhausted. The teenagers eyed each other, delighted their teachers did not embarrass them by denying them the sophisticated beverages. Micah and I knew teenagers fairly well, and we didn't have to exchange words to know what behaviors to allow. So amidst cocky teenagers away from home for the first time, experiencing their first taste of freedom, for some literally their first taste, we signed up for scuba certification training, dolphin lessons, and then hurriedly followed our guide to our rooms.

The cabins were even further up the mountain; it was hard to believe we were not already at the top after climbing the seemingly endless amount of steps. Jared and Adam stayed in the first set of bungalows, about fifty steps lower than the rest of us. As it turned out, Rachel, Stephanie and I shared a room at the mountain's top, and Micah and Joe, our dive master and instructor from Berkley, California, the one who glued Micah's head in Eleuthera, stayed in the room right next to ours. Our two rooms shared a porch with two hammocks and a large star-gazing deck, which jutted out in front of the two bungalows. We could see miles and miles across the inlet out into the Caribbean. "Ms. Scott, are you going to unpack before it gets dark? Our luggage is here," Rachel said.

"I'll be there in a minute." I was tired from the hike up to the cabin but the view almost made me giddy. I stood near the edge of the deck and soaked in the darkening sky, the remnants of the orange sunset, and the rhythm of the lapping waves below.

"Beautiful, ain't it?" Micah's voice was behind me.

I was so moved by the wonder of it all that I couldn't speak right away.

After a few minutes, I said, "I wish I could stand here forever."

Micah placed his hand around the curve of my waist, and I could feel his hummed breath on the back of my neck. We stood in silence, the warm Caribbean wind filling our faces and lungs and hearts. After a few minutes, Micah broke the silence. "See the sky over there? It is only a few hundred miles from Cuba. And this way," Micah pointed to the left, "is the Yucatan Peninsula, less than a hundred miles from right here. Amazing, huh? You know, that's where they think the asteroid hit that killed the dinosaurs."

"Yes, it is amazing." I smiled at Micah under the now indigo and gray striped sky and grabbed his hand from around my waist. I squeezed his hand tightly and wanted to throw myself at him and suggest we make wild passionate love beneath the stars, but the sound of adolescent voices stopped me in my impulsive tracks. "I guess we better unpack before it gets too late," I said.

Micah gently caressed my chin with his thumb and forefinger. "Hurry up, I'm ready for dinner and a cold beer."

Nestled in the slopes of the mountains, the dining rooms protruded over the quiet cay, giving us a panoramic view of ocean and sky. The sun was now barely below the horizon but its influence spread back over our heads as sheared clouds turned rose, peach and back to slate gray all in just a few minutes. A tiny silhouette of what was probably a cruise ship sat upon the horizon line. The reflecting remnants of light illuminated the dark waters of the cay. The raised and lowered tones of the diners and the scolding from the parrots and macaws that strutted along the beams of the ceilings muffled the repetitive sounds of the waters slapping the piers and docked dive boats. A damp tropical breeze cooled our faces as we seated ourselves at the only table big enough to accommodate our group of seven. The teenagers all scrambled to sit together at one end of the table, while Micah and I sat at the other end, saving a seat for Joe, who was making last minute arrangements with our week's boat captain and crew.

Micah and I drank Port Royal beer with dinner, which consisted of grouper and yellow fin tuna. "We may not find the fish too appetizing after our dive tomorrow," Micah said. "Might be like eating one of our pets." Ignoring Micah, I ravished the fish and fresh vegetables. The local beer tasted wonderful and went down fast. Halfway through my second one, Micah commented on my bliss. "It's not good to drink too much before diving in the morning."

"I'm watching what I'm doing ... Dad." I noticed Micah was only about one quarter of the way through his first beer. He shrugged at me.

"Hey, Mr. Marlowe, tell Ms. Scott about what you did with the Mountain Dew in science class last year," Jared shouted from the other end of the table.

"I thought you taught math," I said.

"I teach all math this year, but sometimes I teach math and science. I was gonna teach English but there was no challenge."

"Right, all you do in math is give worksheets," I said.

"Stop fussing! Tell us about the Mountain Dew," said Stephanie.

Joe arrived in time to hear Micah's outrageous but believable story. "Right before my fifth period science class, I filled a test tube with Mountain Dew." Micah paused to laugh. "And I added teeny weeny raisins. Because of the carbonation that sticks to them, the raisins go up and when the bubbles pop, the raisins go down. When the kids came in, mostly freshmen, I told them the raisins were sewer lice, and they would suck up all the contaminants from the sewer water that I had in the test tube." Joe started to laugh; he knew what was coming.

"And I told the kids that the lice would actually make the sewer water drinkable." He had the rest of us at the table laughing now. "I told them that I would drink the water to demonstrate just how safe the lice made the water. You should've seen their faces. They were all staring at me like I was either crazy or full of crap."

"I know which it is," I said.

"Anyway, right before I put the test tube to my mouth, I said, 'Now don't ya'll try this at home, because drinking one of them sewer lice would be disastrous.' Then I slowly put it to my mouth and a few of them groaned. Then I took a big sip and I let one of the raisins go into my mouth. Oh man, I started choking and hacking and they're screaming 'Oh, my God, oh my God'; some kid gets up and hits the intercom button. Panic is prevalent, you might say. Then I started laughing so hard, I really did kinda choke. I had to tell the office that all was well in between coughs. It was beyond funny to see some of their faces."

"Was Dr. Blackwell mad?" asked Rachel.

"He acted like he thought it was funny, but I didn't score any points with him either. Don't much care if they don't like the way I teach anyway."

"You're too much, man." Joe shook his head and chuckled.

"Man, I got something in my eye. Where's my fork?" Micah picked up his fork and started prodding at the edge of his eye with one of the prongs. Before any of us could stop him, he gasped as a white filmy liquid ran out through his fingers. The students jumped backwards in their seats and screamed for help. Joe wasn't sure what to do and I thought the trip was as good as over. I grabbed my napkin and placed it firmly over Micah's eye. "Here, hold this on it," I said.

"Quit, you *are* gonna poke out my eye," Micah said. "My eye's fine. It was a joke, see?" Micah said, holding up a thumbnail carton of coffee creamer. "You guys are too easy. And right after I told you about the sewer lice. Geeesh."

"You really are a brat," I said as I hit him in the arm.

"This'll be a fun week," Micah said with a mischievous grin.

"I don't know if I'm going to survive the week with all of you adolescents," I said. "Especially the one over forty." My adrenaline hadn't yet calmed down from the absurd and juvenile eye trick. I was mad at Micah for scaring me so badly, and mad at myself for falling for the stunt in the first place. This man was not the serious and walled Micah with whom I rode around in the truck and combed the clay looking for artifacts. The person sitting next to me at the table was self-assured and full of himself; in the soft moonlit room, Micah's anxiety dissipated and in repose his facial features softened into those of a wise and kindly father.

"Where do you get your ideas?" I ask.

"The same place you get yours, Miss Ratched. I just think them up at the spur of the moment. I should really keep a notebook and start writing some of 'em down."

"Do you ever actually teach?" I joked.

"Mr. Marlowe's the best teacher I ever had," said Jared. "I learned more in his trig class in one month than I learned in Algebra II all last year with Miss Ulrich."

"Mr. M. makes learning seem like fun. His class goes really fast," added Rachel.

"I've interrupted Mr. Marlowe's classes a few times."

"A few too many," Micah interjected.

"You're right. He doesn't teach half as bad as I thought he might."

The conversation moved from teaching to diving, and Joe reassured us that diving was easy if we just used common sense. Stephanie and I shared our fears about diving and at one point I said I might not even try it. Joe said if I felt any discomfort about diving I could either snorkel or stay on the boat and help the divers with readying their equipment. Micah leaned his head back while scratching his chin as if talking to the sky and said, "Oh, she's gonna dive. I'll make sure she has a hand to hold the whole time, if necessary."

"You'll be Cat's buddy then?" Joe asked. "That will be one less person I have to keep an eye on."

"I thought the four of them would buddy-up to finish their certification, and I'll help Cat with hers. I think she's going to need extra help, if you know what I mean."

"Micah, I'm really not sure I can go in the water, with or without you, so don't plan on it."

"We'll see. You'll be fine. It's not that tough." Without saying goodbye to anyone, Micah abruptly left the table and walked out of the dining room. I wondered if he were mad about my indecisiveness, especially after he said he would personally help me with my diving, or if he did not want to give me another chance to back out.

Shortly after Micah left, we all got up and headed back to the cabins. I still had some unpacking to do, plus I was exhausted from getting up at five in the morning and traveling all day. We had two sets of bunk beds in our bungalow; Stephanie and Rachel took the two top bunks, while I claimed one of the bottom bunks. It was only nine o'clock, but it felt like midnight, and in Atlanta time we were only an hour from midnight. It would feel good to go to bed early and get a good night's sleep before the stressful next day of certification classes and diving. Stephanie sat in one of the hammocks on the porch and wrote in her journal, while Rachel talked to Micah and Joe in the cabin next door and I continued unpacking. When finished, I settled comfortably in my bed and read until Stephanie climbed into hers, and we talked about school and our fears about diving. Rachel finally returned and climbed up to the top bunk across from Stephanie and me. "Mr. Marlowe says goodnight to everybody," Rachel said.

"Did you have him as a teacher, too?" asked Stephanie.

"Yeah, I had him for Algebra II and Physical Science. We moved to Atlanta my sophomore year, and Fulton County requires the P.S. course. I was the only sophomore with all the freshman, but I had so much fun. The freshmen are all so clueless and Marlowe made fun of them all the time."

"Mr. M.'s the only math teacher that taught me anything." Later I found out Stephanie had a learning disability in math, and was in Micah's Concepts class, a class for low achievers in math, and he helped her overcome her handicap so much, she was placed in Algebra II and was doing fine.

"My boyfriend had Mr. M., too. That's where I met him."

"I didn't know you had a boyfriend, Stephanie," I said. "What's he like?"

"He's really sweet and cute. We've been together for about a year. He wanted to come on the trip, but his parents said he had to work all summer for getting busted for smoking pot. He really doesn't smoke it much. I don't let him smoke it in front of me at all."

"Have you ever been busted for smoking pot, Stephanie?" I asked.

"Just once. My parents about had a stroke. I came home from a date with Allan and they smelled it on me."

"Sure you tried it just once," said Rachel.

"I bet you've never done drugs, have you?" Stephanie said to Rachel, deflecting attention from herself.

"I've never really gotten into all that. I don't think my mom would care if I did. She was really understanding when my brother tried it. She would probably be glad if I did try drugs. She thinks I study too much."

"Not my mom. She had a fit when she found out I tried it. Are you married, Ms. Scott?"

"Well, of course. I mean, I'm surprised you'd ask that, Stephanie."

"I wasn't sure. You're not wearing a wedding ring; I thought you and Mr. Marlowe might be a little more than just friends."

"No, we're just friends. Not only am I married, I have kids older than you. Sammy and Elizabeth—they're both in college now. As for my ring, Mr. Marlowe told me to leave it at home. Cold water makes your hands shrink. You might want to take yours off."

"Okay. So did they smoke pot?"

"I'm sure Sammy does from time-to-time, and Elizabeth smoked some in high school. She got high in her room with a couple of her friends, and I smelled it. She thought I was going to disown her."

"Did you smack her?"

"No, Stephanie, I don't believe hitting kids helps much. It just makes them mean."

"Did you ever spank your kids?"

"Probably a few times, but not if I could help it. I usually sent them to their room or grounded them."

"I wish I had you for a mother. My mom spanked me all the time. She used a brush and, boy, did that sting."

"Well, you don't seem too scarred for life because of it. Couldn't have been that bad."

"I hated it though. Rachel, did you ever get spanked? "

"I remember once, at my grandma's, I was running around trying to catch my brother. I think I knocked something over that was valuable. But my mom's pretty cool; she doesn't get too mad at much, except my dad. Thank God he doesn't live with us anymore."

"Where's he live?" I asked.

"He lives in Atlanta, but on the other side of town. No one in my family can stand him. Thank God my mom met Dan. He's really nice to all of us."

"Good. Do you girls mind if we turn off the lights and go to sleep now? I can hardly keep my eyes open."

"Sure, but you have to turn off the lights; you're on the bottom."

"No problem." I threw my legs over the side of the bed and climbed down from the lower bunk. The light was on the wall next to the door that led into the bathroom, and I decided to use the facilities while I was up. I flipped off the light on the way out of the bathroom and groped the wall on my way back to bed.

"Shit!" I yelled. "I smacked my head into this damn wooden post. Damn, that hurts."

"What a klutz … I can't wait to tell Mr. Marlowe."

"I hope I don't get a black eye."

"I don't think you get a black eye if you bump your head," said Stephanie.

"Thanks for your concern." Laughter came from the dark.

"Let's go to sleep and just forget about it, okay?"

"What's the klutziest thing you've done, Ms. Scott?"

"There're too many to choose from."

"Just pick one, then we'll go to sleep."

"Okay, one. Then no more talking. One of the most embarrassing things I've ever done was fall off a boat ladder at a boat show. My husband and I were on the fly bridge of a Bayliner—we were in this huge convention center in Cincinnati, and it was full of boats and people looking at boats, and instead of turning around and walking down the boat ladder backwards, I walked down the ladder frontward, and after a few steps fell to the floor of the boat. Lucky for me I landed on my hands instead of my face, in front of a line of people waiting to get on the boat. Instead of quietly walking away, I started explaining to the crowd why I fell—you know, that I went down the boat the front way when I should have gone down backwards. "

"God, that's so stupid. Why'd you even talk to anybody?"

"Because I didn't want them to think I'd been drinking."

"I would rather have them think I was drunk instead of goofy," Stephanie said. Both girls started giggling and couldn't stop.

"What's so funny in there?" Micah yelled from the cabin next door.

"Someone's making us laugh," shot back Stephanie.

"Okay, girls, I'm really tired. Please, I need to get some sleep, and you do too. We have a hell of a long day tomorrow."

Their snickering continued for a few more minutes and then to my relief, finally stopped, and I sank into a blissful sleep. It felt so good to be a mom again, or at least cast into the mother role. I really missed Elizabeth, and being with Stephanie and Rachel brought back the days of a little girl teasing her mother, giggling with a girlfriend. When Elizabeth was eight years old, she loved to hit me on the bottom and call me "watermelon butt." She always got the much looked-for reaction from me when she did that. "Do you really think I have a big butt, Elizabeth dear?" I would ask. "It's so big you could put out a fire with it," was the usual response.

"But not big enough to put out all the lights in Cincinnati, is it?"

"Mom, you could moon the entire state of Ohio with that thing."

Then I would chase her around the house and we would both laugh. When she was not around, I would get my hand mirror and check out my backside in the full-length mirror. When Marshall came home, I would ask him if he thought I was putting on weight, especially in the back. He always answered correctly. "You look the same as the day we got married, dear. One of the reasons I married you was because of your great butt."

I must have drifted off to sleep for about fifteen minutes when I was awakened by the low rumbling chuckles of Micah and Joe. Just as suddenly as it started, it stopped; then the sound of soft, low voices started to lull me back to sleep, then the jolt of loud laughter, this time for a longer period. Quiet talking for about five minutes, then more, obnoxious roars.

"What the hell? Don't they know we are all trying to sleep?"

"They won't be up for too much longer, Ms. Scott. Marlowe told me he was really whipped," soothed Rachel.

After ten more minutes of listening to the ongoing irritation, I couldn't stand it any longer.

"I'm going over there."

"Ms. Scott, I wouldn't. Mr. Marlowe will make a fool out of you."

"I can take care of myself around Mr. Marlowe, of all people. Joe and Marlowe are so damn inconsiderate." I strode purposefully over to their cabin, listening to the sounds of Rachel and Stephanie's convulsed laughter into their pillows.

"Did you see Ms. Scott's pajamas? They have penguins on them!" Their laughing became even more unrestrained.

Who gives a damn? It's dark anyway, I thought.

The slats on their windows were open, and I could see Micah and Joe sitting in their queen-size beds, talking and joking as loud as they pleased, oblivious to the rest of the world around them, especially the sleeping world. "How'd you guys rate these big beds? We all have narrow bunks."

"The important people get the most comfortable beds," Joe said. "Is that you out there, Cat?"

"None other. Hey, if you guys have such comfortable beds, why don't you all go to sleep in them? We've been listening to you for half an hour, and we're ready to go to sleep. "

"Micah's telling dive stories. They're hilarious. Come on in and join us?"

"No, I was checking to see what all the commotion was about. You think you might go to bed sometime tonight? Weren't you the ones talking all this shit about 'long day tomorrow'?"

"Wasn't me. Was that you?" Joe looked at Micah.

"Nope, not me."

"Besides, I still need to organize my lesson plans," said Joe.

"Lesson plans? You teaching a class?"

"You don't just jump in the water and bing, you're certified; you have to know all the diving rules and regulations. Plus, I'm going to teach you and the kids all about the reef and fish so you know what you're seeing when you are, hopefully, underwater. Class will be held in between dives and a couple in the early evening when we aren't on a night dive. You'll learn about dolphins too. San Pedro's Cay has special dolphin instructors from the Marine Institute that teach those classes. Didn't Micah tell you?"

"He didn't tell me our vacation would be so much work."

"Having fun is hard work, my dear," said Micah.

"Well, I need to get some sleep even more now. So, are you guys about to quiet down?"

Micah walked out of his cabin and motioned me towards the star gazing deck. "Hey, Ms. Scott, come out here for a few minutes and look at the stars before you turn in. They're really something to see."

"Micah, I need to get some sleep, like everyone except you and Joe are getting."

"You can sleep anytime. It isn't often that you get to see stars like this."

Micah was right. When I went out to the deck and beheld the vast expanse of sky, thousands of stars tapped their flickering codes above us and the brilliant infiniteness took my breath away. I thought about waking up Rachel and Stephanie, but I selfishly wanted to savor the sight alone, or almost alone. "Micah ... I've never ... "

"I know ... let's sit for a few minutes." My tired eyes grew wide-awake as we lay in the lounge chairs searching the sky.

"Do you see the Big and Little Dipper over there?" Micah pointed towards the North Star.

I nodded in the dark then realized I needed to speak. "Yes ... amazing. I was a little girl the last time I saw the night sky this clearly. So many ... they go on forever. I can almost feel their wings in my fingers."

"Wings?"

"My dad told me on hot summer nights the stars come down from the heavens to cool off for a bit, but since stars don't have wings they have to jump on the backs of damselflies. Together they become a firefly. He said catching one was like catching a falling star. I believed him for the longest time."

Micah's soft laugh whispered across the star-gazing deck. "That's wonderful. Your father was very creative. When I see as many stars as these, I feel the same way I do on a night dive. You'll see what I mean if you don't chicken out."

"I have never been in the ocean, much less at night, but I can imagine what you're talking about. I can see how the water could be like the sky. If it looks like this, it must be beautiful." Only under the cover of a dark though heavily starlit sky, and only with Micah, it seemed, could I again consider the duality of one of nature's strongest forces: the soft rains flow through the earth with the pulsating rhythms of life's blood; yet blind storms rush over the earth like the angry ravages of multiplying cancers.

"You've heard of Lucifer, right?"

I nodded and mumbled, "Of course. He was the archangel God threw out of heaven. Satan. His name literally means light-bearer. Why?"

"You'll see. I'll take you on a night dive and then you'll know why."

"I don't think I need to go on a night dive. I feel as if I am in the middle of the sea right now."

"Well, you kinda are."

"Yeah, but it feels different surrounded by all these stars. It's as if I am in a small boat, like the ones the Bora Borans were on when they crossed the ocean to Hawaii."

"Not all them Bora Borans made it across the sea, you know. Some of them drowned."

I could not speak and did not for a long moment. "I've always wondered what it feels like to drown. Do you suppose before the water fills your lungs, you actually enjoy how it feels floating around free and light in the waves? "

"I hope so, for *their* sake. I've heard people experience a feeling of euphoria right before death, so I guess it's no different with a drowning. Hey! You see that? A shooting star just split in two."

"I'll be damned … look, another one just went. Should I wake the girls?"

"No, there'll be other nights. Let them sleep."

"Did you see how long the tail was on that one? Incredible."

"Pretty amazin', ain't it?"

"I could lay here all night."

"You better have some bug spray if you're gonna do that."

"I put some on just before dinner. I should be alright."

"I thought you were *tie*-yerd."

"Not anymore. I feel so … so alive right now. So part of the universe. So … "

"Beautiful … "

"I didn't know you thought I was beautiful, Micah," I said.

He must have been caught off guard for a moment, because he quickly explained his "beautiful" compliment away. But it was too late, for even though it was dark, there was enough light for me to observe the way he looked at me when he called me "beautiful."

"I meant you are beautiful because you are part of all of this. You're another star, adding your spirit to nature … and you'll be even more beautiful when you go diving tomorrow."

"It would have been fine if you had stopped after the first 'beautiful,'" I teased. His quiet chuckle drifted down the side of the cliff, and I knew if it were not for Micah, I would be sound asleep in my bungalow instead of wide-awake in the middle of an island surrounded by near-infinite stars. I felt a flush of gratefulness come over me.

"Stephanie said you are the best teacher she has ever had."

"I just do my best."

"Hey, what happened to the thick Southern accent?"

"I can talk Georgia thick just like my mama, or do the Ohio thing like my daddy."

"Where did your dad grow up?"

"Newport, right across the river from Cincinnati. He was a wannabe gangster. You and him would have lots to talk about if you all got together."

"How'd he end up in Georgia?"

"He was in the Army and met my mama at a dance just south of town, place called Fort Gillem. He married my mama and they had me in Germany, and returned to Georgia when my daddy got out of the service. I was a one-year-old when they moved back. My daddy wanted to move back to Newport, but my mama didn't want to live that close to Yankees, so they moved to Ben Hill, a little town near the airport. You wanta hear something cool?"

"What might that be?"

"When mom saw my dad walk in the little dance area at the get-together, she told her friend, 'That's the man I'm going to marry one day.' Pretty nifty huh? Mom is quite a pistol."

"I guess you were, too, since they only had one child."

"My mother had trouble giving birth to me—there were some complications, so I guess that's why she didn't have any more. How many are in your family?"

"I have two sisters and two brothers. I was born smack in the middle of them all."

"At least you weren't lonely."

"I got lonely, a lot. Ever hear about feeling alone in a crowd? That's how it was sometimes. Most of the times. Even now."

"Hey, there's another one, see that? Man, it's ... almost like watching fireworks."

"One after another, it seems. The whole sky is lit up with stars."

"More pebbles to put in your sack."

"Now what're you talking about?"

I could sense Micah smile in the dark. "Haven't you ever heard the pebble story?"

"No, why would I?" He certainly could be an odd man at times.

"I just figured ... maybe ... anyway. It's a good way to approach life."

"Okay, tell me the pebble story so I can be part of the enlightened crowd."

Micah cleared his voice and sat up in his chair. From that, I gathered this story would be rather long. I leaned back, put my bare feet up on the wooden deck rail, and breathed in the salty night air. It had been a long time since anyone had told me a bedtime story.

"A band of weary men were traveling by camel through the desert."

"Only men?"

"Yes, just listen. So one night at camp a magnificent being appeared before them and in their thoughts. They were waiting for some revelation to give them power and prestige but all the vision said was, 'Gather as many pebbles as you can and tomorrow's evening will find you glad and it will find you sad.'"

"Pebbles? Pick up pebbles?"

"Shhh ... that's kinda what they said. But because of the brilliance of their visitor, they bent down and put a few pebbles into their saddle sacks. They traveled for a day and when the next camp was made, they opened their bags and each pebble had become a diamond. They were glad they had diamonds but wished they had picked up more pebbles."

I was quiet for several seconds. "How beautiful! I'm sorry I interrupted. So, is that what we are doing here?" I said. "Gathering pebbles?"

"I can't speak for you. I can only speak for myself."

"So are you gathering pebbles?"

"Trying to, always." And that was all he said. Micah could be very disconcerting at times; he talked when I wanted him to be quiet, and he was quiet when I wanted him to talk.

"So how do you relate the story to your life?"

"I don't know. It's just a story. Look, another shooting star catching a ride." I let out a long, frustrated sigh. "It ain't for me to tell ya what the story means. It's for you to figure out. You're the English teacher, not me."

He had a point and this time I started laughing. "You are so right." For a few minutes I stared at him as he continued to gaze at the stars. He had a familiarity about him I could not quite put my finger on. Finally, it came to me. "Do you know who you remind me of?"

"Ain't no telling, Paul Newman?"

"You wish. Better actually. Atticus Finch. You know, *To Kill a Mockingbird*, or I guess more accurately, Gregory Peck's portrayal of Atticus Finch. He was the wise Southern father who told his children it was a sin to kill a mockingbird."

"I know, I know. I read the book. He said that it was a sin to kill a bird that sang so beautiful and didn't harm nothing."

"You look just the way Gregory Peck did in the movie. I bet he was the same age as you are now when he played Atticus."

"That's so funny you should bring that movie up. When I was about ten, I met in person the two people who played Scout and Jem. They was adults by then."

"They *were* adults by then."

Micah continued, my correction unnoticed. "Mom and Dad drove me to Birmingham to see them. Do you know who played Boo Radley in the film?"

"I can barely remember what Boo Radley looked like. He only was in a few scenes at the end."

"Robert Duvall. It was one of his first films."

"No kidding, I never knew that." We sat there a little longer, and I must have dozed off in the chair, because the next thing I knew, Micah was shaking my shoulders.

"Hey, Scout," he said. "You better go inside and sleep, the mosquiters will eat you up." Before I could get up out of the lounge chair, Micah was already gone. I took my time walking back to the bungalow and savored the sweetness of the night air and the sounds of scurrying night animals. I had no clue what they were, shadows hid them. As I approached my cabin door, I felt the eyes of the puffer on me. I could now see they were sad eyes asking why. He clacked his teeth in frustration that somehow I, and not he, had escaped.

#

Right after the sun came up, Micah called to us between the half-closed louvered windows of the cabin. "Hey, anybody alive in there?"

Half-awake because of the constant crowing of the roosters down in Sandy Bay, a small village about half a mile down the road, I remained comfortably relaxed under the soft cotton sheets, savoring the last few minutes of relative peace. I looked up and could see Rachel sleeping soundly, oblivious to the noisy racket of the puffed-up Chanticleers, and there was as yet no sound from the bunk directly above. I twice reached for my watch on the floor under my bed and saw that it was not yet six. "Go away, Micah," I mumbled. "We don't have to get out of bed until six. We have at least ten more minutes."

"I brought you all some coffee. Open the door, before I drop it all over me."

Reluctantly, I climbed out of bed; I knew Rachel and Stephanie were not going to fly down from their bunks to grab for coffee. But a steaming cup of Honduran coffee sounded like the right kind of brew to get my sluggish body moving; no more late nights star gazing for me, or at least no more nights past ten o'clock.

"Hurry up in there. What's taking you so long? Open the stinking door."

"I'm hurrying," I said as I tried to comb my disheveled hair with my fingers and pull a pair of shorts on at the same time. I opened the door to blue sky and the saw-grass smell of the ocean and a smiling Micah holding three glorious cups of coffee.

"Good morning, Scout. I take it you had a good night's sleep. You obviously did not move around much in bed, the way your hair is all matted down on one side."

For an instance, I touched a hand to my hair, and then laughed. "I guess I'm not so beautiful after all."

"Here, drink some coffee. It'll help. There are rolls over in front of our cabin—I picked them up at the cantina. Jared and Adam are already down there having a big breakfast. You females sure are lazy. Anyway, I thought you all might want to have something fast to eat before you get all fixed up."

"Are you saying there is something wrong with the way we look?"

"Well, look, another female's up. Where's Rachel? Still snoozing away?" Micah stuck his head in our cabin. "Hey, time to get up. You can't see anything purty if you stay in bed all day."

"I'm getting up," Rachel mumbled beneath the covers. "I would've gotten more sleep if you all didn't stay up all night talking. We could hear you two laughing out there. You," she pointed at me, "were just as bad as those other two."

"We were trying to be quiet," I said. "I can't believe you heard us."

"We didn't hear anything," said Stephanie. "Rachel's giving you a hard time. You fall for anything, Ms. Scott."

"I'm going to see how the others are doing," Micah said as he hopped down the steps two at a time.

"Ladies, do you want some coffee and rolls? We have to be down at the dive dock at eight sharp. I suggest you get a move on."

"Okay, okay."

"So, Scout, you have some s'plaining to do. What were you doing up so late?"

"Shut up, you two, and get ready. And its *Ms. Scott*, if you don't mind."

"Can we call you Cat like Mr. M. does?"

"If you stop calling me Scout."

The six of us made it to the dining rooms just before seven o'clock. The concierge had assigned us a permanent table overlooking the right side of the cay. A tall black waiter took our breakfast orders of pancakes, French toast, eggs and bacon and filled our glasses with freshly squeezed orange and pineapple juice. Beyond the ferns, broad leaf plants and wild avocado trees lining the ridge of the cloud forest, the Caribbean waters shimmered in the morning sun, God's original Gaugin. The warm breeze melted over my body and invoked peaceful etchings of long go. An eleven-year-old girl with red pigtails, dressed in a lime green poplin dress and heavy brown shoes leapfrogged into my daydream that morning. Over her dress, she wore a white cotton apron with cross-stitched flowers along the edges. *She skips toward an open field full of long-leafed tobacco plants, and grabs a young boy's hand and almost pulls his arm out of joint swinging him around. When he freezes into a statue, she rolls in the freshly cut grass, her face turning green as she washes it all over with the sweet-smelling clumps. A woman calls for her to come home, and she hides in the cattail marsh. When the woman stops calling, she removes her socks and shoes, and walks barefoot in the running creek adjacent to the cranberry bog. She hikes up to Lone Tree Bluff where trout can be seen in a small pool below the waterfall if the sun hits just right through the trees. The young boy catches crawfish and salamanders and polliwogs in the small spring in the ravine just below. At dusk she faces with uncertainty the old gray farmhouse. She pulls on her jiggered socks and steamy shoes, straightens her mud-soaked dress, and faces the cross-armed warden standing on the long porch.*

Before I had time to place these memories, I felt Micah's silent stare. When my eyes met his, I held them there for longer than I intended. His eyes were not just observing me but searching for something in me. I was the first to look away. I turned my attention to Joe who was giving the group a brief history lesson of the island.

"Mainlanders speak Spanish," Joe was saying, "but most of the Bay Islanders speak English ... well, in a way."

"Why don't they speak Spanish?" asked Adam.

"Because the Mainlanders are mostly Metizos, descended from the Spaniards and native Hondurans. Most of them are farmers. The islanders are mainly fishermen and mariners and boat builders. Can anyone guess who the islanders might be descended from?"

"Pirates!" Stephanie piped up.

"Good guess, missy," Joe said. Not yet thirty, Joe seemed mature beyond his years. "The islanders are descended from Africans and Englishmen, from slaves and buccaneers and pirates. The original population of the Bay Island's was the Paya Indians; you can still see many of the old dwelling sites and pre-Columbian pottery around here. Some of the natives try to sell the ancient ceramics they dig up to us gringos."

"Yaba-ding dings," Micah interjected. "That's what the natives call the pottery pieces."

"French toast and bacon?" interjected our waiter.

"Over here," said Micah. The rest of us patiently waited as the tall Carib placed our orders around the table. At home, a cup of coffee and a roll would have been plenty for breakfast, but the fresh air and sun enlivened my appetite.

Joe continued his lecture telling about the coming of Columbus in 1502 and the Spaniards carrying off the Indians to slave for them in Mexico and the West Indies. But too many reefs blocked the Spanish approach from the sea, so they rejected the Bay Islands as a site for permanent settlements. The pirates and buccaneers had smaller ships so they could navigate the shallow reefs and easily hide from the large Spanish ships behind the reefs. Plus, the islands were close to Trujillo, where the Spanish stockpiled their gold.

"Are we going to see any pirate ships on our dives?" Rachel asked.

"Probably not. But I heard if you search the cay you can find remnants of English pottery."

"Why English pottery?" I asked.

"Early English settlers colonized Roatan around 1638. They were Puritan farmers from Maryland, mostly. They called the island Rich Island and grew tobacco and indigo for export. Later the Spanish threw them out. The English probably colonized in what today is Port Royal. The Spanish couldn't keep the pirates out though. The folklore on the island is that the loot from Morgan's 1671 raid on Panama is buried on Roatan. Cool beans, huh?" Joe said.

"Is it illegal to dig for treasure?" Jared asked. "Maybe we can go looking for some after we dive, huh, Mr. M.?"

"I don't think there would be any harm in digging through the sandy beaches," Joe said.

"I brought my metal detector. We can go looking on some of the small cays around here," Micah added. "There are plenty of small canoes for us to get over there."

Joe laughed at Micah's never-ending artifact quest. "You could probably find plenty of buttons and ceramic pieces from old English dishes, maybe even some old coins. Anyway, back to the history lesson. It's almost time to go down to the docks." Joe leaned back in his chair and cleared his throat. "Around 1797 the English soldiers dumped thousands of Black Caribs on the Islands. After the abolition of slavery, white Cayman islanders settled here because they were afraid of retaliation from the former slaves. Then in 1838, black Caymans started coming to the islands."

"Wait a minute," said Stephanie. "I thought slavery was abolished in the 1860's."

"We're talking about Central America, dear. Slavery was abolished almost forty years before the US. So today the people here are mainly English-speaking Protestants, unlike the people on the mainland who are Spanish-speaking Catholics."

"I've heard some of the people working here speak Spanish," said Rachel.

"Well, there are Spanish Hondurans living on Roatan—especially since tourism has increased on the island. Many Spanish-speaking mainlanders come over here looking for better job opportunities, and there have always been small pockets of Spanish Hondurans on the islands. They make up the small group of farmers and live inland. But the true islanders live on the edge of the water in small houses built on stilts to protect them from the hurricanes, like down in Sandy Bay and West End. They are mainly fishermen."

When the waiter cleared our table, we looked at him with new insights. He had no trouble understanding or speaking English, most likely a descendent of one of the Black Caribs or the later Black Caymans.

Breakfast over, Joe and Micah reminded us to be down at the dive deck at eight sharp, and with fifteen minutes to spare, the teenagers played with the nervy parrots and macaws that were walking on the tables scavenging for food, while I ran up to the bungalow to change into my bathing suit, lather myself with bug spray, and pack all the sundries needed for a day in the sun. It seemed the older I became, the more paraphernalia I needed to do just about any activity. In my younger and simpler days, I would have thrown on my swimsuit in ten minutes and not worry about sunglasses, bug spray, towels, moisturizers, lip balm, sun hat, decongestant, eye drops and whatever else I felt I could not live without. By the time I slipped on my suit, it was already eight, and I only had enough time to grab my shorts and dive bag. As I ran down the endless steps, I rationalized that the bug spray and sun tan lotion would wash off in the water, the salt water was as good as any moisturizer and the scenery was too beautiful to be dulled by sunglasses. It was amazing how the warmth of the sun could toss vanity aside. A few wrinkles were worth the peace and well-being the sun inspired.

When I got down to the dive deck, Micah was pacing back and forth, checking his watch. "Hey, you're late! Joe's already in the dive room. You've missed the first part about the tanks. I guess I'll have to show you how to hook it up."

"We have to hook up our own tanks?" I asked.

"This isn't the country club. You have to tote your own clubs here."

"Oh great, I'll probably hook it up all wrong and run out of air in five minutes."

"That's the price you pay when you're late. You cannot be late. It messes up the whole day. These people run on schedule. The boat will leave and there is nothing I can do about it. Go get a tank."

"Alright, Mr. Ahab."

For the rest of the morning, Joe and Micah taught us all about steel and aluminum tanks, p.s.i. units, service pressure, hydrostatic tests, and tank serial numbers. We learned how to attach our regulator to the valve, and the importance of the O-ring, the rubber gasket between the tank valve and the regulator. We practiced turning our air off and on, and tested the quality of the air by smelling and tasting the air coming out of the second stage. Fairly confident I could manage the equipment and suit up for the afternoon's shallow dive, I still did not know whether I would actually go into the water. One step at a time, I kept telling myself. Keep your pants on, and maybe you can do it. Somewhere in the back of my mind, I had the faint notion she might have been drawn to the water the same way I had been drawn to this diving trip. Yet, the thought of jumping into the sea turned my stomach into a sack of dry ice, a freezer burn that would last until the moment of truth. Still, I told myself, if I cannot jump into the water with all this gear, at least I have learned something today, nothing wrong with that. Just because you milk the cow doesn't mean you necessarily drink the milk.

By the time we broke for lunch it was after one, and Joe had scheduled the dive boat to pick us up at two. That did not give us much time to eat. So we hurriedly went through the buffet line without taking time to carefully choose the largest shrimp or the ripest fruit. But since my stomach was running cold and hot, I didn't eat much.

"I didn't think you were supposed to drink alcohol right before a dive." Adam had seen me sneak a beer.

"Yeah, no kidding," Stephanie said.

"One beer isn't going to hurt her," Micah said. "She's used to a whole lot more."

"What's that supposed to mean?" I said.

"Are you saying Cat has a drinking problem?" Joe finally asked.

"He doesn't know what he's saying," I said. "Nothing like a cold beer on a hot day. You guys don't know what you're missing."

"Have another," said Micah. "When you throw up underwater, don't blame us or expect me to give you all my air."

"Throw up?"

"Let's go, it's one forty-five," Joe said.

"We just sat down," the girls whined.

"Throw up?" I asked again to no one evidently.

Jared and Adam had picked up the exasperated and impatient tones of the older "men."

"How long does it take to eat a salad and shrimp? I thought we came here to dive, not eat. We'll never get in the water. Why'd you invite them anyway, Mr. M?"

"The boat's not going anywhere without us. Just hang loose. Why don't you guys go on ahead and get your gear on the boat, while the girls finish up," Micah suggested. He turned to us with a hard look after the boys left. "Do not be late, no one wants to wait on you all week. Besides, this is gonna be beyond cool. You should be eager to go. Meet ya at the boat." He left to catch up to the others.

It was after two by the time we were all assembled at the dive dock, and Adam and Jared were all too glad to tell us that the boat's captain and crew were disgruntled because we were a few minutes late. "They're really pissed at you," said Jared.

"We're five minutes late, thank you," said Stephanie. "They don't look all that pissed to me. You're making all that up just to rag us."

"Hey, pay attention, knuckleheads. Joe's trying to talk," Micah scolded.

"Okay, everybody," Joe said, "the number of your tank is on the dive board. As soon as you find your name and number, get on the boat and start attaching your regulators. The first thing you are going to do after you jump in is learn how to clear your masks."

"Cat's going with me," Micah said. "She needs individual attention."

I looked at Micah askance, and before I could reply to his comment, he was on the stern of the Delphin making small talk with the captain and his crewmen.

Once aboard, the girls hovered around Joe, asking him endless questions about diving, and Adam and Jared readied their equipment and donned wetsuits, bantering back and forth, flicking towels at each other.

"You guys are such dumb asses," Stephanie said. "I feel sorry for Joe, trying to certify you guys."

"Us? You'll be the ones freaking under the water."

"Okay, listen. I want you to practice some of the underwater hand signals, then we'll be heading out," Joe told us.

The girls were beginning to find Joe irresistible in his tight dive pants and shirtless chest; his muscular physique did not escape any of us. In the afternoon sunlight his close-cropped red hair shone more blonde than red, and his blue eyes were the color of the sea. Besides his handsome face and great body, his self-confidence and position of authority added to his sex appeal, at least to the girls. Micah, by contrast, hid his thin physique under baggy swim trunks and a long white t-shirt. His stance giving the impression of a secret service agent responsible for the lives of several top officials, he remained in the background while Joe ran the show.

"Lucky you," I said to Micah. "You get the paranoid schizoid to take into the water."

Micah's response was lost in the start-up roar of the boat's engine.

"I don't know if I am even going in the water," I yelled above the noisy motor.

"You're going in even if I have to throw you in," Micah said in a voice too calm, his face an uncomfortable deadpan.

"*You* will not be the one who makes that decision," I said, my face turned away from Micah, not really caring whether he heard.

"Enjoy the ride!" Joe yelled. "It takes about thirty minutes to get to White Hole. We'll be going under about twenty-five feet on this first dive."

"Cat, watch this. Jared and Adam have been giving the girls flack all day. I'll get 'em back for Stephanie especially." Micah moved to the center of the stern area where the kids and Joe were sitting. "Joe, did I tell you about the time I took Jared and Adam fishing?"

"I don't think so," Joe replied. The youngsters knew something was coming.

"Yeah, we went fishing with this guy that had a majorly crooked nose. This fellow catches one and takes it off the hook. He holds it in front of his face and just stares and stares, then the fish's nose turns crooked just like his. These two are just amazed, so they watch carefully as he does it again with the next one."

"Don't listen to this crap," Jared told the group knowing full well it was too late to protest.

"Then what?" Stephanie urged.

"So Jared asks this fellow how he does it. He tells them that because his mind is so much more powerful than the fish's, he can make it look just like him. Well, they gotta try it, so they catch one and hold their fish up in front of their faces and just stare and stare. After a bit, both of them go…" Micah held an imaginary fish in front of his face. He opened his mouth wide then closed it while raising his eyebrows several times. He looked like a fish out of water.

"Yukk, yukk," Adam said as he got down off the rail and punched Micah in the arm while everyone else hooted and pointed at him and Jared.

"I always knew that about you two," Stephanie said.

"Hey, no wonder you avoid eye contact with all the fish we've been seeing," Rachel joined in.

We all had a good laugh at their expense, and it helped lessen some of the anxiety in myself and probably the others as well. Adam was embarrassed but he and his roommate took the ribbing good-naturedly.

We had hung our towels and shorts on the wooden beams of the dive boat, and they waved in the wind as the Delphin jettisoned us away from San Pedro's Cay. I sat up on the portside edge to get a better perspective of the disappearing islet and stilted bungalows. In the far distance I could see the colorful shacks of Sandy Bay and a few horses meandering down the beach unattended. The wind breezed through my hair and the ninety-degree weather temporarily melted my anxiety; I sat in silence heralding the beauty all around me. The teal blue water spread an intricate pattern around the speeding boat, splashing sprays of white foam high into the air, sometimes high enough to splatter our arms and legs. The waves pushed away from the bow as Micah pointed to flying fish escaping the water a split-second before the boat passed over them. The girls giggled and squealed in glee, while Adam and Jared let out cries of "Faster, Alonzo. Hey! Faster!" But instead of faster, Alonzo, the boat's captain, slowed the boat down, and the crew, Marcos and Julio, dropped the anchor and line.

"Before you get your gear on, check your buddy's equipment and air. We'll be under the water about forty-five minutes, time for an anxious beginner's air to get low. Be aware of your dive buddy at all times ... Jared and Adam, pay attention. You both will be completely dependent on each other under the water. Same goes for Stephanie and Rachel. You and your dive buddy will be very important to each other this week," Joe added for emphasis. "Cat, Micah will be your dive buddy and teacher, so he will be especially valuable to you, but you have a responsibility to him as well. Remember if your buddy runs out of air, you can either share your regulator until you get to the top, or use your octopus. Don't make me give you the dumb ass sign underwater," Joe said, putting a circle of thumb and forefinger on his forehead.

"How about out of the water?" piped up Stephanie.

"I don't care what you do out of the water. That's Marlowe's problem. Just be cognitive while you're under the water and we won't have any problems. So listen again to what we are going to do. Help your buddy with his tank. Cat goes in with Marlowe, and the rest of you come in with me. We'll go off first since we're the bigger group. As soon as everyone's in, we'll drop down slow. Don't forget to clear you ears. If you forget, the pain will remind you real quick. Then we'll go down about twenty-five feet and swim under the boat and follow the reef to the right until we come to a sandy opening called White Hole. Micah, we'll meet you and Cat there."

"Don't run out of air waiting for us," Micah said.

"Thanks for your support," I shot back at him.

"Did you hook this up in the dark? This is all mixed up. The O-ring is supposed to be at the back of your BC, not in front of it. And change your weight belt around; it's supposed to be so you can open it with your right hand if you need to. Did you pay attention to anything Joe said this morning?" Micah asked, his brows furrowed with impatience.

"I'm trying, Micah, but I told you the whole notion of going in the water scares the shit out of me. I listened to as much as I could, damn it."

"Okay, okay. There, you're all set; just make sure you keep your regulator in your mouth and support your mask when you jump in. You'll be all right. "

"Okay, guys, the pool is open," Joe said right before he did a long stride off the stern.

Micah and I waited as Marcos and Julio helped the four teenagers shuffle up to the edge of the stern and plunge into the open water. Jared and Adam entered the water almost at the same time, the girls following, having no trouble, making it look easy.

When they cleared the entry of the boat, Micah eased me to my feet, the heavy tank on my back and long fins making it difficult to maneuver to the back of the boat.

"Get your hair out of your mask. It's going to leak."

My hair caught on the mask's metal side clasp, and it took several minutes to untangle the mess. Exasperated, Micah cupped his hands in the bucket of ocean water near the end of the boat, and then slicked my hair away from my face with handfuls of water. "Now put your mask on," he said. "I'm going to go off first, and I'll wait for you on top of the water over there." Micah pointed to the left of the stern. "Make sure you take a long stride getting off, otherwise you might hit your head on the ladder. Marcos will help you. Let me check your air. Okay." He peered around my shoulders to look me in the face.

"Okay?" My stare answered for me.

"You're good to go. See ya in the water." And like an aerial gymnast, Micah vaulted over the edge and into the water. As promised, he floated to the port side, his head and shoulders just above the water's surface.

"Okay, lady," Marcos announced. "The pool is open; he's waiting for you."

Marcos steadied my tank in his hands as I shimmied towards the stern and stood between two ladders hanging off the back. I readjusted my weight belt several times, the ten pounds of lead feeling heavy around my waist. I wondered if I had on too many weights and imagined myself sinking to the bottom, anchored in the dark sand, too heavy to be pulled out. Logic escaped me as I stared into the slow moving current. The movement of the others could be seen through the crystalline water.

"Problem?" Micah yelled up, the motion of the waves bouncing him away from the boat. "Hurry up. Everyone else will be back on the boat before we even get in."

"I think I might have to take a couple of these weights off," I shouted. "They feel too heavy."

"Not now," Micah said. "Do it later. Just get in."

"It's too much weight. I'm afraid I'll sink."

"That's kinda the point. Marcos, help her get in … please?"

"Oh all right, I'll keep the weight on," I mumbled under my breath. I contemplated the distance from the boat to the water, and even though it was only about six feet, to me it might as well have been sixty. My legs began shaking so badly I couldn't move if I had wanted to, not even backwards to the safety of my towel and dive bag.

"You coming in some time today, Ms. Scott?" I could hear the exasperation in Micah's voice, and I wanted to jump in, but my pink fins held fast to the deck, and I began to feel dizzy watching the ever-increasing roll of the waves.

The pulsating rain could not block out the sound of the screeching wheels under the milk truck. The driver must have tried to turn the horses away from the running boy, but the thunder frightened the horses causing their forelegs to vault high in the air before their hoofs came crashing down on the young Kentuckian. Oh operatic screams! Drown my feelings forever.

"I can't do it—I'm not coming in. I'm sorry, you go ahead on down. I'll stay here with Marcos and Julio." I could not bring myself to go into the water; my fear was paralyzing and I felt like crying because of my failed attempt at diving. "Marcos, could you help me back to my seat?"

"Don't go near her, Marcos. She's coming in."

"I can't do it, Micah!" I screamed from my frozen position.

"If you don't jump in right now, I'm coming up there."

"That's not going to help. I'm sorry, I shouldn't have put you through this."

Micah immediately began swimming towards the ladder. Marcos and Julio helped him in, shaking their heads at the ensuing scene.

"What's the matter with you?" Micah asked, his breathing labored from not only the extra weight of the dive tank but also the added emotional load.

"I'm terrified of water. I've been like this for a long time. I was hoping it would be different because of you ... I don't know why I thought that. I'm pretty embarrassed."

"What if I hold your hand and we jump in together. I swear, once you go under, you won't be afraid. I'll hold your hand the whole time, and we'll forget about the drills until you feel okay under there."

"Don't you understand? I am *not* going in this fucking water."

"Mr. Micah, maybe you should let her go. She'll be better tomorrow. She can stay on the boat with us."

Ignoring Marcos, Micah stood behind me, placing his two hands on my shoulders. "If you don't go in the water today, you never will. This might be your only chance to overcome your fear."

"Maybe I don't want to."

"Then why are you here?"

"You don't understand, she died underwater ... I can't stand the thought of it..." My eyes teared under my mask, and I was glad my face was already wet.

"Take a look out there—not down, out there." I lifted my eyes outwards across the sea.

"You can see miles and miles of water, right?" Micah was almost whispering in my ear.

"Yes."

"Keep watching the horizon and listen." I noticed a small boat with a single person in it far out from land. "Remember the time my fortune cookie said 'we dropped your fork in the toilet'?" I laughed through my tears and nodded. "What did yours say that day?"

I knew what it was because I had read it many times since. *Follow the advice of your heart.*

"Yes, I remember."

"It said to trust your heart, not your fears, didn't it?"

I nodded again.

"Does your heart tell you I will let anything happen to you?"

My relaxed shoulders revealed my answer.

"You aren't going to find anything bad in there. Most of what you see down there is some of the most beautiful sights you'll ever see."

"But I might die down there."

"You're gonna feel more alive than you ever have. You can hold on to my hand the whole time."

"You don't understand, Micah. My little girl, I let her go ... once ... I can't."

"What if you didn't bother to look further than your own warm bed last night? Would you have seen the stars and remembered your dad telling you about fireflies?"

I could not respond.

"You don't strike me as one who gives up so easily."

"It's the water. Anything else I can deal with."

"You might find what you're looking for. Give me your hand." And then a memory ghost shot past me and I started shaking again, but not because I feared the water. For a fleeting second, I had the feeling that someone I once loved came back from the dead. Holding Micah's hand, I jumped off the edge of the boat, the emerging memory, and the love that memory held, far outweighed my fear of the water.

I guess I let the air out of my BC, because I did have the singular sensation of descending rather quickly under the water, the pressure of the descent hurting my ears, relieved only by holding my nose and blowing hard to equalize the pressure. When he saw I had managed to clear my head, Micah held my hand and led me through paths of sand enclosed by reddish-brown coral. My hand clung tightly to his and he waved our entwined fingers to loosen the grip while at the same time questioning me with his eyes and asking with his free hand if I were okay. I returned the sign indicating that I was fine, and gradually relaxed my fingers as I became used to breathing through a regulator and floating thirty feet under water. And even though my eyes were as open as Micah said later he had ever seen them, I did not see the breathing coral, anemones, sponges or lingering sea creatures near us. I could only *feel* on that first dive. Levitating through the water, I was overcome with the sensibility of freedom, as if I were unchained from a dying animal and its bodily torments and desires, as if I were all spirit and soul, an uttering consciousness clear and defined. The only sentience of any corporal presence was the pulsation of Micah's wide hand covering my fingers.

It was the first time I had been under the water in over twenty-five years, and I questioned why it took me so long to feel what she briefly must have felt. The euphoria of your first plunge, the fast beating of your heart, the exhilaration of floating out of your body, and the autonomy she must have felt for the first time in her life, like a birth into an aqua uterus, but without the umbilical cord. And then the fear and disbelief of being abandoned, and then the hope and the final realization that there is none. Because in death, you see, there is no regulator.

#

Cat used to hold me all the time and read to me. Now she just reads to Tessy and takes Tessy in the pool and spins her around. I brought my beach ball today and asked Cat to throw it to me in the water, but she had to watch Tessy and when I asked her to leave Tessy with one of her girlfriends, she told me to go away, find some of your friends to play with and I started to cry and Cat said I was too big to cry about nothing. And Cat took Tessy to see her boyfriends and they all thought she was so cute and she swam with

Tessy to the other side and Ken walked in and Tessy is on the edge and Cat does not see me and Tessy sings that stupid song and I want her to stop it…

Itty bitty pider … mommie … look … mommie … look at tessy … bye-bye … papa … papa home … mommie patty take … patty … baters man … mommie stay … stay tessy … play tessy … meg … meg play tessy … meggie? … hurt tessy? … mommie … meggie play hurt … tessy fall … water … meggie … why hurt tessy? … water hurt … tessy love … meggie … tessy no swim … no swim … water hurt … mommie … see tessy … help tessy … look mommie … help … mommieee! … tessy hurt … oh mommie … dark … help me … tessy fraid … meg? … why? … tessy play doggie … tessy bath … tessy blow … candles … mommie hold tessy … tessy … love … mommie … mmmmom … ieeeee … mom –

Chapter 20

Life teaches us what we already know and what has always been there for us, what we saw but did not pay attention to, what we heard but did not recognize. And in the corner of that memory stands little Meg frightened and shaken, watching the paramedics take me and Tessy away, little Meg crying alone along the tall metal fence, her bright beach ball deflated in her hands, her stringy brown hair hanging in her eyes. No one knew how Meg must have suffered—Meg the child who caused the least trouble, Meg who had the most friends, the only one who could make my mother really laugh. Yet, Meg was the one who at thirty suffered a nervous breakdown and was hospitalized, who had cancer before she was forty and begged to die because the chemotherapy hurt so bad. Meg was the good child, the happy child, the one who made sure she caused no trouble, the one who tried to take care of everyone. Oh little puffer fish, you had to get out of the tank someday.

The sudden movement of Micah's hand letting go of mine reminded me to see. So I tried to see as much as a person could who had been emerged in the wellspring of feeling, and when I finally looked into his eyes, I could see they were smiling. He must have known that the splendor of the magnificent coral and rare sea creatures had passed me completely by. He held his body in front of me vertically and tapped on my mask, and when I looked at him askance, he filled his mask with water. I watched as he then blew air through his nose while leaning his head back, the water slowly moving down and out of his mask. He indicated for me to do the same, since part of becoming a certified diver involves clearing your mask safely and efficiently.

Ridden with anxiety, I overloaded my mask with saltwater and sputtered and choked and thrashed about so much that Micah had to hold on to me. I focused on Micah as he signaled for me to watch him again. He tipped the top of his mask and allowed water to invade half his mask, then leaned his head back and applied pressure to the top of the frame, while again blowing through his nose forcing the water out. I remembered from Joe's instructions that in order to clear a mask, you have to fill the mask with air to replace the water, and it is important to exhale while pressing the top of the mask frame. In trying to duplicate Micah's actions, I let too much water in and struggled getting it all back out. I did manage to finally remove most of it, but my eyes burned from all the saltwater. To make matters worse I now had problems with my buoyancy because of the additional breathing from flailing around so much in the water, and my tank felt as if it were falling off of my back. I somehow managed to clear my mask, not one time, but several times, to Micah's satisfaction. He told me later he wanted to make sure I did not just get lucky; knowing how to clear your mask can make a difference between life and death.

The drill completed, Micah gestured for me to follow him, and for those minutes we were more than an arm's length apart, I lost control of my buoyancy once again and drifted upward. Soon, my head was completely out of the water, and I bobbed up and down in the waves nervously scanning the endless miles for signs of the Delphin. Before I had time to panic, Micah's head shot out of the water right behind me. "Never allow that to happen," Micah said, his brows furrowed. "If we were any deeper, you could have burst an ear drum or worse. Do you want to spend the rest of the trip in the decompression chamber?"

"Well, no. How do I make myself stay down?" It didn't seem so easy to me.

"You're sucking in too much air. Breathe slowly. Stop using your arms to swim with. When you wiggle all around like that, you lose control. Go under. We have to catch up."

Watching each other, we lifted our inflation/deflation hoses above our heads, our thumbs pushing down on the deflator to vent our buoyancy compensators, and as the air left the BC's our bodies began to sink. I exhaled slowly to continue the descent, and then took a quick breath and exhaled again. We cleared our ears and neither of us had any problem sinking to thirty-five feet, even though I had to kick my fins vigorously not to sink any further. To my relief, Micah pushed my inflator button a few times to help me achieve better equilibrium, and he signaled for me to relax and pointed to my air gauge. When I compared my air gauge to his, I could see that I was using up my air way too fast.

I exhaled slowly to calm myself, and then propelled my body to a comfortable horizontal position in the water. When I used my hands to move myself through the water, Micah grabbed them and placed them on either side of my body. Again, he pointed to my air gauge, and when I reached for him to hold my hand, Micah shook his head and motioned for me to follow him. So we cut through the water as gracefully as we possibly could considering the preponderance of unnatural equipment we were wearing.

Micah was almost unrecognizable, his features distorted into a frog's face under his blue mask, his body covered with a black dive suit and lugubrious black fins, a turtle's body, the buoyancy compensator and aluminum tank his shell. And had I been able to see myself, I would have seen the same amphibian mutant. Like fish out of water we were the humans in the water, trying carefully not to disturb the peace of the natural inhabitants. As I slid through the sea, the airy suspension mesmerized me until I had a sense of calm and peace I never suspected I could feel under the water, almost alone, without holding anybody's hand, and though I had a faint recollection of apricot-tan coral and wheat-colored sea grass, my thoughts were on maintaining buoyancy, preserving my air, and trying to clear my mask which was beginning to fog. I did notice two large gray-and-black grouper with wide luminous eyes that appeared to view me peripherally. They had eyes like Wayne Willet, a skinny boy in my third grade class who wet his pants while standing in front of the chalkboard. Wayne had those large "fish eyes" with watery, protruding corneas, and when he puddled the floor they watered even more. Sister Mary Corde ordered me and Annie Brennan to get a handful of brown paper towels from the girl's bathroom to clean up Wayne's spilled water, because we were the ones sitting in front of the class when he peed all over the floor. I remember it was a very sunny day, and the light made little rainbows in Wayne's pee.

Wayne and I did not make eye contact after that day until high school. Even then, we could not look at each other for long, and though I had developed all the feminine parts in correct proportion, and I knew how to display them well, to Wayne, I was still the auburn-haired girl with freckles who cleaned up his yellow flood.

Wayne's face disappeared and then the two grouper hovered directly in front of me. I tried to whisk them out of the way with my hands, but they moved only slightly to one side. Ignoring them, I strove to maintain my buoyancy and keep up with Micah on the way to White Hole. And still they lingered by my side, filling me with an uncanny sense of familiarity. For a fleeting second I thought of my deceased mother and father. Maybe they returned as two fish and were now guiding me along the coral road. Every two seconds, I glanced over my shoulder to see if they were still there, and sure enough they were. I then tried to communicate with them through underwater telepathy. Mom, Dad, I mentally addressed the pair of grouper. I hope you are adapting well to your new life. I suppose if I did not have to carry this scuba gear around all the time, swimming beneath the waters wouldn't be all bad. I just hope you don't end up as my meal one of these nights. I wonder if you had something to do with my coming on this diving trip. I suppose you know I almost didn't get into the water and made a fool out of myself. I'm still cursing up a blue streak; it gets worse with age. So, now that you are fish, and you've been to the great beyond, I don't need to hide anything from you anymore. You know the truth about everything, that it was Edward and not Perry, and that's why I couldn't walk downstairs by myself for so long, and now you even know about Meg. Or maybe you've known about her all along, and that is why Mom gave her so much more attention than she gave me. Meg should have been in therapy with me after Tessy's death, but we didn't know much about psychiatry in the seventies. But somehow Meg and I survived, and the further I removed myself from the truth, the easier the steps became. I still have to hold on to the rail, but I'm the only one who notices that. But now I've reached the end of my rope and I don't want to live in lies anymore.

Despite all my telepathic skills, the two grouper never responded.

And seemingly out of nowhere Micah appeared in front of me. His narrow blue eyes gently sought my green ones, and I wondered if he could read my hidden thoughts. He held out his hand, either out of support or impatience, and secure in his hold, my reverie dissipated and I forced myself back to reality. When we caught up to the rest of the group, Micah dropped my hand and waved me over to join the rest of the group. Before I swam over to the group, suspended over the coral's edge, I looked for the grouper one last time. They were nowhere in sight; I guess they had other things to do.

Joe led us all to a flat sandy bottom on the other side of the reef, and since it was fairly shallow, the sand and surrounding coral and sea grasses appeared white and ghostly. Joe positioned himself on his knees, and indicated for the rest of us to do the same. Jared and Adam were first to accomplish this feat, while Stephanie and Rachel had trouble staying down long enough to maintain their position. After kneeling for a few seconds, they would lose their balance and fall over. Joe calmed them down, and they finally stationed themselves in the sand along with the guys.

I was just plain spastic. I had trouble getting into a standing position in the sand, much less a kneeling position. At one point I had worked myself into such a dither that I started shooting up to the surface again. Micah flew up and caught the bottom of my fin with his hand and pulled me down. Holding me around the waist, he pushed me into position and then held me there until I found my balance. We novices then discovered if we moved our arms and hands back and forth, we could maintain our equilibrium better, but Joe shook his head as he watched the five novice divers fluttering our arms like ballerinas practicing to be swans. One by one he called us over, and showed us what he expected us to do. He noted our reactions and the time it took us to find our air supply. The first time Joe pulled the regulator out of my mouth I panicked and grabbed my octopus, but at least I knew how to get air when I needed it. He then worked with each pair of buddies, drilling us on how to save each other if one of us ran out of air. Micah told me later I almost knocked out his teeth with my flailing arm. Joe then drilled us for the rest of the dive on mask-clearing and buoyancy.

We spent the rest of the afternoon in class with Joe going over all the things we did wrong on this first dive. Joe used one of the rooms that was part of the Marine Institute for Dolphin research. The walls displayed large charts explaining how dolphins breathe, create sounds and even copulate. According to one diagram a male dolphin has two genital folds while the females have only one. They have a three-chambered stomach, like a cow, and have no sense of smell but excellent vision. One of the charts showed how a dolphin's eye is split in two, the top half for seeing above the water, the bottom half for below. That's why they always tilt their head when looking at their trainers. They have a crescent-shaped pupil in dark light, and an almost unperceivable line for bright light. We also learned that because of multiple frequencies, they can carry on two conversations at once. I told Joe that that wasn't so special, women have been doing that forever, to which Micah chimed in, "Two times nothin' is still nothin'."

When Joe asked Micah if he had anything to add about the time we spent alone in the water, Micah pretty much kept his mouth shut. "Ms. Scott had a little trouble getting off the boat," was his only comment. I did catch him laughing to himself several times throughout the class, however. Noticing the class' curiosity about the dolphin charts, Joe interrupted his "what you all did wrong" lecture to inform us that not only would we be taking classes on diving but also on dolphins and other Caribbean marine life. One of the instructors at the institute would be leading the dolphin instruction and also introducing us to Copan, the alpha male, as well as Rita, Maya and Enzo, the other adult dolphins. Joe had even scheduled a day for us to swim with the dolphins. But our excitement waned as Joe veered back to his critical assessment of the day's dive.

One of the underwater snafus Joe objected to most was the flailing of arms.

"Keep your arms at your sides. You just waste air by moving them all over the place. And when I ask you to kneel in the sand, stay put. Maybe more weight will help." I thought that with anymore, I would not be able to make it to the back of the boat. "You looked like witches reciting spells around a cauldron," Joe continued.

"Ya'll were some strange underwater creatures," Micah added.

"You did okay with mask-clearing and watching your air and depth. Cat, congratulations on getting into the water," Joe said.

"Micah helped a little," I said.

"Next time, you might want to send us out thirty minutes ahead so we can all jump in at the same time," Micah said.

"Last one in, first to run out of air. Nice," Jared offered.

"At least it will make for good dinner conversation," Rachel piped up.

"And don't let your hoses hang loose. You looked like a pod of spiders under there. Besides, a hose dragging over the coral can do irreversible damage." When he told us the years it takes for the reef to repair itself, we said we would help watch each other's hoses, too.

Stephanie brought the attention back to me. "Way to go, Ms. Scott."

"Well hell, at least she got in. And she learned how to clear her mask. But you cannot keep shooting up to the top, Cat. If we were any deeper, you'd be hurting, as in 'serious trouble'," Joe told me.

"Along with everyone else chasin' you," Micah added.

"That's the biggest problem for new divers." Joe continued on about buoyancy while we took notes and tried to absorb his words. We shared our individual problems with buoyancy and tried to determine whether we needed to add or subtract more weight from our dive belts.

By the time Joe let us out of class, the sun was going down. The teenagers ran towards the steps that led to the dining room. "Let's stop at the bar first and get a beer to celebrate our first day of diving," I said to Joe and Micah.

"Mr. Marlowe, can we all get a beer? There's no drinking age here," said Jared.

"I guess you can all have one. Just don't drink any more than us. I don't want ya'all getting sick and puking all over the place."

I trailed behind Micah and the kids, and noticed Micah holding a hand over his head, as if to block out the sun.

"What are you trying to see?" I asked.

"Ah'm trying to see how long it is going to be before sundown. The number of hand widths between the sun and the tree line gives how many hours of light are left. Looks like only one hour of light left this evening."

I held my hand between the sun and the tree line as Micah did, and though smaller, the width of my hand covered the space, the distance altered by my own perception. "I learn something new every time I talk to you," I said.

"Stick around me and I'll teach you all sorts of new things. Hey, see this flowered tree? These blossoms are real pretty, ain't they? Eat one of these, and it could kill ya. It's called Oleander. Some people call it the Boy Scout bush. The scouts would use the limbs to roast marshmallows and get real sick. A few died."

"Well, I don't eat flowers anymore, but I did when I was a little girl. I especially liked to put four-leaf clovers in my mouth."

"Is that why you are so lucky?"

"I don't know if I would call my life lucky."

"Hey, you met me!" He held his arms out like an evangelist.

"You did say lucky, didn't you?" I teased. "I guess if it weren't for you, I wouldn't have gone into the water," I admitted.

"I had to come up with something creative, though, to get you in there. You English teachers always fall for that poetic stuff. Hey, come on, I hear a beer calling my name."

It was almost nine by the time we finished dinner and headed up to the star gazing deck. Micah reminded the students they had to get up early; he had made plans to visit the small elementary school two miles down the beach in Sandy Bay. "We have to get there and back before our first dive. School opens at seven, so ya'll have to grab a banana and roll before then."

"I didn't know we were visiting a school," I said.

"It's something I do every year. The kids bring school supplies and old clothes from home, and we give them to the teachers to hand out to the kids. I brought some kites along this year. I thought they might have some fun with those."

"I brought packs of colored pens," said Stephanie. "Mom packed a bag of my little sister's old clothes."

"My mom's sending a bunch of stuff to the school, but I brought the notebooks with me," added Adam.

"Hey, Jared and Rachel, did you remember to bring your supplies?"

"Yeah, Jared showed me all the funky pencils he bought. I bought some of everything, even erasers," said Rachel.

"I wish you would have told me," I remonstrated Micah. "I would've liked to have contributed something."

"I really do it for the kids. They need to see that not everyone lives as well as they do. Besides, you had enough to worry about." Micah turned to the four adolescents. "You need to have all your dive gear packed and ready before we leave tomorrow morning. I suggest you get to bed early tonight.

"You're one to talk. You and Ms. Scott stayed up later than anyone last night," said Rachel.

"And I can feel it," I said. "I'm ready to go to bed now."

"You have to see at least one shooting star before you turn in. How about we sit on the deck till we all see at least one?" Micah said.

"You've twisted my arm. I'll stay up for one shooting star," I said. The whole group joined Joe, who was already comfortably settled on the deck, and watched the stars from hanging hammocks and old loungers.

"How many shooting stars did you see last night, Mr. M.?" asked Stephanie.

"At least a dozen. Just keep watching, you'll see 'em."

"Hey, Stephanie, did you see that hermaphrodite in the water today?" Jared asked. "It reminded me of you."

"No, what's it look like?"

"It's a cross between an angel fish and an eel," David said with a straight face.

Rachel started laughing and couldn't stop, and Stephanie chased David and Jared around the deck.

"Come on, you guys, what's a hermaphrodite?" she whined. "Tell me, you two. Stop laughing." Stephanie turned to me. "Ms. Scott, what's a hermaphrodite?"

"God almighty, Stephanie," Micah said. "You better learn how to spot one. Hermaphrodites are the most dangerous creatures in the sea. I'll point one out to you tomorrow."

"Hey, did you see that? Over there. You can kind of see the tail."

"If you guys hadn't been fooling around, you would have seen it," said Joe. "Did you see it, Cat?"

"No, I missed it. Hey, there's one. You can't turn your head for a minute or you'll miss them."

"Did ya'll see that one?" Micah asked the kids.

"Yeah ... Wow, that's cool. Get off, Jared, I had the hammock first," said Stephanie.

"You weigh too much. You're going to break it, hermaphrodite."

"What's a hermaphrodite really, Ms. Scott?"

"Don't tell her!" yelled Jared and Adam.

"It's a creature that has both male and female parts. It's not necessarily found underwater. Remember Hermes and Aphrodite from mythology? That's where the name comes from, and I don't think they're very dangerous," I said.

"You idiots!" Stephanie yelled at Adam and Jared. "I'll make you pay for that." She dumped Jared out of the hammock and hopped on Adam's back, trying to wrestle him to the ground. Rachel and Joe laughed at the spectacle, and Micah told them to settle down, other people might be sleeping. My head was spinning from lack of sleep and I was tired of adolescent play.

"I hate to be a party pooper, but I'm going to bed. Don't wake me when you come in," I said to Stephanie and Rachel.

Opening the door to my cabin, I felt a presence behind me. I quickly turned and there was Micah.

"You're not going to bed yet," he said. "I want to show you something really beautiful. The kids will be fine. Joe said he'd watch them." I started to decline his invitation, but he put his arm around my shoulders and led me away from the cabin. In the starlight I could see Joe horsing around with the four students, the five of them enjoying one another's company. They were not likely to miss either Micah or me, so I followed Micah down the long wooden walkway that led to the steps. At the bottom of the cliff, we climbed aboard a small skiff and motored across the cove to the cay. Once there, Micah took my hand, and in the dark we maneuvered our way through date palms and avocado trees, ferns and vines, orchids and broadleaf plants until we came to a small path and followed it to the ocean's edge.

"Sit over here, Cat. It's buggy, but a few bites are worth this." And Micah was so right, indeed. It was a beautiful spot at the edge of the sea surrounded by nature's wilderness. The indefinite stars obliterated the shadow of night, and under the crocheted sky, the swishing sounds of the waves lingered over the diaphanous sands.

"This is one of those places where you can sit and wonder strange things like who we were in our former lives."

"You know, if we truly believe we are reincarnated and the things we say and do reflect that person, isn't that the same thing? They're still here if they're in our hearts." He paused and continued, "I found this spot a few years ago, just wandering around the island by myself. I've always wanted to find someone to share this with." Micah smiled, and we sat close enough for our knees to touch, blanketing our fingers in the soft sand, listening to the waves.

"You did a good job in there today," Micah offered. "You have a lot of guts."

"Thanks," I said, almost choking on my words. Micah caught me by surprise with his rare compliment. "I'm glad you talked me into the water. It was a long time coming."

I leaned back on my elbows and searched the sky for shooting stars and found the moon instead. I stretched my arm to the sky and held the moon between my index finger and thumb. "Look, Micah, the moon is only two inches long. What is it when you hold it?"

Micah reached out his hand to measure the moon. "Two inches, same as yours."

"How can the moon be the same in your fingers as it is in mine? You have bigger hands."

"My hands are larger than yours, but my arms are longer, so proportionally we are equal, which gives us the same perception of the moon."

"And that's why we both saw one hand width between the sun and the horizon yesterday afternoon." I understood.

The rushing sound of the tropical breeze mingled with the susurrus breakers, and tiny ripples from feeding fish sparkled in the shallow waters just beyond the edge of the sand, and in the winter sky a shooting star dropped across Orion's sword. We drank the beauty in silence, like blessed wine, and felt the warmth of the universe tingle inside our bodies.

"What happened to her?" Micah finally whispered, interrupting our quiet communion.

Micah's face hid in the darkness, so I addressed the starlight reflected in his glasses.

"It's a very sad story. One that you might not be ready to hear."

"We all have a sad story. And we don't think anyone is ever ready to hear what we have to say. But most of us don't have an understanding friend to tell the story to." The air steamed with humidity, yet Micah placed his arm around me, as if to protect me from a cold wind.

I stared into the sea, the dark waters woven with ribbons of reflected starlight. The ocean presented a calm face to hide its intimidating force.

"I had a child who drowned. And it was my fault," I whispered, trying not to submerge my words with years of untrained emotions.

"Are you sure it was your fault?"

"Yes, I'm sure." And in faraway words, I told Micah the story of Tessy. Her birth, her short-lived life, and finally her death slashed across the night air. And the white light came again as I relived her death, but the strength of Micah's arms kept me from sinking into the safety of its unscripted oblivion.

"You were so young," he whispered, his lips against my wet cheeks. "I think you acted like most teenagers would have acted under the circumstances. You didn't hurt her on purpose; many parents do, you know. So, who was the father? Marshall?"

"That's the worst part. I went to bed with my boyfriend's father. I really didn't want to, but Perry, my boyfriend at the time, left us alone. I guess his father asked him to leave, and I had too much to drink, and he asked me to take off my clothes." My voice broke and I could not finish.

"You were only fifteen. He took advantage of you. Today that's called statutory rape. He should've gone to jail."

"Perry made me say the baby was his, even though he and I had never had sex. I was a virgin when I made love to Edward, Perry's father. Marshall's the only one I ever told the truth to, besides you and Perry, of course. Edward only suspected he was the father of my child. In later years, he sent me money, and then willed a yearly trust fund to me after he died. A way to save him from years in Purgatory, I suspect was his reason. My parents adopted her, though I don't think my mother ever forgave me for getting pregnant and humiliating her in front of all her church friends. And when she drowned—well, my family treated me like I had some rare disease. Everyone but my dad. And they put me in the loony bin, and I don't think they thought I would ever survive, but I did. Because I met Marshall who was doing a law project there. Something about insanity cases, and his professor made his class go to the asylum to see first-hand what we crazy people are like. And he interviewed me and we became friends and I told him her story."

"So you fell in love and married and had two more kids?"

"I married Marshall because he asked me. I didn't think there would be many marriage proposals coming my way. We made a nice life for ourselves, but we both expected more, like the love that never came. I didn't leave much space open for him. I suppose that's why he buries himself in his work so much. It's a terrible way to live, and some days the tension and anger is hard to bear, but I have caused Marshall so much pain, I don't want to cause him more hurt by leaving him. I'm in a real predicament, Micah."

"You don't have to be in that predicament. You might even do Marshall a favor by leaving him; he could still find someone."

"I've thought of that a million times. And more so even now. I never thought I'd survive the dive. All day I've been trying to put my finger on the feeling I had under the water, and now I think I know. It was the feeling of abandonment of self, a sort of giving over to nature. It was a feeling filled with joy, and I never want it to go away, and it scares me to go back to Atlanta ... to Marshall ... to the fish tank. I don't know what to do with the rest of my life, and I don't know what I'm going to say to Marshall. I just want to exist here and now and worry about the rest of it on the plane going home. Let's pretend we're alone on the cay, and the stars are just for us, and the night is just for us, and the only laws are the ones we create ourselves."

Micah smoothed my wind-blown hair and pulled me closer to him. "And I have you all to myself tonight, Catherine," he whispered. Micah held his arms tightly around me, and I wished I could have cried, but what filled me inside was another emotion, not a sad, sorry-for-myself emotion, but a raw, intense passion fueled by an atmospheric connection of sky, sea, and earth, and the human connection of understanding, forgiveness, and love. And because the darkness freed us, we found each other's lips, and in the soulfulness of that first deep kiss, I finally understood what love could be between a man and a woman. And it was then that I wept.

Buried in Micah's arms, I cried until the slight convulsions of my body stopped, and then he lifted my face with his hands and kissed me again and again, his tongue deep inside my mouth, his breath warm with the humidity of his feelings.

"Catherine ... my Catherine," he breathed. His hands ran up and down my back, and I guided them to my breasts, and his hands searched my body with the longing of a prodigal son. And we reclined on the soft sand so we could know more of the other's body, and I felt his hardness against me, and knew I had to be complete in his arms. My hands reached under his shirt, and the surge of voice and breath escaped from his lips.

"Let's go in the water," I said, my body tensed and awakened, especially the moist, liquid places deep inside of me. We walked out of our shoes, Micah abandoning his glasses inside one of them, and entered the ocean fully clothed. Under the water, I slipped my sleeveless shirt over my head, and Micah struggled to unleash the clasp of my Bali. Frustrated, he tore the clasp open, and tossed the contraption out to sea, both of us overcome by laughter and heightened ardor. His hands fully on me, I struggled to slip out of the rest of my clothes, and, pushing his hands away from me, I indicated for him to do the same. Standing naked in the water, Micah pretended to throw his clothes far out into the water. Reason winning out over passion, Micah made his way to the ocean's edge and hung our clothes on a mangrove root, giving me the opportunity to see his naked body in the starlight. And the secret knowledge of his thighs and tight stomach and curved buttocks filled me with the power of my own sexuality, and when he came to me, I embraced him with the impassionate collectiveness of my sex. Free in our nakedness, our bodies slick and wet like afterbirth, Micah entered me wholly, sacredly, full of universal energy, and I cried out from the ecstasy pulsating from the extreme part of my body, a place filled with ancient fire that only Micah had found.

Exhausted yet fully awakened, reveling in the aftermath of our lovemaking, we swam over to the mangrove root, found our clothes and covered our naked bodies. We could not keep our hands off each other as we made our way to the boat, and sat with our bodies touching until we crossed the lagoon and landed at the base of the cliff. Once off the skiff, we pulled away from each other's touch and climbed the stairs in single file. Not a word was spoken until we reached the door of my cabin. Micah's eyes rested on mine, intense, questioning, and warm, and the power of his eyes made me quiver with excitement and joy, yet my happiness was mixed with the guilt of loving him as well as the guilt of surviving the day's descent. My own eyes clouded with tears as I beseeched her forgiveness for ignoring the burden of my retribution.

"I don't deserve to have such joy," I struggled to say.

"You deserve it more than most people I know," Micah said, and he kissed my tears, and I hugged him as if my life depended on him.

"Tears have the same salinity as the ocean," he said quietly. "Maybe that's why most humans are so drawn to the sea. Sometimes our tears are a reminder of where we came from. I don't know which I'm tasting, your tears or the ocean." And he continued to cover my face with his lips, but I made him stop when I heard one of the girls stir in her sleep, and then he reluctantly said good night, and we entered our cabins only to relive the night in our dreams.

Chapter 21

"Where did *you* and Mr. Marlowe go last night?" Rachel asked after the alarm roused me from my short sleep. "We waited until way after midnight; then we got tired and went to bed."

"We were planning ways to bug you." I tried to make light of the fact that Micah and I wandered off alone in the middle of the night and to deflect any romantic suspicions.

Rachel swung her long legs around to the front of the bunk and sleepily climbed down to the floor. "Why are your clothes all wet?" she asked, moving my discarded shorts and tee shirt from out of the middle of the floor. "You go swimming with your clothes on?"

"Isn't that better than with them off?" I joked.

"I would like to see Mr. M.'s face if you did that," she said.

"It's time to get up already?" Stephanie moaned from under the sheets.

We heard footsteps pounding down the wooden walkway in front of the cabins and recognized the sonorous notes of Micah's voice. "Here, take the coffee over to them. Did you guys grab enough rolls for everyone? I bet those goobers aren't even up yet."

"Hurry up in there!" Jared yelled. "We want to get a head start so we have more time with the kids."

"It's not even six-thirty yet. We don't have to be there until seven," Stephanie yelled back.

Jared peered in between the wooden window slats. "It takes fifteen minutes just to walk there. It will probably take your lazy butts thirty minutes."

"Nice talk, Jared," Rachel said.

"Quit looking in here. We're not even dressed yet," Stephanie said.

"Like you have anything to see."

"You wouldn't know what it is if you saw it. Hey, Mr. Marlowe, Jared's trying to see Ms. Scott in her nighties."

"Shut up, Stephanie," Jared said. "Just hurry up and get ready."

"We'll be good to go in about ten minutes. Tell Micah we'll meet you all at the bottom of the steps," I said. "Don't worry, I can get these girls outa here fast."

Once assembled, we dropped off our dive gear in front of the Delphin, and headed down the dirt road towards Sandy Bay. Established about a hundred yards above the ocean's edge, the village consisted of colorfully painted but weather-worn shacks built on stilts to protect the inhabitants from high tides, their wooden sides shaded by rusted tin roofs. Handmade drainpipes ran down the sides of the houses and into large plastic water barrels used to catch the rain that ran down the pipes. They were crude but functional cisterns. A few of the shacks doubled as residences and bars, the front of the houses appearing to be the living quarters, the back of the houses having a separate entrance for those wishing to imbibe. Even at this early hour, a few patrons hung out the windows of the back entrances waving half-full beer bottles in their hands. But mostly we saw men washing in the cisterns, readying themselves for the work day, and women chasing chickens and pigs in the front yards while half-dressed children watched from the steps, partially eaten tortillas in hands, drinking milk from small paper cartons. The smallest children ran naked under the stilted shacks, playing with dogs and rotting mangoes in their outdoor basements. One little girl, not more than ten years old, pushed a wheelbarrow carrying a crying baby down the road.

"Hola," I said and smiled at her. "Bambino?"

I reached in to try to soothe the distress of the crying baby and saw that the infant was wrapped in soiled towels, flies attacking the newborne skin. I waved the flies away and called to Micah for help. When he saw the baby and her small sister, he stooped down and spoke gently to the little girl. "Dónde está su casa? La niña necesita agua."

"Mama fue a encontrar la vaca para leche. Me dijo que cuidára a la niña. Ésa es mi casa."

The mother called the young girl and her baby sister over and scolded the child for talking to us. "Come on, we need to get to the school before seven," Micah told me.

Already, some of the school age children walked down the beach towards the school, dressed in uniforms of white shirts, navy skirts for the girls, navy shorts or long pants for the boys, carrying satchels of schoolwork on their backs. They eyed us curiously as we neared the school, Stephanie, Rachel and I trying to keep up with the long-legged strides of Micah, Jared and Adam. I thought it strange that

Micah barely said a word to me on the way to the school, and the one question I asked him about the size of the school, he answered without looking at me. Maybe it was my imagination, but he seemed gruff and withdrawn as if he had second thoughts about the night we spent together. Before I could reflect too much on the behavior of Micah Marlowe, we were on the periphery of the yard of the Roberto de Staley School. Uniformed children congregated on the hill that led to the utilitarian structure of concrete walls, whitewashed the faded color of pistachios. Several small children held hands in front of the building's two open doors, and some of the older children crept close to us and stole furtive glances, whispering and laughing to one another. Others ran to the windows from inside their schoolroom to see the strangers.

Micah approached the cluster of teachers seated on a small cement porch adjacent to the doors and spoke to them. "Buenos días, damas y caballeros. Nos gustó tanto nuestro viaje a su escuela el año pasado, que trajé mis amigos para encontrarles." They smiled as if they remembered him and invited us into one of the three classrooms. The room was dark with small windows cut high into the eight-foot ceiling. The high windows provided the only lighting in the room, and like the frameless apertures in the rest of Sandy Bay and San Pedro Cay, they had wooden shutters inside of them instead of glass. Very little air circulated in the room and the heat was stifling. I wondered how the children withstood the heat during the long school day. Instead of chairs, they had to sit on backless wooden benches in front of long gray tables haphazardly placed on a rough cement floor. The teacher's desk sat separated in a far corner under one of the windows, offering one person at least some respite. The room was bare of any decoration ; a slate chalkboard was placed in the middle of one wall, a small shelf containing a few mismatched books next to it.

"Pueden dejar los artículos allí en el pupitre," one of the teachers directed us.

"She said to put the pens and papers over here. They'll pass them out to the students later. Stephanie, put the clothes next to the desk. She'll figure out the sizes."

The four teenagers proudly opened their bags of pens, pencils, and notebooks, and Micah opened a bag with over thirty paper kites, and when he did, Bay Island children appeared as if out of nowhere and swarmed around the teacher's desk, their eyes open wide, their faces smiling.

"Yo quiero ésta," a small face said in a quiet Spanish voice.

"Puedo tener un bolígrafo?"

"Yo necesito un cuaderno."

"Yo quiero lo de Mickey Mouse."

The teacher pushed their hands away as they tried to grab the Mickey Mouse notebooks and Pokemon and Daffy Duck pens. One small child hid a kite up under his shirt, and I did not have the heart to tell on him. Micah must have seen him, too, for he engaged the child in conversation. I hoped he wasn't going to scold the boy for taking the kite. From the response he received from the child, I knew he didn't. "Puedes decirme, cual es cinco por seite?" Micah spoke to the little boy who seemed no older than seven.

"*Si*, senor, treinta y cinco."

"Sí, eres bueno en las matemáticas. No te olvides hacerle volar la cometa después de las clases, bien?" Micah laughed at the boy's surprised expression and patted him on the head."Here. Let's shake, as one math buddy to another."

Micah shook his hand, the smile on the angelic brown face as wide as his ears were apart. Reluctantly, we left the classroom, the children converging around us, asking us questions in Spanish, their hands grabbing at our shorts. The teachers chided them and shooed them away from us. "Niños, siéntense y pórtense bien. Vayan a los pupitres," they said. Their voices were not harsh but demanded respect. Young eyes full of wonder moved away toward their seats. On impulse I grabbed one of the small-boned little girls and hoisted her in my arms. Her laughter tittered past my shoulders and I told her she was very pretty as she covered her giggling mouth with her hand. Her brown eyes glistened. I put her down on the hard cement and turned away from her innocent gaze.

"Adiós. Gracias," she struggled to tell me, and I followed the others out the door.

"Did you want to take her home with you, Ms. Scott?" Micah asked.

"I wish," I mumbled.

"They have a good life here. They don't have many things as we would judge but they have a lot of people who care about them … moms, dads, brothers and sisters. These kids are the lucky ones. They don't need much to make them happy. They will be thrilled with the stuff we brought them. Leave it at that."

"Did I say I thought they needed more?" I asked.

"I saw the way you were looking ... like you were sorry for them. They'll probably end up happier than most folks, especially the ones who have so-called everything."

"I know that."

"Do you, Ms. Scott?" Micah asked pointedly.

And with that he walked ahead, joining Jared and David, leaving me behind to wait for Stephanie and Rachel who were still saying goodbye to the school children. We went directly from the school to the Delphin. Micah and I hooked up our dive gear in silence, and he did not seem to notice that I was having trouble pushing down the large clasp that secured my BC to the tank. When I broke the silence between us by asking for his help, he ignored me and turned to check on Stephanie's gear instead. That was the last straw; his hostility postured in the nuances of his movements and lack of response bewildered and infuriated me. How could two people spend a beautiful night under the stars together, confide in each other, make love in the ocean, and then the next day act as if it not only didn't happen but could never happen? For my part, I thought we would share accidental touches, smile warmly at each other, share looks and words that only we understood, but Micah shattered those thoughts with his irrational behavior.

"Micah, you completely ignored me," I said, grabbing him away from Stephanie. "I told you I needed help with my BC."

"I thought you knew how to take care of yourself. I'm not helping you; you have to learn how to push it down yourself." Tears stung my eyes and when I still could not manage to push the tight buckle down around the tank, Joe casually came to my rescue and even he had a hard time pushing the buckle in place.

"He can act like a turd, huh, Cat? Sure you want to keep him as your buddy?"

"I'm tempted not too," I said. "Especially since my buddy doesn't seem to like me anymore."

"Whatever you want to do, Ms. Scott, is fine with me," Micah said with tight lips.

Something inside pulled me out of the adolescent game we were in and lifted me above the words and behavior, and I glimpsed a broken little boy who had no voice in his life, not even over his own body. "I think it's too late to change now, since all the buddies are taken. Guess we're stuck with each other, Marlowe." I looked directly into his eyes and dared him to continue his rude behavior. When he didn't respond, I asked him how his stomach felt.

"What's that got to do with anything?"

"I just thought you might be constipated and that's what's making you act so pissy."

Micah's grim mood lightened and he finally smiled at me. "Maybe I'm just acting constipated but actually pissy." Stephanie overheard and giggled.

"Did you fix what you needed on your BC? Here, let me check it." Micah wiggled the vest in place around the tank and checked my air hoses. "All set, ready to go. You think you can get off the boat this time without making a big production out of it?"

"Of course. I had a good teacher yesterday," I said, glad he was over his dark mood.

And the second day, I shimmied to the back of the boat, took a long stride into the water, and met Micah at the surface, and when we went under, I opened my eyes beneath the sea. Joe had told us that for this first morning dive, he would not have us do any drills. We were to practice swimming with our buddies and try to identify as much sea life as we could. It was another clear and sunny day, the surface temperature of the water eighty-two degrees. Joe had told us that our maximum depth for this dive would be sixty feet.

Once under the water, I searched for Micah's hand, but he waved it away, indicating with his eyes that I did not need his protective hold. We glided side-by-side, and I could see Micah's laughing eyes and realized how much our thoughts were expressed through our eyes. Released from doing drills, I no longer felt the weight of my earthbound body; I was an astronaut in underwater space. Free in the water, I twisted around in circles and moved my arms up and down as if I were flying. Micah opened his hands to ask what I was doing, but I catapulted my body away from him and turned somersaults until I began to lose my buoyancy. No wonder astronauts train in massive tanks for shuttle missions, I thought. I brought my buoyancy under control in order to reach the same depth as Micah.

Sinking down, I noticed the way the light changed the color of the water at different depths. The rays of light reflecting off the sand combined with the sky to create a soft aquamarine hue in the first ten-to-fifteen feet of water, while the deeper waters changed to a softer brushed blue as the longer wavelengths of red and yellow were absorbed. I met Micah at around thirty feet and we glided along with the rest of the group towards the emerging coral reef which jutted at us like a desert of moon rock full of crenellations, crevices, and pockmarks, an eerie oasis beneath the water. From a distance the reef looked grayish white beneath the pale blue water, but once within a few feet of the reef, I could see the brilliance of the multi-colored colony.

As my goggled eyes adjusted to the intricacies of the reef's surface, I became aware of the vast variety of organisms contributing to the reef's colonization : hard coral, skeletal shells of protruding gray cups, elk horns, purple fingers, brownish-green brains, encrusted red and orange clumps, and mustard fire coral. It was a living mosaic cemented to the ocean floor.

Micah tapped his knife excitedly on his tank, and the suddenness of sound caused me to kick my fins too hard, and I lost neutrality and began to shoot up to the surface. In a panic I hurriedly tried to let out all the air in my BC, but my breathing was so hard I still continued to rise to the top. Micah saw my flailing legs and arms, and again grabbed my right fin and pulled me down. He asked with his hands if I were okay and signaled for me to calm down. I regained my composure and checked my air to see how much that panic-attack cost and slid with Micah into one of the endless canyons of the reef. Whatever creature Micah wanted me to see was either long gone or impossible to find again. We worked with the prevailing current to conserve energy. While the reef was on one shoulder, the opposite direction was an infinite haze beckoning us. As my imagination ran wild, the reef seemed to offer me security much the same as it offered the myriad of ever-anxious creatures within it. I identified with their wariness.

Back along the ridge of the canyon reef, the current directed Micah and me toward the dead-man's fingers and purple and yellow sea fans moving hauntingly back and forth. Micah tapped on his tank again, and this time I remained calm as I let him guide me to a flamingo tongue snail attached to the stalk of a purple sea fan. A tiny jewel hidden in an expansive reef, its checkerboard mantle exposed itself and wrapped around its oblong shell. How many people in the world would ever see what we just saw? I felt overwhelmed and awed that I was now sixty feet under the water in Central America, miles from my past hurts and current struggles, hidden within the reef like the gobies and the blennies burrowed deep within the sponges, peering from the inner recesses only to retreat at the first sign of danger.

Released from the heaviness of my sins, I become a sprite, airy and timeless, a sea nymph in Neptune's realm. I bid adieu to the sea fans and coral and welcomed the green and brown tube dwelling anemones, their curvaceous upside-down legs tantalizing the surrounding sponge cakes and chimneys and cups. "Leave a kiss but in the cup and I'll not look for wine," the poet Ben Jonson wrote.

I dove down to leave a kiss within the cup, but my regulator stopped short of the sponge. Because the water magnified the reef, I seemed closer than I actually was. Micah gave me the "What are you doing?" hand motion, but I ignored him and dived back down to kiss the cuplike sponge. Before I could reach it, the ever-watchful Micah grabbed my leg to gain my attention. He pointed at the reef and shook his forefinger "No!" He pushed me away from the sponge, not understanding my poetic connection to the universe, and I swam away embarrassed. Later, Micah informed me of the large amount of damage caused by divers and snorkelers who touch and often break off the coral for souvenirs, and that many reefs are endangered because of carelessness. Jolted back to reality, I realized what a neophyte I was, but my chagrin lasted as long as it took for a small school of silvery fish with protruding lips and barely discernable yellow stripes to swim in front of me. They fed on tiny wormlike creatures attached to the inside of cupped sponges. Amidst the exotic beauty of the reef there are the eaters and the eaten, the visible and the hidden, the strong and the weak. The silver fish devour the small worms hidden in the sponges, and unless the small fish find a safe place to hide, they also will be devoured, as a larger fish demands its place in the reef's ecosystem. Yet, even predators are prey, and even they need to find places of refuge in their darkest hours.

As on land, the sea houses more than the struggle to eat and not be eaten. There are the one-sided parasitic relationships in which one creature benefits and the other is harmed. Then there are the partnerships in which one animal benefits and the other is neutral. And finally there are the relationships in which both fish gain, one fish cleaning the parasites from the host, benefiting the host fish, while at the same time obtaining food for itself: shark nose goby, golden coral shrimp and spotted cleaning shrimp search the nearby grouper, parrot fish or angel fish for signs of irritating parasites and infected tissues. I think of my own relationships: the ones that are parasitic and start to eat away at my integrity and spirit; the ones in which I am the nurturing partner, the protector; and those relationships where the whole is greater than the individual parts. I often look at Micah hovering above a zone of wavy coral, and I acknowledge that relationships often change. Hopefully ... thankfully.

And I know there are storms to survive above and below, and no matter what our size or beauty we are always someone's potential victim. We learn how to manipulate our way in the universe in order to survive, yet the most unsuspecting, most enlightened can be attacked from all sides, the coated tentacles waiting to attach themselves and draw the victim in. And, as long as the mantle is not completely torn to shreds, we can go back inside our shell and rejuvenate ourselves, next time armed with the sagacity of the predator instead of the naiveté of the prey.

And in the deep waters I am conscious of a father and a son, a son who left the house to allow the father to be alone with a fifteen-year-old girl who was still a virgin. And when he came back the girl was quiet and defeated and full of shame. And when the son drove her home he could not look at her eyes, but stared straight ahead, full of his own misery and shame.

And in the deep waters I am conscious of a small boy who was taken to the woodshed. *A boy who hit the barn with such force his knuckles bled ... a field ... of tobacco ... freeze!* Micah is tapping on his mask. He wants me to see something. It is a small black-and-white striped fish, extremely long dorsal fins and tail. It swims a figure-eight in a space the size of my palm over and over and over.

And in the deep waters I am conscious of another little girl given up to an aging music teacher by her dominant mother. And who had her innocence shattered and her life torn apart by the appetites of her perverse partner, and who remained filled with guilt over the untimely death of a boy she loved. And she became the great diva her mother proclaimed she would be, and when her voice could not protect her anymore, she withdrew from the world and lived imprisoned by the things that were and those that were not. She died alone, her fame forgotten.

And in the deep waters I saw. And when I looked at Micah, I saw.

And when my tank was empty, I emerged from the water, and by the time I reached the ladder, I had changed.

Micah helped me out of my equipment, and we sat next to each other on the short ride back to San Pedro's Cay. I gently touched his well-worn face and placed my arm around him to keep him warm. Before he could question me, I leaned my head on the inside of his neck and pretended to sleep. His throat hummed with laughter but his breathing was content.

Chapter 22

We undertook two more dives that day, both laden with drills and final mask-clearing tests. By the time Joe released us to our cabins it was after three o'clock. My body had the limp and rubbery feeling of exhaustion; incredulously I made it up the steep stairs before the rest of the group. Not bothering to shower the sand and salt water from my body, I grabbed an empty hammock and sank down into the soothing cotton threads. The pulsing wind caused the hammock to move slightly, enough to tease my tired body into a state of seeming levitation. My head pounded too much for me to make much sense out of my intruding thoughts, but I did know that something inside me had changed. My eyes closed, it did not take long for me to fall into a deep sleep, the kind that lasts for minutes, but leaves you refreshed nonetheless, and I dreamed about the great Jumbler of multi-cast lives, and when I opened my eyes Micah hung over me, gently swinging the worn ropes of the red-and-yellow striped hammock. The sun now peeked between different branches.

"We have some free time before dinner," he said. "The kids and I are going to the Cay and hunt for artifacts with my metal detector. You don't look like you want to go."

"Thanks for asking. I might take a break and read or just do nothing for a while. How long are you going to be?"

"We'll be back in time for dinner … before six."

"That sounds good. Have fun. Find something."

After Micah left, the sway of the hammock slowed, and I reached over the side to push my hand against the wooden porch to make the swing fuller. Lazily, I swung back and forth, and after a long stretch of time I thought about finding my journal and writing about the day, but instead stayed right where I was and thought about Meg, and what I would finally say to her, and considered Marshall, and how hurt he would be when I told him I could not stay married to him anymore, at least not the way we were. Meg, I would call on the phone and tell her what I remembered about Therese's death, and if what I remembered was true, she was not to blame. After all, a little girl of four should expect adults to save a baby who had been pushed, and a girl of four should expect an older sister to keep a better eye on her baby; a girl of four would be jealous of a curly haired baby who usurped her place as the wide-eyed youngest of a large family. And I would tell Meg I loved her, and that I was so sorry she suffered because of my mistakes.

And as I hoped to free Meg of any debts she felt she owed me, I hoped to free Marshall of his obligation to care for me, thereby freeing him to find his own happiness. It would not be easy; Marshall, as sons are irrationally apt to do, blamed himself for his parents' unhappy and emotionally controlled marriage. If he saved me, he eased his guilt for not saving his parents from years of marital pain. And he did not know he had the courage to live without me, someone who suffered a worse fate than he, and he did not know I had the strength to live without him, someone who made it so easy to hide behind. I didn't consider running off into the sunset with Micah; Micah showed me what I did not want to live without for the second half of my life. Neither did I think the second half of my life would be with Micah; I could not envision him living any way but alone. I did consider how happy Marshall and I would be if we found other people who could fully love us, not because we had wounds, or because we survived our wounds, but because of the compassionate people our wounds freed us to be.

A crying Stephanie interrupted my meditation. "Jared and Adam are two of the biggest assholes," she said. "All they do is pick on me."

"Did you tell Mr. Marlowe about it?"

"He and Rachel were off with the metal detector somewhere. We couldn't find them."

"I thought you all left together."

"We did, but they went on ahead and didn't wait. We stopped to get some Cokes. Jared and Adam blamed me, and I told them to fuck off."

"Blamed you?"

"Yeah, for taking too long in the bathroom."

"I think Marlowe and Rachel should've waited for you."

"Jared and Adam think I made Mr. Marlowe mad."

"Because you stopped to get a Coke? That doesn't make sense."

"Mr. Marlowe just wanted to be alone with Rachel. I think she has a big crush on him."

"Do you think he has a crush on her?"

"I don't know ... he kind of acts like it sometimes."

"Well, it's probably nothing. Hey, why don't we go down to the bar and watch the sunset? You can finish your Coke and I'll get a cold beer."

"Would you care if smoked a cigarette?"

"Why don't we buy some cigars instead? Let's live on the edge, shall we? I'm going to comb my ratty hair out and put on some red lipstick. Want to borrow my red, sensuous lipstick?"

"You're so weird. Can I fix your hair?"

"Make me look cool. I mean *really* cool."

Stephanie giggled and piled my hair on top of my head and fastened it with a large tortoise clip. We reddened and glossed our lips and sauntered down the steps to the bar. "May we have two big Honduran cigars?" I winked at the tender. "And we will also have one Dos Equis and a great big sexy Coke. We are two wild women who want to let loose tonight."

"Ms. Scott, you're crazy. You'll have some 'splaining to do to Mr. M.," Stephanie said as the bartender grinned.

Adam and Jared found us sitting on bar stools and sharing a fat Honduran stogie. The sweet taste nauseated me and the smoke stung my eyes and throat, yet the stunned looks on Jared and Adam's faces made it all worthwhile. I hid my urge to cough.

"Hey, can we smoke a cigar too?" Jared asked.

"Sure, help yourself," I said, pointing to the packs behind the bar.

"Hey, Stephanie, it doesn't surprise me you smoke with your filthy mouth. I don't know any girl who swears as much as you," Adam told her.

"Get a life, Mama's boy," Stephanie shot back. "Most girls swear as much as I do."

"Yeah, if they're ho's like you."

"Okay, knock it off," I said. "Most people swear sometimes. It's just that some people are more select about it than others. How can you guys waste time fighting when the sunset is so beautiful? Enjoy the moment. It will be time to leave before you know it."

The kids calmed down, and we discussed religion. Adam said he wanted to be a minister like his dad; Jared really liked mythology; Stephanie did not believe in a heaven or hell and was not even sure she believed in God. Adam tried to change Stephanie's mind, and quoted from the Bible, while Jared and I discussed Greek and

Egyptian mythology. We became so engulfed in our conversations we did not notice two still figures standing behind us.

"You could have left us a note. Rachel and I have been searching all over the place for you knotheads," Micah scolded.

"That's interesting," I said. "It seems Stephanie and the guys were searching all over the place for you two."

The bartender leaned over the counter. "Another Dos Equis for you?" I nodded.

"They weren't looking for me; they were looking for you so they could sit at the bar and smoke cigars," Micah said. He caught the tender's eye. "I'll have what she's drinking."

"You and Rachel could have waited for us," said Stephanie.

"You all were taking too long. The sun'd been down by the time you stopped your squabbling. You knew where we were going."

"We looked all over the cay for you, Mr. M.," said Jared.

"You couldn't have looked very hard."

"It's all Stephanie's fault," said Adam. "She has to flirt with the dive guys every time we go anywhere. That's why it took us so long to get our Cokes."

"You guys could have gone ahead with Rachel and me. You didn't have to chaperone Stephanie."

"We were trying to make sure nothing happened to her. She's so stupid she could be talked into anything."

"See? See what assholes they are? I hate you jerks! It's not funny Mr. M." Stephanie stomped off behind the bar, and I could see her fuming on the far side of the lower observation deck. I started to go after, but Micah placed his hand on my arm.

"Let her cool off. She'll be all right. We'll get her in a minute."

"So," I said. "Did you and Rachel find anything with that contraption?"

"It's called a metal detector," Micah said. "As a matter of fact we found some colonial buttons and a Spanish coin. They're kinda mucked up, but they'll clean up after I work on them. These coins are hundreds of years old. Rachel, show 'em the buttons."

"Here," she said. "These are really neat. They have an etched flower on them. Marlowe says they're probably late 1700's English." Rachel and Micah passed around their treasures, and I studied the two of them, trying to make sense out of the inexplicable bond between them. There was no doubt she was attached to Micah, more than seemed normal for a student to have towards her favorite teacher, and he treated her with a special tenderness, different from the jovial affection he showed his other students. Like me, Stephanie had good instincts, and I was surprised I had not picked up on their closeness earlier in the week. But I wasn't overly concerned, and more than likely I was jealous of the attention I thought was solely reserved for me. Besides, I thought, he could very easily feel a fatherly pull towards Rachel, a quiet girl with too few friends. She was not raucous and lively like Stephanie; Rachel had trouble fitting in and appeared vulnerable, as if she needed someone to take care of her. The incident left me with an uneasy feeling, and the vague notion to make sure they didn't spend too much time alone, if any.

"You need to come with us next time, Ms. Scott. And the rest of you goobers need to make sure you keep up next time," Micah said.

All through dinner I covertly watched Micah and brooded over any attention he gave Rachel. I felt like such an idiot, a middle-aged woman competing with a teenager for a man who indicated in so many ways he loved me. But it had been so long since I allowed myself the vulnerability to feel love for a man that any possibility of betrayal and hurt sent me into a dark, downward spiral. So when Rachel mentioned she collected old maps, and Micah suggested the two of them visit the Archives of the Atlanta Museum one day after school and excluded the rest of us from their conversation, I left the table and ran all the way down the steps until I reached the diving docks. I found a pier not obliterated by the large cumbersome dive boats and sat alone, feeling hurt and foolish for reacting badly to what was more than likely an innocent and natural comment.

Beyond me the clear aqua waters of the Caribbean lined the western horizon, and out of the corner of my eye I could see the lush tropical mountains pointing eastward. In between the western waters and the eastern mountains stood the cay with queen palms bowing their quivering fronds to wind, sand and sky; scuffs of hibiscus sprouted pink clusters along the border of the cay's sandy edge, strewn with broken conch shells and coral, and an occasional large root working to unsettle the sand beneath it.

My head reeled from the confusing two days; I wasn't sure I could deal anymore with Micah's mercurial moods. Before the trip, we talked almost every day, walked in the mud for hours, shared stolen moments before and after school; yet, when we fly to Central

America and make love in the sea, he acts like nothing happened between us, and to make matters worse, he dotes on an eighteen-year-old. His jokes, silliness, immaturity and insensitivity contradicted the wisdom, understanding, and yes, even passion, he showed me. It felt like a ten-foot long python was squeezing my stomach; my face was hot and sweaty and my breath hard.

"Something wrong?" Micah's deep voice should have startled me, but it did not. I knew he would find me here.

"I have a hard time understanding you," I said.

"I have a hard time understanding myself."

"But ... after that night in the ocean ... you act like nothing happened. I don't know what to think ... about us."

"It's too hard to think about us."

"What does that mean? It's not too hard for me."

Micah laughed quietly. "C'mon. I have something I want to show you."

When I started to protest, Micah grabbed my hand and pulled me to my feet. "Hurry or the kiddies will find us."

"Is that how you and Rachel got away?" I asked.

He did not seem to hear my question, and I followed him in silence down the long gravel road that led to the main street. Micah hailed a taxi for us, and we rode in the dusk for several minutes until we came to the entrance of a gated park.

"Are you sure it's smart to leave the kids?"

"They aren't going anywhere; they're stuck here. And they sure as hell don't know anything about tracking down a ride. Have any pesos on you?"

"A few."

"Good, it costs about fifteen pesos to get in here. They lock the gates at dark, but I can get us out easily. We just need to get in before it closes. We're going to climb to the top of the cliff."

"Isn't that a dangerous thing to do? It'll be dark before we get to the top."

"The moon and stars will be enough ... you have to see this. It'll bring tears to your eyes."

At the foot of the large hill, Micah pointed to a trail of ants carrying tiny leaf fragments in their mouths. "Look, they go clear up the path. I bet they started near the top. Let's follow their trail back and find the tree they started from."

I followed Micah up the path stepping carefully to avoid the long line of ants marching along the path's right side. It was almost dark and the moonlight provided little relief from the shadowy palms and poinciana trees of the cloud forest. My eyes were slowly adjusting to the shadows.

"I hope you know where you're going. I can barely see three feet in front of me."

"Can you make it without holding my hand?"

"I think I can manage. Just don't get too far ahead."

We twisted our way around the slippery slopes of the cliff, planting our feet in the ditches along the sides dug out by the rain. As we got closer to the top, Micah told me to grab the exposed tree roots to help keep my balance, the procession of ants still descending on the path's other side.

"There are so many ants they're cutting a trough in the path. Bend down so you can get a closer look."

My feet slipping a little, I squatted down to see better, and I realized that not only were there thousands of ants descending the hill, but just as many were climbing up the hill, only the ones ascending were empty mouthed. "Those are the ones going back to the tree," said Micah. "It's a never-ending job for them, gathering food for the queen and the colony."

"Think we'll ever find the tree?"

"Sure, as long as we keep the ants in sight," he said.

We followed the ants to the top of the cliff. Free from the overhang of fernlike branches, the moonlight appeared brighter allowing us to see miles of forest emptying down into the rolling waters. I could not imagine a place more spectacular than what branched out out before us.

"Micah, I can't believe how high up we are ... at night. Another one of your well-kept secrets."

"It's pretty alright, but come over here, this is what I want you to see. The ants have just about stripped this sapling. They only attack young trees. See how they cut the leaves and carry them away with their mouths? That's why they call them the cutter ants."

"They're killing the poor tree."

"No, they're not. A few leaves always remain, so the tree can rejuvenate itself. Nature's way of keeping balance."

"If only human nature were so kind."

"No kidding, we do have our own ants—ever hear of corporate ants?"

"Yes, I'm married to one," I said. "He cuts down his leaves for the Margin of Profit. I'm not sure how much the corporate ants leave behind for the next wave though."

"I guess it depends on the Margin of Profit they need. The cutter ants work to please the Queen Mother—these female vandals of the night can displace half a tree in one night. They strip the tree but fertilize the soil with the leaves they drop all the way to the nest. Most people don't realize how logical the circle of nature is. The corporate ants need to take a lesson from these small creatures and replace what they devour."

"Yeah, corporate ones only go in one direction, huh? Away from the tree."

"It's going to be hard to go back to the strip malls and subdivisions after all this beauty. I shudder to think what our world will be like a hundred years from now," Micah said.

"Maybe we'll get some sense and slow our lives down enough to want to protect all this," I said, spreading my hands out towards the sea.

"Yeah, maybe."

We sat on a small observation bench, curled up in each other's arms.

"Did you ever have to collect and identify leaves when you were in school?" I asked.

"In fifth grade. We glued the leaves on cardboard for a project. I guess everybody had to do that."

"I bet you got an A on your project."

"I was a good student. I didn't have much of a choice; my daddy would have beat the tar out me if I didn't do good in school, or at least I thought."

"I was always in trouble with the nuns. I wanted to know more than just the names of things, and the nuns didn't like to give reasons."

Under the moon and stars, I told Micah how I grew up in Lower Price Hill, a predominantly Catholic community of Irish and German descent on Cincinnati's west side. The Sisters of Charity, ox-like women mostly of German descent, ran the elementary and all-girls high schools on the western side of the city. Also called the

Daughters of the Immaculate Conception, founded at Paderhorn, Germany in 1849, these women had little tolerance for creative disorder and little charity towards inquisitive classroom wards. I managed to avoid trouble in kindergarten and first grade, but in second grade, almost daily, I sat in the corner of the basement classroom, my mouth taped for asking inappropriate questions or making comments that had nothing to do with the subject.

Once, Sister Mary Irmengard took me into the coat closet and spanked me with a ruler because I stood up during math class and announced that my Uncle Bill was a drunk. My feelings hurt more than my behind because, after all, I had told the truth. My mother and aunt talked about what a drunk Uncle Bill was all the time. They called him the family skeleton before he was dead, and he literally became the family skeleton on my tenth birthday when he died of a combination of cirrhosis and diabetes. When my older brothers, Eugene, an eighth grader, and Paul, a seventh grader, heard on the playground from one of the older sisters of another second grader that Sister spanked me in the coat closet, they immediately called my dad at work. They also told him that every time they walked past my classroom, they saw me in the corner with my mouth taped shut. Before the school day was out, my dad marched up to the principal's office and told Sister Mary Richard some of these old biddy nuns needed to broaden their horizons. My brothers heard him say a whole lot more, but they were not allowed to tell me the rest.

I was satisfied because the nuns stopped bothering me for a few weeks, but Sister Irmengard marched me next door to the church confessional when I raised my hand and very seriously informed her she had a broad horizon. I was seven years old and was just beginning to learn about the confessional. I didn't know why repeating what my dad said was such a sin.

Just the night before, my dad said he regretted not moving to the northern suburbs of Cincinnati, where the more tolerant Mercy nuns taught. "You would've gotten along better with them," he maintained. "The good Catherine McCauley of Dublin gave up all her riches to teach poor Irish children. She started the Sisters of Mercy in the homeland and brought the order over to the United States at the end of the Civil War. Those nuns knew how to answer children's questions. They even built schools for the poor Southern children without any regard for race or religion. Bless their souls for tolerating all those Baptists down there."

"Do they have broad horizons, Dad?"

"If you are talking about their minds they sure as hell do. But if you're talking about their girth, there is no broader horizon than Sister Irmengard."

Sister Mary Irmengard pushed me into the confessional and told me to kneel silently while she got the priest. I could hear Father Gallagher's shoes clicking on the marble floor that led to the confessional. Once inside the middle partition, Father opened the small wooden window and blessed me. "Now child," the holy profile said. "Sister said you have a mortal sin to confess."

"I only told sister what my dad said."

"And what was that?"

When I told Father what my dad had said about girths and horizons, he sighed and told me to come outside the confessional box. He clutched my hand and walked me to his office in the rectory.

"Would you like a Pepsi with ice?" he asked. I told him I would, and when he left the room, I sat down in a large leather chair that spun all the way around. By the time he came back with our Pepsi Colas I was dizzy, and the carbonated drink soothed my head. Father Gallagher then read some passages from the autobiography of St. Therese of Lisieux, the Little Flower. In the first passage Father read to me, Therese described an episode of her childhood that echoed the mystery of divine choice. Therese wanted everything offered by her older sister who had said, "Choose one." Therese replied, "I choose all."

When Father read me her words, I giggled because Therese had said what as children we all want to say. Children naturally embrace the illimitable treasures of the universe, while world-weary adults too often enclose themselves in factitious straight jackets. But it was her words about the flowers that made her the only saint whose holy card I wanted to keep. "I understood how all the flowers He has created are beautiful, how the splendor of the rose and the whiteness of the lily do not take away the perfume of the violet or the delightful simplicity of the daisy. He created the child who knows only how to make his feeble cries heard. The poor savage who has nothing but the natural law to guide him. Just as the sun shines simultaneously on the tall cedars and on each little flower as though it were alone on earth, so Our Lord is occupied particularly with each soul as though there were no others like it." I did not know what the words meant at the time; I only knew I liked them and would read her words over and over through the rest of my grade school days. And years later when the sisters would see that sweet little girl in my arms for the first time, I would open her tiny curled fingers and say, "Just like a little flower." She would be Therese the Little Flower for the duration of her short life.

Father Gallagher finished reading the words of St. Therese and suggested I model my life after the Little Flower. I promised him I would try, but in my heart I knew that was impossible because Sister Mary Irmengard told me I was a little girl who would rather spit in the cup God gave me than to drink from it. And I reasoned she was right, because once, after a rare round of harsh words passed between them, I heard my Dad tell my mother the Irish like to spit in their vinegar, not drink it. Then he grabbed her around the waist and the two of them danced to their own silent music in the small rectangle that was our living room.

"You might begin by listening to what the Sisters tell you to do," Father admonished.

"Oh yes, Father, I'll listen." He was so kind, I did not want to disappoint him.

He folded his hands and smiled gently at me. "Now let us pray." We prayed the Act of Contrition together, and then he reached behind his desk and brought out a large peanut butter jar of Worthen's candy. "Reach in there, child, and take a handful. But don't eat them until after school's out."

"Yes, Father," I said.

He tweaked my freckled nose and guided me back to Sister Irmengard's classroom, and when she scowled at me across her desk, I sneaked a Worthen's into my mouth and savored the delicious taste of rebelliousness.

The words Father Gallagher read so impressed me, I checked her autobiography out of Our Lady of the Assumption's library the next day. St. Therese died at the young age of twenty-four and, for me, her young words fired my unquenchable imagination.

Because of St. Therese, I had trouble memorizing plant phylum or identifying trees by their names. Ordered learning did not fit with St. Therese's disorderly curious nature, nor did it fit with mine. In the autumn of my fourth grade year, Sister Mary Corde assigned us a leaf identification project. We had to collect as many different species of leaves as we could find and neatly paste them on poster board with the correct name listed beneath each leaf. I failed the project because I identified only three leaves: ash, oak, and tulip. I could not concentrate on the project because the fallen leaves made me think of death.

When it came time to present our projects, I asked Sister why the tree still lives if its leaves are all dead. She told me I had missed the point of the entire assignment and that I was a very lazy little girl. I kept my head down on my desk and refused to show my face as the rest of the class presented posters covered with twenty, thirty leaves, all perfectly glued and labeled in alphabetical order. Sister rapped me on the head with her rosary beads and told me to sit up, but I adamantly refused to budge. Then she sounded her clicker in my ear and threatened to send me to the principal's office if I did not pay attention. I stuck my fingers in my ears, more to get away from the grating sound of the clicker than to be stubborn, but that was the last straw for Sister Mary Corde. She pulled me by my right arm and led me down the hallway to Sister Mary Richard's office.

"Catherine Faith O'Connel is a lazy stubborn girl," she told our principal. I tried to explain that I wanted to know how a tree could live with dead leaves, but Sister Mary Richard taped my mouth shut and made me kneel on the cement floor in the hallway for the remaining two hours of the day. Alone in the hall, I mentally rehearsed the nun's story I would tell my Dad during one of our heart-to-heart talks in bathroom. My dad still didn't care much for the Sisters of Charity; he thought anyone who did not have a single bill to pay had some nerve accusing children from low income families of mortal and venial sins. "It's easy to stay free of sin when you don't have to worry where your next meal's coming from. The kids in their classrooms know more about the world than those damn penguins. Any Irishman worth his salt knows you can't help but commit sin when you step outside the church door. Just get a good education and ignore all the talk about sin and damnation." I could really get my dad riled up with my almost daily confrontations with the nuns. I didn't even have to exaggerate that much.

"How much of that did you make up?" Micah asked when I finished telling him my story.

"Not a single word. It's exactly as I remembered it."

"Those nuns must've been something. I tell my kids all the time the relationship between man and nature is more than the simple naming parts. Names are manmade tags that explain nothing. Understanding comes from more than a label. Like these cutter ants here. You have learned more by watching them tonight than you would if you had seen their scientific name in a book. I still think they are the most amazing creatures."

"It looks pretty dark down there; think we should spend the night up here?"

"We don't have enough bug spray with us for that. Here, you can hold on to me on the way down. But before we go ..." Micah held me close and kissed me for a long time under the stars.

"I wish we were in the ocean again, Micah."

"We'll be in there all day tomorrow," he whispered.

"That's not what I mean, and you know it."

"Ahhh, yes, now I understand. It is all so clear to me," he tried to sound like Peter Lorre. "If you tempt me like that we'll never get back. Let's go before I lose control and ravish you."

"You can ravish me; I want you to," I said in between giggles.

"Not now. Give me your hand."

And like Sacagawea and Captain Clark, we carefully made our way down the long hillside, my hand squeezing Micah's, our lips touching every few yards, but nothing more. We waited by the edge of the road for almost an hour for a taxi to come by, but it seemed more like minutes, and when we finally arrived back to our cabins, it was quiet and all the lights were out.

"So, did you and Marlowe find your favorite spot by the ocean again?" Rachel asked when I slipped back into the room.

"We found a place that we can all go tomorrow. We had to check it out first. I hope you didn't miss us too much."

"You could let us know the next time you guys are going off somewhere. We just hung out and read and talked with Joe. He was kinda wondering where you all were, too."

"Fair enough. We won't wander without telling you. So, did you have a lousy time without us? I know your enjoyment depends solely on having me around," I said with a big grin.

"Whatever ... Jared and Adam were actually pretty funny. They really were ripping on Stephanie, but she gave it back to them. It was great for once."

"Good for her. I take it she's asleep."

"She's dead to the world. I can never go to sleep until after midnight, no matter how tired I am."

"We'll it's about midnight now. Let's try to get some sleep, and I promise we'll not run off tomorrow night without you, okay?"

"Right," a groggy voice said.

Chapter 23

San Pedro's Cay offered night diving trips for certified divers, and after another rigorous day of drills and testing, Joe suggested that we go on one that evening. Adam and Jared thought night diving sounded like a great idea, Rachel wasn't too sure, Stephanie had little-to-no reaction about the idea, and I absolutely refused to go.

"Come on, it's no big deal," Joe said. "Plus, you'll have Micah as your partner. He won't let anything happen to you … probably." He winked at Micah.

"She's going," said Micah. "She has to play these little games so we'll all beg her to go and tell her everything'll be all right." He turned to me, "Oh, please go, Catherine, pleeeease."

"Oh, shut up. I really like the way you speak for me, Micah," I said sarcastically. "I don't know what I would do without you, since I can't think for myself."

"At least you finally admit it. You do not, do not, do *not* want to miss this. Creatures come out that you don't see during the day. It will be another amazing experience … "

"How different can it be?"

"Have I been wrong about the last two nights?"

"Well, no. Are you absolutely certain it's safe? It looks too scary at night."

"I'll admit, it's different but not that bad. Once you get to the bottom and have something to focus on, you'll be fine. The first five minutes are the hardest." He looked for acceptance of his words in my eyes but only got a stare so he turned back to Joe and the others.

"Everyone will wear lights on their tanks, those kind you snap and shake, and everyone needs a flash light. Micah's right, Cat. You'll be annoyed by too much light, not the lack of it," Joe said. "We'll all meet at the dock at six sharp. Don't be late. And Cat, definitely no drinking."

"Let's rinse off and go over to the island with my metal detector," Micah said. "And this time, you knuckleheads, make sure you keep up."

"Count me out," I said to the group. "I need to recuperate before I go on another dive. Three dives were exhausting enough; I can't imagine how I am going to feel after four."

"I'm going to hang back with Ms. Scott," Stephanie added.

After quick showers, Micah, Jared, Adam, and Rachel took off for the Cay, while Stephanie and I luxuriated in hammocks for a few stolen hours. We read and slept and wrote in our journals.

"Do you see your kids much, Ms. Scott?"

"Not as much as I would like. I really miss them. What about you? Do you miss your parents?"

"Just my mom, a little. I can't talk to my parents like I talk to you and Mr. Marlowe. My mother would definitely not smoke a cigar with me. She expects me to be perfect all the time, and when I do try to talk to her about stuff she freaks out. Like I could never talk to her about smoking pot. She would send me away to a boarding school if I did."

"Well, she's just acting like a mom. She's a little scared you might get yourself into some trouble and get hurt."

"She doesn't care about me. She just cares about what her friends will think. She's all mad because I pierced my belly button. She doesn't even know about the tattoo. I can't believe you have one."

"Well, I got mine when I turned forty. Right after my dad died. I got it so I could keep him with me all the time. He used to call me his wild Irish rose. That's why I got a rose tattooed on my shoulder. You really can't see it unless I have a bathing suit on."

"I still think it's really cool."

"Thanks. You know, your mother really does love you. And she cares more about you than her friends. She let you come on this trip, didn't she?"

"So she could get rid of me."

"I doubt that. But guess what? I'm glad you came along on the trip. It's fun to have someone else along who likes to swing in hammocks and smoke cigars."

The sun was starting to set by the time the rest of the crew came back from their expedition. They carried pocketfuls of old pottery shards and more Spanish coins. Micah could not wait to show me a weathered silver belt buckle he found. "Must be from the 1600s," he said exuberantly. "John'll date it for me. I swear it looks like an old buckle pirates used. Cool, huh?"

"It's awesome," Rachel agreed.

Micah grabbed my ankles and lightly tickled my feet. "Better think about getting ready for that scary night dive. There are some big old monsters under there at night."

"Shut up, Marlowe!" we all yelled. The thought of participating in a night dive made my stomach churn; this slice of diving threatened, yet compelled. I knew I had to conquer yet another fear.

It was dusk when we boarded the Delphin, and I sat on the side of the boat and watched the sun once again drop into a gold-freckled ocean. With our group of six along with eight other divers aboard, the captain started the engines and released the hawsers, and the boat pushed away from the dock. Wearing a Lycra suit for extra warmth, I broke the inner tube of my glow stick and attached it to my tank.

Stephanie and Jared spoke nervously to each other, and I realized I was not alone in trying to quell my rising fear. Joe, the dive master for the evening, emphasized to everyone on board the need to stay in sight of him and not to venture away from the assemblage of divers. I planned on being in Micah's shadow for the entire dive, if that was even possible in pitch-black water forty feet under the waves.

Micah reassured me that everything would be all right. "This is going to be one of the most exciting things you've ever done. Just relax and stay close by me. I like to hang at the back of the group because too many folks wad up at the front. It can be kind of crazy when they get in a tight place."

"Is my equipment the way it should be?" I asked, focusing on my plight and half-listening to his efforts to calm me.

"Yeah, you're fine, just relax; otherwise, you'll suck your tank dry and make us all come up early. Here, let me check your air." He reached over my shoulder and gave my tank valve a slight left-turn twist. Micah then checked his equipment as the boat slowed and shut down her engines.

At the back of the boat, Joe, feet spread, bracing himself to counter the gentle rock of the boat, called us all to attention with a voice that spoke of experience and authority. "Everyone get ready. We'll go against the current at first. When you get to 1500 PSI, let me know and the group will turn around." Micah gave me a look as if to say 'that better not be you.' "Be aware of where you are. Do not touch any of the reef and stay with your buddy. When you get in, go down under the boat and wait for me. My strobe light blinks red. Look for it. And pleeeease, don't shine your light in anyone's face. If you find something, make circles around it with your light so we can see it. Unfortunately, this does attract sharks." I could see a big grin in the dim light. "Any questions?" Joe had spoken those words many times during the last three days. He pushed the ladders down, and they splashed into the obscurity behind the boat.

"The pool is open," he announced. I secretly wished to be back at the bar awaiting the return of the foolish night divers.

I noticed Stephanie did not seem to be getting ready with much urgency.

"Is everything alright?" I asked.

"I'm not so sure about this." She forced out the words as if she were out of breath.

"Stephanie, if you're too worried, just stay on the boat. No need to make you learn to hate diving. You can do the next one. Rachel can go with me and Ms. Scott."

"That's okay, I can do it. I don't want to stick Rachel with you, too," Stephanie said.

"If you have any problems, let me know or Joe." Micah turned to me. "When we get in, let's drop down quick. Jellyfish hang around the surface. Ready to go?"

"Just wait till I'm ready," I said.

"We're not jumping out of a plane behind enemy lines. It's the same place we went in yesterday. After you do this, you won't shut up about it. You'll be amazed at what we'll see, and when I ask you to turn off your light, just trust me."

We were two of the last ready to spread-eagle off the back of the boat and I could see the lights of the other divers awaiting us under the water. At the stern, the depths revealed a swarm of beacons. A yellow-green beam of light in the frantic submerged play defined each diver. My tension heightened as we leapt off the stern and submerged our bodies into the black current, quickly releasing the air in our vests. Descending, the darkness enveloped me and I stabbed it with my light to keep it at bay. Micah came from behind and touched my shoulder. I jumped at first and then spun around with, as I was told later, eyes quite wide. He asked with hand signals, "Are you okay?" and I signaled back ,"I'm okay."

As we were the last ones in, the other group had already discovered an octopus hunting the reef. Nearing the corals and the sponges, colors I had not seen before burst forth due to the intensity of our lights. The octopus did its best to ignore us as it moved effortlessly through the reef. Changing rapidly to match the background, its skin mottled gray, brown and blue in quick succession. Its eyes kept watch as it hid in a crevice beyond our reach. My fears subsided as child-like fascination with this hidden world took over. Micah tapped two fingers on his mask and pointed in the direction of the octopus to make sure I saw, and after he received my positive response, we set off against the current to explore. Keeping our distance from the others, but not too far away, the formations cast shadows as our lights illuminated only a small fraction of the foreboding landscape. Filled with hesitant anticipation, I swept my light across the reef, wondering if I would encounter beauty or threat.

The loosely defined group continued through the reef with Joe as the focal point. Tiny wormlike creatures wriggled in the lights as thousands of translucent microbes shifted with the current. Micah and I moved effortlessly along, Stephanie and Rachel directly in front of us, Jared and Adam up front right behind Joe. Because of her apprehension, Stephanie's buoyancy became erratic, and she struggled to stay at the same depth as the rest of us, and soon she rose out of control to the top. Rachel motioned for me to help, since Micah was slightly ahead of us, and there was no time to get his attention. I ascended enough to catch Stephanie's fin and pull her back down, and when she was safe, I checked her BC and motioned for her to breathe easy. Her eyes were wide with panic, so I held her hand and glided over to Micah and Rachel who were patiently waiting our return. I released Stephanie's hand only to have her grab mine again, this time more tightly, and we remained in tandem for several minutes, Rachel and Micah right beside us.

The sudden clanking of a scuba knife caught our attention. Sound travels so much faster through water than air, making it difficult to find its exact origin. We spun our bodies until we found a group of lights encircling the target. This time, a huge king crab had moved out from under a massive over-hanging ledge to feed. With hand-sized claws and yard-long arms folded at its side, the crustacean alerted his senses to the strange creatures surrounding him. A misdirected finger could quickly become lost. I made sure I was never the closest diver to our temporary companion.

As the four of us hovered over the crab, the others already were moving over the reef wall. Their lights blinked out one by one, and we seemed to be alone in the deep. It occurred to me that at this moment we were the most important people in one another's lives. The infinite darkness created a dependency in a profound way. Relationships with people are forever changed when you place your possible existence into their trust.

Time passed quickly under the water and after more encounters with octopi, crab, and spotted eels, Joe signaled for us to follow him to the anchored boat. Stephanie finally let her hand slip from mine, and she and Rachel swam ahead to catch Jared and Adam. Micah and I moved off to the side, comfortable in our trailing position. Lobster emerged from their nooks, beaked camouflaged parrotfish in their self-made cocoons rested among the rocks, and red-eyed shrimp kept a wary sentinel as guardians of the coral palace. We witnessed flashlight fish, whose retinas reflected our lights so well they sent a beam back into the gloom. The elegant brittlestar with its spindly legs danced its way across a basket sponge larger than an oil drum. The threats of the night had become hidden treasures, coal into diamonds. We entered a hidden world and saw the miracles of a foreign land. But one miracle still awaited us. Micah turned to me and signaled he was turning off his light, and he expected me to do the same. I hesitated as it not only concerned me but it felt profane to silence this scene. Still, I relinquished control and plunged into blackness, void of definition.

In seconds, my eyes adjusted to the barely discernable shadows ahead as the lights of the others flickered to and fro, in and out of the pillar corals. Micah grabbed my shoulder and rotated me so that I faced the most intense darkness. His hand reached out and swept quickly in front of my mask. Hundreds of tiny neon yellow specks sparkled in the water, tossed by the force. He repeated the motion and they were there again. The angel of light was Lucifer, and I now know these microscopic invertebrates contain the compound *Luciferon*. Friction causes them to fire. But as I passed my hand through the dark, they were stars flung across the heavens. I was God creating the Milky Way. The entire trip was worth this moment. I did not want it to end.

Before we became too far behind and lost the path, we turned our lights back on and propelled ourselves forward. I missed my small glittering friends yet felt excited to have known them even so briefly. We glided along and soon the anchor line appeared; it seemed to be pulling itself from the mooring. A large u-shaped piece of iron had been driven into the coral so that all dive boats could secure themselves in the same place each time. As in many cases, a small piece was sacrificed so that much of the reef could be preserved. The mooring line rhythmically went from slack to taut as the waves above heaved the boat from crest to trough.

At this depth of only thirty feet the vessel's underbelly protruded through the mirrored surface and offered us comfort. We knew we were not lost. The other divers had all but disappeared above the surface, and we stopped at fifteen feet to do a five-minute safety stop, allowing us to hover over the reef and explore it from a long distance. Before we finned upward, we needed to create a circular curtain of bubbles by rotating our bodies with a free-flowing regulator held at arm's length. We hoped to clear a shaft of water free from jellyfish. Having been stung on one of the day dives yesterday, this procedure was not one to forego.

I instinctively touched my blistered forearm as I noticed we were the last two divers in the water. Micah moved closer to me and signaled to "look down" and again he turned off his light. I followed suit but questioned why as I had already seen the wonder of the *noctiluca.* He appeared as a dim ghost as he pointed below. In seconds a fluorescent green flash several inches wide emanated from within the recesses of the reef and then another and another. It reminded me of a WWII film of bombing runs over Europe as the incendiary night raids devastated Germany. The midnight world had given up another secret while we hung in the darkness above it. Fireflies condemned to the sea, they called out for acknowledgement from one another or perhaps just to say, "I am here."

The solitude caused me to wonder how many struggles for recognition had I been blinded to. How many people had passed by in my life who have cried out the same message and also went unnoticed? What else did the shroud of this shadowland seek to teach me? I chose to listen to the silent voices. A gentle brush on the arm told me it was time to leave this place. Bubble rings surrounded me as I surfaced and reached for the ladder. It rocked back and forth, and Joe took my flippers, and with his help I pulled myself upward and struggled free from my tank. The unlit boat moved with the waves and I peered over the side. Excitement and sadness mixed as I relived the inspiring visions of my first night dive. I longed for more miracles and reluctantly settled back against the railing as the engines started. As we turned for shore, I glanced into the water and reminded myself of the lessons revealed. The water shone not from within but from above. I looked up and there were my night-lights. The stars reached across the sky placed there by my hand. They are with me still and I listen when they speak.

#

Cold and trembling, the timid seamstress knocks on the door of the tiny garret. "I'm sorry…my light has gone out." She holds the unlit candle towards him. "Would you?"

"Come in for a moment."

"There's no need."

"Please … come in."

The orchestra murmurs a touching phrase of tenderness and fragility as Mimi enters, then clangs in agitation as she collapses in a fit of coughing.

"You're not well?"

"No … nulla."

"Impallidesce!"

"I'm out of breath … the stairs." She faints to the melody of a single oboe.

"Che gelida manina! How cold your little hand is! Se la lasci riscalder. Let me warm it for you."

"Mi chiamana, Mimi."

On the stage of the Metropolitan Opera House, Nellie sings the words of her most cherished composer. Her beauty heightened by the sadness of the role she plays, her voice electrified by talent and dark emotions, she draws long applause and bravos from the New York audience after the first act. It is the opening night of Puccini's La Boheme *at the Met, four years after its premier at the Theatro Regio in Turin on February 1, 1896. By the end of the performance, the critics will laud her as the world's greatest new diva.*

The second and third acts escalate with arias and love duets as the melody becomes warmer and higher, Rudolfo inflammed by his love for Mimi, the actor beneath the beard and Parisian costume tortured by the beauty of his titian-haired leading lady.

"What? You're going?" Rudolfo sings to his Mimi.

"Back to the place I left
At the call of your love,
I'm going back alone
To my lonely nest
To make false flowers.
Goodbye ... no hard feelings.
But listen.
Please gather up the few things
I've left behind. In the trunk
there's the little bracelet
and my prayerbook. Wrap
them ...
in an apron and I'll
send someone for them."

"Adio, sogni d'amor!" Rudolfo cries.

Before the final act, Gabriel praises her performance and gently suggests she ride to the Waldorf Astoria with him for dinner and champagne.

"There can never be a Rudolfo for me outside the stage," she says, her eyes refusing to meet his.

"Then you play your part too well," he recriminates as he adjusts his beard. "Mimi is dead off-stage as well."

Gabriel ties the strings hanging from the collar of his white blouse and awaits the signal marking his entrance.

Marcello once more is at his easel as Rudolfo sits at his writing table. They start working, but quickly throw down brush and pen. Characters come in and out, until Rudolfo discovers the hiding Mimi. He holds her bonnet over his heart.

"Mimi.."

"Have they gone?" she quavers. "I pretended to be asleep because I wanted to be alone with you. I've so many things to tell you, or one thing, huge as the sea, deep and infinite as the sea ... I love you ... you are all my life ... "

"Ah! My beautiful Mimi...!"

"It was dark. You couldn't see me blushing."

"Please don't talk.
Why are you crying like this?
Here ... beloved ... with you always!
My hands ... the warmth ... to sleep.
What does this mean? This
Going back and forth?
Mimi ... "

Nellie lies still in her bed upon the stage, her long red tresses curling almost to the floor as the heavy velvet curtain closes to the screaming static of applause. It is December 26th. Her mother begged her to come home for Christmas, but Nellie declined, loyal only to her voice and to the stage.

Chapter 24

"Was this trip everything you expected it to be, Ms. Scott?" Micah asked me over breakfast the next morning.

"Incredible, to put it mildly," I said, "and enlightening. I can never go back to the fish tank."

"Fish tank?"

"The guilt and shame. Therese's death will always be with me, and the sadness will never leave, but I feel I can have a real chance at life. I don't have to live in a loveless marriage, and I don't have to do destructive things to make the past go away. In the ocean I found her, like you said I would. I found her in Stephanie and Rachel, Adam and Jared, the grouper, the coral, the noctiluca and fire worms ... and I found her in other places too ... the high cliff with the cutter ants, the stars, and myself ... you ... and the past voices that live within me. I know she will always be with me, and for that I'm grateful."

"You are a remarkable person, Catherine Faith Scott. She helped make you that." Micah smiled and tears welled in his eyes. He reached across the table and held my hands in his.

Stephanie was the first to arrive, breaking the shield of invisibility surrounding Micah and me. "Hey, Ms. Scott, you conked out early last night. You missed all the fun. Adam and Jared and Rachel and I went back in the water after dinner. I think we found that secret spot you and Mr. M. went to that night."

"I was so exhausted after four dives, I had a hard time keeping my eyes open through dinner. Plus, I had so much to think about. This has been an overwhelming week."

"Mr. M. and Joe were grading tests when we got back, but you were sawing major z's."

Rachel was the second one to appear. She pulled up a chair and stretched her long arms over her head.

"Hey, Rachel, you think maybe it's about time you got out of bed? Even Stephanie beat you here this morning," Micah said.

"Funny," Stephanie replied.

"I can't believe it's the last day. The trip is almost over," Rachel reminded us. "I have to buy some more film before we do our dolphin snorkel. It sucks that we can't dive today."

"What time do we swim with the dolphins?" Still shaking the sleep from his eyes, Jared arrived just after Rachel. "Adam's still in bed. I told him to get up, and he told me to shut up."

"We don't swim with the dolphins until two, so Adam can sleep awhile. We'll have time to do some exploring this morning for a change. Because of pressure, you can't dive within twenty-four hours of getting on a plane. Tonight we go to West End and celebrate the new certified divers. Me and Joe graded all your tests last night."

"Did we all pass?"

"Well ... I think there was one of you who didn't."

"Was it me? Please tell me it wasn't me," said Stephanie.

"I don't think it was you."

"It's probably Jared. I know he didn't study the manual at all before the trip."

"Stop joking Marlowe, and tell us we all passed," I said. "That's the least you can do for all our hard work this week."

"You all are no fun ... Yeah, everybody passed and you are all certified divers now. You all need to do some small dives from time-to-time when you get home. There are some places off the coast of Georgia to dive that are real easy to get to or the Crystal River in Florida where you can see the manatees. That's not too far from Atlanta, but wherever, you need to practice."

Carrying our test booklets under his arm, Joe sauntered in appearing as if he hadn't slept in days. "It looks like all you knuckleheads passed, and I don't mean just the written part. You guys really improved from that first day. I'll get your certification card in the mail as soon as I get back to California. Way to go, and especially you, Cat."

"Well, thank you, sir," I said. "You must have stayed up grading those tests all night. You doing alright?"

"Since we weren't diving today, I went into town last night. I asked Marlowe to go, but he said he wanted to stay in and read."

"It looks like you had a real good time," Micah said. "You just getting here? I didn't see you when I got up this morning."

"I spent the night out," Joe said, his grin wide. "Man, I could use some strong java this morning."

"Need any aspirin?" I asked.

"I took about five already. I was fine until I started doing tequila shots. You guys order breakfast yet?"

Breakfast was uneventful as we chatted about the week and shared stories of our dives. Eventually Adam showed up, and we gave him a hard time about sleeping late, and then afterwards we all dispersed to enjoy a few hours of free time before lunch and the dolphin swim. Jared and Adam decided to kayak, while Stephanie and Rachel raced to sign up for horseback riding. Micah and I walked back to the bungalows, both of us quieter than usual.

"So, you stayed in last night," I said when we reached the porch. "Even if I hadn't fallen asleep, I wouldn't have been much company."

"I sat on the deck and watched the stars for awhile. I looked in your room, but you were out cold."

"I saw some beautiful stars last night, only they were underwater," I said. Micah held my hand and guided me to one of the hammocks. We lay side-by-side and rocked in the gentle breeze, comfortable in our closeness, our hands caressing each other's arms and shoulders. At one point I ran my finger along the edges of his face and lightly kissed his lips.

"What's going to happen to us when we get back?" I pondered aloud.

"You have to figure out your predicament before there's an us, my dear."

"Could there ever be an 'us'?"

"That depends. I don't know if I'm really what you want. And I don't know how much I have to offer a woman, I've been by myself so long. Let's worry about that later. We don't have much time left here. Since you're a diver now, you have to go river diving with me in the Tennessee River."

"You're kidding! It sounds dangerous. I thought you said the visibility was bad."

"It can be, but just sitting in the boat floating along is beyond cool. Especially late afternoon just before dusk; this time of year, the sun sets right between the mountains downriver ... You'd like it, Catherine."

"I seem to like everything you suggest." Micah moved his body towards me and hugged me so hard we almost fell out of the hammock.

"Let's go back to our spot on the other side of the Cay," he suggested. "I want to take a picture of the gumbo limbo tree in the daylight."

"The what?"

"Gumbo limbo. Isn't that the coolest name? It was right there on the edge of the beach. Near the mangroves where we hung our clothes. You saw it, but didn't I guess."

As soon as we arrived at our secluded stretch of beach, I saw the tree. Near the bottom, its massive trunk split into four thick limbs each about three feet in diameter, and they stretched for about six yards before they split into many more snaking branches that wound endlessly upward and out. Enough storm-blown sand had been piled against the base so that each limb was essentially its own tree. Cluttered with leaves the size of tulip petals, the tree, majestic in its solitude, resisted years of drought, torrential rains and devastating hurricanes. The sun poured through the branches, shimmering the leaves into casts of metal.

"I don't know how I missed this old soul," I said when I spied the gumbo limbo.

"Maybe you weren't ready to see it," Micah said. "Now that you finally can, go over there and sit on one of the branches. I'll take your picture."

Instead of climbing on one of the branches like Micah directed, I stood behind the trunk and popped my head out between the divided middle, grinning like a Cheshire cat. "Gumbo limbo, gumbo limbo, find me in the gumbo limbo," I half sang. Then I playfully climbed on the lower branches and posed like Jean Harlow, my lower lip pouted out.

"Who are you supposed to be?" Micah asked snapping pictures.

"Jean Harlow ... no, Veronica Lake." I tossed my hair over one eye and swung my legs seductively. "Do you want to go into the water with me again, Mr. Marlowe?" I teased. "Why don't you take my picture now," I said, pulling my tee shirt over my head and off.

"You better not do that," Micah said. "I might not be able to control myself."

"That's what I'm counting on."

"It's broad daylight. Anybody could see us if they wanted to."

"Well, then maybe I should really give them a show." I climbed down off the limb and behind the trunk, unzipped my shorts and threw them out on the ground.

"I don't think you want to do that."

"Stop being such an old fuddy-duddy, Micah Marlowe," I said and stood before him in my cotton jockeys.

"You're killing me," he said laughing. "I can't stop looking at you, you know that."

"No, I don't know that."

"Well, you should." And his body pushed me against the trunk of the tree, his hands reaching for my breasts and then down between my thighs. "What are you doing to me?" His mouth covered mine, and he groaned when my hands touched his ready body. His fine hair felt soft and warm in my hands and I wanted to kiss him in his most private place, but he pulled away before I could even start.

"Get dressed. We can't do this. Not here, not now." He breathed deeply and gave out an exasperated sighed. "I need to swim and burn off energy. You can sure get me stirred up. I'll be back in a minute." So, disappointed, not to mention frustrated, I leaned against the gumbo limbo and watched Micah swim out into the sea. By the time he emerged, wet and exhausted, I was fully dressed, my arms crossed over my chest. He shook his wet body all over me and laughed when he saw my angry face. "You have to get a little tougher. We can't jeopardize our careers and lives because of our hormones."

"You must be made of steel," I said. "I've never been turned down before; I must be losing my sex appeal."

"You're much more to me than sex. We better go back now. You don't want to miss the dolphin swim."

We walked back in almost silence, Micah occasionally pointing out a hidden gecko or Jesus lizard, my answers monosyllabic, my brain reeling from his last words. I felt like Alice who went through the looking glass and found a whole new world; only instead of a looking glass, I broke through my reflections in the sea and found a new way to live.

When we got back to the bungalows, we barely had time to get our gear together and run down to the dining room to catch a quick lunch. The dolphin pens could only be reached by boat at certain intervals, so there was no time to spare. Needing only mask and snorkel, we scurried down the familiar steps and through the palms. We stepped over their roots to the shed at the cay's edge. At the covered boat slip, we rang the hanging empty scuba tank with a whack of the small metal tube attached. A special boat from the marine institute pulled into the berth and in seconds we were motoring toward the lagoon with special pens.

San Pedro's Cay hosted some of the most renowned researchers of dolphin behavior, and after several lectures concerning the latest discoveries, we were ready to meet the subjects of these findings up close. As our boat pulled alongside a much longer dock, we hopped out and took a short walk to a wooden shack from which we received a quick orientation. The handler instructed us on how to respond to the dolphins in the water, and he also prepared us for how the dolphins would act and react around us. My complacent attitude, caused partially by the exhaustive week, dissipated as George, our guide, split us up into pairs and directed us to the beach area of the lagoon.

Using a whistle to call the dolphins, George told Micah and me to sit in the shallow water next to one of the three handlers. Ricardo introduced himself to us, and then presented Maya to us, one of the female dolphins who had given birth within the last year. He explained that she might respond to her child's call at any time during our visit. "If she bolts away on a seeming whim," Ricardo told us, "nothing is wrong other than she feels compelled to check on baby Mitch every several minutes."

Mitch was so named because of his birth during the horrific hurricane that uncompromisingly punished and changed the lives of so many people. His entry into this world helped in a small way to temper the losses of the islanders and their relatives on the mainland, which was hit the hardest. Maya's concern for her child bonded us immediately. I identified with her nurturing instinct and wished that all of humanity could love its offspring so well. Until now, Maya and her companions had been frolicking further out from shore, chasing, caressing, and tormenting one another. Then there was a push of water reminiscent of the waves created by a surfacing submarine, and a smooth gray dorsal fin and slightly curved back was lying in the shallow water beside me.

The actual size of Maya was staggering compared to her perceived size in deeper waters. Almost nine feet long and weighing 500 pounds, her sleek wet skin was spongy to the touch. Being a mammal, breathing was not a problem as long as she was kept wet in the one-foot of water. Ricardo gave her a small fish as a reward for responding to his call, and her clicks and squeaks seemed to thank him for the snack. At first she focused her attention on the disseminator of food, but she soon accepted her role as an instrument to educate and entertain.

Ricardo methodically lectured on Maya's unique biological make-up, locating and naming her most noticeable parts. Maya rolled over in response to Ricardo's gentle touch, and we could see where Mitch still suckled each day. As if reminded of her duty to her child, Maya turned slowly from us, and then at a respectful distance bolted for the deep waters to find Mitch. After a quick swim by and a soft nudge from the mother for her son, she returned to her place beside us. I could see her full expression of contentment and joy or perhaps pride in her son, and her eyes were close enough for me to see the intricate details but they revealed so much more.

An intelligent and silent soul spoke from within and acknowledged my own motherhood. For an instant, we were not separate species but were of one mind, having the same struggles, desires, heartaches and passion for that which we would give our lives, our children. She returned to the task at hand as her gaze focused forward. Ricardo allowed Micah and I to feel her tongue, which was rough to the touch, and we learned how the noises we had heard Flipper make actually came from the blowhole and not his mouth. After a few more minutes of forced interaction, Maya sprinted back to Mitch. He had been moving closer to her during our brief encounter with his mother but was hesitant to come into the extremely shallow water. Ricardo told us Maya would be back instantly since adult dolphins have unbounded trust for their trainers, a mutual faith developed through years of dolphin and human experience. The natural naiveté of youth, overshadowed by mankind's reputation of considering himself the owner of nature instead of its caretaker, animals depend on us for their continued survival as a species since man is the only creature who can decide if another shall exist or not. A heavy burden, and I wondered if we had the resolve to consider the implications for our own existence. Were we so blind to think we were exempt from the consequences of actions that created havoc in the natural order? Micah handed me my snorkeling gear, cutting short my reflections.

"Make sure you keep your hands at your sides. Let the dolphins come to you so they feel comfortable having you down there with them," Micah reminded me. "They are intensely curious creatures and will investigate behavior which looks odd."

Swimming to the deepest part of the lagoon, I watched Micah dive to the ten-foot bottom and pretend to dig in the sand. Almost immediately Maya crept close beside him, curious to see what he found, but soon her interest in him was lost when he swam to the surface for much-needed air. Turning in the opposite direction, I snorkeled along enjoying the possibility of coming face-to-face with one of the beautiful long-nose creatures. I could see Mitch hanging in the shadows, and instinctively I dove down to gather blades of turtle grass, and when I waved the grass in Mitch's face, he ventured towards me and gently tried to take it from my hand, like a puppy grasping for a stick. The sparkle in his eye suggested youth at play. Maya soon came behind him and lightly nudged him away.

There were at least four more adult dolphins swimming with us, and luckily I had been forewarned of their favorite ploy or certainly I would have been a victim of their deviousness. Coming up quickly toward the swimmer, the dolphin would get directly in front of one of us and open his mouth while making threatening gestures and noises. If we pulled back in fright or surprise, the thrill of creating fear would be seen in the movement and attitude of the culprit. Once a reeling victim was found, the human would be tormented to no end. Communicating with clicks and whistles, the word would get out that a sucker had been located and other dolphins would converge on this poor soul who now had serious doubts about this wonderful dolphin experience.

On guard against the teasing dolphins, I sensed a presence beside me. I twisted my body to the left and gracefully matching my movement was Maya. Even though I did nothing to warrant her attention, she had chosen to be alone with me for a brief moment. Being much longer that I, her eyes were nevertheless within inches of mine as we moved in rhythm. Was she trying to look into my soul? My dolphin companion was a sentient being deserving of my attention and benevolence. Do I think well of her child? she seemed to ask. I swam on my side and brushed my hands lovingly along her gray rubbery back, hoping she understood my complimentary response. Slowly, she moved away to join Mitch, but not before one last respectful glance in my direction. Never again would I feel unmoved at pictures of dolphin carcasses tossed aside as a consequence of tuna fishing.

When the dive was over, we swam to the shore to gather our shoes and headed toward the boat. On the ride back I told Micah how futile it seemed for people to dedicate their lives to the search of intelligent life on other planets, when we had discovered it here on earth. Looking into Maya's eyes produced a feeling of wonder and appreciation for the miracles of life and all its companion mysteries. This short week had given me much, possibly too much, to consider as I prepared to venture back to the confines of my home.

My energy depleted, I fought off the first jabs of depression and growing thoughts of futility. The trip was over, and there was nothing left except a taxi ride to West End. No more late-night hikes to follow cutter ants, no more long strides off the stern of the boat, no singing on the limbs of gumbo limbo trees or clothes hung on the roots of mangroves. Marshall would meet me at the airport and together we would go home and confront the fish tank.

The boat shuttle dropped us back at the covered dive pier, and not bothering to wait for the rest of the group, I made my way up the steps to the bar. Glumly, I carted two Dos Equis up the rest of the steps to our cabins. The cold beer went down easy and the alcohol gave me some relief from the heat rising inside me. The rest of the group still not back, I sat alone on the star-gazing deck, a cold beer on either side of my chair. Another swig, and the bottle was almost empty; I enjoyed the buzz and sniffed the air in momentary contentment. Live in the moment, I told myself. Don't think about the past or the future, but the sun high in the sky, the waves curling their toes along the sand, the clanging of dive tanks, the geckos poking their heads out from under the louvered cabin doors.

"So, here you are," Micah's voice said. "You don't believe in waiting for anybody, do you?"

"You want a beer? Here, this is for you. I was sure you all would get here before me."

"The kids wanted to go to the Marine Institute and buy some of the books on dolphins. They're in the gift shop now." Micah pulled a chair next to mine and relaxed with his beer. "It feels good to sit down for a couple of minutes. I don't get to do that often."

"You choose not to, Marlowe. I'm surprised you're not out with your metal detector or taking pictures of gumbo limbo and mangrove trees."

"I thought about it."

"You're about as restless as I used to be. What are you running from?"

"What makes you think I'm running from anything? Maybe I just like doing things."

"You don't have to tell me if you don't want to. Just remember, it takes one to know one."

His face expressionless, Micah's eyes became hard, and then he turned away from me. He crossed his arms as if to build a fortress around him, and the intensity of his silence made my body shiver.

"Micah," I whispered. "I think I know."

"Is it something bad?" he asked.

"Nothing about you is bad, Micah." I reached across his chair and squeezed his hand; this time it was my turn to quell his fears of troubled waters.

The rest of the afternoon passed slowly, as if time decided to take a long coffee break; even Jared, Adam and the two girls slowed their pace to a government crawl. Micah strolled down to the bar and took forever to bring back two more beers, and when he finally handed me the sweaty bottle and I took my first sip, my mouth seemed to savor each drop of the grainy liquid. The girls read in the hammocks, flipped through each other's journals, while Adam and Jared hung out on the porch shuffling card tricks and studying their dolphin books. We welcomed the endless hours, holding on to them like precious jewels, pebbles turned into diamonds. But the endless hours had to end. Dusk lingered on the horizon, and before we knew it, our last full day was gone.

Dinner that night was a sad affair, even though Stephanie, Rachel and I had fun dressing up for our night out in West End. Micah wanted to catch a taxi straight from the dining room, which meant if we wanted to dress up, we had to do it before dinner. And dressed up we were, at least compared to the khaki shorts and sometimes smelly tee-shirts we wore all week. The girls curled my hair, swept it up with a tortoise clip, and pomaded and lined my lips in a deep shade of reddish brown. We laughed as we all pulled out our one short dress for the trip, all held together with spaghetti straps, and all black.

"What're you all supposed to be?" Jared asked. "The Spice Girls?"

"You all are dressed alike," Micah noticed. "It's good to know you all clean up alike."

"Ms. Scott," Stephanie whispered in my ear, "I think Jared's drunk. You better tell Mr. Marlowe."

"I think Mr. Marlowe's aware of it. We'll keep an eye on him. Besides, we'll be leaving before he has time to drink any more."

It was just beginning to get dark when we hailed a taxi, which was more like hitchhiking, since anyone with a car or truck could instantly become a taxi for a few dollars. A rusted white mini-van with an entire family stuffed inside stopped and the six of us squeezed among the father, mother, and three small children. Everyone's arms and legs overlapped with the person beside them. The mother held a baby on her lap, and after about five minutes the other two children were sitting on Micah's and my laps. There was no air-conditioning in the van, and by the time we arrived in West End, the Spice Girls were all disheveled.

"Here's your clip back, Stephanie. I think I'll just leave it down," I said, half of my upswept hair fallen down my neck.

"I like it down better, anyway. I don't know why you had to get all dressed up. Those shoes are gonna kill your feet," said Micah, comfortably dressed in shorts and Tevas, as were Jared and Adam.

"We're used to walking in platforms, Mr. M. Anyway, we can take them off if they hurt, huh, Ms. Scott?" Stephanie expertly advised.

"I don't think you want to walk barefoot in West End," said Micah. "There are stray dogs and rats around."

"Then why are we going there in the first place?" I asked.

My question went unnoticed as the mini-van pulled over to the side of a gravel road. "Okay, amigos, we're here," the driver of the van said. "One dollar each." We handed him the money and climbed out of the tight space. I felt like we had been playing TWISTER in a truck.

"Where's the town?" Rachel asked.

"We're in it. The place we want to be is just up the road a little ways. We can't go too far; the town's not that big, but for those with the wrong shoes it might seem like a long hike," Micah said, glancing towards the girls and me.

Micah knew what he was talking about. West End was a small, sleepy town built, appropriately, on the Western coast of the island. The first building we passed was an old church, the white paint chipped and weathered, the stained glass windows beautiful in their humbleness. The lights were on in the old church, and we could hear the voices of children singing, the Spanish words melodious and haunting. It was a Catholic church, a remnant of early explorers. A dark, plain, certainly hand-hewn, wooden cross sat atop the primitive steeple. Those of us who were shorter had to stand on tiptoes to see inside. I could see the simple wooden pews and the massive supporting buttresses. Dark headed people peppered the chapel, prayer books in hand, while soft sounds and shining eyes spread comforting faith from the front. The devotion to their God seemed more sincere than the churchgoers in my neighborhood that was so far away at this moment. The prevailing opinion back home was that a healthy donation to the plate was more important than behavior in their search for redemption.

Diagonally across from the church were clapboard houses and a small general store, chickens and roosters roaming freely on the store's porch and steps. Beyond the church and general store, a long stretch of souvenir shops and open market stands, the tops of palm trees their only cover, fringed the sands leading to the Caribbean Sea.

Micah and Rachel stopped at one of the small stands to barter for ancient pieces of jade and ceramics, while the rest of us scoured the shops for cigars and other booty to take home. Stephanie found a small woven purse for her mother while Jared, Adam and I bought assorted Honduran cigars and coffees for friends and family. I found a jade turtle necklace for Elizabeth, the cigars a more appropriate gift for Marshall and Sammy.

We could hear loud music from afar, and Jared and Adam lit cigars for all of us as we patiently waited for Rachel and Micah to pack away their artifacts. Jared bought a Dos Equis at one of the little bars that dotted the dirt-and-gravel road, and as we sauntered down the road to Foster's, Jared developed the need to inform us how seldom he drinks at home. "Ms. Scott, you won't tell my mother I was drinking on the trip, will you? She would be so disappointed in me. I don't want her to think I drink all the time, because I never drink at home."

"Your secret is safe with me," I said. "As long as you don't get too carried away."

"He's already too carried away," Stephanie said. "Think they have AA down here?"

"I never drink at parties," Jared continued. "I put water in my beer bottle and pretend like I'm drinking as much as everyone else. I never drink; I wouldn't want to disappoint my mother. She'd be so mad if she found out I was drinking here. She expects me to be perfect." His anxiety was becoming quite funny.

"What she doesn't know won't hurt her," Micah said trying to stifle a chuckle. "Relax. You'll be the only one here who would tell her."

The sheer freedom of being miles away from home in the middle of Central America affected us all in different ways. A microcosm of the world at large, the island was a safe place to try ourselves out.

A bar and restaurant suspended on pillars in the water, Foster's came highly recommended by some of the locals who worked at San Pedro's Cay. They informed us the place had live music and dancing on Friday nights. The interior, built entirely of pine and oak, had no walls but tall beams supporting the floor and ceiling so the ocean could be seen from three sides. Stairs on the main level led up to the roof, which doubled as a second bar and star-gazing deck. Even though it was already after ten, the line to get in Foster's was long, and by the time the bouncers at the front door stamped our hands and let us in, the place was packed and the dance floor crowded.

Micah bought us a couple of beers at the bar, Jared right behind him.

"Make that your last beer," Micah said. "We don't want to have to carry you home."

When Jared didn't respond, I grabbed him by the shoulders. "Jared, you really do need to slow down."

"Sure, Ms. Scott," he said, putting his hands around my waist. "Will you save a dance for me tonight?"

"Of course, Jared," I said. "So, how many beers have you had tonight?" Jared ignored my question and left the bar. Without much trouble, he found Stephanie and Rachel, who were dancing with some of the young locals. Soon Adam joined them and it was hard to tell who was dancing with whom.

The main attraction was a sixty-year-old black woman who sang a combination of reggae and blues; a younger man with long dreadlocks sang the background while guitars and perfectly hammered rusted steel drums accompanied them both. The crowd swayed back and forth to the rhythm of the high-pitched voices and soon the dance floor filled with so many people, those of us watching near the bar were caught in the middle of gyrating bodies. I moved my lips to the haunting words, the singers' voices vibrating through my body, and felt as if I were the singer on the stage blasting out my feelings. I half-closed my eyes to see the kaleidoscope of people, lights, and movement. My entire body felt sensual and I wanted to make love to the music.

"I think we should dance, Mr. Marlowe."

"I don't dance," Micah said. "I just watch."

"I think it'd be good for the kids to see you dance."

"I don't know how to dance."

"That's a shitty excuse. It's easy. You move your feet and hands around a little and keep time to the music. Like this." I barely moved my feet and let my hips sway back and forth.

"I need to have another beer first," Micah said. "I wish Joe didn't have to leave today."

"He's gone already? I thought his flight left the same day as ours."

"He had to get back to certify a group in the other ocean. If he were here, you could have danced with him."

"But I want to dance with you." I didn't know if Micah heard me, because Marcos, one of the crewmen of the Delphin, swung his big-bellied body over to mine and grabbed me around the waist with both hands. My body undulated to the soft Caribbean music and caressed the soulful words. I tried to gyrate my body like I imagined the Carib islanders would move and Marcos pulled me close to him and spun me around until my feet were off the floor and shook me until I felt as limp as a rag doll. We wriggled our bodies through two songs until Marcos put his hands on my shoulders and told me to slow down and take it easy.

"You dance too fast. Go slow like this and move with the rhythm." I slowed down and mimicked the motions of Marcos' hips and shoulders, lowering my body with his, my hips pivoting left and right, my arms swinging above my head, my shoulders and chest reeling back and forth. I was caught up in the sensuality of the dance, made even more so by the dark shimmering lights of the ocean and the warm night breeze running down my skin. I was slick with sweat.

Marcos pulled me close to him and I followed every flex of his body, Stephanie commenting later that it looked like I was grinding with him. In actuality I was orgasmic in the euphoria of total abandonment. I didn't give a thought or care to anyone or anything except for the current of my flesh. I felt energy inside me I never knew I had and gave in to an irresistible urge to walk up on the stage and sing my heart out. Micah stopped me two-feet shy of the stage.

"What do you think you're doing?"

"I want to sing."

"How much have you had to drink? You can't go up there! They're taking a break anyway."

"I know; that's why I want to sing, and Micah, I've only had one beer."

"C'mon then, I'll buy you another one."

By the time I walked back to the bar with Micah, the euphoria I felt from the dance and the music diminished.

"I thought you had a lousy voice. Why'd you want to get up there?" Micah said.

"I do, but I wanted to sing tonight. I have a fantasy of becoming a great singer some day. When I was little I would close the door of my closet and sing my lungs out. It didn't sound to me like I had a lousy voice. Oh well, I must've done something in my past life that was really bad, and now I'm being punished for it by having no voice."

"So you grind with the natives instead, nice."

"I was feeling my wild dancing spirit. I just let my body move where it wanted to move." The music started up again, and I pushed Micah into the middle of the floor before he could refuse. Dancing with Micah seemed unnatural and forced, and I swayed uncomfortably beside him.

"Why don't you dance with me the way you danced with Marcos?" he said. "I thought you were going to be arrested for lewdness."

"Well, you don't dance the way Marcos dances, and I wasn't dancing lewdly with him. I was letting my body fall into the pattern of the music."

"You were letting your body fall, alright. All over him."

When a slow song came on, Micah retreated to his table overlooking the sea, and before I could challenge him to a slow dance, Jared caught me by the arm and led me onto the dance floor. I had the distinct feeling he hadn't heeded Micah's words to stop drinking.

"You okay?" I asked.

"I'm fine. You said you'd dance with me. 'Member?" He put his face close to mine and shook his head. "You're so beautiful, Ms. Scott. You know what? If I were your husband, I wouldn't let you go on trips all by yourself. I'd be afraid another man would fall in love with you, like Mr. Marlowe has."

"Jared, Mr. Marlowe's not in love with me. We're just good friends."

"Is that why he always wants to be alone with you? I don't blame him, but he should find somebody who's not married."

"Jared, please stop drinking. You're going to feel really bad in the morning." The song over, I left Jared alone on the dance floor, and silently thanked him for the reality check. Out of the mouth of babes, my mother used to say.

I didn't dance with Micah anymore that evening, and later when he invited me to go to our secret spot behind mangroves and the gumbo limbo, I declined. For the rest of the night at Foster's I joined a circle of local women and stomped and clapped until Jared was falling over and we had to go. And after tucking the besotted Jared in bed, I slept soundly in my bunk with Stephanie and Rachel above me. Micah did not question the abrupt change in my behavior; he quietly withdrew and before he closed the cabin door behind him, he said, "It's been a good trip, Cat." I had a faint recollection of his light being on for a long time, but then again I may have been dreaming. The next morning Micah joked with the kids, and later, on the bus to the airport and, finally, on the plane, we sat apart, readying ourselves for the separation that lay ahead.

Chapter 25

Predictably Marshall greeted me at the airport, and we exchanged a perfunctory hug and kiss. "It's good to have you back, Cat," he said. "You won't believe what's happened since you left. You were right about the jerks in the neighborhood. They're all a bunch of losers. Neil moved out and Debra's caused all kinds of scenes. Rob called while you were gone, and said everyone has seen Debra's true colors and they want us to come back to the group. I told him to go to hell."

"I guess we both had epiphanies over the week," I said. Out of the corner of my eye I could see Jared give his mother a big hug. I wondered how long it would be before she found out her 'perfect' son was not so perfect. I hoped it would be soon. Stephanie and Rachel called me over to meet their parents and excitedly talked about the incredible trip. Soon the whole group was together, parents and kids, Adam teasing Jared about the numerous trips to the bathroom he took on the morning flight to Miami, Stephanie hugging everyone, Rachel wondering what happened to Mr. Marlowe.

Amidst the confusion of mass arrival, Micah hung back from the rest of us as if he were trying to make himself invisible. He seemed nervous and detached. Then I knew why. A thick-armed woman in her late sixties appeared as if out of nowhere and gave Micah a half-hug and then beamed a smiling face at the rest of us. Micah didn't bother to introduce her to anyone. She obviously was his mother; she had the same close-set blue eyes that seemed at one minute to sparkle, while the next minute keenly observing. She had the same pointed nose, though larger because of age, and the same high cheekbones that made her skin crinkle around the edges of her eyes when she smiled. Absent of make-up, she had short bleached-blonde hair, those over-sized glasses grandmas wear, a body thickened by too much Southern cooking over the years, and a laugh that would make you feel loved. She had Micah's same curvaceous legs with wide ankles, meaty fingers on the ends of her wide hands, and the same pronounced Southern drawl that was not quite redneck yet not quite the genteel South either. A skinny gentleman with silver hair moussed back to expose a strong but wrinkled forehead remained passively beside her. He was handsome for his age, which I guessed to be about seventy, and I surmised he must be a vain man, because he had a small brush tucked in his back pocket.

We rode the train to baggage together, and I introduced myself to Micah's parents. His mother gave me a hug; his father politely shook my hand and smiled widely at Marshall and me. Before I could introduce Marshall, Micah told his father that I grew up near Newport, the senior Mr. Marlowe's hometown.

"I used to dive in the Ohio River when I was a kid," he wanted me to know. "On the Kentucky side. We didn't have any fancy equipment like ya'll back then. We just held our breath and jumped in." His voice was thinner than Micah's, and the Southern drawl not as long as Micah's and his mother's, but it had the same mellifluous rhythm.

"Good Lord, Frank," said Micah's mother, "I wouldn't call what ya did diving."

"It was the only kind of diving for po' boys from Kentucky," he said. "We always took our dog Bonehead with us. He was better at it than most of us people. He loved the river so much that sometimes he'd go so far down the river he'd get lost and couldn't find us when he came up. I don't know what he was doing down there, he was like one of them diving ducks. But he liked rabbit hunting better than diving, and as soon as he heard us stickin' our guns in the hunting truck, I could hear that hound barking as far away as Lexington. We hadn't seen him for days and along comes Bonehead, tongue hanging with drool, ready to go. Smartest dog I ever seen. Track down anything. Some kid that lived down the street shot him." My eyes widened. "Didn't kill him. Bonehead was running a rabbit and Larry pulled the trigger a little early. His ear got tore up, pretty ragged. He wasn't too thrilled about hunting rabbits after that."

"Dad," Micah said. "These folks don't want to hear all that." Before I could contradict him, Micah held out his hand to Marshall, and my stomach began to burn.

"You must be Marshall," he said. "Thanks for sharing Cat with us this week. She's a good sport and a good diver. We're all proud of her."

"I've always been proud of Cat," were the only words Marshall ever spoke to Micah.

The wide doors of the airport tram opened and Micah put an arm around his father's shoulder and led the garrulous old man up the escalator to meet the students and their parents. That simple gesture made me fall in love with Micah all over again, and later I would fall in love again when he made a toothless old man feel important or gave a hunched-over small child his Ziggy eraser, wore his buck teeth from the trick store in a fancy restaurant, spent all week individualizing bookmarks for 150 students, and washed large soup pans for tornado victims in Gainesville, Georgia. In the days before the long river diving trip to Tennessee and before the trial, I would go begrudgingly with Micah to help the tornado victims in North Georgia; we would dig down deep in sudsy water to clean the pots and pans used to feed the displaced and homeless. Alongside of us would work a sprightly octogenarian, whose entire face could light up a room. Micah would whisper in my ear, "That man is an angel. We're the only ones that see him." And as long as Micah keeps falling in love with the hearts of people, I will always fall in love with him.

But for now, I noticed a closeness in the small Marlowe family I didn't feel worthy to share, and because of my love for Micah, I did not want to interfere with the devotion of a son to his parents, and I resolved to never do anything to break the bond between parents and their only child, and watching the sweetness of the older couple made me feel like a Jezebel who had tempted Micah with her worldly ways.

Having been married for twenty-five years to a high-powered executive, I was used to a man independent of his parents. Marshall had separated from his mother as soon as he started elementary school and never regretted letting go of the apron strings. That was why I initially did a double-take when Micah's parents were waiting for him at the airport. I thought it strange a forty-year-old man would not drive to the airport himself or have a woman waiting for him somewhere in the wings. But after meeting Micah's parents and sensing the deep affection between them, the situation did not seem odd at all. Micah Marlowe was a caring man, and he cared and protected his parents with vigor unmatched by most adult children.

"The puffer's dead," Marshall said as we wheeled off highway 285 onto GA-400. It was a rainy night, and in the drizzle the glare of headlights pricked the highway like heavy gauged needles.

"How'd that happen? Did you forget to feed him?"

"I fed him twice a day. Once in the morning and once at night. Just like you said."

"Are the other fish okay?"

"They seem to be."

"Maybe the puffer died of a broken heart. He missed the soul mate he left behind in the ocean."

"He was raised in a pet store."

"Do you think he had some kind of infection?"

"There was probably something wrong with him when we bought him. I put him in a plastic bag so we could take him back."

"We've had him for over two years. Just bury him in the yard, poor thing."

"We'll buy another one."

"I don't want to buy any more fish. Not after swimming with them in the ocean."

"Does this have something to do with Micah? I bet you and nature boy had a good time."

"We had a *wonderful* time, actually. He taught me how to dive and how to see far beyond the stars. He helped me with her, Marshall."

"You told him? I can't believe you'd do anything so stupid! How do you know he's not going to tell people at work?"

"It was an accident, Marshall. A horrible accident … and Micah understood all that."

"You've gotten too close to this guy. Way too close for our comfort. You're probably in love with him." Marshall was an excellent lawyer and over the years had fine-tuned his intuitive perceptions of people. The only person whose behavior he could not predict was ironically his wife, but tonight he appraised the situation between Micah and me accurately. I was taken aback by his comment; I have had many male friends over the course of our marriage, and Marshall never questioned my intentions with any of them. His words stung as if he had slapped my face, not because he suspected I was in love with another man, but because I was in love with another man.

"Marshall …" I began.

"Save it, Cat, we're almost home." We drove home the way we went to the airport, in silence. The geometric colors of the foyer solicited us from the top of the street, and the proximity of the oversized houses to each other lent a heaviness to the night air I had not noticed before.

"Home sweet home," Marshall said, as he slammed the door to his Porsche. "Need help with your bags?"

"I've got them, thanks." Marshall already had fixed himself a drink by the time I lugged my couple of bags to our room and unpacked enough to find the box of cigars I bought for him.

"Hey, guess what I brought you—Honduran cigars. They're supposed to be better than Cubans. The word on the street is that the Cubans learned the fine art of cigar-making from the Hondurans."

Marshall checked out the Panatela label on the side of the box, opened the lid and read the gold and white inside cover: El Paraiso, Havana Reserve, Handmade and Imported from Honduras.

"So the cigars are handmade in Honduras, imported to Cuba, and then shipped back to Honduras. That makes a lot of sense."

"I guess you could say you have both Honduran and Cuban cigars," I said.

"Did they have cigars made in Honduras that haven't been imported to Cuba first?"

"I suppose. I can check the other ones."

"Don't bother. I'll light one of these babies first." Marsh sat in his favorite kitchen chair and lit a cigar and stared at the *Atlanta Journal-Constitution*. I was not ready to end the conversation; there were things I needed to say to him.

"Put the paper down, Marsh. We need to talk."

"Here it comes ... so, you're going to leave me."

"Oh, good lord, Marshall, just listen. Something happened under there. I don't know if I can explain it. Something like forgiveness or maybe peace ... I started to think about life in a different way. I've changed in a way that I can't put into words just yet. I want *real* things."

"What're you talking about? You *have* real things. Just walk around this house."

"I know I do, Marshall. I have a real family and a real job, but I want for you and me to have more than that. I want us to speak real words to each other so we can be real friends and have real love."

"What kinds of words are we speaking if they aren't real?" Marshall rolled the corners of his mouth into a half smile. He blew smoke to the ceiling.

"We talk in circles and evade things. For years we've ignored the wall sitting between us. We never mention her death; hell, we never even mention her *name*. We both pretend it never happened and we never deal with those real issues we should've dealt with a long time ago. It's a wound that has festered for so long we can't see the limb it sprung from anymore. I feel like I'm walking around in ether."

"So what're you saying? You don't love me? I didn't think you wanted to talk about her."

"I love you, Marshall, because I know you've been kind and mean well. But I want to love you the way a woman loves a man. Freely and without guilt and sadness ... soul to soul."

"Look, I know I'm gone a lot and I did a lot of thinking when you were gone. I've decided to try to find a way to stay home more. And when I have to travel overseas, I want you to go with me. This neighborhood has really been bad for us. These people aren't friends. They're leeches."

"I don't think we can blame our problems on the neighborhood. They just gave us an excuse not to deal with anything. Like how we married each other for the wrong reasons and used each other to cover up what we couldn't face. You protected me from the horror of Tessy's death; I took the place of your emotionally starved mother. If you helped me, you eased your guilt as a failure because you couldn't help her. Marsh, we need to give each other a chance at life, before we forget who we really are."

"Catherine, I don't want to let you go. I love you. I've *always* loved you."

"But it's a destructive love, don't you see that? We need to find another way to love each other or get out."

"Are you leaving me because of Micah?"

"He helped me find some things out about myself. But I'm not leaving you for Micah. I want to make it work between you and me, Marshall, but it has to be a different way. We cannot stay trapped in each other's needs anymore. We need to be honest with each other."

"Okay. I'll be honest. I don't see how you say you were ever trapped in my needs. I don't have needs left because I've spent my entire life meeting yours. I'm the one who found you rolled up in a ball on the chair in the asylum, remember? And I'm the one who got you out of that place and took you home and married you. You'd be nothing without me."

Marshall's words made me feel like closing up into that ball again, but I knew too much now for that to happen. "You and I both know that's not true. I've always had the strength to put my life together alone; I just didn't know it then. But I do now. What you did for me was wonderful, but in the end, we have to choose as individuals how we want to live our lives. We have a chance, if you understand that. If I leave, it won't be because of anyone except me."

"I don't understand anything about you. I thought we were doing okay, living the good life, and then some math teacher comes along and changes everything. You would fall for some goddamn guy who likes to go digging around in mud. You'll always be crazy."

"This has nothing to do with Micah. It's me. I'm unhappy with our life and what we've become. You don't want to believe that I could be unhappy with Marshall and the great life he gave me. Someone must have come along and changed my mind for me. That's not it, Marshall. The truth is that I feel like I'm living in a glass full of formaldehyde and I can't breath anymore."

Marshall smoothed my bangs away from my face. "I can't imagine life without you." He buried his face in my neck and began to undress me. "I've missed your body so much this week." He held my breasts in his hands and pushed his hips against mine.

"Not now, Marsh, please. There are no temporary fixes anymore. We have to work this out with our minds, not our bodies."

Marshall pushed me hard into the pantry door. "You must have got your fill in Honduras," he said. Marshall slammed the door to our room, and I hid among the large pillows of the white couch. It seemed strange to stare at the fish tank without the puffer clacking his large front teeth at me. The blue tangs and nassos swam back and forth, like lifeless dummies on a track in a carnival booth. The loss of the puffer hurt, as did the loss of Marshall, and of Micah, and I felt restless in my pain. I fell asleep fighting off the impulse to drink a bottle of wine; my pain was one of the real things in life I could count on.

The rest of the weekend passed without drama, Marshall keeping himself busy with work, and as usual, business golf on Sunday, while I planned the last three months of the school year, graded papers, and attempted to write Marshall about my wishes for us, but ended up throwing the words away. If he wouldn't listen to me, why would he take seriously something I wrote? Micah called once to ask if I had experienced any aches or pains from the food or diving; apparently Rachel had an ear infection and Jared had diarrhea so bad he had to go to the emergency room. I answered his questions politely but with an uncharacteristic curtness, not lingering on the phone with added words or anecdotes. He paused before he hung up, as if getting up the strength to ask me something hard, but in the end merely said goodbye.

I can't see you anymore or listen to your voice, I said to myself. It stirs up too much trouble inside of me, Mr. Marlowe. I cannot focus on important changes with you around. But one thing's for certain, it's not going to be easy staying away from you.

A few times I missed him so badly I picked up the phone to dial his number, but then I forced myself to think of his mother and father and the love they had for their son, and I easily put down the phone. His parents deserved someone better for their son, I thought. A younger woman who would give him children, give his parents grandchildren, who understood math and physics the way he did; a woman with a less complex past, a woman whose psyche remained unfettered by voices, a woman who could live loud and free and joyful. All I had to give was love and honesty, and some people say that's enough, but I looked at myself in the mirror and saw the lines around my eyes and the knowledge those lines hold, and I knew it was not.

#

And the angel mother and father looked at each other and sighed. "Now what?" Lola spoke first as she always did. "We send her the man she's been searching for all her lives, and she throws him away, just like that?"

"A temporary setback, Lola. Not to worry. Catherine Faith won't let him get away, especially with a little nudge here and there."

"What're you up to Jamie?"

"Nothing of *my* doing. Nature will take care of everything. You forget whose little girl she is."

Lola smiled and nodded.

#

The first day of spring quarter was wet and cold, yet the students piled in the classrooms wearing shorts and sleeveless shirts to show off their tans from winter vacation. Technically, it was still winter. March had barely begun, but to those of us involved in education, student, faculty, or administrator, the end of winter break meant the start of spring. Throughout the day, I glanced at the door to my portable, half expecting Micah Marlowe to come through the threshold at any minute. A part of me was disappointed; a part of me wanted him to kick down my door and carry me away in his truck. But he never came.

After a few weeks, I became inured to the routine of my life without Micah. Teaching filled my days, and Marshall's growing moodiness, the few evenings he was home, annoyed my evenings. I continued going to my Friday afternoon circle, which was turning into therapy sessions for me; Linda, Ester, Shelly, Eileen, and even Marie supported my endeavor to change the life I led with Marshall.

"He's become more walled since I got back from the trip," I said. "The more I want to change things between us, the harder he resists. I don't understand."

"He's in control this way," said Eileen. "You're the child who needs taking care of and he's the protector. He doesn't want a grown-up. Have you suggested counseling to him?"

"He'll never go for that, or if he does, he won't be honest. We've gone that route before. Part of the problem is Micah. He thinks I'm in love with him."

"*Are* you in love with him?"

"I can't allow myself to think about Micah right now. My marriage is in serious trouble, and I need to do something about it."

"How could your marriage change so drastically in one week?" asked Marie.

"I've changed. I want to live in my soul, and I want Marshall to live in there with me."

"What happened on the trip to make you this way?" asked Linda.

"You didn't!" said Ester.

"Please! How do I get Marshall to see things the way I do? Tell me!"

"Maybe you *can't*. And maybe the way you see things isn't the way he should see things. Why don't you quit worrying about

Marshall and just keep on going where you're going and see what happens," said Eileen. "Things have a way of falling in place."

"Why don't you leave Marshall and start all over again?" Ester suggested.

"She's not getting any younger," said Marie. "It's hard finding men when you're over forty."

"Cat won't have any problem finding a man," countered Linda. "You exude sex, Cat. You'll be fighting off the crowds."

"This is not about finding another man," I said. "It's about making what I have work. It's about *me*."

"Have you fallen out of love with Marshall?" Ester wanted to know.

"I never *was* in love with him. I have always cared for him and tried not to hurt him. I don't know how to explain our situation. We feed off of each other in a way that's more hurtful than helpful. We're stale together, like the walking dead. "

"Sounds like you should get out of the marriage with your running shoes on, Cat dear," said Eileen.

"She wants to see if she can try it a new way," said Marie. "Cat, I wish I had done that. I left Charlie without giving him a chance to explain his affair. He wanted to come back to the marriage. It's been a really hard life, Cat."

"How do you truly want to spend the rest of your life?" asked Shelly.

I closed my eyes and pictured the next forty years. A vision of who I wanted to be came to me and I laughed out loud. "I want to yell, belch and fart as loud and as much as I want for the rest of my life. By myself if necessary, but if perchance Marshall or some willing partner wants to do the same, there would be joy and freedom multiplied by two. I want to throw guilt and shame and all those punishing years out the window and laugh until my guts hurt. You know, I have screwed up big-time in my life, so big none of you all would believe it. You'd cry if I told you my story. Hell, it makes *me* cry. But now the sad, serious part is over, and I want to have some fun, and if it's a sin because I haven't paid all my dues, well, then it's too God-damned, fucking, son-of-a-bitch bad."

"You go, girl."

"Amen!"

"Tell it to us!"

"You all sound like God-damned Holy Rollers."

"Now we know what to call ourselves." The name stuck, thanks to Marie, and at every opportunity we all made a point to tell people we belonged to the Holy Rollers. It was funny to everyone but the pew-jumping, tongue-speaking originals.

Going home to Marshall after my Friday night sessions with the Holy Rollers was glum and I had only myself as an outlet. I tried to reopen the conversation I'd begun about making a new start, and suggested we take up a hobby to get to know each other in a different and even romantic way, but ever since I came home from Honduras, he grew more secretive and isolated. He communicated even less than before and shut himself in his office when he was home and spent hours on the phone. It did not surprise me when women began to call the house and asked me to give Marshall messages, as if I were his secretary.

One woman called and curtly told me she had made reservations at Bones on Saturday night for her and Marshall, and would I please give him the message. "I'm sorry," I said. "That's his wedding anniversary, and we already have reservations at The Diner." Click. I wasn't being ornery; it *was* our anniversary and I really *did* make reservations at The Diner. Marshall appeared ashen-faced when I told him what I had said to the woman, and then he stumbled over his words and said she was a business associate who would be in Atlanta at that time. I offered to cancel the dinner reservations, but he quickly declined my offer. I have never known Marshall to lie, and she probably was a business associate, but it wouldn't have surprised me if Marshall were hoping it might turn into something else. We hadn't had sex in a long time; Marshall had not initiated any ever since I rejected him the night he pushed me against the pantry door, and I had no desire to pursue him. The thought that Micah ruined any sex I would have with another man faintly crossed my mind, but I pushed that thought aside as ridiculous, and knew things would change with me and Marshall as soon as we started finding new ways to reach each other.

In comparison to Marshall's hectic life, mine was rather dull, especially my social life. After school, I graded papers, wrote in my journal, read, attended the Holy Rollers, and occasionally went out to a movie or dinner with a few teachers. But I was learning how to fill the empty hours with myself, and as I began to enjoy the quiet time alone, I felt confident and peaceful, as if I were on that tiny Honduran island again, memorizing the constellations.

One evening, I reached for the phone and called Meg.

"Hey, baby sister, how are you? We haven't talked in forever."

"Hey, Cat," said Meg. "I'm a little stressed, but at the moment things are calm. What's going on?"

"I wanted you to know I love you, Meg. I always have. You were the sweetest little girl, always making us laugh, especially mom. She really needed you after the debacle I caused the family. I should've been jealous of you, but I was as charmed as everyone else."

"What brought all this on?"

"I went diving, Meg."

"Cat … I can't believe it. I thought you couldn't go in the water after … that."

"I didn't think I could either, but I did and … then I remembered everything, clearer than ever before." Meg did not respond and the silence between us cut into my heart.

"I forgave us, Meg. We were all children, not just Tessy, not just you, but also me. Funny, how I never looked at it that way. I was a child myself when she died; I was even more of a child when Perry's father … "

"Perry's father? What does he have to do with …" Meg grew silent and then started to cry.

"Oh my God, Cat. I didn't know … Oh my God! What are you telling me?" I could hear her long sobs over the phone, and I felt bad, but I had to continue.

"All of us drowned in some way that day, not just Tess. I want to let you know, I'm coming back. That's why I told you. I don't want the others to know, but you had to. You're the one I have always been closest to. You never shut me out, Meg, not like the rest of them. I want you to come back with me so you won't get sick again."

"Catherine … Oh, Catherine … I'm so sorry." Meg choked on her words, and I knew she was still crying.

"The next time I go diving, I want you to come with me. "

"I could never go, Cat. I'm not as strong as you."

"You'll see how innocent you were, sweetheart. And then you can be Meg again, and not have to try so hard to please all the time."

"You have to make everything deeper than it really is. You went diving and it was a great trip. Leave it that."

"But Meg, something happened to me under there. I understood so much about me, you, life. It changed me."

"Cat, not everybody can be like you and get meaning out of things like that. And not all of us want to. Why dig it all up? It'll just hurt you all over again. But thanks for caring about me. You'll always be my favorite sister. I've gotta pick up Jimmy from basketball and I'm already late. I have to go. Sorry."

"That's okay, Meg. Love you."

Chapter 26

Heavy storms come through northern Georgia in the spring, and the first week in April, a tornado ripped a path wider than a football field through Gainesville, destroying hundreds of homes and killing over a dozen people. Relief funds for the homeless and the displaced were set up in all the northern counties, and Dr.Blackwell, the principal of Tecumseh High School, encouraged the homerooms to collect money for the victims. Micah had posted a sign-up list in the faculty mailroom for volunteers to help with clean-up and food services at several churches in the Gainesville area. Only a few students had signed up, and on impulse I added my name to the list; after all, I reasoned, it's not like we will be alone. Enough time had passed for me to gain control over my emotions, I thought, and I did want to do my part to help people whose lives were in such chaos.

"Be at the truck as soon as school's out," Micah's voice said behind me. "Gainesville's about an hour away and we need to get there in time to help serve food, maybe even cook some of it."

"Boy, I timed that just right," I joked.

"I came by to see how many people signed up. Doesn't look like too many people are willing to help those in need. Glad to see you care, Ms. Scott."

"It's a great idea. At least a few people can be helped." I should have walked away immediately, but stayed and fumbled with my papers and briefcase.

"I've missed you," he said. Before I could reply, Dr. Blackwell called Micah over.

"Make sure the kids have permission slips from their parents; otherwise, you can't take them."

"It's after school hours. I didn't think they needed them."

"They do at Tecumseh," Blackwell said brusquely. "Don't take them with you unless they have permission slips."

Micah turned to me. "Well, Ms. Scott, looks like today will be just me and you … together again," he half-sang as he closed the mailroom door behind him.

The school day dragged in anticipation of the afternoon drive up to Gainesville. My excitement was reminiscent of those elementary days when I knew my parents were taking me to the circus or Coney Island after school. I always have liked carnival acts and joy rides down one-way tracks.

"So," I said, when Micah and I finally sat side-by-side in his truck. "Together again." Micah stared straight ahead, his response an octave below a groan, his hands like lead on the wheel.

"What have you been doing lately?" Micah asked after a long silence.

"Oh, nothing much. Teaching, grading papers. Life goes on." Talk was awkward between us. What I really wanted to do was scream and yell and shake him into recognizing how much I had changed. But it didn't seem like the right thing to do at the time.

"It's hard coming back from a trip like that," he said. "I always get a little depressed afterwards."

"A little depressed ... I thought you might have a different reaction ... especially after the night we spent in the ocean," I said coyly.

"Oh, you're going to acknowledge that, are you?"

"Why wouldn't I?"

"You've hardly acknowledged me since the trip."

"I'm not sure what you expected from me. What happened, happened. Like an out of body experience, and now it's over." I paused long enough to see his rigid and inscrutable profile. It was enough to keep me from going any further.

"What have you been up to since we've been back?" I finally said.

"Beau and I went to South Carolina a few weeks ago."

"What's in South Carolina?"

"We went river diving in the Cooper River. I told you about some of our trips before. Another time you weren't listening."

"I remember ... you go looking for shark teeth down there. Find anything?"

"Oh, baby doll, we sure did. Some really pretty points and shark's teeth as big as your hand. Megalodon, like you saw in my classroom. The current was about as rough as it's ever been."

"Isn't that dangerous?" We turned off State Bridge Road onto the highway. Gainesville was about an hour away.

"Not as dangerous as the alligators," he said. "Sometimes they sit on the bottom, but not during mating season. They were hovering near the top this time; during mating season the males get kinda defensive of their territory."

"Alligators? No way. You see any?"

"Sure as shit did. Almost as soon as we got in. Visibility was only about two or three feet and right after I dropped down, there sat one. I got about a foot away before I recognized it. 'Bout messed up my wetsuit. I was shining my light right in an alligator's mouth."

"Damn! What'd you do?"

"I froze until the alligator got bored and backed away. I climbed up my hose and sat on the boat and caught my breath. I had to force myself to go back in. I knew if I didn't go in right away I would never go in that river again. Those last couple feet before I crawled into the boat were the scariest. They have the advantage on the surface."

"Did you see any more after that?"

"No, just eels, some crabs, and catfish the size of my mama's dog. They must have been three-and-a-half feet long. But no more alligators. The current was a bitch, though. We were down there when the tide was going out which makes the current doubly strong. You cannot stay in one place for long when the current's like that. It's better when the tide goes in, sorta balances out the river. It's so cool during slack tide. You can literally see the tiny particles in the water move slower and slower, then they sit still for about thirty seconds. You know that at that moment it is exact high tide and the moon is directly overhead or directly underneath the Earth. Then they start to ever-so-slightly go back the other way." He moved his hand slowly forward and backward to represent the small flakes of dust and dirt in the river.

"Sounds pretty neat, but I still don't know why you'd take such chances."

"Our motto is 'If we live through it, it was fun.' Alligators and currents aren't the only troubles in the Cooper. The bottom is limestone with pockets about fifty feet deep. If you hit one of those, you go sliding into space. You hope the current doesn't pin you against one of walls surrounding the pocket."

"And you call this fun?"

"One time the current was so strong and we were sliding along, the tide taking us backwards, and it pushed me into a big tree, and my hose got caught on the limbs, and I had to pull myself upriver in order to get my hose loose. That was major scary. Almost panicked."

"Have you ever thought about taking a trip where you sit under palm trees and drink piña coladas and mai tais all day?"

Micah laughed. "It's not always that dangerous. The Tennessee is much calmer, especially up by Chattanooga. Most of the time the visibility is as clear as a swimming pool. You could dive in there without much danger. It's chilly up there now, but you could wear a wet suit."

"I think I'll pass on that one."

"You need to go."

"And why is that?"

"So the circle will be complete."

"What circle?"

"You'll understand when we go."

"I don't recall ever saying I would."

"You've only seen one side of diving. You need to see the other half. It'd be good for you to see the same stars from a different perspective."

"That's certainly sounds interesting, but couldn't I just see the stars from a different perspective without risking my life at the bottom of a river?"

"Hey, did I ever tell you about the time I almost died in a cave?" Micah changed the subject, assuming the topic was settled. "… and so that's why I'm now claustrophobic," he finished ten minutes later.

"My God. Can you ever have a normal outing?" I asked him, being serious.

"Evidently not. I don't know what it is but things have a way of happening around me. Maybe it's because me and Beau are out there trying stuff that not everyone else does."

"Probably so. You got me convinced. Okay, enough stories for one day. Let's talk about us, not rivers, caves, catfish, but the big white elephant sitting between us."

"Oh my God! Where?"

I hesitated for a couple seconds. "We had sex, Micah. We changed things between us. You can tell all the stories you want, but that will always be there."

"I'm not the one whose been ignoring it. I tried to talk to you the last night, remember? I don't think you know what you want, so how can I know? Hey, we're here."

"So, we're not going to talk about it."

"There's not much to say, not now at least. Unless you want to bring it up in the church." Micah pulled the truck into the lot adjacent to a pointed church with a high-pitched roof. The parking area was full of pick-ups with an assortment of dirty and damaged household items in the back of each. Attached to the church was a one-story complex; both the church and surrounding buildings were the purple color of a newly formed bruise. A large sign in front announced, "Jesus loves all sinners."

"I'm in the right place," I told Micah.

"Boy, no kidding. Take those heels off and put on a pair of my old boots." The corners of his eyes wrinkled.

"They won't go with my outfit," I said with a straight face.

"I've got some old jeans somewhere in the truck. You can wear those so you don't get your dress dirty."

"What do I wear for a shirt? I don't care if I get this dress dirty; I've had it forever. And these heels are low. I'll be fine."

We were met at the church door by an old man with sparse hair and baby fine cheeks above his sagging jaw. He wore a t-shirt with I'M OVER 80 AND YOU CAN'T GET RID OF ME on it, but his spryness belied his age.

"We're here to help wherever you need us," Micah told him. "The Red Cross sent us here."

"Oh, we need all the help we can get. There are over a hundred people staying here, and another hundred who come here to get a meal. Some of these folks lost everything in the tornado; most of 'em were too poor to afford insurance. We have plenty of people to serve the food. What we really need are people to collect the silverware and trays, and helpers to wash the pots and pans. The cooks can't get clean ones fast enough. Either of you good with kids?"

"We're both teachers," Micah said.

"Teachers. Great! You could start by giving the moms a break. Some of them have been cooped up in here for days."

"What do you want us to do?" I asked.

"Why don't you go in and stay with some of the kids so the moms can get a meal in peace. Then we'll call you for dish duty.

People are all over the church. Most have their bedding and personal belongings in the auditorium behind the cafeteria."

We walked through a labyrinth of halls, not knowing exactly where to go, following the mixed sounds of pulsating voices and clanging dishes. As we passed the cafeteria and neared the doors to the auditorium, the sounds became distinguishable, and we recognized the high-pitch wails of a baby and the disgruntled whines of young children.

The food lines in the cafeteria were long, and weary people resigned themselves to the long wait. The shock of recent loss was still on the faces of many. Middle-aged women with children hugging them around the waist made up the bulk of the line; heavy men with protruding stomachs, skinny bearded men and the elderly filled out the rest. These souls had no family to take them in and some were the only members of their family not injured or killed.

The doors to the auditorium were open revealing a chaotic jumble of sheets, suitcases, toys and toiletries. People were scattered everywhere, some seated quietly on rolled-up bedding, others talking boisterously to a group of willing listeners. Mothers scolded unhappy children, a few men of assorted ages hung around the periphery of the room, and frail old ladies knitted the frantic fabric of their upturned lives. One young mother surrounded by several scruffy children tried to appease the squalling baby in her arms. The other children, not too long out of infanthood themselves, pulled on her wrinkled blouse, pleading for her attention. "We're hungry, Mama," one toddler said. "Can't we go stand in line by ourselves?"

"No, you cannot. Just be quiet till I give your sister her bottle."

I wanted to help, but did not want to upset the delicate balance of the family. Micah graciously made the initial contact.

"You have one unhappy baby, there, Ma'am." The young mother kept her eyes down and barely responded. "Let us help you. Would you like us to bring some food back here for the children? My name is Micah and this is Catherine." His soft tone even soothed *my* anxiety.

"We were told we cain't have food in here," one of the little boys said.

"We could take the kids for you, and get them something to eat," Micah offered.

"No, I want to keep them with me," she said, this time darting her eyes towards me and then back to Micah. The baby started crying again, its red face scrunched up like a toothless old woman.

"It's been a long time since I held a baby that small," I said. "May I?" The young woman smiled and placed the squalling baby in my arms. Her diapered bottom and pudgy legs weighted my arms down in a comfortable, familiar way. Her tiny nose was running and her wet blue eyes stared at me curiously, her crying stopped for the moment. I guessed her to be fairly new to this world; she couldn't be more than three-months-old.

"What's her name?" I asked.

"Her name's Winona, like one of the Judds," the mother said.

"She's a pretty baby, oh yes, you are, you sweet pretty baby." I smiled at the chubby-cheeked and curly brown-haired infant. "Are you hungry?" I cooed. "Would you like someone to feed you?"

"What do you think she's been fussing about?" Micah said. "Of course, she's hungry."

"Like you would know," I said. "How many babies have you been around?"

"I used to be a baby. I have personal experience. Maybe she's upset with your unkindly way towards me, Miss Scarlett." The mother couldn't help but laugh.

"Since it's so easy, here, you take her."

Micah backed away. "She's fine right where she is, Ms. Scott."

The young mom giggled again at Micah's reticence to take the baby. "I was about to get her bottle ready, but every time I put her down she wails up a storm. Some folks're trying to sleep in here, and I felt bad just letting her cry."

"I'll hold her while you get her bottle ready. She's such a little angel." I held her so Micah could see her better. "Look, Micah, wouldn't you like to have one of these someday?"

"You're the one stuck on babies," he said. "You want me to take the rest of 'em to get something to eat?" Micah redirected his attention to the mother. "They might run out of food if you wait much longer. We can save you and Winona a place."

"Can we go with him, Mama? We're starving," the oldest boy said.

"Me too," the one who appeared to be about three added.

"I guess, but you boys look after Keely. And ya'll best behave yourselves."

"They'll be fine. Alright guys, what's your name?"

"I'm Jackson and he's Colquitt," the oldest boy said. "She's Keely."

"Those are mighty important sounding names. Jackson and Colquitt, are you two lawyers? Your name is wonderful too, Keely. You guys ever see a real shark's tooth? I got some in my truck. I'll get them after you eat something, and if you clean your plate, I might have to just give you one." Micah held two fingers up and pretended to poke them in the eyes, Three Stooges style. The boys smiled.

"Micah," I said. "I don't think that's something you want to teach them. If they start doing that to each other and their friends, they could poke an eye out."

"Yes, Ralphie's mother," Micah said. "I promise I won't teach them any more bad things. Otherwise, she might spank me," he said to the boys who now laughed out loud.

I had a few choice words of my own to say to him, but restrained myself for the sake of the young mother and her children. Micah carried Keely to the cafeteria, the two boys lagging behind, mimicking the two-fingered antics Micah had taught them. I furiously turned to the young mother. "I am so sorry he taught them that," I said.

"Shoot, that's nothin'," she said. "Don't worry about them. Your husband's a nice man. He was just having fun." I did not bother to correct her mistake. It would take too long to explain my relationship with Micah. So, I watched the baby while the mother traipsed to the kitchen to mix the baby's formula, and found a few clean Pampers and changed the baby and wiped her nose. When the mother came back, I offered to feed the baby while she joined the kids to get something to eat. "I can stand in line with you, if you want," I said. "That way you will know your baby's safe."

"I trust the good Lord," she said. "I know my baby's in good hands with you being a teacher and all. I've always wanted to be a teacher, but I had too many babies to finish school."

I quickly replayed all the conversation we had had with this woman. "How did you know we were teachers?"

"I thought you said so. Maybe I just felt it."

"Well, you are a teacher," I said. "Your kids soak in everything you show them. A teacher cannot replace a good parent."

After drinking almost the whole bottle, the baby fell asleep in my arms, and several women came by to admire little Winona. I sat on the makeshift bedding and lay Winona down on a small comforter and curled up beside her. I don't know how long I lay there, but the sounds of children's voices roused me out of my semi-conscious state. "Look, Mama, a shark's tooth. The man said I could keep it if I kept my fingers outa' people's eyes."

"He gave us all one, and some pretty rocks."

"Those are crystals," Micah said. "Found 'em myself."

"Those *are* pretty. You know it's almost seven. You haven't done your reading yet." She turned to us. "He's in the first grade and is behind in his reading. We have to practice every night."

"I'm gonna start kinnergarden soon," Colquitt said.

"Not for a couple years, honey," his mother said.

"Mr. Micah said he was going to tell us a story, about getting lost in the woods," the older boy said.

"After you do your reading."

"He has to tell it now, cause he's gotta go do dishes soon."

The mother laughed. "Good Lord, a man who does dishes. You've got you a good man," she said to me.

"Yes, I do," I said, watching Micah's neck turn a dark shade of pink.

"I'll make it short," he said.

"Since when?" I asked.

"Be quiet and listen, Ms.Catherine. Now get over there with the other children, and I'll tell you a story."

"Is it true?" asked Jackson. Keely put her thumb in her mouth and lay in her mother's lap.

"Yes, it's true. It was one of the scariest nights of my life. About a year ago," Micah began, "me and my digging buddy… "

"Who's that?" Jackson interrupted.

"Beau, that don't matter. We'd been looking for arrowheads down in South Georgia and were headin' home. We didn't find much. Anyway, we had our detectors in the back. You know what a metal detector is?"

"Yeah, our daddy had one. It got tore up tuther night in the storm." The young boy's eyes lowered.

Micah quickly continued the story. "That stinks, so, I knew about this old fort site but I had kinda forgot exactly where it was. Beau," he looked at Jackson, "wanted something to show for the day so somehow I let him sucker me into looking for this old fort. Well, by the time we found it, it was 'bout dark and it was miles from anything. Way back in the woods. We had already seen a couple rattlesnakes that day, and I wasn't too thrilled about finding a musketball in the dark with snakes and who knows what else around."

"D'ja have a gun?" Jackson asked. Both boys stared at Micah intently.

"Nope. I had a shovel and my knife, that's it. Well, being the geniuses we are, we head off into these thick overgrown woods with a dinky-ass, sorry, flashlight that couldn't light up my foot much less the path. Beau found a couple musketballs and I told him 'c'mon man, let's go, it's creepy in here.' See, there was no moon and in thick woods it gets really dark. So we tried to leave and even though the truck should have been no more'n ten minutes away, after twenty minutes, we knew we were going wrong. A little later, I could feel panic trying to set in. Beau's wife was pregnant and he already was panicking. He kept saying 'I can't stay in these woods,' like I wanted to. After a few hours of wandering, the light started to go out and we're sitting there and I hear a siren way off in the distance. And then a dog howls like its ears hurt. And then another one but closer and then real close. Guess what?"

"What?" three of us said in unison.

"It ain't dogs; it's coyotes and we can hear them all around us. Now, we're thinking we might have to climb a tree to spend the night and then we hear cannon fire from the military base nearby. That's all we need cause the firing range is south like we need to go. So, we start running through the bushes, and stickers, toward that sound. Beau's in front carrying our feeble light and right when he looks back to ask me something, I see it right beside his leg."

"Oh, God, what?" I asked.

"An old well, a big black hole. If he had fell in or I had, we coulda died in those woods. I still have dreams about that well." Micah gazed over our heads at something behind us. "Then the guns stopped. We just sat there. In the dark, with coyotes all around us. We didn't know what to do."

"What happened next?" Jackson had to know.

"The guns start back up firing and off we go. All of a sudden, the trees kinda stop and there is a clearing ahead of us. Luckily we both sense something cause we both stop and about ten feet ahead of us is a cliff about eighty feet high. If we had kept on running, well, who knows. We peeked over the cliff and there are the railroad tracks that will lead us back to the truck. We never went back to that spot. It gave us one chance and I'm taking it."

"Man, what a story. That really true?"

"Every word."

"How long were you lost?"

"Eight long hours. We were exhausted, cold and hungry when we got outa there."

"Did you think the coyotes woulda eaten you?" asked Colquitt.

"The thought crossed my mind, and probably theirs, too," said Micah.

"He almost didn't get back in time for the baby to be borned," added Jackson.

"You can sure tell a story," I said, skeptical of the facts.

"Well, Catherine, you ready for clean-up duty?"

"It's mighty comfortable here," I said, "but I guess I'll roll up my sleeves and give it a go."

"You kids be good. Do your reading like your momma asks, you hear?" admonished Micah. "She works hard for you."

"Thanks for your help. I'll keep you in my prayers tonight."

"Thank you," Micah and I replied. We patted the children on their heads and turned for the kitchen. We never saw this family again but for a few moments we had been able to take their minds off the loss of a husband and a father.

The soft-cheeked octogenarian who met us at the front door was now in the kitchen, his hands deep down in metal tubs filled with soapy water. "Well, just what we were looking for, kitchen relief," he said when he saw us. "Agnes and Clifford, you can take a break for the night. These young people will take over for awhile." Stacks of dishes and large, ugly utility pots covered almost every inch of the kitchen. My heart sank as I glanced at my newly manicured French nails and clipped cuticles.

"The water's real hot right now, but it'll cool off. You need to change the water every ten stacks or so."

Taking a deep breath, I carried a stack of dirty trays to one of the tubs. Micah wore an amused grin as he watched me plunge my hands and arms in the dishwater.

"A first for you, Ms. Scott?"

"I've washed plenty of dishes over the years, thank you very much." I said."Of course, never quite this many all at once."

Micah laughed then directed his attention to the older gentleman. "When are you taking a break?"

"Not tonight. I'm the one in charge of volunteers."

"Lucky you, huh?" Micah asked.

"You got that right. I live up the road a piece, you see. I was one of the fortunate ones who didn't get his house blown to Kingdom Come. The only thing the wind blowed over was an old fence that needed fixin anyways. By the will and grace of God Almighty, I only lost one old evergreen. The houses on either side of me, up the road, got wiped out. That's why I decided to run the volunteer group here. God spared me for a reason, and I know what that reason is alright."

"Well, we're glad we can help you out," Micah said.

"We sure are," I agreed, while scrubbing the dishes vigorously.

For well over three hours, we washed and dried dishes, but the time passed quickly. Micah and Harold, as the old man's name turned out to be, traded stories of their Southern childhoods and discussed the best places to hunt for fossils and Spanish coins.

"Do all Southern men have to go artifact hunting?" I asked.

"Those who are worth their salt," said Harold. "And the boys up here do a lot of woodworking. I like making birdhouses. Been selling quite a few of them up in Helen. Ever been there?"

"Yessir, we have. I'd like to see some of your birdhouses," said Micah. "I bet you make real sturdy ones, not like the ones you find in those mall stores."

Harold beamed. "Come by any time. I live two blocks up the highway and then left down the gravel road a ways. You turn off the highway right by Subway. Can't miss it. I usually charge twenty bucks a house, but you can have 'em for half price, with you helping us out and all."

Micah turned to me. "Another trip, Ms. Scott. My lady friend and I will be sure to come by."

"I thought you two was married."

"We got to be good friends because we teach together," I explained.

"Could have fooled me," the old man said.

I smiled at Harold and caught a mischievous light in his timeworn but practiced eyes. "Somehow, I think not much else fools you."

It was close to midnight by the time we put the last dish on the shelf, and for the second time in the last few months I was exhausted yet enervated. Being with Micah had that kind of effect on me.

"Believe me now?" Micah said as we walked to the truck.

"What?"

"We got to work with an angel. Kinda neat, huh?"

Micah made me half-believe that if I turned around, Harold would be gone and no one would know of him. I didn't dare risk that not being true so I walked straight ahead, not looking back.

"Kinda neat, I would agree. What a meaningful day. Harold showed me a few things about life."

"We can learn a lot from people like him if we only listen. So, did you get your delicate hands all chapped up, Ms. Scott?"

"Yes, and I am beyond tired but I loved every minute of it, my dear Mr. Marlowe."

Micah laughed and unlocked the door on my side of the truck. "Just picking up pebbles," he commented as he shut my door.

We sped down the road for a few minutes before Micah took one hand off the wheel and rubbed my shoulder. "I bet you are tired. It's not everyday you wash 300 dishes. Think you'll make it through the day tomorrow?"

"I probably won't be able to sign my name but I'll be fine. I can do anything after a natural high. It's those wine highs I have trouble dealing with the next day. Mmmmm, that feels good ... You're going to put me to sleep if you keep doing that." The stars were out and the moon was full. Tired as I was, I wanted to stay up all night.

"Micah, I'd like to complete the circle you were talking about." I grabbed his hand from my shoulder. "Take me to the river," I whispered.

"You're sure you want to?" he said.

"I couldn't be more sure," I said gazing into his eyes.

"Well, let me check with Beau to see if he's using the boat this weekend. The weather's supposed to be perfect for diving, but I think Allison made plans for her parents to come over. I know she won't let him out of that." The two had pooled their resources and purchased a fishing boat, outboard motor, hoses, and compression tank.

"What do we need the boat for?" I taunted.

"How else are we going to get out there? They're kinda handy when traveling on water."

"Never mind," I said. "I didn't think we'd be going so soon. I don't know if I can get a wet suit by this weekend."

"You can wear Allison's; she's about your size."

"When and what time?"

"We won't leave until Saturday morning. Early. You need to be at my house by six."

"Unless it rains."

"It won't rain. We need to stop by Beau's first and check out the boat. He's going to have a fit when he hears I'm taking you diving. "

"Why's that?"

"His wife's been asking to go for years, and if she catches wind of your going, Beau won't be able to put her off any longer. Plus, every Southern male knows women are bad luck on a river. You don't know how special you are Ms. Scott for me to be taking you on the river. I have decided just to suck it up and take my chances with fate."

"Oh, come on, when did you make that up? Just now?"

"My daddy was raised in Newport, Kentucky, and has stories about women on the river that would make you shiver."

"I guess so, since Newport is famous for its prostitutes."

"Not *those* women. He told me one story about a group of men working the Ohio on a coal barge." He rambled on about Hand-Me-Down Simpson and how a woman in a stranded boat caused poor ole Hand-Me-Down to wreck his barge. "And so," he finished, "they were fired because they followed the cry of a woman on the river. 'Don't you boys know the first rule of a bargeman is to stay away from women on the river? Women are the devil's curse to men on the river,' their bossman scolded."

"That's the most ridiculous story I ever heard," I said. "One man could never run a barge anyway."

"My daddy swears that's true. And he has plenty more stories about the bad luck of women. One time he and my granddaddy—"

"I don't want to hear any more stories. If you feel that way about it, I'll wear my scapular and that will cancel out any bad luck you encounter."

"What's that?"

"My scapular? It's a necklace made out of felt and a holy picture to protect Catholics from bad luck."

"How's *that* going to help me? I'm not Catholic."

"It doesn't matter. My superstition will cancel out yours and then we can dive in peace."

"Whatever. Damn, it's after midnight, and we still have to drive home. We ought to just get out and sleep in our classrooms."

Micah walked me over to my car. "Make sure you bring your skins and booties. I'll tell Allison you need her wetsuit. You'll need a change of clothes and shoes. And an underwater flashlight if you have one, just in case the one we have for you doesn't work. If I think of anything else you need, I'll call you. Don't forget your mask."

"Do I need my fins?"

"No, you don't need your fins."

"You're kidding!"

"We stay on the bottom the whole time. You shall become a turtle. I know I told you that."

"Well, I guess I forgot."

"Well, I would think common sense would tell you that."

"Stop being such a man, and give me a hug." He wrapped his arms around me and breathed heavily on my neck. "I've missed you, Micah. I forgot how good the world seems when I'm around you. What are we going to do about us?"

"I'm not getting into all that right now. We both need to get some sleep. I'll see you tomorrow ... probably."

God damn him, I thought. I slammed my car door and drove home.

Chapter 27

It was five minutes after six when I arrived at Micah's house Saturday morning. The door to his truck was open, and his dive gear and extra hoses were piled next to it in the driveway. I entered his house from the side door as always and yelled up the stairs. "Hey, you ready?"

"Give me five minutes," he called down. "Start putting your stuff in the truck. Help yourself to some coffee."

The strong Costa Rican coffee awakened my senses, and I drank almost half a cup before I set my mug on the kitchen table. Mail, sticky notes, and stacks of ungraded papers cluttered the table. In the middle of the disarray lay Micah's copy of the high school yearbook that comes out in the early spring. Because it was sitting there, I opened it. The inside cover was full of comments from Micah's students, most of them short notes about how he was their favorite teacher. I flipped through the rest of the book, smiling at the memories and creative student ads.

I was about to shut the yearbook when the inside of the back cover caught my eye. There was a letter that took up almost a full page, much longer than the other student messages. I should not have read the page, but the opening sentence drew me in.

Dear Micah,

Since I met you in Algebra II class last year, my life has never been the same. The hours we've spent talking on the phone, our private jokes, and the late night "meetings" have meant the world to me. Even though I will be going away to college in the fall, it does not mean we have to lose touch with each other. I will still come home at breaks and we can still take day trips together. You can come up to Georgetown and visit me. We could have so much fun. I can't bear the thought of not talking to you on the phone, so we will have to look for cheap long distance rates. You wrote in my yearbook that I am your inspiration; well you have

> been mine also. I will never forget the first time you showed me the stars. You will remain in my life always.
>
> Love forever,
> Julie

"Your gear in the car?" Micah asked from the hallway.

I slammed the yearbook shut. "I was just about to do that." Clumsily picking up my coffee cup, I spilled half of it on the floor. I searched the cupboards for some paper towels and hurriedly dabbed at the brown puddles. My hands were shaking as the adrenaline rushed through my body. My God, Micah, I thought. What have you been doing these past three years? And with a *student*? Maybe she's just taken with him and he likes the attention. Maybe it's just a father-daughter relationship, and I'm jumping to conclusions. Yet some things in that letter were familiar. I could have written those exact words, and there was nothing less than innocent that went on between the two of us ... at first. And teenagers were always so melodramatic. Micah was a very giving man. I could see him spending time on the phone helping out an unhappy adolescent with parental or boyfriend problems. And, the more I thought about it, Micah had many students who confided in him. The late night meetings could be anything. If Micah did anything he shouldn't have done, he wouldn't have left his yearbook out on his table for me to stumble across.

Micah bounded down the stairs into the kitchen. "Is something wrong?" he asked.

"No, nothing. I'm ready to dive into a river."

On the road to Beau's, we opened the windows and let the early morning breeze blow through our hair. "I'm so glad we only have a few more weeks," Micah said. "I need to get away from school for awhile." By school, he meant administrators. Even though he was one of the best teachers in the school, he was always in some kind of conflict. He was considered too controversial by several of them and frowned upon by some teachers who thought his style was excessively loose. But I knew better.

"Did you get called in again?"

"Yes, Jesus, I bet some kid a dollar he would fail the test and damn if he didn't anyway. Usually it works the other way."

"And?"

"Well, his mom thought I flunked him just to prove myself right or that I'm being stubborn. Can you believe that? Dr. Blackwell just sat there fidgeting."

"So, what happened? Do you have to apologize, let him pass, what?"

"I told her I did it so he would prove me wrong, but I think he got so nervous, he went blank. I know he studied a bunch. I told the mom I didn't even take his dollar. She didn't think that was very funny. Dr. Blackwell just rolled his eyes."

"Only you," I offered.

Beauregard, Beau for short, was tinkering with the boat when we pulled up. He was shorter than Micah but wiry, around thirty-five-years-old, it appeared. He was the brains behind the diving expeditions. "Do you think you can take this baby out without me?" he asked Micah.

"If the motor's in one piece, we can manage. What can she do?" he said pointing to me.

"Well, someone has to be in the boat when you back it in. Can she start the engine?" I hated it when someone talked about me in the third person. I had met Beau a few times before, and he never did seem very comfortable around me. Every time I made eye contact with him, he looked away. I wondered what Micah had told him about our relationship. At first I thought he had told Beau I had a glass eye like the stunt he pulled with Bobby. Later, I found out Beau was generally suspicious of women. He did find someone to marry, yet from what Micah had told me, Beau controls his household, especially Allison. Like the nursery rhyme, he stuck her in a pumpkin shell and there he keeps her very well.

"Well, I guess that's me," I said, trying to sound upbeat. "What do I do after we back the boat in?"

Reluctantly, Beau showed me how to choke the engine before I pulled the cord and how to steer the boat. I thought it seemed fairly easy and didn't anticipate any problems.

"You're going to have to get the boat back on the trailer when it's time to go. Think you can do that?" Beau had two vertical lines burrowed in the middle of his brow.

"Don't worry. My husband and I have a boat, and I help him dock it all the time. We had a sailboat on Lake Michigan." His eyes brightened at my comment. What I didn't tell him was how petrified of the water I used to be, and that when Marshall and I went sailing, we had horrible shouting matches because more often than not, I hooked the sails on upside-down. All hell would break loose, and Marshall would bellow about my incompetence and lack of common sense. I'd scream back he's right, I was incompetent, so why didn't he leave me and find someone who could put sails on right. But Marshall would never leave me. I did a damn good job of making him seem like a superior member of the human race. What he never found out, however, was after Micah talked me into the ocean, I drove up to the new marina on Lake Lanier and single-handedly took the boat out and docked it without any major episodes.

Before we left, Micah and Beau checked the compression tank to make sure it was working, organized the air hoses, and placed the life jackets under the seats with the wetsuits. Black storage boxes for holding artifacts were put there, too.

"Hook her up. We're finally ready. You okay with all this before we drive three hours for nothing?"

"Let's go river diving, Marlowe."

Beau lifted the trailer onto the hitch on the back of Micah's truck. A decal of the Confederate Flag adorned the side of the boat. "Oh, you have a Rebel flag on your boat." I couldn't help but state the obvious.

"Yeah, so?" Beau said.

Micah grabbed my shoulders and shoved me towards the shotgun side of the truck. "Why don't you get in before you say something that might get you into trouble," he suggested. I took the hint and got in the truck, but I was not happy about it, and I felt frustrated because I couldn't tell Beau that the war was over and there isn't a Confederacy any more.

"Micah," I said when we were on our way to Taylorsville, "how can he still hold on to the flag like that? Doesn't he know what it represents?"

"I think a flag means something different to everyone. Besides, it was on the boat when we got it. Too lazy to take it off."

"I'll do it for you," I offered.

"I don't think so," he said as he turned and implied with his gaze that the discussion was over. I didn't give in just yet.

"So, what does it mean to you and Beau?"

"Well," he paused for effect, "I see it as a decal stuck on the side of a boat that gets people who think they know everything all riled up and possibly ruining a perfectly good day."

"Alright, later. So, does your mom worry about all this diving in rivers?"

"That woman worries about everything I do. It's a wonder she doesn't make herself sick. She does sometimes, actually."

"What mom wouldn't be concerned with all you do?"

"Yeah, but she frets over stuff you can't change, like the weather. Every time a storm is near, she calls. I have my own personal weather station."

"Isn't it about time you cut the apron strings?"

"You sound like Beau. The price of being an only child," he said quietly.

We talked our way up the interstate through north Georgia past Canton, Rome and on towards Chattanooga. Finally, we came to the exit for Taylorsville. According to Micah, the town had once been a Union distribution point during the Civil War. At the end of the war, the citizens dumped tons of ammunition and guns into the Tennessee River. There had once been a bustling community here with steamboats sounding their whistles as they churned against the current. Now, over a century later, the streets were almost deserted and the descendants of those days stayed inside the run-down houses while the ghosts of soldiers faded into the mist along the river. Painted advertisements for the local bread company and one for Coca-Cola were barely noticeable on the sides of the elderly brick buildings. We went through the tight railroad underpass and onto a small road leading to the river.

"We're almost to the ramp. It's right past the steel plant; you can see the fire in the blast furnace day or night. We always stop and pay tribute to the fire for good luck. You have to do it. No choice."

"What do you do, sacrifice a virgin?" I asked.

"I suppose we could, if we knew any."

"Funny."

We drove down a narrow gravel road, a variety of overgrown weeds on either side, a few lopsided clapboard shacks cluttered with old tires and junked cars. A large tin-and-brick building loomed ahead and to the left. In the center of the complex was a large girded window for ventilation, allowing us to view the bowels of the inferno. The fire spit flames through the vent, easily visible from the road. We parked alongside the drainage ditch, careful not to go too far into it. Micah and I moved close to the chain-link fence where there was a small grassy area. As the disturbed air rose and distorted reality into ripples of energy, Micah began to chant his so-called tribute.

"Hayanana ... hayanana," he intoned, while stomping around in circles. I didn't know what to do or how to react, so I remained motionless and watched him gyrate all over the place. He was making such a fool of himself, I felt embarrassed for him.

"I feel so connected to the universe when I dance," Micah said when he stopped. I caught the glint in his eyes, and put my hands on my hips.

"Very funny," I said. Micah laughed one of his rare belly laughs, and his grin stretched his cheeks.

"Ever hear of the green corn ceremony?" he asked after he calmed down.

"No, would you expect me to?"

"Guess not. Every spring the Southeastern Indians held what they called the Green Corn Ceremony. It's a rite of thanksgiving for a successful corn crop. To them, the ceremony was a way to achieve purification. They always went into the river after the ceremony."

"So you thought you'd have a little ceremony of your own."

"No, I thought we'd have a ceremony together, Ms. Scott. We're going to get rid of all our old sins today."

It was my turn to laugh, not because it was a ridiculous idea, but because Micah thought so much like me. "Okay, Mr. Marlowe, how do we celebrate the green corn?"

"Okay, first, we have to fast. We didn't eat much this morning, so that kinda counts. You bring any food with you?"

"Just crackers in the car."

"Good enough. We'll pretend it's the third day of fasting, and the women have cooked a pot of food and placed it outside for us to eat. The men partake of the food slowly; it's bad form to hurry, and then when they're done, the women clean the empty vessels in the river. All the fires in the village must be extinguished, so a new holy fire can be made." Micah pointed to the incinerator inside the steel factory. "The high priest wears white buckskin, a carved gorget made from a conch shell, and white swan feathers. Then he takes a dry willow and a stick of white oak and rubs them together until they begin to smoke." Micah grabbed two sticks from the ground and rubbed them together. "Then he adds splinters of pitch pine to the smoking sticks and fans the flames with the wing of a white bird."

Micah motioned for me to move closer to the blazing furnace. "An old woman brings a basket of opened corn and places it near the fire," he told me. Shuffling along like an ancient hag, I pretended to set a basket on the ground by the fence. "The high priest rises and walks around the basket three times, tastes the corn and rubs bear oil on it and throws it into the fire. He pours snakeroot medicine into the fire and purifies the tribe. Then the whole bunch dances around the fire and immerses themselves in the river according to the order of their prominence. Warriors always rank higher than women, which means I must go in the river first. Come, my dear. We must dance in front of the fire before we immerse ourselves in the river."

Micah held both my hands and twirled me around and around until I was so dizzy and laughing so hard, I thought I would fall to the ground. We were radiant when we climbed back into the truck. "You're almost as crazy as I am, Micah," I said.

"You must be rubbing off on me."

We continued our journey down a gravel road and up a slight hill. The ending tree-line foretold a wide-open area just before us. We crested the rise and there, moving left to right, was a gently flowing river two-hundred yards across. Its vastness was instantly intimidating and anxiety washed over me. A black Ford pick-up with a couple of teenagers smoking cigarettes sat in the gravel lot facing the river. Shaved heads hung out the truck's windows and turned as we drove up with our boat. They spied the Confederate flag on either side, and gave us the thumbs-up signal.

"Be nice, now. You're in the South. You have to be friendly to folks," Micah said when I turned away from the skinheads.

"Let's just get in the river," I grumbled.

"Yes, ma'am," Micah said tauntingly.

We threw bottles of water, snacks and masks into the boat. "Okay, you can direct me in. Tell me when the trailer is almost completely in the water."

I clambered into the boat and unhooked it from the trailer. "You remember how to start the motor?" Micah yelled. He backed the trailer with the boat on it and me in the boat down the ramp. Seconds later, the small aluminum v-hull slid into the river.

"Of course I do. Have a little faith in me." But once the current moved the boat away from shore, I felt the old sailing anxiety coming back. I pulled the choke like Beau showed me, and yanked on the motor cord several times. Nothing. I tugged harder and faster. Still nothing. No matter how hard or how many times I pulled the stupid cord, the motor wouldn't turn over. By this time, Micah had parked the truck and was standing on shore, his hands on his hips. "What's the matter?" he hollered across the water.

"I can't get the damn thing to start. Do you think it's broken?"

"No, I think *you're* broken. Hurry up! You're floating away!"

"I can't. My arm's worn-out."

As we yelled across the water, the boat drifted further away. I was about to be stranded in the middle of a huge river in a small aluminum boat with a motor that didn't work. And, from what I could see, there wasn't anyone else on the river.

"Jesus. Hang on," Micah yelled. "I'm gonna have to swim out. Dammit, shit." As he was cursing, he took off his shoes and glasses and laid them on a large rock along with the truck keys. He had to swim roughly fifty yards to get to me. "Put the ladder out the back." When he reached the boat, he held onto the railing. "Damn, 'Sure, I know how to start a motor, I know how to start a motor,'" he mocked. "Good grief, I don't know about you."

Micah climbed in and started the engine on the second yank of the cord. "What a weakling. I should've known. Those two guys in the truck were cracking up when they saw you pulling on that cord." He steered us toward the rock where his belongings were ; the two locals were there ready to lend a hand. As they were about to toss the keys to us Micah yelled, "No!" They threw them anyway and the jangling mass bounced off the center console and landed against the back transom. We almost spent the day diving for keys. "I'll come get the rest, guys. Thanks." The boys handed Micah his glasses and shoes when we got close enough.

"Sorry 'bout the keys. I told him not to," the older-looking fellow said in a soft voice that contradicted his appearance. "He just wanted to help after seeing all the trouble ya'll were having." He turned to me, "Don't let him fuss at you like that, ma'am. Sometimes these old motors just won't start no matter who's pulling. But you were pretty funny trying."

"Gee, thanks. Glad I could amuse you guys," I replied.

Micah placed his glasses back on and pushed his wet hair up off of them. These were the glasses I had picked out for him a few weeks before the diving trip. His eyesight had gotten worse, and he needed bifocals. The glasses he did have were too big for his face, a convenient hiding place. So one afternoon I met him at the mall and convinced him to buy glasses with smaller frames. They not only revealed more of his face, the lines, strong bone structure, smooth skin around his cheeks, but also his emotions. His eyes even showed up more, allowing me to read his reactions on those rare occasions he let his guard down. Yet, his unguarded eyes unnerved me, especially those times when I saw someone other than Micah in them. But now only sunlight reflected in his eyes as we waved goodbye to the teenage pair and eased the boat down the river.

Micah steered us through the soft current and somehow I felt he was hiding from me again. I sat on the raised bench in the middle, my back towards Micah, my hair flapping in the warm late spring wind. "Watch for logs," he warned. I assured him I was, but actually I was admiring the expanse of the gentle river beneath a crayon blue sky. Trees that had once been well away from the river were now at its edge due to the TVA and their damming of the formerly smaller waterways. Greenness rushed by as I leaned back and stared straight ahead, absorbing the entire scene instead of parts or pieces. The colors were so primary I think I could have painted it all without blending and mixing like artists do to get the shadows just right. The river ran brown, and yellow sun exploded on its surface like leftover fireworks. The shoreline caught shy licks of waves that barely crested into the shallow water, and I turned around to see that we were pulling behind us a massive V that reached to the river's edge. There was not a cloud in the sky, and the feel of the day reminded me of a childhood song we used to sing in the prairie grass: *Rainbow round the moon and sun means the rain is on the run.*

We slowed and moved closer to shore. I needed to understand something. "You know, those guys back at the ramp didn't seem like bad kids. You'd think they would understand tolerance with the way they dressed. So how come this hanging on to the old times, the Confederate flag and all that?" I asked.

"I don't know for sure. It's more a feeling than anything. Feelings are hard to get over. The little town here, they had sons that died in their own backyard. How can you expect them to forget? This country was formed by our not wanting others to tell us how to think but somehow that doesn't seem to apply to Southerners. We fought just as hard in the Revolutionary War as we did in World War Two. We're passionate about everything that means home to us. The Rebel flag doesn't mean slavery to me and Beau or those kids. It just means home, that's all."

"I guess." We didn't speak again until we reached a part of the river Micah called "Wade." Micah explained that he and Beau had found a type of spearpoint called Wade here, therefore the creative name. He guided the boat between two fallen trees onto the narrow shore, grabbed our skins and wet suits and climbed out. Before we put on our gear, Micah suggested we walk the shore just in case something interesting had washed out of the riverbank. "I have to go to the can. Go the other way."

"Where ..." Before I finished my question, Micah grabbed a roll of toilet paper and walked into the woods.

"I thought you were supposed to use leaves," I yelled at him.

"Don't worry, its biodegradable. Now leave me alone. Gee."

I picked up a stone from the shore and heaved it into the area near Micah.

"Hey! Stop it! Can't I go without you bugging me? Just wait till I get outa here. Go look for something or I'll make you have to start the engine, you little weakling." He came out of the woods a few minutes later. "Some people," was all he managed to say.

After a twenty-minute search up and down the narrow shore and finding nothing more than broken mussel shells and scattered pieces of unworked flint, we stretched on our dive suits, freed the boat from shore, hoisted ourselves in over the side, and guided it into knee-deep water. Micah put up the red-and-white dive flag and started the engine that ran the compressor which in turn supplied us with air. The compressor forced air into a sealed aluminum cylinder, identical to the soft drink cylinders used at Little League ballparks, except that fitted to the top were two valves connected to our fifty-foot hoses. The engine ran constantly, so we had an endless supply of breaths, allowing us to crawl like turtles for hours along the bottom. As long as we kept gas in it, we could stay down there all day.

The Honda engine made a noise like a lawnmower, which grated on my nerves soon after Micah pulled its cord. "That sound is enough to make anybody want to get off this boat," I said.

"You want out? Here, grab one of the hoses and hook it to your weight belt. I gave you twenty-five pounds. I think that'll be enough."

"You think that will be enough? I usually dive with only six or eight on."

"You need at least that much to keep you on the bottom. You *don't* want to be flying around in the water. This isn't ocean diving where you float around and look at the pretty coral in clear water. The river isn't that clear. You could get your hose tangled in a tree if you don't stay down."

The air hoses were rubber with interlocking nylon sheathing. They reminded me of Chinese finger toys with a regulator attached to the end, making the high-pressured air a breathable force. Micah informed me that originally shell divers used the contained breathing apparatus we were hooking to our dive belts; they designed the contraption so they could stay on river bottoms for hours to collect the eight-inch mussels indigenous to Southern rivers. They then shipped the mussels to the Japanese who used the shell's mother of pearl lining to start cultured pearls. The pearl makers punched the opaque linings into varied shapes and placed them inside the oysters. But with the decline of the Japanese economy, the shell divers lost their businesses, and their diving apparatus quickly became unneeded, so they sold their equipment dirt-cheap to amateur divers like Micah and Beau.

Micah helped me hook my weight belt to my air hose; I tightened it around my waist and put the regulator in my mouth.

"Make sure it's tight on your hips. When you're ready, grab your light and follow me. Stay next to me, I mean right beside me, till you get comfy. Remember, we're pulling the boat along with our hoses under there, so if you need to come up, find me. Focus on what you're doing. You might look all day and not find anything. It's a skill, so don't get discouraged. Ready?"

"Yep." I positioned the mask comfortably over my eyes and climbed out onto a sandy ledge. Initially my head was above the water, but I took one step to the left and slipped down a muddy slope, losing Micah in the sediment. The strength of the flow had gouged a severe channel, and I was instantly twenty feet underwater. Visibility was poor and I could only see about six feet in front of me, but even then, it was six feet of nothing. Anxiety crawled into my gut as two water snakes disappeared into the gloom, but then the dark ends of Micah's booties passed before me in the muck. I followed after them until they stopped; then I crawled up the sediment and positioned myself right beside Micah.

Like Micah had directed, I crept hesitantly along the rocky bottom, shining my flashlight from side-to-side, hoping to find signs of ancient Indian cultures. Most of the old villages lost to the river had been washed away by years of rain and erosion. On the murky bottom, I watched first-hand as the river water continued to erode the dirt upon which long forgotten societies walked, leaving behind remnants of the tools and weapons they used and the bones of people they loved. Catfish and bass swam hauntingly in front of me as I placed my fingers in the dirt and sand, picking up mussel shells.

My light cast an eerie glow in the dusty water, and I arched my back to push my stomach more firmly against the river's floor. It was dark, but not black, and occasionally I caught the moving shadows of trees overhead. Crawling to the left, I came to a spot filled with several pieces of bone. Most were small, possibly parts of a deer skeleton, but one might have been human, and as I shone my light further to the left, I found what was perhaps the jawbone from a child. It had what looked like the teeth I used to take from under the pillows of my children. Who was this little person from so long ago? I thought. Why did he die so young? I tried to picture him running along the banks of the river, teasing his sisters, hiding from his father or maybe being held by his mother during his illness. I was certain she cried at his untimely death. The bone frightened yet fascinated me. I had come face-to-face with remnants of people who had occupied the same space as me. Whatever petty concerns or nightmares filled their lives had vanquished in the abyss of time. Their jealousies and slights, status and beauty were lost to us now; pottery shards and discarded flint dropped in the silt were the only truths left. I stuck a few deer bones in my pocket along with several pieces of flint. Time passed quickly under the river, and after an hour-and-a-half, Micah signaled it was time to come up. It took me about thirty seconds to climb up the hose, and when we broke the surface, we hung on to the sides of the boat, our masks dangling around our necks. Without its human anchors, the boat slowly drifted downriver.

"Find anything interesting?" Micah asked.

"A few deer bones and flint pieces. Not much. What about you?"

"I found some broken points, but look at this. What do you think it is?" Micah placed a small opaque glass object in my hand, and I turned it around a few times before I admitted my ignorance.

"It's an old perfume bottle. Got to be old, probably from before the Civil War. I'll look it up when we get home," Micah told me as he carefully laid the bottle inside the boat and shook the water out of his ears. "I bet someone on the steamboats chunked it overboard. So, what do you think about all this?"

"It's truly beautiful. I like putting my hands in the past. It feels like what I always thought church should feel like."

"I never thought of it that way, but I guess this *is* my church. How much closer to God can we I get than here on the river?" Micah took a deep breath and pulled his mask back up over his eyes. "Ready to go back down?"

"Ready, captain," I replied.

The second time under I located more flint pieces and some pottery pieces with distinctive shapes and markings. Even under the water, I could see the beauty of the ancient designs in the hand-worked borders. The second dive was easier and I understood how to manipulate my body sideways to search more thoroughly in the silt. I sighted more deer bones, and kept the one that was tapered to a point, an old button, and finally, a golden brown spearpoint that was almost perfect. I was beaming the second time we came up.

"Man, you found some good stuff," Micah complimented me. "I think you brought me luck, too. Look at these points I found, and an old pair of scissors. These could have been barber's scissors during the Civil War."

"I guess women aren't such bad luck on the river after all."

"Yeah, maybe so, but we aren't through on the river yet," Micah said.

We went under one more time, but this time Micah stayed under much longer than either time before. I was getting tired, and the coffin-like atmosphere was starting to make me claustrophobic. As I hovered around the bottom waiting for Micah to signal our ascent, I looked to my right and saw a vague outline in the gloom, then the body of a four-foot long catfish snapped into focus. It was swimming almost parallel to me and moved closer with each second I lay frozen to the bottom. I screamed into my regulator and frantically searched for the outline of Micah's wetsuit.

My psyche spent and my muscles aching to the point of pain, I knew I could not take this one more minute. Micah had shown me how to find him by moving sideways under the river until I encountered a cloudy debris trail. Then, I was to crawl up the silt, my light pointed straight ahead, while I searched for his shadowy silhouette. But that involved way too much energy, so I opted for the easy way out by going up to the boat and tugging on Micah's hose. Twenty-five pounds of weights wrapped around my waist hindered even this maneuver, but I managed to repel up the nylon rope to the bow. Micah now had the boat and me to contend with against the current and soon his bubbles were moving towards the boat. Within seconds he popped to the surface, his face contorted with exasperation beneath his math.

"What's wrong?" he pleaded.

"I'm tired and I can't get in the boat. These weights are too heavy."

"You've got to be kidding me! I thought you were stronger than that."

Micah worked his way to the stern by hanging onto the side. With neither of us on the bottom, we were now a floating tangle of hoses and dangling feet. Micah pulled the ladder from inside the boat and slid it into its slot attached to the transom. He deftly hopped one knee onto the bottom rung and was soon up the three-step device. The small ladder looked like it belonged more in a GI Joe kit than on the back of fifteen-foot dive boat. Eventually, I would have to do a Shamu stunt and belly-flop right into the boat, but all I could manage to do was sit on the step and rest, grasping the back railing. Micah now had his weights off and moved to assist me.

"Well, are you going to get in the boat or just ride the ladder home?"

"I can't move. These weights are exhausting. Can you get them off?" I tried to sound pitiful so he would hurry. He stood over me with a mischievous grin.

"I suppose I could use you as an anchor," he laughed with himself and at my plight.

"This isn't funny. Just help me."

Micah laughed harder yet and told me to release my weight belt while he grasped my hose. Free from too much gravity, I bounced up the ladder while he struggled to get twenty-five pounds of lead over the side and into the boat.

"To think that all along, I thought going *into* the river was the problem," he commented as he put my gear in its proper place, away from where we needed to sit. I relaxed upon the carpet-covered center console, Cleopatra's sofa at the moment. Micah unsnapped the shoulder straps on his wetsuit and slumped back into the seat in front of the engine. After wetting his hair and combing it back with just his hands, he looked up at the scene gliding by and then at me.

"I suppose, and it pains me to say this, but I suppose you did pretty good. You're either a lot tougher or more stubborn than I thought at first. I know lots of divers that wouldn't have jumped into this murkiness," he begrudgingly stated. I knew it was difficult for him to acknowledge my achievement but he had his moments of grace.

"Of course, most everyone else I know can actually get back into the boat." And his moments of retribution.

As the sun slid down the western sky, the river pulled us along on an easy current. Unseen shapes on the bottom created swirls and eddies on the surface. With no more diving this day, how pleasant and serene it was to just enjoy the beauty of an isolated arc in a mighty river. We were like the molecules of water that make the unending journey to the Gulf of Mexico only to begin again as they are deposited into another field, forest, or creek months later as rain.

The mountain ridges of the southern Appalachians bounded us to the immediate left. Hundreds and thousands of summers ago, people wintered at the headwaters of small streams in the hillsides. I was sure they also marveled at the blood of the Earth transporting silt, trees, fish and hand-hewn canoes to the horizon and beyond. To have lived in a time when miles were not charted and to have ventured forth across untainted land and waters created envy in my emergent spirit.

"Isn't this great? Just being out here, it is so peaceful," Micah said, interrupting my thoughts.

"It's really wonderful. I can't remember when I felt so isolated from civilization."

The sun was now at the horizon, the eastern sky darkening. A few brushstrokes of icy clouds hung miles overhead.

"Should we be heading back?"

"Nah, we can drift along for a bit."

Minutes of silence passed.

"Have you always taught at our school?" I wondered.

"Nope."

"Well, where else?"

"At a school on the other side of town."

"How was it?"

"Alright."

"Don't elaborate so much, I can't absorb it all."

"What else is there to say? It was a school with students and we taught them and went home. Satisfied?"

I knew when he used his humor to deflect unwanted probes. Now the darkness enveloped us. With no moon yet tonight, stars began to sprinkle the sky like shining salt on a black cloth. The silent river continued on, and a beaver slapped the water with his tail near the shore.

"You had your yearbook sitting out on your kitchen table," I said. I tried to read his reactions in the shadowed light.

"It's not as good as last year's, but it's tolerable."

"I read the note from Julie. You two must be really close."

"She's had some tough shit to deal with over the last few years. I've tried to be there for her whenever I could."

"It sounds like she wants you to always be there for her."

"What're you trying to say?"

"The note made it sound like you two were romantically involved, at least from her end of it."

Micah's back stiffened and I could hear his angry breathing. "First of all, you had no business reading the letter to begin with. And just because the yearbook was out doesn't mean you have permission to open it. That's the second time you put your nose in places it doesn't belong."

"I didn't mean to snoop. It was just … *there* and I looked through it, like I would any book. And I read the letter, and what I read concerned me. So, just what's going on with you and her?"

"It's none of your business. Move, we're going."

"So you're in love with her? My God, she's not even eighteen."

Micah wrapped his arms around his chest and sat back down. "I have to calm myself down before I throw you out of this boat."

"But—"

"Shut up, and listen. That little girl has been beaten so badly by her daddy, she ran away from home the first year she was in my class. Twice she came to school with black eyes, and when I talked to the counselors about it, they called her parents, and found out her daddy's a minister with his own radio show. He is so respected 'round here, no one would do anything about it. I took her home after school one day, and sat and talked to her dear old dad for a long time. I told him if she came to school with bruises ever again I'd take my story to the papers. And while she was listening, I said that maybe instead of that I could round up some guys to just kick his ass so bad he'd be whistlin' Dixie out his ears. So, she's been my buddy ever since. And yes, Cat, I'll be there for her as long as she wants. I might be the only adult male in her life who has treated her with any respect. Certainly the only one that stood up to her daddy."

"I'm sorry, Micah. I didn't understand."

"No, I suppose you didn't but you did a pretty good job of filling in the gaps. You, of all people. I thought you knew me better than that."

"I'm sorry," was all I could get out. We sat in silence for a long time. Stars reflected on the water and reminded me of my nightlights. The faintest remaining glow of this day could be seen just above the western trees.

Micah stirred in his seat. "You know when we stopped for gas and I didn't have much to say for awhile?"

"Yeah, I noticed."

"Well, that kid there reminded me of someone a great deal."

"Someone you taught?"

"A kid on my basketball team, one of my most favorite people I ever taught or even knew."

"Do you stay in touch with him?"

"I speak to him some and visit when I can."

The curtain of night is easy to hide behind while the heart speaks. I suddenly felt his unease at continuing, yet knew he wanted to talk of this now and perhaps never again.

"One day at practice, he smarted off and made me really mad. After practice I had gone back to my room to do some paperwork.

William came down to the room and stood outside my door. I knew he was there, working up his nerve. He finally came in and told me, 'Coach, I'm sorry for talking back. I just got angry with myself for acting so stupid. You know I didn't mean it.' This kid had such a big heart; he'd run through a wall if I had asked him to. He didn't have much at home and tried to do his best just because of the relationship we had. I thought that day would be a good day to teach him a lesson, so I told him to get out and think about what he had done. My other players said he was crying in the locker room. I went to look for him cause usually I'd give him a ride home. He had no one around at that hour to pick him up. We usually had meaningful talks on the way home and this would have been a good time to chat about our problem." The words were forced and robotic.

"I would've never left him there. When I got to the locker room, he was gone. His friends told me he had just started walking. I didn't see him on the road anywhere, so I went on home. I didn't know what else to do."

I wanted the story to stop. I wanted to talk about something else. The river, diving, school, anything. I didn't know what this story had to do with the other, and I didn't understand how Micah could so abruptly change the subject. But I couldn't stop him, because Micah had retreated into an unattainable place.

"The next day he wasn't at school. They told me his mother called to say he never made it home. She asked for me. She knew how we got along. Several days later, he was still not to be found. Search parties were formed, his mother frantic."

Micah leaned on broken words and tears glistened on his cheeks in the soft starlight.

"A week after he disappeared, they found his body tangled in tree limbs in a river not too far from where he lived. He had been strangled. Someone had used his trust to kill him. I can still remember his eyes when he said he didn't mean it. He believed in me so much ... I try to tell him how much I believed in him each time I visit."

"Micah ... "

"And I've promised myself I will never turn my back on another kid the way I did William."

The warm breeze swept Micah's words into the empty night, and I knew it would be a long time before I would hear them again. Only when I tasted the salt did I realize my own tears. Micah had his head down, certainly judging himself, replaying the events of his life. No solace could I provide, but I understood and loved him as never before. My life would forever change because of this man sitting in a small boat on an immense river.

The stars were now piercing the darkening sky as we moved silently along. The glow from the lights of a nearby small town lay upon the treetops and gave the only indication of people within miles. Bold crickets on shore played a rhythmic tune in an effort to soothe the souls of those listening. The river was quietly alive. I could feel its strength reaching into me. It was easy to feel insignificant in this setting, but I knew that once we left, I would take a small portion of its power with me. And with Micah beside me, I would always be reminded of its complex and vital force. For Micah was the river, his resolve matched by this arena. Moving through the world on his own terms, affecting many, an unforgiving dispenser of fate, a loving parent to those with none, an innocent pawn in the hands of power, he reflected that which he sought. The river never gives in; we perceive it as being controllable but only when it lets us. It will quickly remind those who are complacent of its presence.

"You about ready to head home?" Micah broke the silence.

"Yeah, I suppose. Are you okay?"

"I'm sorry I ruined your day by telling you all that."

"I'm glad you told me. Maybe now you can start forgiving yourself. None of it was your fault."

"It's the eyes you don't forget."

"Sometimes things happen for no reason; we could drive ourselves crazy if we tried to understand. Who knows how many kids you have saved. We don't know about them because nothing happened to make headlines."

"Thanks. No one has ever really talked about any of this with me. Somehow they always talk around it. I don't think it would've helped back then anyway." Micah grasped the rope to start the engine, and his shadow shifted with a new attitude. The mountain ridge to the east was lit from behind as if another city skyline approached, but there was none in that direction. We had drifted beside a large outcropping covered with fir trees on its summit.

"Watch the mountain and you'll see that it's not only the ocean with magical lights." Micah released the rope and turned his seat to face the silhouetted scene. Within seconds the light spread and intensified; a blinding beam peeked through the trees as a glorious full moon rose to greet us. The pure air gave it clarity unseen in the city as it instantly gave shape to the valley while reflecting off the swirling water. It felt like this was the first time I had ever seen it rise.

"You know something?" he thought aloud. "Every person that has ever lived has at some point in his life watched the moon do that very same thing. How could you not feel amazed and thankful that you're alive and a witness to it? I'm glad you're here with me, Catherine. It helps to not be alone when the world makes you feel so trivial."

"Micah," I said, my heart breaking, "you are not trivial."

"I guess it seems no one is, then. You think it's time to roll on home?"

Though I felt I could float along till sunup, I realized we had a long ride ahead.

"Let's go. Besides, I think I've seen enough for one day."

Chapter 28

The morning fog hung low over the marsh at the bottom of the hill. By the time I approached the stoplight leading out of my neighborhood, my attitude shifted towards the task of teaching a class within the hour. As usual, I had tentatively planned the week the Friday before and didn't take home more than a few stacks of quizzes and essays to grade. Pulling into the teacher's parking lot, I noticed several of my colleagues trudging across the damp pavement to the canopy-covered sidewalks leading to the school building and surrounding trailers.

An astute observer could tell from a teacher's posture whether it was early or late in the week, and carrying my paper-filled satchel, I joined the sluggish troops and stepped through the maze of trailers toward my second home. Crushed gravel covered the ground in front of my rickety portable, but I had to be careful to avoid the occasional patch of red Georgia clay; it was next to impossible to get the red stain out of shoes, clothes and carpeting. I unlocked the door and turned on the lights, and set my books and satchel next to the broken arrowheads on my desk. On the shelf behind my file cabinets, I kept my better, unbroken spearpoints in a Riker-mount Micah had given me.

In the two weeks since the river diving trip, Micah and I spoke a few times on the phone, but neither of us suggested getting together in person. I supposed we were both too busy sorting out our feelings about what we had shared with each other. Until we calmed ourselves down about the gravity of that night on the river and the thought that we could never go back to what we were before, it would be hard to face each other for any extended period of time. But I hadn't heard from Micah all weekend, so I left my papers in my room and headed out to the office to sign in and then to Micah's trailer.

The outside light of his trailer was still on, while the inside light was off, unusual for him this time of morning. Micah usually arrived way before the rest of us, and his classroom lights were always on. Certainly he was around somewhere; perhaps he had a meeting or was copying worksheets in the math office. As I approached the departmental office, Janet Watson, one of the two Calculus teachers, pushed open the door.

"Have you seen Micah this morning?" I asked. Janet was a good friend of Micah's, yet unaware of our evolving friendship.

"No, not yet. He might not be in anyway after Friday." Her face betrayed concern and frustration and wrinkled with tension as she prepared her words of explanation.

"What do you mean? What happened Friday?" A second is enough time to generate a multitude of possibilities. Did someone die? An accident? Something at school? He did live on the edge of the handbook and the accepted protocol in education. The qualities that set him distinctly apart often ruffled someone along the way. As Janet spoke, her words moved around me, as I was reluctant to let them land and affect me.

"A parent complained about his speaker and Micah got called in by Dr. Blackwell. Whoever it was, I'm not really sure which parent, but they said the slides Micah's speaker showed were pornographic. Even called the police and tried to get him arrested."

"Tried to get *who* arrested? *Micah*?" I envisioned Micah sitting in the back of a police car. My heart fell to my stomach at the thought.

She glanced over my shoulder and down the hall to see whom, if anyone, was listening. The student body had an uncanny way of ferreting out information way before the teachers. They probably knew about the incident already but didn't know the recent details.

"It didn't happen, but a report was filed. I can't believe this. Nobody has seen Micah. I think he has a sub for the day."

"What did Dr. Blackwell say? Why didn't he just tell the parent it was okay? You know, beneficial and all that." I was unsure of what to ask or think. Should I run to a phone and call Micah at home or go to the front office and find out what they knew? I wondered how much of the situation our principal had resolved.

She continued, "What I understand is that Dr. Blackwell said he didn't know it was going on. He's laying it all on Micah."

"You have to be kidding me! Can he get into any major trouble over this?" I already knew the answer to my question. Exposure to school systems for so many years taught me that when problems arose, teachers were pretty much on their own. I had to call Micah, and without speaking further to Janet, I turned toward the parking lot to get my phone. Half-sprinting, even in my heels, I found my cordless lying on the passenger seat. Micah's number was on my speed dial and within seconds it was ringing his house. I really didn't expect him to pick up, and I practiced my message of concern and urgency to leave on his answering machine.

"Hello?" he answered as if it were another uneventful day. The fact that he was home said a great deal.

"I just spoke to Janet. She told me about what happened. What's going on? Why are you home?" Micah couldn't answer my questions fast enough.

"Well, I'm not really sure. It's happened so fast. Last Thursday, my medical examiner buddy came in to class to talk about solving murders, blood-splatter analysis and DUI teenagers. I told you about some of it, I think. Some of the slides are graphic but they have to be. Anyway, Julie, the girl I told you about on the river that night, went home and mentioned to her dad about the slides. She told him he ought to see the slides, and when he pressed her for more information, she told him about the dead bodies and the nude corpse and now he's after Doctor Blackwell to get me fired. Her father's been after my ass for a long time. Now he thinks he's got something on me and he's going for the jugular. I guess I know too much about the 'man of the church.'"

"She must've known how her father would react. Why did she tell him?"

"I don't know. I think she was trying to get him to stop the violence against her and the rest of the family, her way of trying to help. If the slides could make the kids wonder about their behavior, maybe he'd wonder about his. She's a mixed up girl. It's not her fault what her daddy does."

"Damn."

"I told Blackwell the kids knew for two weeks about the slides, and they were told they didn't have to watch them or even stay in the room if they needed to leave. Her dad now says I made her watch all the slides. He's accusing the school and me in particular of trying to corrupt his daughter and comes to school Friday looking for me, goes to the police, calls the superintendent, Dr. Blackwell and anyone else he could think of." The more he talked, the more frustrated he became.

"So what'd they say? What did Dr. Blackwell say?"

"When he called me down to the office, he says, 'Gosh, I sure wish I had known this was happening.' I just looked at him with disbelief. I told him he had eaten lunch with Randy and that he'd been coming to school for several years now giving his talks. Blackwell was immediately distancing himself from blame or more exactly the school system. He told me last night to stay home today. Probably to get his facts together without me around. So I don't know what's coming out of all this. The nut even called the Professional Practices board. They can take my teaching license away. You know what really gets me is that all this could be fixed if Dr. Blackwell would say it was okay, but he won't do it." Disdain had given way to exasperation.

"They'd never do that. Stop talking crazy. All this will be okay." I wasn't sure how to calm Micah; soothing words were difficult with my own anxiety rising.

"Who knows? My stomach's in knots … Everyone is going to think I got fired because I'm not there. Tell them that's not the case. You know schools are big rumor mills." His voice was strained and was perhaps on the verge of breaking. I felt I needed to go to him but I stayed at school; the institution that seemed to be deserting Micah had trained me to be hesitant about abandoning it. One of us needed to be there to keep an eye on Dr. Blackwell, I rationalized.

"Are you going to be alright? I can meet you for a drink after school. Why don't we meet at the Cellar?" I hoped he'd agree for my sake as well as his.

"We'll see. I don't know what I should do. I didn't do anything wrong. Trying to save some of these kids from themselves, and now this." He was pleading for me to understand, but I already did. He envisioned his world to be crumbling around him.

"I have to go to class. I'm already late but they'll get over it. I'm going to call this afternoon. Let's meet at around 4:30. I'll see what I can find out. You sure you'll be okay?" If I hurried out after school, I could get to the Cellar before heavy traffic congested the streets. It was to be a long day; the minutes would be interminable, frozen.

"Yeah, I guess. I don't think I'll grade any more papers for now, just in case. Man, this is just crazy. I can't believe I'm sitting at home with a sub in my room right now."

"Hang in there. People who know better will help. I'll see you this afternoon." As I hung up, I couldn't imagine what Micah was thinking as he worked through every possible outcome. This situation wasn't as bad as it seemed. I had to keep telling myself that, but I'd personally seen minor conflicts with parents turn distasteful and mean-spirited. When the image of the school system is at stake, its sense of loyalty often is misplaced by pompous bureaucrats covering their asses.

My thoughts a blur and my concentration in flux, the day crept along. My students noticed my inattention and guessed the reason. They were aware of my friendship with Micah and freely discussed his situation with me.

"Is he going to get fired because of the slides?" his students asked.

"I heard he showed nasty pictures to his classes. Mr. Whitaker is our minister, and he told my mother Mr. Marlowe showed male frontal nudity and that Julie had nightmares because of it."

"No way! Really? I wish I were in his class."

"It wasn't like that. I saw them, and the only thing we saw was a dead guy with a little bit of his dingle showing. It was nothing," said another student.

"And Mr. Whitaker said there were naked bodies of females."

"Same thing. They were mutilated bodies. The M.E. that showed the slides was trying to make a point. He wasn't going to show nice bodies to us. After seeing those pictures there is no way I'm getting in a car with a drunk driver. Julie's a skank for ratting on Mr. M. He didn't do nothing."

"I noticed she hasn't been in class lately. She probably knows no one will talk to her. Mr. Marlowe is the best teacher in this school, except for you, of course, Ms. Scott."

The entire class laughed, but it was nervous laughter. Except for a few, the entire student body was worried about Micah; his students had talked enough about him for the other students to appreciate his innocence. It was the one or two students I tried to reach that long day.

"Just because Whitaker is a minister doesn't mean he's right or that he necessarily got his facts straight. Julie's devoted to Mr. Marlowe. She would never do anything to hurt him. She probably mentioned the slides to her father in passing, and he took her remarks the wrong way. It's just a matter of time before Whitaker understands that Mr. Marlowe'd never do anything to hurt a child.

He was trying to save lives. Unfortunately, there are people who always believe the worst."

Most students were concerned for him and wanted to know what would happen and what they could do. Telling them "things will be fine" and "wait for this to pass" was easy, but I wasn't sure I believed it myself. I did go to the office and ask around but no one was offering much. One of the secretaries told me that last Friday Mr. Whitaker had been incredibly upset, almost to the point of being frantic, and he had to be refrained from pursuing Micah in his room. He informed all who would listen of his intentions to prosecute Micah and prove him unfit to teach. This Mr. Whittaker infuriated me, but what bothered me more was the acceptance of this tirade by the administration and the apparent complacency it bred, almost as if this happened each day. In small groups at the copy machine, teachers commiserated about Micah's situation and his subjection to such harsh accusations, but none offered more help than lip service. At lunch, the faculty whispered to each other about Micah's precarious present and uncertain future.

"Well, I can't believe it hasn't happened before now. He always thinks he has to do more than teach the curriculum," Darla Miller, one of the Spanish teachers, offered loud enough for everyone in the lounge to hear. Whenever I'd get stuck eating lunch with her, she always complained about the students and how they could not do the work. I wanted to ask her why, with such a stained attitude, she was a teacher. If working with young people could not be found rewarding, what a sad life this person led. Unfortunately there are teachers in schools all over the country who equate their own shortcomings with those of their students, but I suppose all workplaces have a certain amount of dissatisfaction. The problem is that a teacher's bitterness can seep through to their students and the love of learning takes another decline.

She continued with her negative comments. "I wonder what he's after. I guess if someone came to school hungry, he'd cook them breakfast. He interferes way too much in his students' lives. We need to stick with the stated objectives and nothing else. No wonder students are getting worse each year." My neck burned with anger and my need to respond became unbearable.

"What do you think he's after? Other than helping his students?" I asked.

"You know what he's after. Why do you think he encourages the young girls to stay after for help?"

"Maybe the problem isn't that he does more than is necessary but that you do so much less. The same old ways like yours don't seem to be working very well and the sooner schools are rid of complainers like you, the better off they'll be. I would hate to be a student in your class. I think I would rather drop out." There, I said it and I was glad. Later, some of the younger teachers told me they were grateful someone had finally put her in her place. Her destructive ways had already exacted too great a toll on the minds of children and didn't represent the vast majority of teachers. On another day I would have let it slide but today was different. She accused Micah of more than showing questionable material.

When not a sound of comfort came from her lunch partners, she gave a slight huff. "Well, just wait'll you teach for thirty years, little lady. You'll feel the same as I do."

"If your years get worse, it must be of your own making because mine get more wonderful." I could've said more, but I could tell by the look in her eyes I was confirming what she already knew. With a defensive stare and a sour expression not endearing to teenagers, her demeanor had created a situation of divisiveness even though her intentions were probably noble at first. Her redemption was still not unreachable but her resentment for life made it unattainable.

The rest of the day continued without incident even though students were still interested in what I knew about Micah. I told them I should have answers Monday and that Micah would certainly return to school then. Finally, the last class filed out amid bids of "have a nice weekend" and my mind focused on the hoped-for meeting with Micah. As soon as the last student bounced down the stairs, my cell phone was out of my purse.

"Hello, porno central. May I help you?" Micah answered. I really hated caller ID sometimes. I'd been creating an ulcer today, and he was home thinking up jokes.

"Are we still going to the Cellar?" The only place in the area with a little bit of character even if slightly artificial, it was a great place to loosen up after a long day. The owner and clientele made it so.

"Sure, I could use a break from sitting and thinking. Find out anything today? What'd everyone have to say?" To no avail he awkwardly tried to hide his anxiety.

"I'll tell you when I get there. Nothing much really. I can be there in about thirty minutes."

The Cellar had once been an elegant older home, built in the twenties or thirties, and had been captured before it became a pile of rubble followed by another pharmacy or video store. Upstairs was a nice restaurant with tablecloths and waiters in ties, but downstairs was reserved for those with a saltier view of life. Each setting provided its own memory but the one in the former basement was a lot cheaper. We had to enter in the back after parking in the cement lot just off the dirt road beside the house. Many years before, the dirt road had been the main avenue of travel between here and the next town. It was said to have been part of the old Federal Road that connected northern Georgia with Alabama, and probably was. Militia troops heading west to force local Cherokees onto the disgraceful Trail of Tears could have passed this way. But now I walked along this road towards a local bar to find a person I wanted desperately to help but was unsure how.

The lighting inside was purposely low even at this early hour. I wasn't certain they would even be open but we knew Harold, the owner, well enough that he wouldn't mind if we just sat at a table for a while. Usually this crowd came in after eight or nine, which made the upstairs management happy. A strange set of establishments co-existed here but each made a small fortune for Harold as it provided two entirely different sets of customers in the same location. While my eyes adjusted to the slim light, Micah leaned back against the scratched wood panel in one of the three booths on the far wall. I had to step up a bit to fit into my side. Micah already had a beer and Harold brought my regular glass of white wine.

"So, my dear Holmes, what have you discovered?" Micah must have been on his second beer.

"Everyone's concerned but not much information to report. Did you call Dr. Blackwell today?"

"Yes, and he was very evasive which makes me highly suspicious. Hey, wasn't 'Highly Suspicious' the king of Ethiopia?"

"You idiot, that was Halie Selasie or something like that. How many beers have you had?" I leaned over to peer closer into his eyes.

"Well, I did have a couple at home. This could be four or five, but who cares?"

"I do and everyone else driving near you. What did Blackwell say?" I could not believe our principal was turning his back on a good teacher. Micah had to be misinterpreting Dr. Blackwell's methodical style.

"After I talked to you, I called Blackwell and he told me the county was debating what to do. Something about ethics. He said I shouldn't worry, that he was doing what he could but for me to stay home again until they dealt with this parent and everyone he had called. I said I would rather return to school so I could defend myself. He made some comment to the effect of 'let's not stir the pot anymore right now,' whatever that means. I don't really know what I should do. What a bunch of pricks." I could see now that his eyes were red and began to tear as he continued to speak. The words were barely audible as he leaned forward and placed his hands against his temples and pushed them back and through his hair.

Sliding out of my wooden seat, I stepped over to Micah's side and slipped into the space beside him. He moved further in without looking up. This time he did not retreat when I placed my arm over his shoulders and pulled him to me. I laid my cheek against the top of his head and focused on the unlit candle in front of me. "We'll get through this together," was all I could say, but to me it meant that once I decided to fight, it was to the end. Within minutes, I would take him home in my car, leaving his truck in the dusty parking lot where ghosts of soldiers and Native Americans walked at night.

Almost a week passed before Dr. Blackwell allowed Micah to return to school. His room was in disarray from having last-minute substitutes each day and some days, none at all. On those occasions, his students were split up among other teachers. With the shortage of competent subs, the disassembling of classes was not uncommon in school systems everywhere and was one of the biggest hindrances to education. Having a warm body calling roll and writing bathroom passes does not constitute a "learning environment," but the needs of the students do not always make for a good sound bite in political campaigns and are thus ignored. Micah survived his first morning back, getting to school early and cleaning up his room. He would be the first to acknowledge that even before his imposed hiatus his room appeared to be in a constant post-tornado status, but he knew where each particular piece of debris could be found. His mother had told me once that he had always been like that; if she cleaned his room, he became frantic that something would become lost. Not because it wasn't in his room somewhere but that by not being in its proper place, it would lose its identity and she might as well have thrown it away. Each morning, students would normally come by Micah's room to chat and work on homework for other classes. This time, the early arrivals were not there, and I watched Micah glance at the door each time we heard footsteps on the gravel outside. I had come by to talk and now sat with my papers and coffee. The students didn't know when he was coming back and had become frustrated at a locked door greeting them the last five mornings.

"I can't believe how awkward this feels. It's like my first day ever teaching," he said.

"The students will be bugging you all day about your absence, you know."

"Tell me something I don't already know. I'll probably be answering questions about my little absence all day."

"That's okay. They should know what happened so they won't be filling in the blanks with their own version."

Before I could agree with him, one of his students entered expecting to see another unfamiliar face. The young boy with shaggy hair and jeans pulled on the metal door that had become tight in the frame from years of overuse.

"Hey, Mr. Marlowe, you're back! We're so sick of subs. We thought you got fired." His face curled up in joy and relief.

"I figured ya'll would, but they had to sort things out. How was everyone acting?"

"We're all pretty ticked. They kept telling us each day that you would be back the next one but after awhile, we quit believing them. Word was spreading that we would have a protest if you didn't come back. Just came by to see if you might be here. Gotta go. See ya fourth period, Mr. M." He bounded down the stairs and was quickly gone. Now Micah and I understood the sudden change in attitude of the administration. They asked him to come back to dispel problems, not because they absolved him of blame.

"Makes sense, doesn't it?" he asked me.

"Yeah. I don't think I'd trust anything they say. Did you get that lawyer you called?" I replied.

"Sort of. I have to call back. We've been playing phone tag. Sounds like I need to sit down with her and cover myself just in case."

"Call her today, don't forget." I emphasized "today." With the school year nearing an end, this could drag on until people became desensitized or were gone for the summer.

As I gathered my papers and walked for the door, I tried to soften the implications of his student's revelation. "Today will be fine. Everything will work out, Micah. You'll see. I'll talk to you later." I closed the door and walked along the concrete path toward the front office.

It could have been my imagination, but the office staff coldly stared at me as I passed through the reception area and behind the three secretarial desks to the teachers' mailroom. I wondered if they were aware of my growing relationship with Micah and knew I supported him wholeheartedly. Maybe they heard what I said in the lunchroom to Darla Miller. She was always hanging around the office staff complaining about someone or something. I checked my mail and walked out the same way I came in, but this time I smiled broadly and shook my hair out of my eyes. "Have a wonderful day, ladies. I know I sure will, now that we have our favorite teacher back." In seconds, I was out the door and on the way to my portable.

The day passed without event, and Micah said after his first few classes, the students acted as if nothing had changed and things were back to normal, as normal goes in his trailer. He did tell me it would be awhile before he had anymore speakers in class. Another thing he mentioned was how my verbal antagonist from lunch had given him the evil eye, and then he thanked me for forgetting to tell him of our little feud about him last week.

As was so often the case, Friday arrived suddenly, and I had only spoken with Micah on the phone. He had conferred in the middle of the week with a lawyer but it was preliminary and minimal. With only two weeks to go until finals, the initial stress of dealing with an angry parent gave way to getting through the end of the year. Summer has a way of cleaning the slate, tabula rasa, and creating the feeling of uneasy forgiveness. Micah had told his students that as far as he knew, nothing had come of the problem. The school system had questioned him about the incident and had him write a letter explaining his side. It seemed to be over.

Several minutes after the bell rang ending the school day, the loudspeaker blurted out, "Mr. Marlowe, please come by the front office." Instantly, my tension and queasiness returned. Friday afternoon proved notorious for broken hearts and numbing one-sided conversations. With students staying after for help with the end of the year Shakespearean Festival, I couldn't leave the room, but while the students practiced scenes from *Hamlet,* my mind focused on Micah's long walk to the office. I pictured Dr. Blackwell escorting him into the conference room to find several men from downtown sitting around the table. Micah's face turns ashen as they speak in low understanding tones and inform him of their decision to terminate his contract based upon recent events. They tell him his irresponsible choice to bring in this speaker did not reflect the true desire of the community or school, and he has not only stepped over the line from which they could help him but has also placed the county in a precarious legal position.

"'There's rosemary, that's for remembrance; pray you, love, remember: and there's pansies, that's for thoughts.'" Ophelia's madcap lines brought me back to reality.

"Remember, Erin," I told my student, "even though she's out of her mind, there's still a sense of intelligence about her. In her crazy way, she knows what she's doing. She sticks it to the King and Queen, but gets away with it because of her madness. Show some deviousness in your manner. Continue with Laertes' line."

"'A document in madness, thought and remembrance fitted.'"

Erin's eyes shifted back and forth as she passed Ophelia's flowers around to the conspirators. "'There's fennel for you, and columbines: there's rue for you; and here's some for me: we may call it herb of grace o' Sundays: O, you must wear your rue with a difference. There's a daisy: I would give you some violets, but they withered all when my father died: they say 'a made a good end.'"

"Much better, but the rosemary goes to Laertes in remembrance for their father's death; fennel symbolizes flattery, so that goes to the King, and the Queen gets the columbines for unchastity, rue for sorrow, and daisies for infidelity. Try it again. Slow down and put your body into it more."

For over an hour the students rehearsed their scenes, the students demanding my attention, giving me a respite from my frantic thoughts. But that soon ended with the sound of footsteps on the trailer's wooden stairs. The door swung outward and Micah entered, but it was not the Micah I knew. Instead, a stranger entered my room, a man stripped of his confidence, a defeated warrior. Stepping further into the room, he gripped the back of the last student desk and with sad eyes he whispered, "They want me to resign." My skin flushed instinctively and adrenalin rushed throughout my blood. Frozen in my seat, I heard the words but did not fully grasp the meaning. His lip trembled as he tried to catch his breath, and he reminded me of my father after Therese's death. He stepped forward and collapsed into the seat, my cheeks already wet and my heart breaking.

"Oh, God, no ... they can't ... they just ... can't." I reached for Micah, his face hidden inside his folded arms on the desktop, and I placed my arms around him, not knowing what else to say or do. My worst fears were no longer dreams, yet I longed to wake up still. He lifted his head and rubbed his eyes with his hands.

"They told me I should resign. That I did things never authorized." His gaze wandered and settled on the floor; he could not yet look at me.

"How can they make you resign? Who was this?" I turned to my spellbound students. "Perhaps you should leave now." They quietly retreated, but not before a distressed survey of the scene.

"Several of them from the central office, plus Dr. Blackwell. No one took my side ... they said if I didn't resign, they'd be forced to terminate me."

"Did you sign anything?"

"No. Hell no, as my mama would say." He bit his lower lip so hard I expected to see blood.

"What then, if you don't?" I asked sullenly.

"Make me stay home, said I'd be fired on ethics grounds. I pleaded my case but no one listened. They just nodded and said they were sorry. I told them that we had probably ... probably saved some kid's life by showing them these slides. I guess that doesn't matter, I asked them. Students first, my ass, was what I should have said, but I was so caught off-guard, I didn't know what to say." As he stood, I embraced him with all of my heart and hoped he could feel by my touch how much he was loved. Pulling away after a protracted moment, he looked for the answer I did not have. "Thanks for being here, Catherine ... but what should I do now?"

"Don't fucking resign," I said. "That makes it too easy for them. Don't let those bureaucratic jerks think they can intimidate you. Make them fire you. Can't you request a hearing?" My mind was free to think more clearly now; a task was at hand that required focus on the solution, not the problem.

"I believe so. They were not very forthcoming on my options. I guess I have to figure that out myself." He hesitated, sniffed, and stared at the floor. "Now I can call the lawyer-lady for sure." Leaning against a desk with his fingers spread out as a brace, his cheeks were flushed and eyes strained red. For an elongated minute, he did not stir. Seldom have I seen a person change in front of me without a single movement of muscle, but I now witnessed this firsthand. Micah had shown to me before his ability to alter his attitude directly and with power. He lifted his gaze toward my eyes, making it difficult to look away. "I will *not* give in. Throughout my life, anything I set my mind to, I achieve. I'll be back in a minute." He left the room via the back door and walked vigorously across the asphalt towards the school building. I could only wait.

Sitting on the back steps of my trailer, I noticed several of the county officials leaving through the front doors. Micah exited behind them and called after those within range. Too far for me to hear anything, I watched Micah approach the nearest two, his face angry, his hands emphatically gesturing. The representative with the dark blue suit nodded and then turned to follow the others. His counterpart spoke to Micah with an agitated posture and then waved him away. Micah searched for me on the stairs and tramped across the overgrown grass to my trailer.

"What'd you say to them?" I thought I knew but needed confirmation.

"I told them they couldn't scare me into resigning, that I had done nothing wrong. Then I said that if they wanted me out, they'd have to do it themselves." His speech quickened with excitement. "Then I spoke to Dr. Carroll, the head of human resources for the county, and he said, 'If that's the way you want it, fine,' so I said, 'Well, actually sir, that's the way it has to be.'"

"Good. The hell with them," I said. "You have to fight them; they're used to people giving in, but now what?" I had no inclination as to the procedure, and Micah probably did not either.

"From what I gather, I'm suspended right here at the end of the year, and I can appeal my firing … Jesus, I can't believe I'm talking about this. It doesn't seem like I'm the one involved but someone I know." Again, his emotions slipped back into despair, and the lines around his distant blue eyes deepened into heavy wrinkles. Sorrowful and dejected, Micah slumped onto the step beside me.

"You can't feel sorry for yourself now," I said.

"Just when will I be able to? Cause I can't think of a better time than now." His humor had not retreated, darker perhaps, but still there. "I need to call my lawyer and see what's the next step. You going home?" I nodded. "Okay, I'll call you later with some information hopefully. I have to go by my trailer before I head on home."

"Micah," I said before he left. "What is it they are so upset about? Were the slides really that bad?"

He hesitated before he spoke. "At the end of the slides, there were some others in the set from a homicide where a couple got their throats slit. It was pretty nasty and they got put on the screen before I could say anything to Randy, the M.E. showing the slides. Both people were naked, and for the few seconds before Randy could turn the projector off, the kids saw the mutilated bodies. Julie Whitaker told her father about it."

"For God sakes why?"

"She called me about it, but we could only speak for a few minutes. Her mom and dad are watching like a hawk. They know she calls me sometimes and, of course, now they have forbidden her to have anything to do with me. But she said her dad was threatening her again and waving a big knife in front of her, and she said why don't you slit my throat like the girl in the slides. He beat her down, literally, until she told him about the slides and who showed them. If he makes me look like the bad guy, my credibility will be shot, and he won't have to worry about me going to the press, the abusive bastard. He's nailing me so he doesn't have to worry about losing his church."

"I wonder if you could get Julie to testify on your behalf. She really seems to love you."

"I couldn't do that to her. Besides, it's too late. He's already told the county he would go to the media with pornography charges which has them looking for a way out of bad PR. So, I guess I'll be their fall guy." Micah's bitterness surrounded his words. "I gotta go to my trailer." He ran his hand along the railing and gazed across the parking lot.

"I'm going that way. Can I tag along?"

"Sure, Ms.Scott. Come on."

We made our way past the circular grassy area that encompassed the flagpole and onto the concrete walkway leading to the back of the school. Micah bounded up his own wooden stairs and into his menagerie of knowledge. Moving toward his desk, he reeled around with awareness.

"Who am I kidding? This could be the last time I'm in here. I don't know anything else but this room, my books, and my kids." His voice trailed off with the realization of what lay ahead of him. The power of the system can be overwhelming, if not intimidating and ruthless. "Well, hell, I always said if anyone ever left teaching, it was because of the adults and not the students. Right again, huh?" He tried to be casual but his words were forced.

"It's okay, Micah ... you'll get through this." We quietly embraced before he confronted the task of calculating the fragments of his room. Dr. Blackwell had told him he needed to leave, or send, lessons for the upcoming week if he were to appeal. Not to do this would be considered insubordination and give the county further cause to sever ties. Micah grabbed a few papers and put away some important folders. Retrieving his teacher's editions from their hiding place, he laid them upon the desk toward the back door.

"Everything I need to take home each day, I put on that desk," he explained. I watched as he rummaged through the drawers and boxes accumulated over the years. Micah searched for necessary items first and then for those more meaningful. I offered to help but he just shrugged, lost in his thoughts. Several times he picked up an object of simple appearance, a lopsided old pot, a broken cup, a gold-and-blue graduation tassel, but of obvious personal significance. The items invoked memories only he knew, smiles remembered and cherished. He came to a laminated bookmark and held it until his hand trembled.

"I make these at the end of each year for my students." He handed me a bookmark so I could read the quotes on either side: "When you go as far as you can see, then you can see further" by Thomas Carlyle and "If you never have dreams, they never come true" by Homer Hickam. At the bottom of one side it said, "Mr. Marlowe, Algebra II."

"You can have that if you want. I've been giving these out for the last few years; I vary the quotes, but the message is always the same. Last summer one of my students was killed in an accident and at his funeral, Dean's sister told me that even though his buddies teased him about having a bookmark from his math teacher, he kept it beside his bed just to remind him to do better. Nothing anybody has told me about my teaching has meant as much as that, and I almost forgot it by feeling sorry for myself. It's time for that to stop," he said. "How about helping me tote some stuff to the truck."

He had redrawn the curtain as soon as he opened it, but his humble words pulled me into his heart's inner reaches where I resolved to stay forever. "Let's load up what you need and get out of here. We can stop for a beer and talk this through. You first should call your lawyer and see what she says." I put some of his paperwork on top of mine and took the three short paces to the back door.

Chapter 29

Monday mornings are often harried, but never would I have imagined the circus atmosphere that greeted me the first day back after Micah's forced departure. The few students who witnessed Micah's distress in my classroom circulated the news around the community, and the enormity of student and parent response spun the main office into a whirlwind. The front desk receptionist slammed down one phone only to pick up another. "No, no, he has not been fired. There's been a complaint filed. Dr. Blackwell's looking into it. We have no more information." SLAM. "Good morning, Tecumseh High School. No, no, he has *not* been fired ..." The phone had not stopped ringing from the moment the first secretary arrived at seven until the time the rest of us came dragging in around eight Concerned parents who never would have considered calling the school flooded the phone lines, and the secretarial staff answered with an administratively orchestrated response. Teachers whose names I barely knew crowded me with questions. "What's he gonna do?" "How's he taking it?" I explained Micah's situation over and over until I grew weary of the whole subject, and after awhile pared my answer down to one word: appeal.

By midday, I had retreated to my room with the door locked to anyone but students. Trance-like, I made it through the day, my thoughts elsewhere and nowhere. Students that had been in Micah's class told me how the slides had impacted them. They indicated something in school finally made a difference in their lives and now adults were telling them it shouldn't have taken place at all. Stephanie came to see me during the day and pressed me for news about Micah. "What's going to happen to him, Ms. Scott? What can we do to help?" Her concern covered her frustration just as her baggy clothes and cranberry hair cloaked her extreme intelligence. "Rachel and Jared heard about it over the weekend. We told Adam this morning. We thought you might know what to do, since you're the closest to him."

"Well, at this point, I'm not sure but perhaps when his appeal happens, he might need someone to speak on his behalf. You can testify for Mr. Marlowe inside and outside of the classroom. You could talk about the school we visited in Honduras and the children and … and his crazy metal detector."

"I know exactly what I'd say. I would tell the judge Mr. Marlowe has been the one person here that sees through all the crap most teachers try to throw at us. He told us that if we leave this school and don't have a desire for learning, then he has not done his job. He showed me that there are so many cool things in the world that a lifetime isn't enough to even get started on them. I appreciate learning now. How can the administration take that away from me?" She was pleading for an answer.

"They shouldn't, but they're trying to. It has a lot of us upset but we must wait for our moment." The sixth period bell rang and my class would be filled with students any minute. "You need a pass back to class?"

"I'll explain to Mr. Ripportella tomorrow. He's pretty cool. He understood when I told him I needed to talk to you."

"Tell the rest of them to hang in there; things have a way of working out," I said.

"If you talk to him, tell him if he needs me, I will be there like he's always been for me. But some of us might not wait too long for our moment."

"Meaning?" I thought I knew what she meant. Whispers of a student protest had spread through the morning hours, and by afternoon openly discussed. Several years ago, a reaction to an administrative decision had led to a great many students walking out of school. It had appeared on the local news which had a definite impact on the outcome and left an imprint upon the often image-conscious educational elite. How others possibly perceive us can cloud judgment even in a dynamic entity such as a school system.

"Is there going to be a walkout?" I asked. The arriving students shared looks at each other and then smiled.

"Should we tell her?" Stephanie said to a few of my juniors.

"Yeah, she's cool," a kid near the door said. "We can tell her."

"So what time is it?" I tried to sound non-plussed by my question.

"We're trying to get everyone to walk out tomorrow at one o'clock," Stephanie confessed.

"You're not going to rat on us, are you Ms. S.?"

"You have a right to your views. Hell, I might walk out with you. I don't like what those pompous-ass bureaucrats are doing to Mr. Marlowe anymore than you do."

"We want Dr. Blackwell to know we aren't doing it just to get out of school. We have a real reason to protest. We're trying to get parents to come, too."

"You don't think this'll hurt Mr. Marlowe's chance of winning his appeal, do you?" asked Stephanie.

"I don't see how things could get any worse." Stephanie left and the students adjusted themselves to the curved backs of their chairs.

I played with the broken arrow points on the top of my desk, then flung them down across my stacks of ungraded papers. "We need to get some work done today," I said. "So, what does Prufrock mean when he says his life is 'measured out in coffee spoons'?" I smiled as hands in the classroom flew up. In light of the impending protest, they were ready to answer that question.

The next day teemed with tension and curiosity about the walkout. My morning classes speculated on how many kids would actually leave the building, and how many parents and teachers would support the protest. "Are you walking out with us, Ms. Scott?" they asked over and over.

"Mr. Marlowe is a very close friend of mine," is the only answer I gave them.

"Alright! Ms. Scott is with us!"

The tension escalated as the day wore on. More and more teachers found out about the walk-out, and the students waved my name as a supportive banner. Linda and several other English teachers asked me if I were going to leave with the kids, and my hesitation gave them their answer. "Why don't you leave with me?" I asked Linda in private.

"I can't," she said. "I'm part of the administration team, and I really need my paycheck. But you do what you have to do. You're not a department head and linked to them like I am. You can get away with it. If anybody can."

Smiling at Linda, I said, "Just practicing what I preach. Or teach. "Civil Disobedience," you know."

Linda gave me a quick hug. "I love you, Cat."

The last lunch ended at 12:45 and instead of going to their classes when the bell rang, the students from the cafeteria grabbed what they needed from their lockers and marched out the doors. Their departure signaled the start of mass evacuation, and in minutes hundreds of students left the security of their classroom seats, slammed locker doors and chaotically piled out of the building's innumerable entrances.

"Marlowe's innocent!" "We want Marlowe back!" "Blackwell's a shithead!" the students shouted as they exited the building and portables. Many had extracted signs from their lockers with words of support for Micah on them, some simply stating, "Bring Marlowe Back" or "Marlowe's the Best." The students migrated towards the red clay washouts of the front hill, at first a few hundred, then hundreds more until only a few were left inside. The students had chosen this meeting point because the hill could accommodate a couple thousand students, and it was within view of Dr. Blackwell's office window. Cars of parental supporters already lined the streets leading to the school, and by the time I closed up my room and joined the protesters, a couple thousand people crowded the hill in front of Tecumseh High School.

Teachers had done little to stop the students once the flow began, and besides me only a few math teachers had joined the fray; Marlowe had kept so much to himself, very few teachers outside his own department knew much about him other than the recent multiplying rumors. The charges against Micah had been distorted to include sexual abuse charges towards his female students along with the original charge of showing violent and pornographic materials to students. Micah would never be the same after this, I thought amid the angry shouts of demonstrators. Against his will, Micah Marlowe was now catapulted out of his private and safe world into the glaring limelight.

The administration had prepared itself for the onslaught. Police with walkie-talkies stood at the periphery of the throng encouraging orderly behavior, while the administrative staff stayed behind the closed doors of their offices. They hoped the whole situation would dissipate with the 3:30 arrival of the yellow buses, I supposed. But the arrival of the local TV and newspapers drew them out from behind closed doors. One by one, Dr. Blackwell and his four assistant principals gave brief statements to the news media, trying to quell the growing alarm of the community.

"Hey, Baby Cakes, I mean Ms. Scott, way to go!" I spotted Joey's red hair across the confluence. "That's my English teacher," he told anyone who would listen. A small group of girls smirked at him across the worn grass. One girl whispered to the others and they all sneered in agreement. "No wonder Mrs. Scott is out here. She's been after Mr. Marlowe all year," a brown-haired teenager said as she turned in my direction. It was Ashley. I held her gaze for a few seconds and then she disappeared into the crowd.

The gathering now spread across the street to the grassy area leading into the surrounding subdivisions. Mothers with young children stood on their porches regarding the rebellious students, their stances rigid, their stares serious. For many students, this foray was their first attempt to fight the system. They really didn't know what to do, and after the initial shouts and rallying, they milled around, chatting and glancing towards the school. Eventually, someone began a chant of "Bring back Marlowe," and it emanated across the assemblage. I found myself joining in.

Getting no response from the Powers-That-Be, some of the students strode over to the small stand of administrators facing the local news broadcasters and addressed Dr. Blackwell. "Hey, we want an answer, Blackwell. What are you going to do about Mr. Marlowe?" they shouted. Behind them, the crowd echoed the question. "What're you going to do about Mr. Marlowe? What're you going to do about Mr. Marlowe?" they cried.

The shouts became angrier and angrier, until Dr. Blackwell was forced to speak. "Quiet down. Quiet down, listen to me," he yelled above the clamor. When the students realized he was about to speak, they calmed and listened. "Mr. Marlowe will be given a hearing in a couple of weeks, and he'll have an opportunity to present his case. The courts will decide his future; it's out of my hands now."

Since Dr. Blackwell had no microphone, the front of the crowd passed his words to those in the back. A loud hiss passed through the dissenting body, and a shout of "Blackwell's a pussy!" could be heard. Several police cars arrived, sounding their sirens as a warning to the smoldering mass. After awhile the students grew tired and many sat on the ground. A feeling of *déjà vu* overwhelmed me, and even though I never actively had participated in the demonstrations of the sixties and seventies, I'd seen enough live protests on television to make me feel as if I had been an active-participant in my generation's history.

Ahead of schedule yellow buses edged the curbs of the school parking lot and reluctant students began to fill them. "Sell out!" some of their classmates called after them, but for many of the young people the buses were their only mode of transportation home. Others had after-school jobs, and slowly but surely the student body dispersed to the school parking lot, until only a few of us remained.

"You going to get in trouble, Ms. Scott?" asked Stephanie, her cranberry hair glistening in the sunlight.

"I hope so," I smiled.

"You think we helped Mr. M. at all?"

"Of course," I said. "I'll let him know how loved he is."

"At least you understand, Ms. Scott." I leaned over and hugged the small group of students around me, and as I did so, I instinctively lifted my head to catch the cold eyes of Dr. Blackwell on me. Our gazes locked in defiant stares before he turned and proceeded back into the building.

You son-of-a-bitch, I thought. It's out of your hands, my ass. No wonder the kids like Micah. One of the greatest gifts he gives the kids—and also me—is his full attention. Young people too often feel adults never listen to them, and Dr. Blackwell proved once again how right they are. Told they are too naïve or just don't understand the intricacies of a situation, a young heart becomes cynical by example. Do we not extinguish one more dream each time we cast doubt upon the hopes of a child? Don't we all suffer the loss of our own stolen childhoods? In the late afternoon sun, the school building cast shadows onto the street, and from its many windows, invisible eyes glared at me for daring to ask why.

Life returned to a semblance of normalcy the next day though Tecumseh High School would never again be the same without Micah. The local news had aired the protest the evening before, and the newspaper carried a brief clip of the event. The county refused to respond to any more interviews and decided not to punish those who left the campus. Students were told, however, no further demonstrations would be tolerated.

Towards the end of my last period, an office aid knocked on my door and handed me a letter marked "urgent." It was on official Tecumseh High School stationery and formally addressed to Mrs.

Catherine Scott. I guessed who sent it before I even opened it. It was a letter of reprimand written by Dr. Blackwell and signed by the Superintendent of Garret County Schools. A short note written by Dr. Blackwell requested I sign the reprimand and return it to him immediately; a copy was included for my personal files, the original would be sent downtown ... to haunt me for the rest of my days, I supposed he thought. The reprimand didn't refer directly to the student protest, but stated that I had acted in defiance of the county's authority. I signed the letter and left my class unattended to deliver it in person to Dr. Blackwell. Ignoring the protest of his overworked secretary, I pushed my way into his office and threw the envelope on his desk. "Marlowe could've used your support." He was on the phone and waved for me to sit down. "No thanks," I said and left the room.

Micah had called me about the walk-out and told me to tell the students he appreciated all the concern for him. He gave me a hard time for jeopardizing my job, but I knew he was touched I had not abandoned our kids. He hoped the protest would prove to be meaningful, but I corrected him to say he meant useful; it was already meaningful. His students wandered in and out of my room all day. They told me how before, if their day wasn't going well, walking into his room would change their moods. Now they said going to his class made their day miserable. They asked me to tell Micah how much they missed him.

"Call him up and tell him yourself, or go to the appeal hearing. It'll be in a few weeks, and he sure would appreciate the support." The hearing had been set for the second week in June.

"We'll be there, for sure. Let us know when. This is all so ridiculous, but nothing surprises me here." Stephanie made my thoughts her own. In front of the students, I was hesitant to say all that I felt. That would come at a later time. Hopefully, I could speak at the hearing for Micah, but thus far, his lawyer had not worked out the proceedings. I wished for a chance to speak and protect the man I loved but with each passing day Micah became more withdrawn. He could no longer inhale strength from his students. He once told me that he felt so alive rambling on about some adventure of his with his "kiddies," as much as when he's lost to the world sitting in a boat upon a glass river. Questioning his own judgment, Micah thought his chances of reversing the county's decision were minimal, and slipped further into despair.

Finals are always given after Memorial Day. Exams one week away, Micah called to see if I could meet him at the Cellar to pick up his tests. He didn't trust anyone else with them. I hadn't seen him in person since that infamous Friday, and I expected to see a defeated and sad man. He was standing in the parking lot waiting for me when I arrived, late as usual, and in the evening light, his broad shoulders and chiseled face had the look of a valiant gladiator resigned to his fate. My body melted with love for him, and before he could speak, I held him tightly, and would have stayed locked in his arms all night, but he drew back his face and lifted my chin until our lips touched, and he kissed me so deeply it felt as though he breathed his very soul into me. Then, he gently pulled me by the hand into the bar. We sat side-by-side and stared at each for a long moment. "So, what did your lawyer say?" I finally said. Micah nodded at the waitress and ordered two Dos Equis before he answered.

"My lawyer has decided who to have speak at the trial. A couple of students who were there along with Randy and maybe a teacher who was there. He said that there's room for one other person, that it should be someone who understands me. Someone who cares deeply for what I'm about." He hesitated and looked toward me and through me. For a second, Micah's face turned into Dr. Craig's. "I hoped it would be you."

Years before, my father had told me that everyone gets a chance to do a truly honorable thing, regardless of the consequences. If I testified, Dr. Blackwell would add another black mark to my file and most likely try to get me fired along with Micah, but I had my dad and his bathroom lectures to guide me now. He had prepared me for this day; the choice was simple. My hands smoothing his tired face, I swallowed hard to fight back tears. "Of course, I'll speak for you. How could I not?"

Micah released his sly grin and pushed back his hair. The blue eyes before me gave a hint of the magic tucked safely away behind them. He started to say something, stopped for a second and then continued. What he finally said was not his initial thoughts, I knew.

"Maybe we can get through this in one piece, huh?" I was caught off guard by his choice of words. "Maybe we" would never have been possible for Micah a year, maybe not even a month, ago. His internal struggles didn't allow another soul within reach of his, until now. Was stress or love the catalyst that brought about the genesis of this new person?

"So when's the hearing? I'm ready to get this going so my life, and yours, can get back to normal."

Micah laughed and flipped the ends of my hair. "Cat, neither of our lives will be normal after this. The hearing's supposed to take place in a couple of weeks. It won't be soon enough for me. "

The "couple of weeks" turned into four, and it was the end of June by the time the hearing to determine Micah's future started. The days before the hearing, my moods swung from feeling everything would be all right to envisioning the worst possible scenario. Marshall made matters worse by attacking Micah any chance he could get. "What kind of guy is this?" Marshall said the morning of the trial." The papers said he showed nude corpses to his students. In math class? You're a fool to testify for this guy. Any good lawyer is going to make mincemeat out of you. The entire city of Atlanta's going to hear all about you and Micah running around together. How's that going to make me look?"

"Micah's job is on the line, and all you care about is how this is going to make you look? Give me a fucking break, Marshall."

"Your job will be on the line too, Cat. Do you think Blackwell is going to hire you back after Marlowe gets fired if you testify against the school?"

"First of all, I don't think Micah's going to get fired, and second of all, why would I want to work for Blackwell after all this, anyway. There are plenty of other jobs out there."

"Do what you want. You always do anyway. I won't be home for dinner tonight."

"What else is new?" I said as Marshall slammed the garage door. Things weren't getting any better between Marshall and me; in fact, they were getting much worse. He was seldom home anymore, and when he was, he spent his time shut up in his office on the phone. Working, I supposed. On occasion, he would come out of his self-imposed cocoon and we would share a bottle of wine. Our conversations would start out civilly, but by the time the bottle was empty, Marshall's mood turned ugly, and he would tell me how much he hated me. Then the next morning he would apologize and promise to go to counseling with me. I should have tried harder and paid more attention to Marshall, but Micah's trial was so much on my mind, I couldn't concentrate on anything else.

The hearing was to be held in the County Office Building and begin promptly at nine a.m. Presenting first would be the lawyer for the county while the judge chosen was from a panel dedicated to ruling on situations such as these. Micah and I kept in constant contact, and he informed me via his lawyer of the specific questions to expect. The bothersome part was that Marshall was right—I could be cross-examined on any topic I mentioned during my direct testimony. One more time, I looked to the heavens for an answer. Okay, Jamie and Lola, how do I handle this? I prayed. I know damn well you had something to do with all of this. Then I recalled something my dad said during one of our heart to heart bathroom talks: "Simply tell what's in your heart and fear will have no place to reside." At the time he was teaching me how to get along with the nuns, but the words rang true now. And, I truly didn't believe anyone knew the private and public Micah better than I. His students could sense how he felt about teaching, but I could give voice to his reflections told softly on a river or in the cold wind of a barren lakefront. Micah had never been one to force his opinions of life upon others, but his message seeped into a person that spent time with him. Penitence came in many forms.

Rachel and Stephanie were the students chosen to give their version of the dramatic day. Randy, the medical examiner, was to be called by the prosecutors since the slides were to be the primary evidence. Micah would speak for himself after the students, and then I would step forward to give balance and closure to the proceeding.

When I arrived at the County Office that morning, the parking lot was full, and dozens of people hung around the front steps waiting for the doors to open. I searched the crowd for Micah, and I caught a glimpse of his profile, but before I could reach him, a county clerk unlocked the doors, and Micah disappeared inside of them. I followed the crowd into the buiding and down the corridor leading to the hearing room. The room was small with several rows of long wooden benches on either side of the aisle leading to the tables of Micah and his adversaries. Micah sat on the right side of the room, his parents directly behind him, students, parents and other supporters behind them. Glass globes suspended from long steel tubes illuminated an otherwise drab, cheaply painted room. A dark mahogany-stained railing separated the onlookers from the watched.

I was not allowed in the room once the proceeding began, as all witnesses were kept right outside the door waiting for the clerk to beckon. I spoke briefly with Micah's mother and father, their backs ramrod-straight in their chairs. His mother wore a beige-and-green checked pants suit, while his father had a sport jacket and tie to match. His father's silver hair was pulled straight back.

"It'll be fine, don't worry. He has so much support," I said to the elder Mr. Marlowe.

"We certainly appreciate you doing this for him ... and us." They did not know what else to say.

"He'll be alright. Common sense has to prevail eventually."

The lawyers and court recorder assembled themselves in the room, and witnesses were asked to meet in the corridor. Waiting outside was excruciatingly frustrating, and I wanted to know instant progress of the county's tactics. Sitting in the hall with the other witnesses seemed endless. We could only imagine how the county's attorney peppered Randy with endless questions about the slides. When Randy exited, he told me that the lawyer was tough on him, asking questions he had not anticipated. "They asked about the slides, and if I had previewed them with Micah. I had to answer 'No' at first, they made it seem as if Micah was doing all this by himself without any consideration of protocol. Micah's lawyer did a good job of making sure the judge knew that I'd been to school many times before and that Dr. Blackwell knew me. He asked if there had ever been any objection before, which is no, so, he planted the thought that all this had implied permission if not explicit."

"Good, good for us. How does the judge act?"

"Rather indifferent so far, but that lawyer for the county is a pain. Oh yeah, Dr.Blackwell sat in back of the county table at first, then he had to leave. He's taking the stand later. Kind of forged his allegiance, don't you think?" he huffed.

"That's okay. At least we know where we stand with everyone. I know you gotta go back to work. Thanks for trying to help."

"Hey, no problem. Let me know something later if they decide anything. Tell Micah to call me at work. He knows the number." Randy pushed open the glass door and walked to the county car parked at the curb, a perk for working for an arm of the police department. As I turned back toward the hearing room, a clerk of the court summoned the assistant superintendent for the county's curriculum. An overweight man with an ill-fitting seersucker suit came down the right-hand side of the corridor. He had uncanny timing about when it was his turn to speak, because he had not been waiting with the rest of us.

"Who's that?" Rachel asked.

"He's the guy in charge of what you need to study in class. Curriculum is what they call it."

"What's he doing here?"

"Guess we'll see when someone comes out." I walked down the hallway to find a water fountain. If I were a smoker, I would be well into a pack by now. The sun had risen past the point where light came directly into the front doors. The morning was quickly ending.

Several students exited the too-large wooden door of the hearing room to inform us that the curriculum guru had been called just before they left. A half-hour later, others came out with a rendering of the testimony. The county lawyer asked him if a speaker on crime scene investigations had anything to with math or with the guidelines established to meet state standards. The superintendent replied that what Micah had done had no place in a math class. To his surprise, Micah's lawyer asked on cross if he knew of *Newton's Law of Cooling*, which of course he did not. His eyebrow rose when Marlowe's lawyer explained the law: time of death can be determined as long as the body hasn't reached room temperature. Then Dr. Curriculum was asked if he knew how to use an ellipse to calculate the place of origin for a blood drop recently emanated from some unlucky victim. He wasn't aware of this, either, and then the lawyer provided other examples of how math works in forensics. Reluctantly, the superintendent agreed that perhaps math had its place in forensics, but he was still hesitant to confirm that the classroom was also its place.

He initially thought everyone would accept his word on the issue but his word had lost some weight in the last few minutes. A small but important victory, but only if the judge saw it that way. Dr. Blackwell came into the hallway and stiffened his posture on seeing us. He gave a cool "good morning" and reentered the hearing room. I wondered where he'd been hiding. Somewhere in this building was the storage place for county witnesses, while the rest of us must pace the area that hosted snack machines and the restrooms.

Focusing on my own emotion and churning stomach, I had misplaced the meaning of the day. At stake was a man's career. He had, unwittingly perhaps, given me my life back, and it would soon be my chance to return the gift. Glancing down, a line of ants leading to and then behind the drink machine caught my attention. Not before this year would I have noticed them, and a slight smile crossed my lips. Through Micah, the world would know the struggles of teachers, the sacrifices for children not their own, and their desire to make life better for another person. My testimony had to be the most forceful speech of my life.

The door swung outward and the present grabbed me. Two parents spoke to each other as they exited. "Dr. Blackwell acts as if he had no clue this was taking place; either he is lying or he should know more of what's happening in his school." The parent, dressed in a pin-striped business suit, looked over his shoulder. "Gotta go. Let me know what happens. Tell Micah I was here but had to go."

"Yeah, yeah. I'll call later. See ya." The other man peered down the hall.

"Bathroom's over there," I said.

"Thanks. Say, aren't you a teacher at the school?"

"Yes, I'm testifying for Mr. Marlowe."

"That's great. He's such a good person and this shit's ridiculous. Schools are such political rat-holes, no wonder we can't get any good teachers to stay—not you, though. You know what I mean."

"I understand. You're right. It's amazing there are any teachers at all. How's it going in there?"

"Well, at first our old buddy said he was unaware of the lectures taking place and that Micah acted without his permission. You know, like all this was done in secret. Micah's lawyer got his ass when he asked if he knew that his assistant principal had sent students to the viewing for their own good. He made some little noise that I think was a 'no.' Then he had to admit that the M.E. guy had been out to do his little show for several years. He was steaming, but, hey, too bad." I liked this man; he spoke his thoughts.

"I bet he was miffed. Wait 'till he hears what I have to say."

"Good luck … I'll be in there. My son insisted at first but now I'm glad he did. Down here, you said?" He hurried down the hall toward the restroom.

I turned at the sound of a person entering the building. An immense man wearing a shirt that was half tucked all the way around his waist walked toward me. His hair was dark, way too long and parted on the side, exposing a thick expanse of eyebrow. Sweat stains under his arms tinted his button-down, and his breathing was labored. He seemed familiar.

"Scuse me, ma'am. Do you know where the hearing room is?"

"Are you here for the hearing with Mr. Marlowe?" I asked.

"Yep, and if I have anything to do about it, his teaching days are over."

Now I knew. My skin flushed and the back of my neck burned. "You're the reason for all this? Why couldn't you just sit down and talk things out? People like you give parents a bad name. All it takes is one lunatic and the schools cave in. Aren't you a minister? What kind of example are you giving your daughter, other children, your congregation?" I half-screamed at him.

"Who are you and *who* are you calling a 'lunatic'?" His face contorted and his eyebrows furrowed. He stepped toward me.

"You, that's who, buddy. I'm Mrs. Scott, and I happen to know Mr. Marlowe very well. So well, in fact, I know all about you and your daughter." Before he could respond, I pivoted and gave the door to the outside a shove. Clouds covered the midday sun, but the humidity was engulfing. Thick arms pushed open the door behind me.

"Hey! Hope you know, Ms. Scott, that we know all about your little affair with Micah. Whatever you have to say about him won't matter much, so who's giving who a bad name? Maybe you should take your immoral ways and go with him! And, you can tell him for me, Ms. Scott, we're going to put an end to his talking to my daughter and encouraging her to write things that aren't true."

The door eased its way shut, and I was left with silence, especially my own. What did he just say? I asked myself. I must have heard wrong, but as I replayed his words, I understood their meaning. My immoral ways … His daughter talking to Micah … The note on my desk … Julie… It was Julie who wrote the note … *It's started again with my Dad* … What a strange sequence of events. The note I found in those first days of school before I met Micah had been written by a girl whose life would cross mine under dramatic and tragic circumstances, all centered around the man I loved. I had turned my back on Julie twice, once in my classroom, and once amid a chorus of tiny frogs. I wouldn't let her down now. By saving Micah, I would save her.

Skipping every other step, I ran inside to find the demon. How dare he say that to me, how dare he think it. Blood rushed through my ears as I pulled open the door. It was now someone else speaking through me; I watched from the sidelines. "That man's a liar!" I shouted at him while looking at no one.

I could have been sued for whiplash as every head turned at my outburst. The large man with the continuous eyebrow scowled, his animosity toward Micah now directed at me.

The judge gave me an exasperated stare but said nothing as the guard politely escorted me out of the room. The county's star witness duck-walked toward the prosecution's table, but stopped first at a row of chairs immediately behind the railing. I caught the briefest glance of over-processed blonde hair and a familiar facial curve. Debra and Ashley shook hands with the slovenly reverend, and my mind spun out of control. First she tried to destroy my family, now Micah. Debra was adept at creating an imperfect world to surround her own. Suspect the worst, get the worst was her creed. Her innocent questions before the Thanksgiving fiasco were not so innocent, after all. *"Who is that fellow I see you riding off with every day? You sure do seem to be spending a lot of time with him. Is he your new boyfriend? And that's a nice truck he's got," Debra snickered at herself.*

So, she's telling people that Micah and I are having an affair. Fine, just fine. I absolutely cannot wait to speak. Out in the hallway, I imagined difficult questions followed by eloquent answers. I hoped my words would convey the deepness of my feelings, but how could words reveal a sunset through a mangrove tree, stars flung across the blackness of the night ocean, or a soul recovered? As I leaned against the wall nearest the room, I heard muffled voices. Within minutes, the crowd, antagonists and the antagonized, began to exit through the doors. The prosecution had finished, and I was now allowed in. I passed by Debra without a glance, and quickly found Micah and his parents. His lawyer and other supporters milled around nearby.

Micah acknowledged me with his eyes as I moved close enough to hear the conversation.

"I think things are going fine, don't you?" Micah asked his lawyer.

"Seem to be, but are you sure you want to speak? Who knows what they'll ask."

"How can I ask others to speak for me if I'll not do so for myself? Hell, I'm almost past the point of worrying. I have to go through with it or I'd regret it forever if things didn't work out," Micah said.

I had to interrupt. "What did the good reverend say?"

"Oh, 'bout what we expected. That I was the anti-Christ for showing his little girl pictures of dead folks. One of a guy half-naked. But Jeff here asked him if he lets his daughter watch the news or escorts her to the movies on weekends. He said, 'My daughter doesn't go to movies, and I screen what she watches at home.' Made him seem rather rigid. We think he has it in for the school, and I'm the means to stick it to 'em. Oh, yeah. It came out he home-schooled Julie until eighth grade."

"Are you going to tell the court what Julie told you about him?"

Micah gave a slight nod toward his lawyer. The young attorney, his body bent over the defense table, spoke softly to the elder Marlowe. "Jeff and I discussed this, and we decided it wouldn't help anybody, especially Julie. We think we have a good argument without allegations of abuse. But after the hearing, I will personally make sure social services gets involved."

"So it went okay?"

"Yeah, we think so. They still won't drop it, though. That knot-head reverend has to, but he won't so the system continues to plod along. No wonder there are such backups in court. Are you ready for your little performance, Ms. Catherine?" His attempt to lessen my anxiety didn't help.

"Yes, Mr. Marlowe, I'm ready." My confidence left as quickly as it came. "Tell me about Dr. Blackwell's testimony. I spoke with someone who said he was squirming."

"It was pretty interesting to watch. Jeff asked some tough questions. Take a seat, Cat. I have to chat with Jeff about something." Micah pulled his lawyer aside, and I sat in the seat next to his mother.

"Hey, Mrs. Marlowe, what do you think? Micah seems to think things are going okay." She looked strong but uneasy.

"I don't know. I watched the judge and he wasn't too pleased. I think we're losing right now. He really needs some good people for his side. Are you still gonna testify for him?" Her voice sounded strained.

"Certainly I am. I'm going to give them a lot to think about. Teachers who never do anything should be the ones on trial. I viewed the slides last night. They're not pretty, but I'll never drink and drive. I hope Micah's lawyer asks me all the things we discussed." My responses began to play again at the edge of my consciousness. I could hear words nearby, but didn't pay attention to them, I was so lost in my reverie.

"Catherine, wake up," Micah said.

"I'm sorry. I was thinking about my turn this afternoon."

His mother continued, "Yes, we're all a bit thrown off right now. I just hope Micah doesn't become a hard person because of this. He has always been gentle but lately his attitude is really different." She spoke to her husband and then turned back to me.

"We're going to lunch with Micah. I guess we'll see you this afternoon. Do you want to go with us?"

"No, but thanks. I have to run an errand." The lie sufficed to cover the real reason. Within several hours, I would be speaking for, and to, a man I cared deeply about. The words I used could easily determine my own future along with his. Somehow, I had denied what lingered beneath the surface of my own ocean but denial does not equal absence. As Micah faced his truth, I confronted mine.

"We'll see you in a little bit then," his mother replied. Micah and his lawyer were still conferring, so I didn't have a chance to say goodbye. Driving alone to nowhere in particular, I stopped at a small park several miles from the courthouse but within view of the city skyline. A narrow stream only inches deep passed over multicolored slates, and small fish darted within the ripples, but the water striders caught my attention. Interesting creatures they are. The sound was reassuring in its pattern and its gentleness. A woman walked alongside its edge with a water-worn stick in one hand. She had white satin hair, sharp features and a slight build. Peeking over her glasses, her eyes danced blue as she approached me.

"Hello. Nice day for a look in the creek." Her voice was soft and husky.

"Yes, yes, it is. What are you looking for?" I asked.

"Whatever I find is what I'm lookin' for, mostly just lookin'," she replied.

"Guess you never get disappointed then, huh?"

"'Spose not. Never seen you before. I walk through each day and know most folks 'round." She was not rude, but just asking.

"I just needed to think about some things and a quiet spot," I told her.

"I'll leave you alone then. Good luck with your problem … bye now." She turned and headed back in the opposite direction.

"No, wait. I'm sorry. I didn't mean you had to leave." She looked back over her shoulder. "How'd you know I had a problem?" I called after her.

"Just seemed that way. Your eyes and your voice. Some guy, ain't it?" She tilted her head and raised her hand to block the sun.

"Well, yes. I feel like a turning point in my life is about to happen. It's pretty difficult," I told her.

"Gotta choose, huh?"

I only lifted my eyebrows and lightly shrugged. How long had I known this woman, several minutes or years? I felt at ease with her. Perhaps she reminded me of some relative or long-ago friend. At her suggestion, we sat at a picnic table nearby. I studied her thin but strong arms; they seemed too pale for someone who frequents the park. She removed her glasses and rubbed her eyes. "Why do you have to choose now?" she asked.

"Because today I'll have a chance to tell all that I feel … "

"Has he ever said how he feels?"

"Not really, but I'm sure I know. Of course, there's always the chance I'm wrong."

"Is he worth the risk for you? What do you have to lose?"

"My marriage. My way of life. But, yes, he's worth the chance. I'm not sure it's the smart thing, though."

"Life has so many turns, often unexpected. We make many mistakes but those of the heart can haunt us forever. I had a friend when I was growing up that moved away when I was twelve. I never saw him again even though I never met a person I ever felt closer to. I tried to get in touch but his family was hard to find. It was the

Depression and his Daddy moved 'em all over trying to find work. Years later, I ran into a person that knew him. He told me that my friend had mentioned me and how he'd been trying to find me. I always figured he forgot me." She gazed out over the patches of dirt scattered throughout the grass, discarded cigarettes abundant in the dust. Her eyes, though, focused only on a memory.

"Why don't you find him now?"

"When Walter, my friend, told me this, Thomas had been dead for several years." We were silent and then she continued. "I still miss him. We used to play in the creek and hunt for tadpoles and crawfish. Now I know which mistakes hurt the most." Her gray blue eyes watered above her wistful smile.

She then apologized for telling me her story, but I assured her how important her words were to me. "You helped me today," I said. "I'm still nervous but now it's because of anticipation."

"I'm glad you came to the park today. I hadn't thought about Thomas for a while; it hurts to remember him but also makes me happy. I should thank you for being here. The times I had with him were wonderful … perhaps we can meet again here," she offered.

"I hope so."

We talked about the trash littering the park for a few minutes, and then I told her I needed to return to my car and head back to the county building. The silver-haired woman seemed so familiar in such a short time; it felt as if shared memories were hidden away barely out of reach. My fingertips brushed them but there was not enough to grasp, no distinct edge. As the sun reflected across the narrow stream, I half-closed my eyes and for a brief instant saw the outline of my mother's face. The caring I needed years ago was here now; all I ever wanted was someone to listen. How different would my life have been had I not had to carry a burden not deserving of a child? The image of my mother rushed forward hindering reality; she spoke within me. *Please forgive me for not listening … I love you each day … and so does David.* My thoughts faded but I wanted them to stay. I needed my mother. A few quiet words lingered and whispered. *Your heart is not wrong.*

Chapter 30

Rachel twisted the silver cross in the v-neck of her white blouse. "I am so nervous, I couldn't even eat lunch. My mom's worse than me."

"You'll do fine. Just tell the truth about the slides," I said. "Your testimony will counteract the lies Whitaker is spreading about Micah."

"Yeah, no kidding. It'll be scary but I do have a few things to tell the county." She had been a student of Micah's for the last two years and was in the same class as Julie. She was an important eyewitness.

"Good luck, Rachel. Micah and I are proud of you."

Her large smile belied her apprehensiveness as she entered the courtroom, and I learned later her testimony shook up the prosecution. Even the impassive judge couldn't help but smile. When asked about the slides, Rachel said Micah had explained the violent subject matter to the students, and he had encouraged the students to leave the classroom as soon as they felt uncomfortable. She added that many students feel schools never prepare them for the troublesome side of their future. The school environment operates as if everything is going to be fine forever. "Yes, the pictures were graphic," she said, "but so is life. Teachers never mention how to deal with an alcoholic parent or how not to repeat the cycle of abuse in the home. Why must I be forced to learn from my own mistakes? Give me a better chance to make a good decision concerning the dangers around me. Or do I have to be in an accident first?" She said she appreciated the fact that Micah cared enough to shock the class into saving their own lives. "Maybe," she finished, "the school should be on trial, not Mr. Marlowe."

Stephanie testified next, burgundy hair flying in short tufts, her spirit for life glowing in her face. Her mother told me afterwards Stephanie confirmed what Rachel had said but showed more disdain for the accusers. "Mr. Marlowe tried to get us not to be another robot," she had said. "He told us those that are the best painters, best physicists, best poets and those that discover wonders beyond our dreams see the world in a different way. If you only see what you are told to see, then you will never see anything for the first time. He's one of the few that can see through the image-driven manure of school." Micah was always an outspoken advocate for his students and now they were his.

Several more adults, parents perhaps, came out of the hearing room doors and passed by me on their way to the parking lot. "I don't know, man, maybe. I can't help but think that he needs to say something to make it all relevant. If he gets on the stand and doesn't do well, it might be over. Emotion can't replace good judgment."

"Isn't someone else supposed to speak after him? What those kids said was good, but who listens to them in court?"

"Yeah, but they should. I sure hope whoever's next is good. I did hear someone whispering about Micah having an affair with some teacher at school."

"I heard that, too. I think she might be the one testifying next. They'll probably bring it up when she gets up there just to mess with her. See ya." The speaker glanced in my direction, and I could see his face tighten and flush. Evidently Debra was spinning tales about me to the community who in turn fed them to the prosecution. People too often believe the worst about each other without bothering to check out the facts or to see the contradictions. Did my presence here hurt Micah? I wondered. Maybe he would be better off if I didn't subject myself to ridicule. I will send word for his lawyer to meet me in the hall since my testimony will be of little consequence if people think I have a hidden agenda. Besides, everyone seems to think things will be fine if Micah does well on the stand. He might not need me, and I can avoid accusing eyes. Yes, that makes sense. I probably shouldn't go through with this. I might say something I will regret or end up getting both of us in trouble. Fine. Good. Yes, that makes sense. I cannot go through with this.

My mind made up, I reached for the door of the hearing room, and my finger touched its brass handle. And then I thought of all that had happened over the past school year. Floating into a world not of this realm, I had created stars within its darkness. A man with blue eyes peered out from under his camouflage hat and into my soul. And I found a person I thought was lost. And I could regret forever words I do not speak. Forever. The hinge creaked and the door swung open several inches.

"May I help you, ma'am?" the clerk asked.

"Yes, I wanted to ask the lawyer for Mr. Marlowe when I might testify. I'm Mrs. Scott."

"Shouldn't be much longer. Mr. Marlowe is finishing his testimony."

"Good. This waiting is killing me."

A half-hour later, the clerk came into the hall and waved me forward.

"It's time for you, ma'am. Just step to the front and into the witness chair."

"Thanks, it's about time." My stomach tightened as I pulled the door handle and entered. Micah, along with the rest of the courtroom, turned to see this last person to speak. Micah's eyes appeared red, his mouth held in a tight thin line. I sensed that his appearance on the stand had not gone as hoped. The time has come for me to speak, I thought, as I carefully edged myself into the witness chair.

Familiar faces become a collective unknown when you are viewing them from the witness seat. At least that's what I thought when I sat there the first and, so far, the only time in my life. Even Micah's face became part of the unfamiliar tapestry facing me. The enormity of the day froze everything around me into a brown-and-white wash of color. The judge in his heavy, black robe and silver-rimmed glasses seemed to be the singular form in the room.

"Could you speak a little louder?" the judge demanded.

"Yes, I swear." My voice cracked, and drops of sweat gathered above my lips.

Micah's attorney Jeff Shepherd shuffled through his papers, then studied me over the rims of his reading glasses. He was about forty-years-old, give or take a few years, with curly black hair that made his pale skin paler. He had a tall, angular body and bad skin, probably a left-over acne problem from his adolescence.

"How are you doing today, Mrs. Scott?" he asked.

"Just fine, Mr. Shepherd."

"You have a good lunch?"

"Actually I spent the break in the park. It was quite enjoyable, thank you. What about you?"

"Enjoyable also." Jeff cleared his throat before he began his questioning. "How many years have you been a teacher?" His soft voice evoked confidence and capability. He immediately put me at ease. I liked the man.

"For twenty-one years."

"Would you tell us a little bit about your teaching experience?"

"Objection, Your Honor." Mr. Alvarez, the prosecuting attorney, rose from his seat. "Only her history at Tecumseh High School is relevant, not her entire career."

"Her teaching experience can help us gain a better understanding of her character, Your Honor. Some background is relevant," countered Mr. Shepherd.

"Objection overruled." The judge rolled his eyes toward me. "Keep it short, Mrs. Scott."

"Yes, Your Honor. Well, I've taught in all kinds of high schools: rural, private, city and now suburban. I've found that no matter what the teaching environment, the students share many of the same problems."

"Would you elaborate on some of those problems, Ma'am?"

"Be glad to. Most of the problems are the same ones young people have been dealing with for decades. Parents not understanding them, peer pressure, drug and alcohol abuse, sex, identity ... the need to prove themselves. Feeling invincible one moment, insecure the next."

"In your opinion, how well are the schools dealing with these problems?"

"Not very well. The educational system has become a bureaucratic monstrosity. The paper trails have gotten out of control. As teachers, we spend more time filling out reports, accountability folders, and surveys to prove we are doing our jobs than actually teaching. For creative individuals, the paper trail is stifling. Sometimes I feel the job of administrators and teachers is to make the school look good—at least on paper—and nothing else matters, not even the kids."

There was a stir in the brown-and-white blur of faces, and for a minute Micah's smile became distinguishable.

"How do you deal with the paper trail, Mrs. Scott?"

"Mostly by ignoring it ... I throw most of the forms away. Eventually, the administration gets tired of asking me for them."

"How do you deal with these problems you say all adolescents have?"

"Like many other teachers. I try to be open so the students trust me enough to feel comfortable coming to me with their problems. I talk about sex and violence and substance abuse through the literature we study, and try to relate some of these age-old issues to their lives. It seems to help."

"Do you ever talk to your students about the dangers of drinking and driving?"

"All the time."

"Does it help?"

"Maybe ... a little."

"What would help?"

"The ghost-out we have before prom helps, but I'm not sure that makes as much of an impact as ..." I paused. I wasn't sure if I should bring the slides up yet.

"Yes? Go on."

I took a deep breath and looked to Mr. Shepherd for reassurance. His face kept its same stoic expression. "As the slides Mr. Marlowe shows the students ... "

"Have you seen the slides?"

"Yes, sir. I have."

"Would you feel comfortable showing them to your students?"

"Absolutely."

"From what the court and I have seen, they are rather graphic, wouldn't you agree?"

"They are realistic enough to make death an inevitability to kids who think they are immortal. I know kids. They don't really pay attention to simulations of death. They see enough of that in movies. But the real thing presented by a real medical examiner has a visible impact on them. Enough to make them think twice about drinking and driving."

"Do you think the slides would benefit all students then? Not just those in Mr. Marlowe's classes?"

"Yes. All teenagers have the potential to get behind the wheel of a car drunk, or to ride in a car with a drunk driver."

"Even though the slides they see contain nudity?"

"The nudity wasn't sexually explicit, at least what I saw. A dead body mangled beyond recognition isn't very appealing. The slides did what they were supposed to do. Make kids think."

"How long have you known Micah Marlowe?"

"Almost a year."

"And you've come to know him fairly well."

"Micah and I have become close friends."

"How would you describe Micah Marlowe as a teacher?"

"Great. He's the best teacher I've ever met, and I've met some great ones. He cares about the kids. Sometimes more than their own parents seem to."

Mr. Shepherd stared at me a long time and started to ask me another question, but cleared his throat instead. "Thank you, Mrs. Scott," he said. Micah's eyes followed Mr. Shepherd as he walked back to his seat; then he caught my eye and nodded. Mr. Shepherd smiled at Micah, and I knew my testimony was going well.

"Mr. Alvarez, do you have any questions for Ms. Scott?"

"Yes, Your Honor, I have some questions for Mrs. Scott." The judge raised his eyebrows at Mr. Alvarez's emphatic pronunciation of *Mrs.* A young lawyer, probably early thirties, Mr. Alvarez smiled at me as he approached the witness chair. Though young, his sandy blonde hair was thinning and he was more than a few pounds overweight.

"How are you today, Mrs. Scott? Uh, it is *Mrs.* is it not?"

"Objection, Your Honor. He knows her name."

"Sustained. This isn't a name game, Mr. Alvarez."

"Just wanted to get it correct, Your Honor." He directed his attention back to me. "You doing okay today, Ma'am?"

"Yes, sir. You already heard me tell the defense how well I'm doing."

"I must have been daydreaming during that time. Pardon my lapse."

"Mr. Alvarez ..." The judge folded his arms and gave the young lawyer an exasperated look.

"I did hear you tell Mr. Shepherd you and Mr. Marlowe are very good friends, did I not?"

"Yes sir, you heard correctly."

"How much time would you say you spend with him in, say, a week's time?"

"Lately, not too much. But it varies. Sometimes I see him a few times a week, sometimes more."

"Sometimes ... like everyday?"

"Not usually. No, not everyday."

"Do you spend this time alone with him?"

"Yes. Often we go places together."

"All day?"

"Maybe … but not usually. We do teach during the week."

"How does your husband feel about all this alone time you spend with Micah Marlowe?"

"He trusts me. He knows we're good friends."

"Does your husband travel at all?"

"Yes."

"A few nights a week? A month?"

"He's gone for a week at a time, sometimes two or three weeks at a time. He travels internationally."

"So this leaves you with plenty of lonely nights."

"Objection! I don't see any relevancy to this line of questioning. It's not Mrs. Scott's hearing."

"Sustained. Get to the point, sir."

"Yes, Your Honor. Mrs. Scott, are you in love with Micah Marlowe?"

Micah's eyes searched for mine and then closed slightly as he turned to the prosecutor. I couldn't tell how he wanted me to answer. I hesitated and by that very hesitation the entire courtroom knew my answer. Mr. Shepherd came to my rescue, but too late.

"Objection. Irrelevant question."

"It's a very relevant question, Your Honor. She's a key witness. If she's in love with him, her credibility's in question."

"Mr. Marlowe obviously used witnesses who cared about him. Whether they're in love with him or not is a moot point," Micah's lawyer argued.

"Objection sustained. Change this line of questioning."

The prosecutor turned back to me. "Mrs. Scott, you've seen the slides?"

"Yes, I've already told Mr. Shepherd that. Were you daydreaming again, Mr. Alvarez?" A collective chuckle from the courtroom.

"Just making sure, Ma'am. That's my job. And you found nothing offensive about them?"

"No, not really."

"Not even a picture of a man with his penis exposed?"

"It was a corpse."

"Do you have any children, Mrs. Scott?"

"Yes, sir. I have two children in college."

"Would you have found it acceptable for them to have seen these slides at the impressionable ages of fifteen, sixteen and seventeen?"

"I would appreciate any help as a parent trying to make my children understand their own mortality. You couldn't be too much over thirty, Mr. Alvarez. Surely, you must understand what it takes to knock some sense into a young person's head."

"There are other ways than showing lewd pictures to adolescents. If a parent wants to show those kinds of pictures, then that is the parent's choice." Mr. Alvarez paused and faced the courtroom. "Not teachers."

"Judge, may I answer him?"

The judge held up his palms to both lawyers.

"I would like to hear her answer, Your Honor," said Mr. Alvarez.

"Go ahead, Mrs. Scott," Micah's lawyer agreed.

"Make it short, Mrs. Scott."

"Thank you, Your Honor." I turned back to the young prosecutor. "You're right, Mr. Alvarez. Parents should be the ones to make important decisions concerning the lives of their children. But the problem is that many parents don't care or don't know how to care, and they leave the important task of raising their children to the teachers or their children's peers. I've heard children in my class joke about how drunk their parents get every weekend, or how their parents are seldom home. They're either working or traveling. Many of our students depend on their peer group for answers to questions of behavior and conscience. Sometimes they ask their teachers for guidance, especially the ones they know care, like Micah Marlowe. He's one of the rare teachers who's not afraid to risk his career to help a student in need. Unfortunately, in today's climate and the all-too-ambiguous interpretation of what is and what isn't sexual harassment, many formerly caring teachers have closed down emotionally towards their students and will only impart subject matter and go home. Micah once told me if the time comes when he's forced to stop showing emotion towards his students, he'd quit teaching.

"Micah Marlowe, like me, has seen too many adolescents killed because of alcohol and drugs. What, as teachers, does society want us to do? Ignore the talk we hear in the halls about who drank the most last Friday, how blind-drunk one of their friends drove home ... and not care? Micah showed the slides because he is tired, like the rest of us, of going to funerals for students. He cares—and they know it. They showed this by the walkout a few weeks ago. Most of the parents appreciate how much he has helped their children, except for one. A minister. A man who should recognize a good soul. But unfortunately, some of us become blinded by our own welled-up anger and past hurts. We have to find scapegoats to ease our own sins.

"Micah Marlowe is a savant, untouched by the hype of power and money. He is a curator of nature who uses his creative gifts to lead those who listen back to the world's heart. To take Mr. Marlowe out of the classroom because of one angry parent and some scared bureaucrats would mean thousands of untouched hearts, young and old. I ask you, Mr. Alvarez, Your Honor, what is worth more?" Silence brushed the courtroom for a few suffocating minutes, and I wondered if I had said too much. The judge quickly answered my question.

"That's not quite 'the short' I had in mind." Another chuckle rose from the courtroom. He paused. "Mr. Alvarez, do you have any more questions?"

"Just one more, Your Honor." Mr. Alvarez drew his face close to mine and spoke in a soft voice. "Has Mr. Marlowe touched your heart, Mrs. Scott?"

My answer came as the defense started to object. "Yes, he has," I said, my voice cracking on the words.

"Can you tell the court how he has touched your heart?" Mr. Alvarez's voice matched the quietness of mine.

"Objection, Your Honor."

"Overruled. She needs to finish what she's started. Answer the question, Mrs. Scott. Briefly, if you can."

"I'll try, Your Honor." Out of the corner of my eye I could see Micah and his parents, their faces lifted towards mine. My hands were clammy and I wiped them on my skirt. I took a deep breath before I spoke. "He ... he changed my life ... he showed me so many things." I cleared my throat. "Like night-lights." I stumbled over my words and forced myself to reach down deep to find the truth. "He... he gave me back the person I thought I lost."

"How'd he do that?"

"By sharing his world with me ... By taking me to quiet places ... We listened to tree frogs together and watched cutter ants climb up a long hill... We sat in the dark and watched the stars fall across the sky ... We ... he ... made me see things in a different way."

"Go on."

"And we sat on a dock under a mangrove tree and felt the sunset on our faces. We found God in a church kitchen at the crest of the North Georgia mountains. Micah took me outside the insanity of all the hype and, for a while, he became my eyes to the world. He gave back to me the gifts of wonder and ..." Emotion halted my words, my tears a blurred wall of protection from the silent courtroom.

"And?" Mr.Alvarez prodded.

"And ... his heart," I finally said.

Mr. Alvarez smiled, opened his mouth to speak but then closed it slowly. With his body turned so that only I could see, I thought I saw the slightest wink. "Thank you, Mrs. Scott."

I stepped down from the witness chair. Concentrating on the heavy wooden doors, I fought against the impulse to glance towards Micah and his parents. My emotions catapulted all around me, and I dared not give any more away of what might not be wanted. Someone whispered, "Way to go, Ms. Scott" as I shakily walked towards the exit. And when the guard opened the door for me to pass through, the word "Jezebel" hissed through someone's clenched teeth. In the open corridor, the natural light of day relieved my eyes of the courtroom's fluorescent glare.

#

"We do not find probable cause to continue this separation and find for Mr. Marlowe." The judge glanced at the school attorney anticipating a response but none came. Micah sat expressionless, as if he already knew this scene but participated for our benefit. Seconds passed before the words echoed their meaning. Then the room erupted with shouts of triumph as Micah and Mr. Shepherd exchanged brief, inaudible words. They shook hands and then embraced as if long misplaced brothers. Parents and several students pushed through the gate and crowded around Micah; I stood behind them waiting for my turn to get close to him. His parents were afforded his first words; Micah comforted his tearful mother and grasped his father's hand.

"Can you believe this is over?" Micah asked himself along with others. The judge had left the bench and the school officials were placing papers in their briefcase while watching the activity.

"It had to end this way, you're right. Finally someone around here had some sense," his father replied. His mother managed to laugh and cry at the same time, while she hugged her only child. Her face was bright red and the stressful days had aged her. Parents and teachers were now swarming Micah with bright smiles, encouraging words, pats on the back, tears and handshakes. Love for this unassuming man broke the dam of anger, frustration, and disbelief. Students, past and present, smacked hands in youthful style.

"We're so proud of you," his father said in broken words. Micah looked into his father's eyes, and they both realized they already knew that. Micah's posture leaned in relief, his movements no longer labored. The sparkle had partially returned to his eyes. I remained standing several rows back, using all my senses to absorb the events. Rachel was now holding Micah to never let go. He pushed his glasses up off his nose, wiped a forefinger across his cheek and then pulled back to do the same for her. Our eyes met over her shoulder, and for a moment we were swimming side-by-side needing to say nothing. The faces of the group between the rail and Micah changed expression and tensed. Dr. Blackwell stepped forward. He displayed forced encouragement.

"I'm so glad this worked out." The principal extended his hand. Micah simply nodded and remained silent, his hand at his side. Micah's mother reacted but his father reached an arm across as restraint.

"We'll talk later," was all the good doctor could say as he retreated. The anxious moment receded, and Micah moved to thank as many as possible for their presence and support. Soon there were small groups discussing the outcome and implications.

"Will he come back next year?" someone asked.

"Man, I hope so after all this."

"He probably doesn't want to come back."

"Could be. Guess we'll see in a couple of months."

I moved up as Micah spoke with his parents again, his back turned to me. His mother's expression still reflected the joy and pain of the hour. His father glanced up and stepped around Micah. "Your words helped so much. We cannot thank you enough."

"We all love him so much." I had to replay my statement in my head to make sure I said "we."

"Well, he certainly feels the same about you."

Upon hearing my voice, Micah walked toward me and openly reached to me without hesitation for once. His eyes spoke before he did. "Pretty exciting, huh?"

"If you say so."

"Did you see Dr. Blackwell come over?"

"Lotta nerve he has."

"Yeah, well, I'm glad this crap's over, should've been a long time ago."

"*You're* glad? Now we can *all* exhale."

"Well, it's never boring. Just another adventure." Micah had changed too quickly for me. For him, the events seemed already to be in the distant past.

"Some adventures I would rather not be a part of, thank you."

He laughed in his way. I could never tell the meaning of it and that often infuriated me. Micah stepped closer to me and gently placed my hand in his. His eyes stared through me as he softly spoke. "What you have done for me I can never repay."

The past months from the moment I first met Micah flashed by. Feelings of freedom, exhilaration, passion, the wonder of my night-lights and our tree in full regalia swept across my mind and heart. "You already have." Before he could respond, another teacher grabbed his shoulder and pulled him away. I didn't know whether I should wait for him to return but then it seemed obvious he wasn't coming back.

"Please call us," his mother told me.

"I will. We need to go to the flea market some time," was all I could manage.

"Now maybe we can relax and do some of the things we want to, and thank you so much. You know he's all we got." New tears filled her eyes.

My voice broke in response to hers. "Let's go have dinner one night soon."

"Why don't you go with us now?"

"I guess not. Marshall's due home tonight. Guess I better be there." I knew where I would rather be.

"Next time then, stay in touch." She turned back to her men.

I chatted with a few students and teachers on the way out and soon the walnut doors of the chamber were swinging behind me. Walking down the hall, I knew I was leaving too soon but continued towards the parking lot. I did not really know what I expected from Micah. Something had changed today that could not be reverted to its original state. Perhaps that was good. I was certain it was; yet I drove home feeling uneasy. My life had changed dramatically, but not enough to free me from the fish tank. Seems like I would remain on the rim of the cup after all.

Marshall would be home before midnight. I had some tuna in the fridge and plenty of lemons. There was a new fish man at Kroger; Stephan had probably moved back to Milwaukee or was in jail again. I had yet to find Jack Burden; instead, I found Micah Marlowe, a man I loved deeply enough to let go.

As I pulled into my driveway, I noticed familiar cars lining the curb next door. I checked my watch, half-past-five. Happy hour was well under way. The dull thud of the car door echoed throughout the empty garage. I stood before the car window looking at my reflection. I had to turn away from my own questioning stare but not before I caught a glint of pink through the window of the back door. I opened the door, and lying on the seat was a watercolor of a rose. It was signed M. Marlowe.

#

The humid New York night sweats on the glass. Light through the window comes from a single gas streetlamp at the end of the alley. The beads of water create an endless number of tiny half-moons within their translucent hemispheres. Musty damp smells hide in the room's heavy drapes and in the tired feathers of the stained bed coverings. Carelessly ajar, a beveled and gold-tacked door to an elegant armoire reveals opulent hats and sequined evening gowns halfway off the padded hangers as if expecting to be worn again. Nellie peers at the window but not through it. Her gaze fixes upon the small droplets as they merge with others and eventually stream to the bottom and are gone. She caresses the dark bruises upon her arm and reaches for the needle on the nightstand, yet she pauses. In the distance, thunder can be heard. The rain is approaching. She remembers running to the barn.

"If that book gets wet, Aunt Sally will kill me!"

"I can see way 'cross the tobacca' field," says a thin tow-headed boy with the only eyes that knew her soul.

"Nellie?"

"Yes?"

"Remember?"

"I want to ... I want to play freeze ... to smell fresh hay in a loft ... to teach a young boy to read ... to be kissed on the cheek again ... to not lose you."

There is no answer.

Her hand reaches to her face; she feels her tears. The more she tries to focus on the pane, the more she cannot. The sparkles with their half-moons jump off the window and swim about her like a cluster of stars. They surround her. She sweeps her hand at them and ever so slightly they glide beyond her touch. And as she watches them dance, she knows. And as she looks at her reflection, she knows. Nellie will not live through the night, but she will not die alone.

The next day a man asks, "I wonder who she was," but no one notices the tangled ball of fishing line in her hand.

Epilogue

The dusty journal lies beneath forgotten lesson plan books and dog-eared math manuals. I brush off the cover and see the hand-drawn picture of a tree. It is a tree I know all too well. Guiltily, my hands turn the pages of the author's private thoughts.

Day 5

The first day of school started with the usual anticipation and anxiety. How would this new set of students respond to my personality and accent? Several parents came by to wish me luck. The first day was full of questions about myself and how I felt about being back. I answered as many as possible and still managed to get some menial tasks resolved so learning could begin. My shirt was already sticking to me early in the morning. All eyes sparkle as the year begins; the challenge is keeping the sparkle alive till the end. Too often, students realize the atmosphere into which they are sentenced is the same as before, just a different desk. I try to change that; who knows if I will succeed this year. The task will be more difficult due to the circumstances of last spring. The students seemed eager to please and to make my first day easier. They certainly succeeded. Several tried to share their meager lunch with me. What wonderful hearts they possess. Finally, the afternoon arrived and the school day was over. On the walk home, several students strolled along with me, some beside me, other shy ones behind. I eventually made it to my front porch and sipped on a beer. I wonder if I have done the right thing. I have to do my best even though I feel an ache inside. My toe also aches due to bumping it against a root on the way home. It evidently is hard to talk, watch the water and walk at the same time. The sunset tonight could be great; the clouds seem to be preparing to pose for a picture. I recognize some of my students playing down by the docks waiting for their fathers to come home with the day's catch. I must prepare lessons for tomorrow, but first I will take a gentle walk to a favorite place ... Sunset was beautiful, azure blue with orange stripes and pink puffs stretching back over my head to the east. It felt strange to watch alone. I kept turning to anyone to be amazed with, but no one was there. Time will make this easier.

Day 8

All is flowing much smoother now. Kids have more energy than I can keep up with which makes the day go rather fast. As any place, some are consistently at school ahead of time and the same ones each day are scurrying in at the last minute. They track sand into the room and there is a constant scrunching sound as feet become active. I now know most names; however, the uniforms they wear make it difficult for the quiet ones. Blue bottoms and white tops. Shorts or pants for the boys and skirts for the girls. There are so many gaps in knowledge that each day requires a different short review over a wide variety of topics. At least they are eager to learn. Many of them know that perhaps their only way out of the cyclical existence here is through education. Today, my newness was wearing off and many wanted to discuss my home and why I was here when in their minds the US has everything a person could ever want or need. I answered as best I could, but they soon realized that this topic was not my favorite. I did try to impress upon them that I was here to help them to become better students and people. We had a nice chat about how it is much more important to have a thirst for learning than to be a repository of knowledge.

The one thing that cannot be looked up in a book is how to think. The desire to know why and its applications have driven mankind to the brink of non-existence and back. It has also given us insight into our beginnings, the ability to almost play God and the opportunity to leave a footprint on the moon. Growing up and participating in the latter half of the twentieth century gives me a good vantage point on the value of education. Many of these students cannot see what it can do for them because often the objective for the week is just to have enough to get by. I feel so lucky, but should I? I suppose it's all a roll of the dice, but who is to say that I won? I see these children with smiles that don't represent their material or social status and wonder if the fates were really on their side. Still, I have to think that all I have seen in my life gives me the ability to contemplate these things. I'm glad that I played baseball for my dad in Little League, that we traveled to California in a beat-up station wagon, that I have looked through a telescope at the breath-taking rings of Saturn and that I can share my visions while making others desire their own. The sunset this evening was not as stunning as yesterday when the storm clouds over the mainland created separated rays, which always reminds me of Japan's flag.

Had lobster tail salad for dinner, thanks to one of the local parents. Hopefully, I can be taught how to catch my own dinner one day. For many here, life cannot be that much different from centuries past. At least now when explorers venture here, they don't plunder and pillage as before. I believe the conquerors are more subtle now, which is probably the only difference.

I fan the pages of the diary and see some pages with only a small bit of writing, others with a full page or more. The longer segments seem to be more introspective than informative.

Day 35

Have been invited to dinner with a family two doors away. You would think the governor of the island was about to make a grand entrance. They're sweeping the dirt yard. The trees are so shady and with the occasional saltwater incursions, grass is not a convenience. No grass to cut is a major selling point as far as I am concerned. A poinciana tree to the house's side is in full bloom. The red flowers in the tree and on the ground accent the turquoise-painted dwelling. Bright colors here come from old beliefs about their intensity keeping evil spirits away. Must work from what I have witnessed so far. Time to get ready. Need to be there in half an hour.

Man, that was good. They almost had to bring me home in a wheelbarrow. Grouper, fresh from the reef, local vegetables, homemade hot bread and tea, lemons from the backyard tree. All eyes were on me at the table. They judged each bite as if gauging my reaction to its taste like the food critic for the New York Times was sitting there instead of me. Finished up with a beer on the porch as the sun prepared for another rest. Perhaps there will be discussions as to whose contribution produced the greatest pleasure.

I had not really sat and talked with the grandparents before, but they are charming and held in great respect. They represent a changing world more than most grandparents. Many items that have been widespread back home for most of the century are still novelties here. Electricity, paved roads instead of horse paths, the anxiety of an iron-fisted government and more knee-deep water lobster than could fill up a five-gallon bucket have either come or gone in the last thirty years. I have a feeling that dinner invitations will be more frequent now as everyone tries to measure up to the Jones (Fuentes). My days are full of life. I think my presence here is helping. It is certainly helping me. I can see things much more clearly now. I called home tonight. Spoke with Mom and Dad. Said everything is okay. They would say that even if it wasn't. Everyone realizes I must deal with the hearing and its aftermath my own way. This is a good night to look for shooting stars and make a wish. A soft breeze is rustling the palms.

Day 45

Have made friends with locals and other Americans working near here in various tourist activities. Have been diving several times with them. How strange it feels not to have Catherine to watch over. It makes me sad when I get back on the boat, and she is not to be found. No discussion of all the wonders we had just seen. I cannot help but expect to see her and the others washing out their gear on the dock of San Pedro's Cay when we pass by in our dive boat. Each graceful turtle or night-time bioluminescence brings back such great memories. How is she feeling now? I know it hurt those I love and in turn love me to have come here, but I could not have continued without this disconnection from the past year's events. I've never been good at sorting out my feelings. Much easier to go diving in rivers and hunt for points. What to do about Catherine ... Don't want to let her go, but don't know how to make her mine.

At sunset, the stars slowly appear, but only if I turn away and do not watch. When I look away and then back, their numbers grow. Much like a life. The days sneak by when you don't pay attention. It is impossible to have no regrets, but I try to minimize the cancer of indifference. A boring life says more about the person than his credentials. Eventually, there will be a moment one million years from now. How will I have used my brief spark of existence? I try to make my life worthwhile, yet I am not the final judge of that.

The Milky Way stretched its placid self across the zenith tonight. It seems so static, but beneath its mask lies a turbulent, elegant existence. The same can be said on many scales of the universe. I feel at ease knowing that the person in my heart is perhaps seeing the same night sky. A beautiful connection as this helps me make it through another day, knowing that only distance separates us. Some people live in the same house and are further apart than friends an ocean away from each other.

Day 72

Thanksgiving approaching. Not celebrated here, so just another day. Class is going fine. The students respect teachers here and problems are minimal. Today in class, someone thought they heard a mouse in the front corner near some boxes. At first, I ignored their pleas, but when they insisted, I was compelled to come to the rescue. Those closest to the front eased their desks away with each step I took toward the suspected hiding place. Squatting beside my desk and next to the box in question, it dawned on me that it was possible in a tropical environment for this mouse to be the size of a cat. The tension building in the classroom, the wide-eyed students strained their necks to watch my heroic efforts.

Pulling the first carton from under the table, I found myself in a situation I would rather not be. I sure as heck didn't want to have a big rat wriggling in my face. The sight of their teacher screaming and fainting would not lend itself to promoting authority the remainder of the year. So I decided to turn their anxiety into terror. Lifting a magazine, I jumped back as I let out a convincing gasp of fright. The wave of hysteria began with those closest and moved across the room like a bomb blast. A collective scream passed from student-to-student and away from the epicenter, which was my rat and me. Many of the students clutched their chests; a few were in tears. The only thing that could have made it worse for them would have been a giant claw reaching out of the box pulling me into it and the inevitable crunching. I was so proud of myself when teachers from adjoining rooms rushed in to see what calamity had struck. I told them we thought we had seen a mouse, but all was fine. By now, laughter of relief had invaded the classroom, and the largest boys were picked on for their miraculous escape from the jaws of a mutated rodent. Several times the rest of the day, someone would start infectious giggling that soon spread to the entire room, like the ripples in a stream. They may not have learned much today, but it would be a day they would never forget.

As I finger the well-worn pages, I notice the entries are becoming more irregular, not everyday represented. I flip ahead several pages, fascinated yet uneasy about what I will find.

Day 92

Christmas is near. Only one other time have I not been home for this holiday. I feel that if I go home now, all the reasons why I came here will be rendered useless. Am I punishing myself, creating misery where there should be none? Why am I here if all I think about is home? I feel very lost and alone. Maybe I am too stubborn to grasp what and who has been in my heart all along. I remember how I would look forward to something for what seemed forever and now it is years in the past. The memory still exists of walking to my little desk beside the table in kindergarten and the day we placed our small hands in the clay. I still have that piece of fired clay on the mantle. It teaches me each time I look at it how swift are the days, the years. My own hesitance keeps the circle broken. How can I both realize my failing and do so little about it? Time is an elusive captor of souls; it is the devil that seeks us. I know what needs to be done. Will I have the courage to tell Catherine all that I feel?

The lightning flash on the horizon is another life come and gone. A bolt must quickly return to the darkness yet the thunder can rumble on for much longer. We cannot help that we are but a streak of light in existence but the thunder comes from our own hand. A bitter fruit can become the most beautiful tree.

I turn the pages of the journal until I come across the jagged edges of a torn-out page. Staring at the irregular contour of the left-hand margin, it looks hauntingly familiar and I instantly know the words that once were there. They spill forth from my heart like a fountain, because I have read them several times a day since the moment they reached me. I am here now thanks to a letter that began with "crawling along a river bottom" and ended with "I know where my heart is." I envision the writer breaking the bonds in the paper as he attempts to mend his isolation, and in my mind I place the treasured page beside the tattered edge. Their union is perfect.

The sun has now hidden itself behind the trees and the light is diffused enough that reading becomes difficult. Perhaps another day I will continue, but for now, I return the journal to its once-forgotten nest. A short walk takes me along a dirt path to a sandy beach peppered with pebbles. A mangrove tree has a small dock built between its two trunks. The slip extends over gentle evening waves and has several planks missing. The roots reach out and down seeking stability and nourishment. Its full supply of leaves and tangle of limbs are silhouetted against a tangerine and cerulean sky. Micah sits on the dock, facing the sunset. I sit down beside him, our dangling feet almost touching the water. He puts his arm around me and pulls me closer without his eyes leaving the horizon.

"When I walked up, you seemed to be inseparable from this scene," I told him.

"It does feel like this is where I belong."

"Micah ... where is your heart?"

He pauses and then turns to me. In his eyes, I can see the sparkle of a reflected sunset and emerging stars. Nightlights perhaps. "It is here, now that you brought it back to me."

Lightning flashes on the mainland, but the slow roll of thunder seems to last forever.

About the Authors

Mary Diane Lang, born and raised in the German and Irish culture of Cincinnati, attended the local Catholic schools. Diane attended the University of Cincinnati and Xavier University receiving degrees in education and English. She has taught English literature for over twenty years during which time she was selected twice as teacher of the year. She also attended the Queen Elizabeth College in London, England and studied Mortimer Adler's philosophy of Paideia education at Xavier University. Diane has traveled extensively and in each of the last five summers has ventured to exotic locations with student groups. These trips have ranged from scuba diving in the Caribbean to hiking through the rain forests of Costa Rica. She has been a certified scuba diver and amateur archeologist since she met Michael Buchanan. Diane has written plays, short stories, and poetry, and *Micah's Child* is her first collaborative writing effort. Diane and her husband Don currently live in Sarasota, Florida. They have two children.

Robert Penn Warrens' writings have greatly influenced Diane, her favorite being "....if you could not accept the past and its burden there was no future, for without one there cannot be the other...."

"I don't mind people tagging along when I take walks in the woods or drives in the mountains, but they have to be silent. I was taught not to talk in church." - MDL

Michael David Buchanan, born in Nurnberg, Germany, and raised in Atlanta, Georgia, presently lives in Alpharetta. He attended Georgia Tech and Georgia State University where he received a Masters in mathematics. From an early age he has traveled throughout North and Central America. His interests include diving for artifacts and fossils in rivers of the Southeast as well as reef diving in the Caribbean. Having been a teacher and coach for over twenty-four years, Michael has been recognized for his creativity in and out of the classroom. He has initiated various clubs, including Adventure and Rocket Club, and for the past ten years has organized student dive trips to exotic sites. Michael recently was featured in *USA Today* for incorporating the book *Rocket Boys* into his high school math classes. Michael has been published in artifact magazines and *Micah's Child* is his first fictional work.

Michael's philosophy is shown best by the words from Thomas Carlyle, "When you go as far as you can see, then you can see further."

"Writing this book has allowed me to uncover in myself a better person. Expressing one's feelings about life is often dampened by the commonplace of each day, but a blank page listens and does not question." – MDB

An excerpt from ***Micah's Child*** appears in **O, Georgia! A Collection of Georgia's Newest & Most Promising Writers.**

Printed in the United States
6347